# Rapture
## of the Deep

L. A. MEYER

# Rapture
*of the* **Deep**

Being an Account of
the Further Adventures
of Jacky Faber,
Soldier, Sailor, Mermaid, Spy

HARCOURT
Houghton Mifflin Harcourt

*Boston    New York    2009*

Harcourt is an imprint of Houghton Mifflin Harcourt Publishing Company.

www.hmhbooks.com

Text set in Minion

Library of Congress Cataloging-in-Publication Data
Meyer, L. A. (Louis A.), 1942–
Rapture of the deep : being an account of the further adventures of Jacky Faber, soldier, sailor, mermaid, spy / L. A. Meyer.
p. cm. – (A Bloody Jack adventure)

Summary: In 1806, star-crossed lovers Jacky Faber and Jaimy Fletcher are kidnapped by British Naval Intelligence and forced to embark on yet another daring mission—this time to search for sunken Spanish gold off the Florida coast.
ISBN 978-0-15-206501-0 (hardcover : alk. paper) [1. Spies—Fiction. 2. Seafaring life—Fiction. 3. Buried treasure—Fiction. 4. Kidnapping—Fiction. 5. Orphans—Fiction. 6. Caribbean Area—History—19th century—Fiction.] I. Title.
PZ7.M57172Rap 2009
[Fic]–dc22
2009019494

Manufactured in the United States of America
MP 10 9 8 7 6 5 4 3

*Again for my dear Annetje.*

*And for Chris and Tuck and memories
of Florida and the Keys.*

*For Betsey, too, as well as for Chelsea and Chelly,
both noble Cockers, who lay by my feet all of these
years and by their loving presence helped me
pound out these words.*

# Prologue

## 1806
## The London Home for Little Wanderers
### England

"Ah, and it's a bonny, bonny bride ye shall be, Jacky. Just look at you, now!" exclaims one of my attending bridesmaids. She adjusts the waist on my bridal gown as I look at my reflection in the mirror and grin. "And in an hour or so, you'll be a fine married lady!"

I am swathed in yards and yards of the finest white cloth on this, my wedding day, and I am consumed with happiness as I am being dressed by my three bridesmaids. The unabashed grin of pure joy spreads over my face and it will not go away.

*Oh Jaimy, it's finally gonna happen!*

"All right, let's see how this fits, then."

As the girls carefully place on my head the veil's coronet of braided posies and adjust the filmy cloth, I marvel at just how I came to be here in this place, when, not five days ago, I was kneeling in the sand of a desolate beach in France, a pistol pressed to the back of my head, waiting for the bullet that would surely end my life . . .

# PART I

# Chapter 1

"You, Miss," pronounces Higgins, "are a complete mess."

I groan and stretch out over my lovely bed on my lovely schooner, the *Nancy B. Alsop*, neither of which I had ever expected to see again.

"Please calm down, Miss. I know you want to be with your young man, but Mr. Fletcher's feet are a mere four feet above your head, tending to the business of getting you and your ship as far away from the coast of France as quickly as possible. Please let him do that and allow me to take care of you."

You might have thought that Jaimy and I would have tumbled into the sack right then and there, as soon as we got back on the *Nancy B.*, but no, such was not to be. While Jaimy assumed the con on the quarterdeck and gave orders to set sail and fly, Higgins hauled my sobbing and gasping self into my cabin, where he stripped me down to clean me up and, hopefully, make me presentable. That's when he discovered that I was covered head to toe with scratches and bruises from when my dear Mathilde had dragged me across that battlefield in Germany, my foot being caught in my stirrup and she being blind with terror. I don't blame her none—she was a good horse and already I miss her.

"Good Lord," exclaims Higgins. "Amongst a veritable constellation of contusions, right there is a bruise the size of a cricket ball. A lovely shade of purple and yellow, as well, I might add."

My mind is still reeling from the events of the past hour. "If you've never been dragged on your back across some very rough ground by a terrified horse, Higgins, then you have no room to chastise me."

"I believe I will take a pass on that particular experience, Miss. Hold still now."

I feel the healing salve being applied to my poor bare and much abused bum.

*Ahhhhh . . . nobody has a touch like Higgins.*

"Turn over, please, Miss."

I give out a low moan and turn over on my back.

"Ah. Your front is not quite so bad. Just a bit of salve on your shoulder and some about your knees, there. Good."

I don't mind being tended to by my dear Higgins. In fact, I'm loving it—that and the fact that I am still alive. I had spent the time in the lifeboat that brought me here curled up in Jaimy's lap, trembling and weeping—after all, a mere hour ago I had been on my knees on the beach, waiting for a bullet from the pistol of spymaster Jardineaux to scatter my brains all over the sand—and I do need some time to calm down.

"But how came you to be here?" I ask, still in wonder at my rescue. "With our ship and Jaimy and all . . ."

Higgins takes my shako and places it on my writing

table. "Yet another trophy," he muses, putting his pinkie through the bullet hole in the front. "I shall tell you, Miss, but first will you tell me about this?" He holds up the medal I had worn about my neck.

"It is the Legion of Honor. I didn't deserve it, but *L'empereur* gave it to me, anyway," says I, once again stretching out and reveling in the smooth sheets on my bed, my own dear bed, which tonight will hold both me *and* James Emerson Fletcher—right next to my own sweet self. *Oh yes!*

"The *Emperor?*" asks Higgins, for once surprised and incredulous. "Napoleon Bonaparte himself?"

"Right. He had given me a ride in his coach after the Battle of Jena. He wanted me to deliver a letter to Empress Josephine. Which I did."

"You never fail to astound me, Miss."

"It was not all that astonishing, Higgins," I say, and then proceed to tell him of Jardineaux, the guillotine, Madame Pelletier, Les Petites Gamines, Jean-Paul, Marshal De Groot, my commission as a second lieutenant in the Grand Army, Bardot, the Clodhoppers, my job as messenger between the generals and Napoleon, my delivery of Napoleon's message to Murat, which ordered him to charge the Prussian line, meeting Randall Trevelyne again, the great and terrible battle, and finally, that dark time down on my knees on that beach, crying, and expecting nothing but death.

"Remarkable," says Higgins, looking off into the middle distance. "However, we might have a problem here. With that message you delivered. If Naval Intelligence gets wind of that, it might be trouble. And they *certainly* will not be pleased to hear of the death of Jardineaux, whom they considered very valuable." He shakes his head and sighs. "I could have told them that when you, Miss, get thrown into any mix, unforeseen events occur, but I was not given that opportunity. Not till later, and then it was too late."

"What do you mean?"

"You asked how I knew you would be on that beach. Well, after I learned, through certain sources, that you had been pressed into the Intelligence Service, I, myself, using my Hollingsworth connections, joined that same service so as to be able to find you. I met and gained the confidence of Mr. Peel, Sir Grenville, and the very delightful Dr. Sebastian. We passed many pleasant hours at dinners and in intellectual discussions. Dr. Sebastian declared himself to be especially fond of you—he greatly appreciated the fine illustrations you did for his naturalist endeavors and hopes he will be working with you again someday."

"So I have confessed to treason in front of an agent of the Intelligence Branch?" I ask, with some dread. Higgins is my dearest friend, but male honor and all . . .

"Never fear, Miss," he says. "I would never betray you, but there are other agents in France, some of whom might have learned of your actions and reported them to my colleagues in the Admiralty. We shall see. Now let us get you back into some clothing. Since we left England in a hurry, I did not have time to purchase any female garments for you. I do, however, have your midshipman uniform, the one you were wearing when you were captured."

"I have a dress, there in my knapsack. It will serve as my wedding dress."

Higgins reaches into my bag and pulls out my white gown, the one dress I had taken with me on my way to join Napoleon and the Grand Army of France.

"Hmmm . . . It could use a bit of ironing, but I know you will not wait for me to do that."

"You are so right, Higgins."

"And your underclothing is not even close to dry."

"The dress itself will be enough. I don't plan to have it on long," I say, popping up and putting my arms in the air so that Higgins can slip the dress over them and then over me. He adjusts it, and then I regard myself in my mirror. *Not too bad, considering . . .*

"May I ask, Miss, if the color of the dress is still appropriate for the wedding you seem to be planning?"

"Yes, it is, Higgins. I've done just about everything else, but not yet that particular thing," I say, getting up from my bed and not taking offense at Higgins's question as to the state of my rather shaky virtue. Higgins has always been my friend and protector, and has often given me gentle advice concerning my often impetuous conduct with the assorted males whom I have met on my travels, but he has never interfered when I finally set a course in that regard.

"Ah. Well. I ask only out of concern for your welfare and what you might recently have gone through."

"I know that, Higgins," I reply, continuing to look at my reflection. "Should I wear my wig?"

"Ohhhh." Higgins shudders. "That awful thing? No. Please. I think you will look fine without it, Miss. Let me give your hair a bit of a brush-up."

I sit at my desk while Higgins applies the brush.

"How did Jaimy come to be here, standing on the deck above us?"

"Upon the arrival of the *Nancy B.* in London, I immediately sought out the Fletcher residence and found to my great joy that your Mr. Fletcher was there in the bosom of his family, recuperating from his wound. Upon his complete recovery, I, as the only senior representative of Faber Shipping Worldwide present, appointed him Captain of the *Nancy B. Alsop* in your absence, as I thought that would be your wish, had you been in my place."

I nod.

"So. I shall finally be married this day." I sigh, beginning to fully come back to myself. "I still cannot believe I was so wondrously delivered again into this world."

"I know you have experienced a shock, Miss, but please relax, and soon you shall be your old self. And as for marriage, may we discuss that?"

"All right, Higgins, let's have it." I know what that means—I'm about to be given a lecture on the proper deportment of a young lady.

"Have you considered getting *legally* married first, before you leap headlong into the conjugal bed? Many people do, you know. We are only a day or so away from London and you could be legitimately married, in a church."

*In a church? Hmmm . . . Little Mary Faber, former street urchin, married in grand style at Saint Paul's Cathedral, wouldn't that be something?*

"Nay, Higgins, I'm going to be married, all right, but it's going to be today. A captain of a ship is authorized to perform marriages," I say. "And, Higgins, if you think for one moment that I am not sleeping next to Jaimy Fletcher in this bed tonight, then you are sadly mistaken." I look up at the ceiling, amazed to think that Jaimy is right up there on the deck, not five feet above me. *Imagine that . . .*

"I certainly know that a captain of a ship is authorized to perform marriages, but can he marry himself, or in this case, *herself*?"

"Well, then, Higgins," I retort, "as Chairwench of the Board of Faber Shipping Worldwide, I will appoint *you*, John Higgins, captain of the *Nancy B. Alsop,* current flagship of that company, for as long a time as necessary, and *you* are going to perform the service. See if you can find a Bible on this bark." *And, oh, that brush feels so good!*

"Yes, Miss," says Higgins. "It would probably be legal, but you must know that the very instant I pronounce you man and wife, you will never again issue an order as the head of Faber Shipping Worldwide, as your husband, Mr. Fletcher, would own all of your property, including this ship, all your shares in Faber Shipping, and even the clothing on your back. You would own nothing, not even your own self."

*What?*

"It is the law, Miss."

"Well, even if it is, Jaimy would never be like that—to deny me my rights and all," I say, fuming about the unfairness of it all. "I know he wouldn't."

"I agree that he probably would not. But I have noticed that he has a very protective nature when it comes to you, and it is possible that in order to protect his frail and delicate flower from harm, he might order her to that rose-covered cottage by the shore to safely keep house and await his return from the perilous sea. Hmmm?"

*Damn! Higgins, why do you have to bring this up now, on the eve of my greatest happiness!*

"I will speak to Mr. Fletcher about that, and we will

come to an agreement, I am sure," I say. "Anything else you might want to burden me with, Higgins, my dearest friend, confidant, consultant, protector, and ever-present conscience?"

"Very colorfully put, Miss, as always," he answers, laying down his brush, apparently satisfied with the condition of my mop. "But, yes, there is something and it is this. If you marry, you must expect to be with child within a year. Though it would be a joyous occasion, welcoming another such as you into the world, are you ready for that particular and dangerous trial? You are, after all, still quite young."

"I am sixteen years old." I sniff. "That's old enough for a lot of things."

"Indeed. I have noticed that, small as you are, you do have all the necessary female equipment, and judging from what I have observed of your amorous adventures in the past, it all seems to be in excellent working order."

"Higgins," says I, with an edge of warning in my voice.

"I am but suggesting that you might think about the change in your life that would occur by your having a child."

"Don't care, Higgins. Jaimy and I have waited long enough," I firmly reply. Then I blush and say, "Plus, I know of some things . . . other things . . . other games that people who love each other play, which do not lead to babies."

"You blush most becomingly, Miss. It is reassuring that your face is still able to don a maidenly flush of pink in the cheeks," replies Higgins, without changing his usual calm expression. "But you do realize a marriage must be . . . consummated . . . to be legal?"

"Well, we will do it, then. Babies are born at sea, as well

as on land. In fact, I helped deliver one on the *Pequod*. Little Elizabeth Ahab, it was, and a perfect little creature was she."

But it turns out that Father Neptune, that unpredictable rascal, is the one who decides my future, and not me.

"Jacky?" I hear from the speaking tube right above my head.

"Yes, Jaimy, I'm here," I reply. I still can't believe I am alive and he is here with me and I am hearing his voice.

"Better get ready. Looks like we're in for a storm."

"I'll be right up."

I had noticed that the sea had been working up, because the *Nancy B.* was beginning to pitch and yaw a little more than normal. I get up and dart out of my cabin and onto the deck. There is a cheer from my own dear crew as I emerge into the light—there's little Daniel Prescott, my young ship's boy, *So good to see you again, Missy!,* and my two stout sailors Smasher McGee and John Thomas, and there's Jim Tanner, and—*Good Lord!* Up at helm is John Tinker, himself, grinning for all he is worth as he spins the wheel . . . And there's Jaimy, lovely Jaimy, looking oh-so-splendid standing there and gazing up at the set of the sails, his dark hair blowing about his face. Hard to believe, but three members of the original Brotherhood of the *Dolphin* are standing on the same rolling deck!

"First, Jaimy, a kiss," I say, wrapping my arms around him and pressing my mouth on his. *Ummmm . . .*

I think he's a bit startled, this not being regular Royal Navy quarterdeck routine, but he quickly gets into the spirit of the thing. His own arms go about me and he hugs me tightly.

When our lips come apart, I lower my eyes and say to him, "I know you for a proper young gentleman, Jaimy, but this is my ship, love, and when I am on it, I do what I want to do, and what I want to do right now is to have you kiss me again and hold me, Jaimy, hold me ever so close to you. Oh, Jaimy, we have been so long kept apart." And the tears are coming again, and again our lips come together and stay there for a good—*oh so very good*—long time.

Then the dear boy takes my shoulders in his hands and looks me in my streaming eyes and says, "I want to hold you like this, Jacky, for the rest of my life, but right now I've got to deal with this. You should go below, for it will be rough."

*What . . . ? Go below?*

He glances over my head and I follow that look and notice that the storm has drawn closer. It looks like a bad one, a bank of storm clouds that stretches across the horizon with nothing but blackness beneath, blackness that is split every few moments by streaks of lightning, followed by the rolling thunder that rumbles across the sea, warning us to beware the fury that is surely to come. The wind has come up even more and my dress flies up about me.

"One more kiss, Jaimy, and I will go below," I say all meek-like. We have that kiss and then I turn to go back down into my cabin.

*Oh yes, Mr. Fletcher, I will go below, but it will not be to cower and hide—it will be to change into my midshipman's uniform.*

I find Higgins setting the table for dinner. "Higgins, I'm going to need my uniform after all. We're in for a bit of a blow and I can't face it in this flimsy dress. And if I were you, I wouldn't set out the dishes just yet."

He nods and lays out my black middie jacket, white shirt, and white pants as I pull my dress over my head and fling it onto the bed.

Higgins helps me into my midshipman gear and asks, "The boots, Miss?"

"Nay, I don't want them wet. I'll just go barefoot. I will have better purchase that way, anyway, and things are going to get slippery. And no hat, either—it'd just get blown off."

As I go to leave the cabin, he says, "Please exercise some caution, Miss. I sense that you have not fully recovered from your recent ordeal."

It's true, I am still a bit trembly, but fighting this gale should cure me of the shakes. I assure him that I will be careful, then go back out on deck, to find my ship's boy, Daniel Prescott, standing next to Jaimy on the quarterdeck. Jaimy appears startled to see me once again on the deck and clad not in my dress, but in jacket and trousers.

"Danny, go below and bring me my oilskins, if you would," I say. All on deck already have on their rain gear. The storm is much closer now, and the black wall of cloud towers high overhead. We are going to be hammered.

"Aye, aye, Captain," he pipes as he scampers off to get my gear. I am sure he did not answer my order in that manner to intentionally get Jaimy's goat, but I can tell that Jaimy's goat is certainly gotten. It is very easy to get used to being the captain of a ship, and I can tell from Jaimy's expression that he is neither pleased with my reappearance dressed as I am nor with his demotion by a mere ship's boy.

I go to him, place my hand on his arm, and peer into his eyes and smile. "Come, love, and together we will get through this storm, side by side, as we will get through other things in our lives, neither one of us in front of the other." I put my left arm around him and give him a poke in the ribs with the stiff forefinger of my right hand and continue to look deep into his eyes. "All right, Jaimy?"

He looks off, takes a breath, lets it out, and then smiles down at me, running his hand through my hair.

"This is not the Royal Navy, then, is it, Jacky?"

"No, dear one, it is not. This is Faber Shipping Worldwide, such as it is."

He laughs and says, "Well, let's get on with it, then."

I jump up and kiss his cheek, then climb into my 'skins as we all prepare to get mauled by the storm.

*Ah yes, Jacky and Jaimy, together at last! Hooray!*

*Yeah, right . . .*

# Chapter 2

"Come, Jaimy, come down with me, and let us go into my bed."

My gallant crew had fought that howling gale the whole night long, but the *Nancy B.* is a stout little ship, she is, and she carried us through the storm. We pitched, we rolled, we yawed, with just scraps of canvas set—just enough sail to keep her head into the wind, so she could take the mountainous seas on her port bow. Her bowsprit tore deep into the bellies of the waves and disappeared while green water swept across her decks; but she came back up every time, the seas streaming off her sides, her bow lifted high to take yet another in her teeth. She held, yes, she did, and so did we.

As the storm lessened in the early morning hours, I had sent Jim Tanner and John Thomas below to get some sleep, and now they have come up to give us blessed relief.

Jaimy and I stagger down to my cabin and prepare for bed. We strip off our rain gear; then we pull off our damp clothes and take up the towels that Higgins had laid out for us—the oilskins had not kept all of the water out—and we dried ourselves.

Completely naked now, I know I am looking quite awful and I am suddenly shy before him.

I put my arms across my chest and whisper, "I-I-I'm sorry, I know I don't present a very c-c-comely sight to you, Jaimy, being banged up and all . . . But I'm your lass, Jaimy, should you still want me." My hair is plastered to my head, my bare feet are blue, my skin is gray from tiredness and cold, and my body is splotched with bruises and scars; I cannot imagine any man wanting me in my current condition.

"My eyes could not behold a vision more lovely," he says, taking me by the shoulders. "I have been waiting and hoping for this moment for years. Now here it is, and here you are." The lovely boy holds me to him and plants a kiss on my forehead. I drop my arms and put them about his waist and pull him to me and lay my head upon his chest. *Oh, thank you, Lord, thank you . . .*

"But you're trembling. Here. A quick toweling of your hair and then into bed with you." He takes up the towels and rumples my hair dry, and I crawl into my lovely bed and pull the covers to my chin.

"Come to me, J-J-Jaimy. Come lie next to me and we shall finally be as one. Hurry, Jaimy, come and warm me. Oh Jaimy, I am so c-c-cold. Hold me to you, please, J-J-Jaimy . . ."

I shudder and the shuddering doesn't stop, even after he slides in beside me and puts his arms around me. I press my face into his neck and wrap myself around him.

"Hold me, Jaimy, it has been so long and I am so . . . c-c-cold . . ."

I feel him take his hand from my shoulder and place his palm on my forehead.

"Good Lord, Jacky! You're burning up with fever!" cries Jaimy. He jumps out of my bed and goes to the door.

*Don't go, Jaimy, don't leave me . . . What are you doing, Jaimy? What . . .*

He puts his head out and shouts, "Higgins!"

# Chapter 3

The fever has left me and I am told we are being tied alongside Paul's Wharf in London. We had a following breeze upon our entrance into the mouth of the Thames, and Jaimy told me he felt it best to come all the way up to the city; we could always ride the tide and the river flow on the way out.

Imagine that, Paul's Wharf, not two hundred yards from our old kip under Blackfriars Bridge.

Jaimy now sits on the bed, by my side, and holds my hand and looks into my eyes.

"You are much better, Jacky, and for that I am very glad," he says, softly.

"I am so sorry we could not have been . . . together . . . last night."

"Actually, my dear, it was the night before last. You've been out for a long while. It is good to see you back among us once again."

I don't remember much of the past few days, but I do know that it was Jaimy who held me to him when my body was wracked with chills and he who held the cool wet cloths to my sweat-soaked form when the hot flashes came.

"It is so good to be here," I whisper, still weak from the fever. I lift my hand and put the backs of my fingers to his face. *Oh Jaimy, you are so beautiful . . .*

He takes that same hand and kisses the back of it. Then he rises. "Well, it appears that we're going to be doing this the proper way, after all. I am now off to inform my family and to publish the banns."

"Oh Jaimy, sit with me a while longer yet . . . It has been so long."

"I would love to do that, Jacky, but I must go. There are many things for me to do. Any number of things to set in train. We will want this done right."

*I don't care how right it is done, Jaimy. I just want you and me to be together for good and ever . . .*

"I'll want my grandfather to marry us."

"Of course, dear. I shall inform him straightaway of your safe return. Your Home for Little Wanderers is on the way to my parents' house, and I will stop there to give all therein the joyous news."

"And if it could be at Saint Paul's . . . maybe . . . well, I'd like that a lot." *Sure I would—the church that wouldn't let my dirty little urchin self in the front door back in the old days will now receive my grown self in all its glory. Money and position talks, even in church . . . Maybe especially in church.*

"You rest up now," he says, placing my hand back on my chest. "It's plain that you've been through a lot."

There is a light knock at the door. "Ah, here's Higgins," says Jaimy, rising, then leaning down to place a kiss on my rather damp and probably very salty forehead, "with your breakfast. Till later, Jacky. Goodbye."

"Goodbye, Jaimy, and be careful. I can tell you, this is a very rough neighborhood . . . And please give your family my regards—your father, your brother . . ." *and especially your mother.*

It is not long after Higgins has propped up my sorry self on pillows and I have ravenously devoured everything on the tray that he had laid across my belly that the door again pops open, and I am overjoyed to see a very familiar mop of flaming red hair atop a hugely grinning freckled face come bursting into my cabin.

*Mairead! Oh joy!*

# Chapter 4

The next week is a flurry of activity. There are old friends to visit—*Oh Grandfather, how good it is to see you!*—provisions to get on board the *Nancy B.*, and much clothing to buy, such as a wedding trousseau, no less! And there's nothing like the prospect of a little shopping to get Jacky Faber up and off her duff, that's for sure.

I am invited by Jaimy's father to come to dinner, and I accept even though Jaimy doesn't want to put me through the ordeal. But I say, *Hey, if she's to be my mum-in-law, then we're both gonna have to get used to it.*

Sure enough, throughout the entire meal, his mother sits there stiff as a ramrod, barely eating a bite or speaking a word. Which is good, for what she wants to say is that I lack breeding and am not a fit match for her son. That I have driven a wedge between him and her, and that he has forsaken her house for mine—the *Nancy B.*, such as she is.

The devilment, though, wells up in me as I include her silent self in my hopefully bright and charming conversation, pretending that she is graciously joining in.

". . . and Mrs. Fletcher, if you could have but seen Jaimy's heroic rescue of my poor self as I was hanging there, choking in LeFievre's noose. Ah, yes, he was every inch the hero while he disregarded the bullets that were flying all about him as he swung his gleaming sword at that horrid rope . . ."

Cheers all around, but nothing cracks her reserve; and I know what she is thinking, for I can see it in her eyes: *Another minute at the end of that rope would have served you very well and done us all a world of good, you insolent little guttersnipe . . .*

Well, to hell with her, then. I think it will always be thus. However, I believe I have won over the hearts of Jaimy's father and brother George, as well as the rest of the company, as they listen raptly to my stories and join me in joyous song.

'Course the fact that Amy's fourth book is a sensation out on the London streets doesn't help much with Mother Fletcher, either . . .

Earlier on, sitting in my cabin after I had fully recovered from my bout with that fever, Higgins looked at my head, sighed, and set to work getting my hair into some sort of reasonable condition. What there is of my hair, anyway—it was cut to a length of scarce half an inch last August due to an unfortunate encounter with bad men, much tar, and many feathers; and here it is November and still it is only about five scruffy inches long. He takes his scissors and trims up the mop to even things out a bit. He casts his eye upon the result and pronounces himself satisfied.

"There. That makes it look like it was intentionally cut short, you see," says Higgins, fluffing my hair with his fingers. "The latest style on the Continent, as it were. Better than wearing one of your ghastly wigs."

"But Higgins, surely women wear wigs as well as men," I counter. "I could wear a wig to the wedding. The powdered white one."

Higgins shudders. "They were in fashion ten years ago. They are *not* in fashion now," he says, firmly. "The look now is au naturel, and you certainly *do* look natural."

"You mean like a natural savage, don't you, Higgins?" I pout, while still enjoying the feeling of his brush in my hair.

"Do not worry, Miss. The bridal veil will cover your shorn locks at the wedding, and till then, when you go out in public, you can wear your mantilla, so as not to cause a scandal," he advises, reaching behind me to pick up a book, which he lays in my lap. "Or more of a scandal than you already are."

I gasp and pick up the book, fearing that I already know exactly what it is, and sure enough, there on the lurid cover is the title, *In the Belly of the Bloodhound, Being an Account of a Particularly Peculiar Adventure in the Life of Jacky Faber,* by Miss Amy Trevelyne. I notice that she did not add the "as told to" bit, since she would have gotten most of the information for this book from the girls of the Lawson Peabody, and not from me, since I was nowhere around. Amy is nothing if not precise in naming her sources.

A lot of the revenues that support the Home, now that I am not out buccaneering, come from the books that she has written concerning my exploits. Amy Trevelyne, well-fixed herself, has directed that all profits from the books go to the Home, so I can't really complain. And after all, I really did do most of that stuff.

I see that the cover is decorated with a pretty good wood engraving, showing a girl who, I reckon, is supposed to be me, stripped to the waist and lashed to the mast, about to be flogged insensible—which I had been. But . . . let's see what else . . .

I open the book and begin quickly thumbing through it, looking with dread for certain things that I fear might be in there. Surely she could not have put *that* part in it, that bit with me dropping my drawers in front of Mick and Keefe . . . Oh, no, surely she did. For a self-described blue-nosed New England Puritan, she sure ain't shy about layin' out all of Jacky Faber's crimes against proper behavior for all to see, and, *Hey wait, I didn't go that far!* And hold on, what about that kiss with Clarissa? Flip, flip, flip . . . Of course, there it is. In detail. *Geez, Amy, couldn't you have lied a bit and reported I had at least some of my clothes on?* And, oh, Clarissa's dad is gonna love the hell out of this if he ever sees it. Heavy sigh. And Mother Fletcher, don't even think about it . . .

Higgins casts an amused eye on me.

"I'm sorry, Higgins. I do try to be good."

"I know you do, Miss, and sometimes you succeed."

There is to be a reception at the dining hall of the London Home for Little Wanderers, and afterwards Jaimy and I shall take ourselves off to a place where no one can find us—I have in mind a cozy seaside cottage at Bournemouth—and we will be gone for a long time. A very good long time. When we get back, we shall get started on things.

I had taken Higgins's advice and had a long talk with Jaimy. Two days after we got back to London, I had him pick me up and take me to the Admiral Benbow Inn for lunch. The Benbow isn't an elegant place, but I wanted us to meet there for it is not on Jaimy's turf, but rather on mine, 'cause we've got to get some things worked out.

We go in, take a table, and order. He looks about at the humble interior, then looks at me and raises his eyebrows in question.

"We gotta talk, Jaimy," I say, "about what's gonna happen to me after we get married."

"Well," he says, "I do have my eye on a nice set of rooms for you to stay in, over on Aldersgate, and I am sure you'll be quite comfortable."

I say nothing to that for a moment. Then I say, "Listen to me. All I want, Jaimy—all I ever want—is to stand by your side, wherever and whenever the world allows us to do so . . ."

He reaches over to put his hand on mine, and I put my other hand on his and continue.

". . . but I just can't sit around and knit when you're far off at sea. You are still in the Royal Navy, you might remember, and no telling when you might be sent off for months, maybe years . . . No, Jaimy, hear me out, please."

He nods and waits, and I go on.

"Here's what I propose. I will continue to run the *Nancy B.* back across the ocean, except this time not carrying cargo but men—Irish men."

"Why? Whatever for?"

"To work in Boston. They're filling in the Back Bay and they're desperate for workers. The Irish are going through another famine, so they are desperate for work. It's to everyone's advantage. The *Nancy B.* could be fitted out to carry a hundred men."

"But if there's a famine, how could these men pay their fares?"

"They wouldn't have to. Faber Shipping would take their indenture, and they could pay us back after they find work."

"How do you know they would pay what they owed?"

"Ha. Woe be to any man who failed to pay his debt. I've got John Thomas and Smasher McGee, remember. They would be quite formidable enforcers."

"You seem to have it all worked out," he says, doubtfully.

"Yes, I have. I've talked to Ian McConnaughey, and he says he could handle the Irish end of things while my Mr. Ezra Pickering would do what was necessary in Boston—making sure there was work for the men the instant they stepped off my ship."

"But the danger, Jacky. Your ship is so small."

"She is a very sound craft, Jaimy, as you well know. And if we make a year's worth of successful trips, we would be in a position to buy a bigger ship—maybe a bark or a brigantine—and then we could haul four hundred men at once and make some serious money. And as for danger, a person can die as easily from a fever caught in the streets of London as from a storm at sea. What do you say, Jaimy?"

"But . . . I don't want a wife of mine . . . working."

I look at him severely. "That's your class talking, Jaimy, not you. I used to stand right outside this place, with my hand out, begging, Jaimy. I ain't too proud to be in trade. I ain't too proud to work."

"I know that, Jacky, and I never want you to—"

"You don't want me to wither and die, do you, Jaimy? 'Cause that's what'll happen to me if I'm put down in some stuffy rooms to be a good, dutiful wife. You know that ain't me, Jaimy. I'm a member of the seagoing brotherhood, too, Jaimy. Don't you remember?"

"I remember, but—"

"Know this, Jaimy," I say, withdrawing my hands from his, "I'll not give up Faber Shipping."

Our eyes lock, and we gaze at each other for a long while.

Finally he smiles and puts his hands back on mine. "So that is the way of it, then? Very well, it is the way it shall be."

"Oh Jaimy! I'm so glad we agree!" I cry, and rise to wrap my arms around his neck. "So glad!"

When I sit back down and calm myself, he reaches over and rumples my hair. "Perhaps I am too much the pessimist, Jacky, while you are forever the bubbly optimist," he says. "But that childhood fable about the belling of the cat comes to mind. Do you recall the moral of that little story? Well, it's that the well-made plans of mice and men oft go awry."

"Aw, g'wan wi' ye, Jaimy," says I, gleefully lapsing back into the Cockney of my youth. "It'll be just prime, you'll see."

After we leave the Admiral Benbow, I link my arm in Jaimy's and put my head on his shoulder, and we walk slowly back to my *Nancy B.*

# Chapter 5

*Something old, something new, something borrowed, something blue.*

I am standing in the middle of the room in my ever-so-white and oh-so-lacy bridal gown, while Mairead and Judy and Joannie are on their knees fussing with it, sewing a tighter seam here, taking a tuck there, making everything just perfect.

I let out a long, happy sigh. *At last!*

"Ah, Judy, will you look at her up there now, all smilin' and dimplin' up, she is." Mairead laughs, winking at Judy.

We are in the rooms of Ian and Mairead Delaney Mc-Connaughey at the London Home for Little Wanderers, making our final preparations. In under an hour, we leave for Saint Paul's Cathedral, where I am to be married this day to Lieutenant James Emerson Fletcher. My ring is back in my ear, and I reach up and touch it. I will be taking it out to put it on Jaimy's finger at the proper time. Yes, my old ring from the time back in that goldsmith's shop in Kingston, when Jaimy and I first plighted our troths.

*Something old . . .*

"Well, 'tis not every day a young girl gets married, Mrs. McConnaughey. Let Mistress Mary have her time," replies Judy Miller, her mouth set primly. She is my old comrade from the Rooster Charlie Gang of Cheapside Orphans and new employee of the London Home. "Let her enjoy her last few moments as a tender maiden."

Mairead gives out a snort on that one. "Maiden, maybe, but tender? I think not. Remember, I've sailed with this one before."

*Yes, you have, Mairead.* I think back fondly to our days on my *Emerald,* freebooting about the Atlantic, waving swords about and taking prize after prize. "We were wild then, weren't we, Mairead?"

"That we were, Jacky. Suck in your gut a bit . . . Good . . . That's got it. All done," she says, making the stitch and then getting to her feet. "And now we're going to be just a couple of old married ladies, sittin' by the fire and noddin' off, the days of our youth past and gone."

I give my own snort at that. Mairead is scarce seventeen years old, married to Ian McConnaughey for only a year now, and no less feisty than when first I laid eyes on her.

"Nay," she continues, shaking her head sadly. "The only rough sailing the renowned sailor Jacky Faber will do this night, and for many nights after this, will be in the good ship *Bedstead,* and won't the springs and stays of that noble craft be mightily squeakin' and squawkin' like any ship's riggin' in a lusty storm?"

I say nothing, but only smile serenely and let them prattle on, the bridesmaids teasing the bride-to-be in that time-honored fashion. I imagine Jaimy is getting the same from his groomsmen . . . and a good deal coarser, if I know my men—and I think I do.

"Tsk!" says Joannie, lifting up the front of my gown. "She hasn't put on her shoes yet."

Joannie—Joannie Nichols, that is—is about the last of the Blackfriars Bridge orphans. She is the third of my bridesmaids and has been a resident at the Home for Little Wanderers for the last year or so. She is turning into a fine young woman—twelve, maybe thirteen years old now, I suspect. I sigh to think of those old days in the kip 'neath the old bridge. I visited there with Judy and Joannie a few days ago, but we found no orphan gang under there now, just a few pathetic old drunkards. We tossed them some coins and left, saddened.

I look at Joannie now, well spoken and dressed all neat, and I allow myself a bit of the sin of pride for having a part in getting her off the streets and setting her on a better path through this life.

"Just like her"—here Mairead chuckles—"to get married barefoot."

That snaps me back into the present, and I slip my feet into the delicate white pumps we had purchased only yesterday.

*Something new . . .*

This accomplished, Mairead twirls a bit of frilly cloth about her finger and says, "Keep your dress up and stick out your leg."

I do it, and she slips the pale pink garter up my right leg to snap it in place on my upper thigh. "There. That is the garter I wore to my own wedding, and I lend it to you in hopes that your man turns out to be as good as mine," she says, with a leer, "in *all* ways."

*Something borrowed . . .*


A little while ago Higgins had stopped by, bearing a small floral box, to give me a bit of a final fluff-up.

"So how is Jaimy?" I asked as he applied his brush. As by custom, I have not seen the bridegroom for several days—it being considered bad luck and all.

"We had the bachelor party at Mr. Fletcher's club last night. There were many toasts raised in your honor," he said, then coughed discreetly. "Many, *many* toasts."

"I hope you all were temperate, Higgins," I said, putting on my own Puritan face and checking for signs of alcohol excess in Higgins's face but finding none.

"Reasonably temperate, Miss. Mr. Fletcher himself did not have to be carried out."

"That is good. After all, I shall expect Mr. Fletcher to be in *peak* physical condition this evening." This got some low chuckles out of my attending bridesmaids.

"Very droll, Miss," said Higgins, "and as always the very soul of decorum. There, I think that is the best I can do with your hair. Now, to pin the blue ribbon back here . . . Done. And, lastly, let me apply this . . ." With that he opens the small box he had brought in with him and pulls out a beautiful blue and white orchid, shimmery with dew. He also draws out a five-inch-long needle and, with it, attaches the bloom to my breast.

"With my compliments, Miss," said my dear Higgins,

"and now I am off to Saint Paul's. Adieu, Miss. Please know you couldn't look more radiant."

The bit of blue ribbon that Higgins pinned in my hair had been given to me this morning by my grandfather, Reverend Alsop. He had come by as we were starting to get ready.

"It was one your mother wore as a child," he said, "and which I have kept over the years in memory of her. I know she would have loved to be here on this day, and I know, too, that she would be, or rather . . . *is* . . . very proud of you, my dear, for what you have done for the poor orphans of this city."

*Something blue . . .*

"Would she have been as proud of the other things I have done in this life, Grandfather?" I teased, thinking of just how I got the money to pay for that orphanage, which he now runs—mainly through plunder gained from something very nearly approaching piracy on the high seas.

"Ah, now, I am but a simple country vicar and have no wish to pass judgment on any soul that spends its allotted time on this earth . . . But yes . . . I believe she looks down with great pride upon you, her daughter, and how you have conducted your life."

"That is sweet of you to say, Grandfather," I said, leaning over to place a kiss on his cheek, "although I know I have a few things to answer for."

"Ahem. Well, maybe it is best that the old do not know everything about the young," he said, putting his own kiss upon my brow. "And now I must be off to Saint Paul's to prepare. I wish you the best, my dear. Mr. Fletcher is a fine young man, and I know you will be very happy together.

When next I see my dear granddaughter, she will be walking down the aisle toward me, and I will count it one of the happiest days of my life."

"There," says Mairead, standing. "I think we've done the best we can with all this. Let's put the veil on. It is about time for us to go."

I stand with my arms to my sides as they place the veil's coronet of intertwined posies on my head and trail the veil's gossamer cloth down my back. Before I enter the church, it will be placed over my face, to be raised only when the ceremony is complete and Jaimy lifts it up to kiss me, and *Oh Jaimy, at last!*

As if on cue, there is a knock on the door.

"That must be the coachman," says Mairead. "This is it, Jacky."

She plants a kiss on my cheek, hands me the bridal bouquet, and I take it as Judy picks up the train to my gown to keep it off the ground. My eyes are starting to mist up, and the door is opened, and . . .

. . . and it is not the coachman, I realize with mounting horror as I recognize who is standing there.

It is Carr and Boyd, two cold-eyed agents of the Intelligence Branch of the Royal Navy, come to take me, yet again. Behind them stand two others, who have hats pulled down over their eyes, but who are strangely familiar. Bliffil *and* Flashby?

*Oh no!*

I turn to flee, but there is no escape. Carr grabs my left arm and Boyd my right, and I am lifted from the floor and hauled off down the hallway.

*"No. Pleeease, let me go!"* I shriek. *"Let me go!"*

But they do not let me go, no, and they say not a word. They merely take the train of my gown and wrap it around and around my face to stifle my cries, and carry me out like a piece of baggage.

"Hands off her, you dogs!" I hear Mairead shout, followed by sounds of a scuffle and cries of pain; but then I hear no more.

I am once again taken.

# Chapter 6

*"How could you be so meeeeeean to meeeeeeee?"* I keen, my hands holding what was supposed to be my bridal veil to my open mouth. Tears course down my cheeks and into the filmy white fabric. *"I was going to my wedding, for God's sake! How could you be so cruuuell to meeeeee?"*

Mr. Peel, the head of British Naval Intelligence, once again stands behind Sir Thomas Grenville, First Lord of the Admiralty, who sits at his desk and gazes at me, while tapping his fingers on some papers that lie in front of him, as once again in a state of abject misery, I am seated before them. The black-suited Carr stands guard at the door, and the identically clad Boyd is at the window, to make sure I don't try that way out. And Bliffil—yes, that very same vile Alexander Bliffil—stands directly behind me, ready to shove me back down in my chair should I try to rise. And, incredibly, standing next to him is the possibly even more vile Lieutenant Harry Flashby. A part of my shattered mind realizes that the pair, indeed, were the other two men at Mairead's door not a half hour ago.

*Good God, could things get any worse?*

"We are afraid that that particular blessed event must be indefinitely postponed," pronounces Peel, without a great deal of sorrow in his voice. "You are going to be assigned another mission."

"Another mission?" I wail. "Haven't I done enough for you? What about my Mr. Fletcher? What must he think?" *Oh Jaimy, we were so close to being united, so close! Alas, poor Jaimy, alas, poor me . . .*

"Why don't we ask him?" Mr. Peel turns to Flashby and says, "Bring in Lieutenant Fletcher."

*What? Jaimy?*

Flashby opens the door and goes out while I return to full-scale bawling. The Black Cloud rolls in and I cannot stop it; I can't, I—

"*Jaimy!*" I exclaim, astounded upon seeing him brought into the room. I try to rise to go to him, but Bliffil puts his hands on my shoulders and pushes me back down. He leaves his heavy hands there and squeezes *hard*, and I wince and cry out.

Jaimy, furious, shakes off Flashby's arm and glares at those about him, especially at Bliffil, who still has his heavy hands on my shaking shoulders.

"Just what the hell do you think you are doing?" cries Jaimy, enraged. "Get your filthy hands off her!"

Sir Grenville now speaks. "Lieutenant Fletcher. You have already been told that you are to hold your tongue when you are in this room. I am First Lord of the Admiralty and, as such, your ultimate superior officer, save the King himself. Do you understand? Good.

"We have brought you here, Mr. Fletcher, for a good reason. You will observe these proceedings, and then both you and this girl will be offered a choice. You will find out shortly exactly what that choice is, but for now you will remain silent. Now, Miss Faber, as for you . . ."

He turns his attention to the papers laid out before him. "Ahem. To recapitulate your rather checkered past—in 1803, Ship's Boy on HMS *Dolphin,* made Midshipman, found to be female. In 1804, sent to girls' school in Boston. In 1805, left said school under a cloud, soon discovered onboard HMS *Wolverine,* made Acting Lieutenant on that ship. Took command upon death of captain, seized prizes, relinquished command of *Wolverine,* departed on the bark *L'Emeraude,* one of the prize ships. Became known to this agency by revealing to us a spy ring she had uncovered and was given a Letter of Marque. Renamed the bark the *Emerald* and set sail as a privateer. The King's Treasury then discovered that she had taken four prizes and turned in only three, keeping the aforementioned *Emerald* for herself. The Letter of Marque was revoked and a warrant issued for her arrest. Captured off the coast of France and her ship sunk, she escaped in the confusion at the Battle of Trafalgar."

Here Grenville pauses to catch his breath and to clear his throat. Now he goes on.

"In 1806, appeared again in Boston and was briefly recaptured, but escaped again and was later found in the interior of the United States, where she interfered with British agents who were negotiating with our Indian allies in the region, causing injury to one such officer"—here he looks up at Flashby, who is looking down at me with a certain amount of pure hatred—"and the possible fatal loss of another. Several months later she was taken from her schooner, the *Nancy B. Alsop,* by our frigate the *Dauntless.* That ship, in turn, was taken by the French, and she spent some time in a French prison. Our operatives in France were able to extricate her from that place, and she was brought here and given a mission to Paris to gather information—"

"Totally against my will," I say, and sniff, looking down at the bunch of poor, wilting flowers that I still hold in my hand.

"—which mission she did accomplish, up to a point. Sometime later, she, on her own accord, got herself up in military uniform and joined the French army as a messenger. In that capacity, she delivered many messages between high-ranking French commanders, even those from Napoleon, himself. At the Battle of Jena, she was given a message from Bonaparte directing Marshal Murat to charge the Prussian line. She did deliver the order, Murat charged, and the day was won for France. Had she not done so, the outcome might have been very different."

He stops and looks at me severely. "Do you wonder why we sometimes grow impatient with you, Miss Faber?" I slump down further into my chair.

"To conclude—we were able to get her out of France but lost a very valuable operative in the process," he says. "And here we are. So, what do you have to say for yourself?"

I don't say anything for a while, but then I lift my head and begin to explain.

"When I went to join the French army—to avoid being placed as a common camp-following prostitute, by this very Service, I might well add—it was my intention to volunteer as a simple messenger. I thought in that capacity I would garner much valuable information, and I was right. But instead of assigning me right off to that position, my battalion commander gave me a squad of poor country boys—raw recruits, nothing more than cannon fodder—to train as we marched toward the battlefield at Jena. I believe he did it to establish my worth as an officer. I did work with them, and I gained their respect and loyalty. They watched out for me, too, and soon I had great affection for them as well."

Here I stop and look the First Lord in the eye. "If you have ever been in a war before, my Lord, which I very much doubt, you would know what kind of affection I mean. When it comes down to it in a battle, you are not fighting for King and country, or for Emperor and empire. No, you are fighting to keep your comrades alive as best you can. When I rode across that battlefield with that message in my hand, I knew that if I did not deliver it, my men would be butchered—and I could not let that happen."

"But your mission was—" interjects Mr. Peel.

"My mission was to be a spy, sir, to gather information, which I did. I did not believe I was sent as a saboteur . . . or as an assassin. If you think otherwise, then take me out and shoot me—or hang me, or cut off my head, or whatever—I don't care anymore. I have faced all those things and I just don't care anymore. You have stolen all of my joy today, so why don't you just go ahead and kill me?"

Mr. Peel regards me thoughtfully. "Did you really meet Napoleon Bonaparte?"

"Yes. I carried many messages for him. I had breakfast with him on the morning of the Battle of Jena. I rode in his carriage. He gave me a medal. I'm sure you saw it when you went through my things."

"Remarkable. You do have your ways, don't you?"

"I try to do my duty. Wherever I find that it lies."

"Ah, well. We shall now discuss your new mission."

"My new mission?"

The Black Cloud comes rolling in again, and I am help-less before it, and, *I'm sorry, Jaimy, that you should see me like this. Any shred of my dignity or courage is gone, but I just can't help it. I can't* . . . Tears pour down my face as again I keen, "How can you be so mean to meeeee?"

"You really should try to calm yourself, Miss," says Peel. "And as to our supposed meanness, I want you to listen to this. You should know that, in a certain way, you have been somewhat under our protection . . . Oh yes, you are doubt-ful of that, I can see. But should we cut you loose, the Chan-cellor of the Exchequer would be most interested in taking custody of you. He is the Lord in charge of the King's Treas-ury, and he wishes to discuss a certain matter of theft of the King's property. I do not think it would end well for you. The judicial branch of government is involved in this as well. They think it sets rather a bad precedent. One judge has declared within my hearing at the court, 'If we let her get away with it, we will have legalized thievery. I am afraid she must be hanged.'"

"I don't care, just do it."

"Oh, you do not care? Very well," says the First Lord, picking up yet another paper from his desk. "Do you care about this, then? We have here a young French royal, a cer-tain Monsieur Jean-Paul de Valdon, with whom you were recently romantically involved, and who, we believe, was in-strumental in the death of our very valuable spymaster Monsieur Jardineaux. Just what did happen on that beach in France, Miss Faber? Hmmm? Do you want us to investigate further? Do you want us to instigate inquiries within the French Republic?"

I shake my head. "No. He is an honorable man. Please don't hurt him." I glance over at Jaimy and see that he is standing ramrod straight, his eyes fixed on the wall. *I'm sorry, Jaimy . . .*

"And then there is the matter of cavalry captain Lord Richard Allen, now stationed in Kingston, Jamaica," continues Peel, consulting yet another damning paper. "It seems there was some sort of . . . affair . . . between the two of you, and there is some question as to whether he willfully disobeyed the orders of certain superior officers last summer. Charges could be brought."

I look up at Jaimy again to find he is no longer looking at the wall but rather at me.

I sigh and take up my bouquet again. Amongst the other flowers, I see a daisy and I draw it out from the bunch. With thumb and forefinger I begin to pluck the petals and let them fall to the floor, one by one, while chanting softly in a singsong way, "He loves me, he loves me not. He loves me—"

"Please don't play the simpleton with us, Miss."

"He loves me not—"

"I suspect, Miss, that in spite of all your depredations against proper maidenly behavior, the poor man does indeed still love you, and is to be pitied for it," says Peel briskly. "But be that as it may, here are the terms."

He directs his attention to me first. I sit dejectedly indifferent. *To hell with him and his terms.*

"Ahem. Miss Faber, you will reboard your schooner and set sail for the Caribbean Sea to gather information on the doings of our Spanish enemies in the area. You will sail under your American colors, so the Spanish will not bother you, as they are not enemies of the United States. Your cover will be that of a scientific expedition . . ."

My chin lifts and my eyes begin to widen at this.

". . . gathering specimens of the local flora and fauna. You will be accompanied by Dr. Stephen Sebastian, with whom you are acquainted and who you also know is a member of our branch of service. He will be both your control and your guardian. We know that you have some command of the Spanish language, picked up during your buccaneering cruise there in the summer of '05 and your . . . association . . . during that time with a certain Hispanic pirate named Flaco Jimenez."

*How many more names from my past can they dredge up with which to wound poor Jaimy . . . or me?*

"Although you will have nominal command of your little craft, you will be under the direct orders of Captain Hannibal Hudson, who has been given command of HMS *Dolphin*, a forty-four-gun frigate with which you are both familiar and which will be on patrol in the area, not only to harry Spanish shipping, but also to accept your periodic reports."

*What? The* Dolphin? *Can it be?*

Mr. Peel seems to be done with me and now looks to Jaimy.

"As for you, Mr. Fletcher, to show that we are not completely cold in matters of the heart, you will be assigned as Third Mate on said *Dolphin*, so that at least you will be in the same area as your . . . lady . . . and you might even get to see her occasionally—from afar, of course. It is an excellent posting, as you well know, Third Mate on a forty-four-gun frigate at your young age. But you might well wonder why we are doing this. The reason is that you have an excellent record and come highly recommended by all your former commanding officers, and you should be rewarded for that service. And, too, we wish to keep an eye on you, Lieutenant Fletcher, to make sure you do not raise a fuss over what has just occurred. You will keep your mouth shut. You will inform all who were involved in that aborted wedding that you each had a change of heart. Oil will be spread on the waters. Is that clear?"

Jaimy says nothing.

"So those are the choices," states Mr. Peel. "Should either of you refuse to comply, you, Mr. Fletcher, will be assigned as a low-ranking officer on an Arctic expedition about to set sail to seek a Northwest Passage around the North Pole. And I would like to point out that the last two such expeditions never returned, so I would also suggest that you invest heavily in foul-weather gear. And as for Miss Faber, should she refuse this present assignment, she will be given over to the Treasury people, who will joyfully receive her into their solicitous care. She will be thrown into Newgate Prison, eventually taken to court, charged with Theft of the King's Property, put up in the dock, given a speedy trial, and then condemned to hang by the neck until dead. She will be returned to Newgate to await her turn, and she will fester there until the day when she will be taken out into the square, to mount the gallows. The rope will be put around her neck, the trap will be sprung, and after a few minutes of struggle, that will be it for her. Well?" inquires Peel of us. "You may speak."

"It is not much of a choice," growls Jaimy through clenched teeth.

"I am afraid it is the only option you have, Mr. Fletcher."

"Why can't we be married and still do all you ask of us?" I say, ever the eager, if not very hopeful, bride-to-be.

"Because we have no use for a pregnant agent, and especially *this* agent," says the First Lord, then sniffs. "And in that regard, you must both swear on your honor that you will not have any sexual congress with each other." Here he looks at me. "And in your case, Miss, anyone else, for that matter, until the mission is over and done."

A flush comes to my face and I look down. *Am I really that bad?*

Jaimy speaks up, addressing Mr. Peel, "I cannot imagine why this girl is of such interest to you and your kind."

"Why, my dear sir, there are any number of reasons. This girl is fluent in French, has some Spanish, is not loath to use disguises—some of them male—has led soldiers and sailors in battle, is a thoroughgoing seaman and expert in both small arms and large, has killed by her own hand a certain number of men, is a passable forger and lock pick, has been in difficult circumstances many times yet managed to get herself out of them, *and* has contrived to get herself into Napoleon Bonaparte's very presence. You may be sure, Sir, that no other operative in this service has managed to do *that!*"

The usually very calm and collected Mr. Peel has worked himself up into quite a lather. Jaimy doesn't reply but merely glowers, and Peel continues.

"You may also wonder why we should hold such a person valuable, in spite of her frequent lapses in judgment. Well, I must say we do—and the fact that she owes King George at least forty thousand pounds and several very sincere apologies, all the better!"

"All right, enough," says Lord Grenville. "You both know the terms of the agreement. Do you so swear to those terms, Miss Faber?"

I take a breath—thinking how much this scene is so like, in a twisted way, the marriage ceremony I was so cruelly denied—and finally say, "I do."

He turns to Jaimy. "And do you, Mr. Fletcher, so swear?"

Jaimy looks down at me, and I nod. *There's no way out, Jaimy . . .*

"I do," he manages to choke out.

*I now pronounce you the world's most star-crossed lovers,* I think to myself, all forlorn.

"Very well," says Mr. Peel. "I think it would be best if Mr. Fletcher left now, to report to the *Dolphin*. She lies down at Bournemouth. Messrs. Carr and Boyd will accompany you to pick up your gear at your home and then escort you to your ship. Once boarded, I suggest you stay there. Good day, Mr. Fletcher."

I speak up then.

"You have had your way with us, Sirs, and now I wish to say goodbye to Mr. Fletcher," I say, and try to rise, but Bliffil's hands hold me fast.

"Oh no, you don't," says Bliffil.

"Oh yes, I do," says I, pulling the hatpin that holds Higgins's flower to my breast. The orchid falls into my lap, but I put the five-inch needle into the back of Bliffil's hand.

"*YEEEEEOOOOW!*" he screeches, lurching backward and away from me, clawing at his hand.

"Do not worry, gentlemen. I will harm no one else," I say to the astounded others, and go to stand in front of Jaimy. "Nor will I try to escape. After all, I have given my word."

I look up into Jaimy's face. "Goodbye, Jaimy. I will see you on the other side, and we will talk about . . . the things that were said about me. Just know that I'm still your lass, Jaimy, body and soul, if you still want me."

He tries to respond, but I put my fingertips to his lips. "Not now, Jaimy. Later."

He puts his hands on my shoulders, draws me to him, and kisses me—and I kiss him back. When we come apart, I pat him on the chest, and with tears once again on my cheeks, I say, "Go now, love. Fare thee well."

Carr and Boyd come up on either side of him. He bows stiffly to the First Lord, takes my hand, and bows over it. "We have been sorely tested, but we will someday come together for good and ever, Jacky. I know that. Till such time as we meet again, farewell."

With that, he kisses the back of my hand, turns on his heel, and leaves the room.

After a few moments of quiet weeping, I return to stand yet again in front of the First Lord's desk. Flashby keeps a careful eye on me, while in a corner Bliffil curses over his hurt hand.

"All right, my Lord. Let us get on with this. I hope you do not think that I am stupid enough to believe that I, accompanied by a fully manned Royal Navy frigate, am being sent on this errand to pick up what little scraps of information I might gather from drunken Spanish sailors in dismal bars in the Caribbean."

Mr. Peel smiles. "We think you are anything but stupid, Miss Faber. And no, we are not sending you on this mission because of your abilities as a spy, which are admittedly meager."

"Why, then?" I demand.

"It is because, Miss Faber," says Mr. Peel, smiling one of his very rare smiles. "It is because you can swim."

*What?*

# Chapter 7

*Swim?*

"Yes, swim. And swim very well, by all accounts."

Mr. Peel pulls out yet another piece of paper. "Ahem. In 1803, teaches self to swim while marooned on the coast of South America. In 1804, dives off main yard of HMS *Excaliber* in Boston Harbor, to consternation of crew, who believe her drowned. Later that same year, leaps off side of HMS *Wolverine* to escape impressment, swimming a good quarter mile before being recaptured, and, in the process, dives underwater to save life of drowning seaman. In 1806, after destruction of the slaver *Bloodhound*, swims to lifeboat with severe wound in leg. And finally," he says, putting the paper back down on the desk, "in August of this year, is spotted diving over side of HMS *Mercury* and swimming underwater, back to her schooner."

*Is there no part of my poor life that has gone unreported?*

"It would seem, Miss," observes First Lord Grenville, "that you are not shy about getting wet."

"From that report, Sir, it would seem that I am seldom

dry," I retort. "But still, I do not see what that has to do with anything."

"Mr. Peel will now tell you what it has to do with, but first, Mr. Bliffil, you are excused. Best get something on that hand."

"Yes, you'd best, Bliffil," says I, "as I believe the tropical orchid that the pin held to my dress is of the poisonous variety." *I wish it were.*

Bliffil glares at me and heads to the door. As he goes out, John Higgins comes in.

"Ah, Mr. Higgins. Come in, come in," says the First Lord heartily.

I do not move to embrace Higgins on his arrival, nor do I greet him. No, I only slide my eyes over to peer at him with some suspicion.

Mr. Peel, noticing my look, says, "Ah, are you wondering if Mr. Higgins knew how and when we were going to take you back into the fold, as it were? Well, no, he did not. We did not want to test his loyalty in that way, knowing full well that he is, for some reason, totally devoted to you. And while we have found Mr. Higgins to be a superb analyst of intelligence information, he is not privy to everything."

"Of that I am glad," I murmur, putting my hand on Higgins's arm.

"Your report on today's events, Mr. Higgins, if you would," demands Peel.

"As you please, Sir," answers Higgins. "I was standing by the altar at Saint Paul's, when there was a commotion and Mrs. Mairead McConnaughey, one of Miss Faber's bridesmaids, burst in shouting, 'She's been kidnapped!' While she related to the shocked bridal party what had happened, I guessed that the bride had been taken by this agency. Seeking to spread oil upon these troubled waters, I advised all there not to say a word about this to the newspapers or anyone else, in the interest of Miss Faber's safety. I assured them all that I would make inquiries and keep them informed as much as I could. All seemed to agree to this plan and went home—much dejected, I might add."

"Well done, Higgins," says Lord Grenville, who seems to have taken a real shine to our Higgins, I note through all my continuing confusion. "Well done!"

"I might further add that the bridesmaid's nose was bleeding quite profusely when she entered the church."

I turn to Flashby, furious. "Did you have to hit her, you bastard? Did you?"

Flashby shrugs. "She wouldn't shut up. And I had my orders."

"Now, now," says the First Lord, "let us get back to the matter at hand, shall we? Mr. Peel?"

Mr. Peel puts his fingertips together and begins to recite as if he were giving a historical lecture. "In 1733, a Spanish fleet, whose ships were filled with gold and silver looted from their colonies located in that part of the world, set sail from South America, bound for Spain. It never got there. It ran into a storm and the ships were wrecked off the Florida Keys." He pauses to clear his throat and then continues. "The ships that sank in shallow water were, of course, stripped of their cargoes in no time, but those that sank farther out, were not, as men could not dive down that far. One ship in particular, the *Santa Magdalena,* which was the largest of the fleet and carried the most gold, was never found. We think we know about where she lies"—here he pauses to let that sink in—"and you, Miss Faber, are going to be the one who is going to find and recover the treasure of the *Santa Magdalena*."

My jaw drops open and I sit back down in the chair.

"The gold could be worth in the range of a million pounds sterling. This war with Napoleon is costing a lot of money and His Majesty's Treasury is growing thin. If you were instrumental in getting that Spanish treasure into the King's coffers, it would go a long way toward getting you back in his good graces again. A pardon is possible and . . ."

Mr. Peel rattles on, but I don't hear him—what I hear is Little Mary Faber of the Rooster Charlie Gang, that greedy little imp who is never far from the surface of my mind, sneaking up and whispering in my ear, *Treasure, Jacky, treasure . . .*

I shake my head to get her out of it. *Begone, you!* Mr. Peel is still droning on. ". . . a Spanish sailor, a survivor of the wreck of the *Santa Magdalena,* noted some rough coordinates on where she went down, and those notes have come down through the years, through family records, to us and we—"

"What makes you think I could dive down that far when others cannot?" I ask, a part of me ever the realist.

"There are new scientific discoveries . . . a new apparatus designed to take men deeper than they have ever gone before."

"Then, why not get men to do it? Professional pearl divers or something?"

"Because professional divers would arouse suspicion and you would not. They would not keep their mouths shut and you will. They are not members of this organization, and you are, however much you might resist that title. Remember, Florida is in Spanish hands, and you might be watched."

"This . . . apparatus . . . what is it?"

"You will see. A respected man of science in Boston has the latest model, ready for us to put aboard. Boston, of course, is considered the hub of what they choose to call civilization over there. He will accompany the machine, to instruct you in its proper use."

I think on this and then say, "A full pardon? And I'd be let go to make my own way in this world without all of you hounding me?"

"It is possible."

*Hmmm . . .*

"What do you think, Higgins?"

"Well, Miss, it has possibilities," he replies. "And I think it is your only option. Plus you will get to see your friends in Boston again."

"Yes, there's that," I say. "And will Mr. Higgins be with me?"

"Yes, Miss, as will your entire crew. Several of them are in jail right now, but they will be restored to your ship. And as a further sign of our goodwill, we have managed to extricate from imprisonment in France your friend David Jones, as per your request earlier this year. Seaman Jones will be assigned to your ship's crew as well."

*Davy?*

My mind is spinning out of control and Little Mary seizes that opportunity to creep back into my brain and I am powerless to keep her out.

*Treasure, Jacky, treasure beyond our wildest dreams . . .*

# Chapter 8

I had resolved early on that, in spite of all that had happened to destroy my happiness, I would be cheerful and make the best of things. After all, I am able to get back on my lovely little ship again, and though I was not able to marry Jaimy, at least I will be able to see him sometimes, which is a welcome change from our usual situation of being half a world apart. And again, there is that possibility of treasure. Plus it's in my nature to be cheerful—whenever I can keep the Black Cloud off, that is—and right now I can . . .

. . . because now . . . there is Davy.

It was the day after my supposed wedding and I was brought back to the *Nancy B.*, with strict orders to behave myself, and there he was, standing on the quarterdeck. And it was so good to see the scrappy rascal again, looking all fine in blue trousers and jacket and red striped shirt, that I clasped him to me, crying, "Ah, Davy, well met, well met indeed!"

"You again," he said with a wide grin. "I thought we were done with you for good and ever, Jacky."

"You see, I do have a way of popping back up."

He put his hands on my shoulders and his gaze softened as he looked in my eyes and said, "Ah, Jacky, when I saw that blade come down and then the executioner lifting up the head by its hair for all to see—hair that looked a lot like yours—well, I thought that . . . I thought the old Brotherhood of five was now reduced unto three, I did." Then remembering his old cheeky self, he looked off, coughed, and added, "And good riddance, I thought at the time. Old Boney has done me a favor and gotten rid of that pest for good and ever."

I gave him a poke with my finger. *And that's not all you did, Davy. You also led a riot in the prison and got yourself flogged for it. That's why you've got these stripes on your back and that's why you have this new tattoo here on the back of your hand.*

I grabbed his wrist and held up his hand, to look at the tattoo. It was of a cat and, from the rendering of the chest and hips, plainly a female cat, wearing boots and brandishing a sword with *Puss-in-Boots* written above and the single word *Vengeance* written below. Mr. Peel had told me about that particular tattoo, the one that was being etched onto various arms and hands about the fleet, in memory of the death by guillotine of the girl pirate *La Belle Jeune Fille Sans Merci,* but that was the first time I had actually seen one of them. And here it was on Davy. Imagine that.

"And now three members of that old Brotherhood will again trod on the same deck, and a fourth not too far off. Ain't life strange sometimes?"

"Aye, it is, Jacky, and stranger yet is the fact that Puss-in-Boots is the boss of that same deck. Don't know how I'll be handlin' that."

*You'll get over it, Davy. I ain't that hard a taskmaster.*

I ran my hand over his back, feeling the furrowed lash marks there. "I heard you were whipped, Brother, and all on account of me. I am so sorry," I said. "I know I am so very hard on my friends." And I hugged him to me again, putting my head to his chest. "But let us speak no more about that." I lifted my head to look into his eyes. "You know we are going to the Caribbean, but we are stopping in Boston first."

And those eyes did light up. "Oh yes, Jacky, I do know that!" he exulted, and I knew he was imagining his reunion—and I do mean re-union—with Annie, my own dear friend and, most recently, his own dear wife.

I gave him a punch and said, "You'd better be good to her, Davy."

"I am very good to her," said the rascal with a saucy wink. "Just ask the lass—after I've been there a few days—just how good I have been."

I gave him another poke and we both turned to the outfitting of the *Nancy B. Alsop* for the coming voyage across the raging sea.

During the week following my involuntary reenlistment in the Naval Intelligence Corps, we made mighty preparations for getting under way. In addition to loading on stores—the usual flour, salt pork, dried peas, crates of chickens, oatmeal, dry soup, and rum—we added a carefully packed cargo of fine Wedgwood china. Jacky Faber may now be an agent of British Naval Intelligence, but she is still a merchant. We also used the time to set up a laboratory under the main hatch, for Dr. Sebastian's use. When we were done, he came to visit and pronounced himself very satisfied with the results and most excited about the upcoming expedition—the scientific part of it, anyway. Dr. Sebastian would make the later crossing, on the *Dolphin,* as he had family business to attend to, and because, I think, he really did not relish sailing across the Atlantic in such a small craft as mine. After all, the *Dolphin* was two hundred and four feet long at the waterline and the *Nancy B.* a scant sixty-five.

It was decided that my schooner would leave a week before the frigate, as I would be ready sooner than they, and besides, for reasons of secrecy, it would not be good for us to be seen sailing together. Captain Hudson decided to pay a call on us as we were preparing to get under way, and I was so very glad to see the good Captain again, he who watched out for me as best he could back there on the *Dauntless,* and later when we all were crammed into that foul French prison. And I was further delighted to find that Lieutenant Bennett was again with him, as he was assigned to be his First Mate on the *Dolphin.*

However, at a final meeting in the First Lord's office, I was *not* delighted to learn that, much to my disgust, Lieutenant Harry Flashby would also be assigned to the *Dolphin,* and as Second Mate, no less!

"You must be joking!" I cried, when I first learned of this. I jumped up and pointed my finger at Flashby, who stood smirking by the door. "The first time we met, he tried to ravish me and I was but fourteen years old and lay unconscious. And the second time he managed to get me in his foul clutches, he tied me to a chair and tortured me! A fine choice for Second Mate of HMS *Dolphin,* I must say!" *That will also make the vile bastard Jaimy's superior officer and you can count on Flashby's doing his best to make Jaimy's life miserable . . .*

"Now, Miss," replied Peel, in what he must have thought was a soothing voice, "those were different circumstances. You understand we must have an agent onboard who has military experience, to watch out for our . . . interests, should the mission succeed."

*And watch me, too . . .*

I was *not* mollified.

The day before we leave, I have another visitor.

At dawn she appears on the dock next to us, holding a small bundle of what I assume to be her clothes, other than those she had on her back, along with everything else she owned.

It is Joannie Nichols.

"Joannie? What are you doing here?" I ask, going to the gangway.

She looks up at me. "I want to go with you," she says, and hands me a letter, which I promptly open and read. It is from my grandfather, Reverend Alsop, Headmaster of the London Home for Little Wanderers.

*My Dearest Mary,*

*As you read this, I know that Joan Nichols stands before you, asking to be taken with you on your next journey. How she knows where you can be found, I do not know, and she will not tell me.*

*Joan is a good child, but she has a stubborn, restless nature—she has already left the Home on three separate occa-*

*sions, but has eventually returned each time. She is polite, has good manners, is good at sewing, and has learned her letters, but she has expressed no inclination for going into teaching, manufacturing, marriage, or service, which as you know are the options open to our girls.*

*If she does not come back, I will know that she is with you and I wish you both Godspeed.*

*Wishing you lived a more settled life, I am*
*Your loving grandfather,*
*George Henry Alsop*

I fold the letter back up and look at her standing, head bowed, on the wharf.

"So. The lure of the street proved too much for you, eh?"

"Sometimes. They were nice at the Home, but . . ." She lets it trail off, and I know exactly what she means.

"You realize it's dangerous out on the sea?"

"I do."

"How did you know where to find me? It's supposed to be a secret."

"We're here in Cheapside. I've been in and out of the Home. I know what's happenin' on my turf, I do. I have friends both in the Home and on the streets. So I know."

Hmmm . . . Scrawny, but with a smart mouth on her. Maybe twelve or thirteen years old. Red rough hands and pointy nose. Awkward. Hands and feet too big for her gangly body . . .

*Just like I was.*

I sigh and think, *She's wise in the ways of the streets, so at least I won't have to baby-sit her. So, what the hell—if I re-*

*fuse, she'll just work those streets till she is devoured by them, and sailing with me is better than that. Not much, but some.*

"All right, Joannie. Come aboard. Your billet will be that of Ship's Girl. You will help Mr. Tinker in the cooking of food, and you will mop and clean and do anything else that is asked of you." I give her a stern look. "Is that understood?"

She nods and runs up the gangway, the joy plain on her face.

"Draw some light canvas from our stores to make yourself a pair of proper sailor's pants, as you certainly cannot perform your duties in that dress. When you are presentable, report to me."

In less than ten minutes I see her up on the crow's-nest, sewing away, and singing.

This morning we cast off, now riding the Thames's river current and the tide down to the sea. It is a beautiful day for a departure, if such a leave-taking must be made, the sky clear, with but a few scudding clouds, the breeze brisk, and the air warm.

As we pass Bournemouth, I see a Royal Navy frigate lying at anchor, golden porpoises entwined about her name on the stern, a newly restored figurehead of a scantily dressed woman on her prow, and my breath catches in my throat.

*It is the* Dolphin, *the ship that took me in and gave me a home when I had none, the place where I was taught all the sailor skills I now have and where I met and joined the Brotherhood and where I first fell in love with a fine boy.*

I force myself to be strong and not cry, and say to Jim

Tanner, my very skilled helmsman, "Bring us close to that ship there, Mr. Tanner, if you would."

We have the wind behind us, so it is an easy thing for him to do, and as we swing alongside the dear *Dolphin*, I see Captain Hudson and Lieutenant Bennett and, yes, Lieutenant James Emerson Fletcher on the quarterdeck. They all look up, surprised, as I cup my hands to my mouth and merrily call out, "We'll beat you over by two weeks, you sorry lot of swabs, just see if we don't!"

There are cheers and laughter from both ships as we sheer away and head off to the rolling sea. I stand there a long time, looking back, and I think I see Jaimy doing the same.

# PART II

# Chapter 9

"Back in good old Boston!" I crow, as the sleek *Nancy B.* slips by the more clumsy craft in Boston Harbor on this fine day, all her sails tight as drums, flags out and snapping, heading for Long Wharf. *Oh, how good it is to be back and, for once, not being chased!*

As we approach the town docks, I see a likely spot. "There, Jim," I say, pointing. "Right behind that merchantman. We'll tie up there. Careful, now."

Jim Tanner is at the helm, Davy and the others tending the sails. Joannie Nichols is by my side, jumping up and down in her excitement at her first glimpse of the New World. Daniel Prescott is there, too, but he affects the more world-weary, seen-it-all-before attitude of the experienced sailor, for all of his twelve years. I know he does this to impress Joannie, but I also know he is just as excited as the rest of us to be back in Boston, our dear home port.

As we edge in, taking down more and more canvas till there is none left up, we let the breeze and the tide nestle our stout little schooner into her berth. *Ah, yes, home again, girl . . .*

While we're maneuvering in, I notice a girl with flaxen hair standing on the dock, dressed in the serving-girl gear favored by Mistress Pimm of the Lawson Peabody School for Young Girls located up there on that hill. When she sees that it is us and that it is Jim Tanner who stands straight and tall at the helm, she falls to her knees and clasps her hands in front of her, her head bowed. *Yes, Clementine,* I say to myself, *once again, your prayers have been answered.* I speculate that she had gotten hold of a telescope and stolen chances each day to climb up onto the widow's walk on the top of the Lawson Peabody to scan the incoming seagoing traffic, and today she was rewarded, and I wish you the joy of it, Sister, I do.

Tink throws over the land lines and a dockhand ties them to the wharf's bollards. We are secure, the *Nancy B.* now a thing of the land and not of the sea. The gangplank is laid across. And no sooner is it done than Clementine hops over the rail and is wrapped around her Jim, and he wrapped around her.

"Clementine! Dear girl!"

"Oh, Jimmy, I'm so glad! So glad!"

"Good to see you, too, Clementine," I say to she who has not spared me so much as a glance. "Ah, well . . . Jim Tanner, be off with your girl. We'll get things shipshape around here and we'll come get you when we need you. Keep in touch, now. See you in a few days." Jim throws his seabag over his shoulder, and they are joyously off without a backward glance.

There is a thump of feet upon deck and I turn to see that Davy has come down from the mainmast, where he has been managing the set of the sails for the tricky way in. His sandy hair is neatly braided in a pigtail—hair the color and texture of which is so much like mine that people have sometimes taken us for brother and sister. That and the fact that we bicker like any two members of the same litter of pups.

*Well done, Davy,* is what I should say for his expert handling of the sails, but what I do say is, "Not bad, Seaman Jones, though there was a bit of a luff in the jib on the way in. Hope no true and worthy seaman was watching and chanced to see that. I should die of shame were it let out that I would allow something like that to happen on a ship of mine."

He knows I am joking with him, so he grimaces and grunts, "Stoof it, Jack-o."

I realize that he is about to jump out of his skin in his fervent desire to get close, very close, to his new bride, Annie, who he knows is working in the Lawson Peabody building right there up on Beacon Hill. *Right there, by God . . .*

"Now, is that any way to talk to your Captain, Day-vee?" I tease, giving him a poke in the ribs.

Yesterday I had given him some money, 'cause I knew he'd be wanting to take Annie off for a few days' romp in a room at the Pig and Whistle, rather than suffer under her father's stern and sometimes not-very-friendly eye at the Byrneses' family homestead. After all, he is taking the man's daughter to bed, and that doesn't always set easy with a dad.

"Your first pay from Faber Shipping Worldwide. Ain't that grand, now, Davy?" I had said, pressing it into his hand and grinning into his face. "It isn't much, 'cause you're only rated Ordinary here, Davy, *very* Ordinary. But it should serve. Ah, yes, I know that in the Royal Navy you are rated Able, yes, I know . . . But here at Faber Shipping, we hold to a much higher standard."

I do love to see his teeth go on edge . . . *Ah yes, just like old times.*

"All right, the ship is secure and I'm off," says Davy now, preparing to leap over the rail and sprint up Beacon Hill to the school. "Do I have permission to go ashore, *Captain*?" the last word spoken with a bit of a snarl.

"Not just yet, Seaman Jones. You must calm yourself." I simper. "We shall go off and visit the Lawson Peabody together. I have to change, and you will stay right there till I get back," I order, pointing to the deck beneath his feet. "I shan't be long."

I give him a bit of a finger wave and go below into my cabin, where I find Higgins laying out my Lawson Peabody School dress. I am out of my working clothes in a moment and into the uniform black dress.

"What else will you need, Miss?" asks my good Higgins.

"Just my mantilla," I say. "And my red wig."

"*What?*" he says, eyebrows up.

"Davy and I are going up to the Lawson Peabody, he to see his wife and me to see my sisters. Will you not join us?"

"No, thank God," says Higgins, reaching into my seabag and pulling out the wig as if it were a large and particularly hideous spider. He shudders as he puts it on my head and fluffs it up. "I must go see Mr. Pickering concerning the disposal of the cargo."

"Ah. Good," I say. "Well, please give Ezra my compliments and tell him that I shall see him later this afternoon. And please inform him and all the crew that we will have dinner at the Pig and Whistle this evening, Faber Shipping's treat."

"I shall convey that message. But how can you wear this thing in public?" he asks, shuddering.

My red wig is undoubtedly one of the more outrageous of the hairpieces I've picked up to hide my shorn locks—short hair on women is a scandal in many parts of the world—and the wig is very high and very long and is decorated with yellow ribbons, and when it is in place, a cascade of ringlets hang by my face.

"It is a joke, Higgins. I mean to have a bit of fun," I say as I wrap the black lace mantilla about my shoulders, ready, should I need it, to veil my face.

"Well, I hope you do, Miss," says Higgins. "Here, you will need your cloak if it grows chilly outside."

"Thank you, Higgins," I say, as he wraps the coat about me and pulls the hood up over my head, completely concealing my fake hair. "And now we must be off."

Regaining the deck, I link my arm in Davy's and say, "Now, my fine young sailor lad, we shall go to see about the Lawson Peabody and all who lie within it."

As we walk through the narrow streets near the docks and then up across the commons, I revel in the old familiar sights and in the delicious cool of the late fall day.

It is not long before we have crossed Beacon Street and are approaching the school. I stop and heave a great sigh while looking at the building, the scene of much grief and, yes, much gladness for me.

Davy, however, is in no mood for such female wistfulness and charges on ahead.

"Wait, Davy," I say, running to catch up with him. "Let's go around back and go in that way."

And so we do, and as I approach the door to the kitchen, I say, "You wait out here, Davy." Then, lifting the latch, I add, "It'll be better that way, you'll see."

I open the door and duck in. Sure enough, there's good old Peggy, working away at the stove. As she turns to look at me, I pull the mantilla from my face and say, "Hello, Peggy," and her eyes grow wide and she drops her ladle and says, "Oh, my good Lord, it's our Jacky!" and comes to enfold me in her warm embrace.

I bury my face in her breast, and the tears come, as I remember all the kindness she has always shown to me, her poor wayward girl, and just then Annie comes down the stairs and into the kitchen, bearing a large empty tray, and I know she has just come down from the dining hall, where dinner is being served to the girls.

Seeing me, she gasps, then says, "Jacky! Can it be you? Is it possible?"

I wipe the tears from my eyes and go over and take the tray from her hands before she drops it, as I know she will when she hears my news. "Yes, it's me, dear Annie, and—"

"Jacky, have you heard anything—"

"I think you had best just go out through that door right now, Sister, and your question will be answered," I say, grinning from ear to ear in anticipation of her joy.

Her mouth pops open and her eyes go wide and she says, "You mean . . ."

I nod and she flies across the room and out the door and then lets out a squeal of pure, absolute joy.

*"Davy! Oh, dear God! Davy!"*

I go over and pull the door shut. "Sorry, Peg, but I think you're gonna have to do without Annie for a few days, and Clementine, too, I'm afraid, 'cause Faber Shipping's back in town."

Peg laughs. "That's all right, Jacky, we've got lots of girls. Oh, it's just so good to see you, dear! Where have you been and what—"

"I'll fill you in later, Peg, but just now let's fill up this tray and let me carry it up to the little darlings."

While Peg is preparing the platter with some very tasty-looking meat dishes, I shed my cloak and shawl and let the red tresses spill down over my shoulders.

"Well," says Peg, with some disapproval in her appraising eye, "ye don't look like half a tramp, now, do ye?"

I give her a saucy wink, like any true strumpet, pick up the tray, and head up the stairs and out into the hall. I meet two other serving girls coming out of the dining room as I head in, new girls whom I do not know, and who look in wonder at me in all my garish splendor. I give my head a shake so that the ringlets hang more in my face and I gaze about me.

The girls are all seated, as are the teachers at the head table, awaiting the arrival of Mistress Pimm. *And here are all my dear sisters,* I'm thinkin', and startin' to mist up. *Here's Martha and Julia and little Rebecca and Rose and . . .*

*. . . there's Amy . . .*

I blink away the tears and head over to where she is sitting. Unlike the first time I laid eyes on Amy Trevelyne, she now has company at her table—Dorothea and Elspeth and Priscilla, among others—but again she has her nose in a book. Well, we'll soon fix *that*.

I see that I am attracting considerable attention. Heads are raised and elbows nudge ribs and pointed glances are cast my way, which is as it should be—I do love being the center of attention.

Dear little Rebecca Adams is seated next to Amy, chattering away, a chattering that stops mid-chat as I approach in all my tacky glory.

She looks up at me, her big eyes round, as I tap her on the shoulder and say, "Well, hain't ye the pretty one, Missy," loud enough for all to hear. "Yes, ye are, but roight now whyn't ye take yer pretty li'l butt outta that there chair so's a real laydie kin sit 'er arse down?"

The room is dead silent as a stunned Rebecca gets out of her seat and I plunk myself down in it.

Amy's nose is now out of the book and staring at what she can see of me 'neath this red mop.

"Allo, Miss," I says, echoing the first conversation we ever had. "Me name is Jacky Faber and I'm new 'ere and perhaps you'll be tellin' me why we gots two spoons 'ere?"

Her mouth drops open in a very un-Amy-like way as I reach up and pull off the wig, revealing my still-short locks and my very foxy grin. "Perhaps you'll be givin' yer old mate a bit of a hug and kiss, then?"

The place explodes with excitement. *It's Jacky! She's back!*

I rise and Amy throws her arms around me and I throw mine around her and Rebecca joins in the hug, too, and there are cries of *welcome back!* and *hooray, Jacky!* and . . .

There is the sound of two sharp raps of a cane on the floor—Mistress Pimm has come into the room. The noise stops. Ramrod straight as always, and no grayer than last I saw her, she casts her eye about till it finally falls on me.

"Take your places, all of you," she says, her voice low, her gaze expressionless, seemingly not surprised by my sudden appearance. The girls shuffle about to again stand behind their chairs. When all is quiet, she continues.

"I see that our wandering child has returned to us, and that is good. I will now ask her to give us the grace. Miss Faber, if you will."

I clasp my hands in front of me and begin. "Thank you, Lord, for this food that we are about to receive and for which we are most grateful," I say, about to sail into my usual glib performance. But this time, as I look out over their faces, I suddenly find I cannot do it. *All my dear sisters . . .* I try, but I cannot. It's all too much . . . too much.

I choke up.

"And th-thank you all for the kind friendship y-you have sh-shown me over the years . . . and . . ."

I bury my face in my hands and sob away. I did not think this would happen, but it did. I thought I was hard, but I am not. I am not . . .

"Perhaps, Miss Howell," I hear Mistress say, "you will complete the grace, as Miss Faber seems overcome with rather unseemly emotion."

Miss Howell, Connie Howell, the very pious girl who has had very little use for one Jacky Faber in the past, steps up and delivers. "Dear Lord Jesus, thank you for bringing our lost friend back into our midst. It needs must make us think of the parable that You Yourself spoke unto us, that of the Shepherd and his Lost Sheep—how ninety and nine sheep were safe in the fold but how the true shepherd went out looking for the one lost lamb, and when he did find it, he layeth it upon his shoulders, saying to his friends, 'Rejoice with me, for I have found my sheep which was lost.'" She pauses, and then simply says, "Amen."

I always thought that I could sling scripture around with the best of them, but Connie sure nailed me this time.

"Amen!" chorus the other girls, and all take their seats.

"Thank you, Miss Howell," says Mistress before she herself sits down. "We shall all take our dinner, and after that we shall call upon Miss Faber for a recounting of her recent travels. I fear that scant other, possibly more worthy, instruction shall take place this afternoon, but so be it."

We have our dinner, and when we are done, I stand up and do it, and I lay it on.

> *"Oh, you my sisters, attend to me,*
> *You who have braved both wild and stormy seas,*
> *and suffered the cruelest of tyrannies.*
> *And you who have suffered durance most vile,*
> *Take a cup and offer it up and listen now*
> *to a happier tale of work, song, and travail,*
> *on a trip down the American Nile . . ."*

I may not be Virgil, but I can lay it on good and thick.

# Chapter 10

*Lieutenant James Fletcher*
*Onboard HMS* Dolphin
*Approaching Boston Harbor*
*Massachusetts, USA*

*Jacky Faber*
*Onboard the schooner* Nancy B. Alsop
*Somewhere in that same Boston*

*Dear Jacky,*

*Well, I shall probably see you very soon, as we are no more than a day's sail from Boston. I say "probably" in the event you have been carried off by Hottentots, wild Red Indians, Pyrates, or somesuch, which, given the happenings of the past three years, is not entirely unlikely.*

*We had smooth sailing on the way over and I only hope that the mission to which you have been committed will play out as smooth, but I have my doubts as to that—there is talk amongst the officers about this device that is going to be loaded aboard and I have uneasy feelings about it. I overhear Dr. Sebastian saying things like "heavy atmospheric pressure" and "being so small, she won't need much air." Just what part this "device" will play in this supposedly purely scientific expedition, I do not know, as I have not been told. But I can imagine who the "she" is.*

*The ship's company did prove convivial—except for Flashby, of course, but he has kept his distance from me, at least for now. I believe he knows I shall not pass up an opportunity to call him out and he does want to provoke me. I know you would not like to hear this, Jacky, but the scoundrel has exercised what turns out to be his considerable, if false, charm, and is well liked by the other officers. Even I have found it hard to suppress a laugh at some of his stories and jokes told at the mess table.*

*Captain Hudson is an excellent commanding officer, firm but fair and a thoroughgoing seaman. He has told me that I will not be confined to the ship when we reach Boston, saying that Intelligence be damned, he's not going to treat a gentleman like a common unrated seaman, and for that I am grateful. When in Boston, I shall be able to take you out to dinner, if not to bed. I should greatly prefer the latter, but I must accept my lot.*

*Well, I must go on watch now, and so I will conclude. Should the Fates prove kind this time, I shall soon be able to place this letter in your hand, and that prospect soothes my worried mind somewhat.*

*In any case, dear one, till we meet again, I remain yr most humble and etc. . . .*

*Jaimy*

# Chapter 11

"...and that is how I almost got married," I say, heaving a huge, theatrical sigh and wiping away an imaginary tear. "End of story. Sniff."

"I am sorry for you, Sister," says Amy Trevelyne. "But I am glad that you found your way back to us and have regained your good spirits in spite of it all."

We are up in the hayloft of the big barn at Dovecote, the estate of the family Trevelyne in Quincy, Massachusetts. It has always been one of our favorite places to lie about and talk and to tell each other our hopes and dreams. We have just gotten back from a fine ride about the meadows and fields in the late fall air and I am lying sprawled on my back in the still-warm straw and it feels oh so lovely. The horses we rode are being cooled and curried and put up by the stablemen below, and I feel a bit guilty about it—for one who was born common and raised as a beggar, I certainly find it easy to slip into the ways of the rich. I pick up a tasty-looking piece of new hay that still has its head of bearded barleycorn on it and I stick it between my teeth and chew on the end, musing on the happenings of the last six weeks—London, the outfitting of my vessel, the leave-taking, the journey over, and our arrival back in dear old Boston.

"Still, Amy, I wish the marriage had happened," I say, shaking my head to get it back in the present.

"You are only sixteen years old, Sister, you have time enough," says Amy.

"Lots of people get married at sixteen. Younger, even."

"Yes, but the quality do not."

"Oh? And I am suddenly of the quality?"

"You'll do," she says, and goes on. "Martha Custis married George Washington at age twenty-nine. Of course, she was a widow, but even before that, when she had wed Daniel Custis, she was two years older than you. And our second president, John Adams, became interested in Abigail when she was fifteen, but they didn't marry until she was twenty."

"Umm," I say, reserving judgment on that. "And what about you?"

"I am not ready for that sort of thing just yet," she says, as she has so often before. I take that with a grain of salt but hold my tongue, for now.

While I'm stretching in the warm straw, Amy sits cross-legged next to me with her portable writing desk balanced on her knees. She bends over the paper laid thereupon, writing away furiously, pausing only to ask me pertinent questions as I relate the happenings on my recent trip down the Mississippi River. Finally, we are done.

"*And with a last, full-throated, stentorian bellow, Mike Fink disappeared around a bend in the river and I saw him no more.* End of story, thank God."

"Well, there are a few gaps to be filled," says Amy, still scribbling away, "but I suppose that will do for now."

I put my hands behind my head and look off into the high rafters. "And just how scarlet will you paint me this time, Amy?" For one who has never yet been caught breathing hard in an amorous situation, she is certainly not loath to portray my poor fallible self in such a way.

"I only write down what you tell me, Jacky."

*Uh-huh, and with a few literary embellishments here and there . . .*

"Well, I'm sure Mother Fletcher will be delighted," I say, imagining the sheer joy that Jaimy's mother must have felt upon seeing my wedding to her darling son turn into a shambles. I look at my dear friend through narrow eyes. "You have become quite the literary sensation, Miss, both here and in London. I hear your works are to be translated into French, even."

"Well," says Amy, "my family is quite mortified, you'll be glad to hear. It's not done, you know. One such as I to publish, I mean." She writes down another few words and sniffs a ladylike sniff. "If the literary establishment will not publish my poetry, then it will have to put up with my . . . prose efforts."

I knew that Amy had sent a sheaf of her poems to a Mr. Thomas Wentworth, the editor of a high-toned Boston literary journal, and he sent them back saying that she "ought not publish," for various reasons, chief of which was that she was a young girl of gentle birth and because of that her efforts could not possibly be up to snuff. Last week I was at my local bookseller's on Cornhull Street and I managed to find some of Mr. Wentworth's writing. I can tell you one thing—Thomas Wentworth may be a fine and righteous Abolitionist, but as a poet, he ain't a patch on Amy Trevelyne's snowy white drawers.

"Your very purple prose efforts, Sister," says I, squirming deeper into the wonderfully warm hay. "And speaking of marriage prospects, quality or not, how are things between you and our fine Mr. Pickering?"

She blushes, but before she can say her usual "I am not ready for that sort of thing right now," there is a bit of a bustle down below, and whose head should pop up at the edge of the loft but that of Ezra Pickering himself.

"And what do we have here?" he asks, smiling his secret little smile. "Two dewy country maidens taking their ease in the new-mown hay. How charmingly rustic. May I join them?"

I laugh and say, "Ah, yes, just two simple milkmaids are we. Come on up." I glance at Amy and see that she is not at all displeased at Ezra's arrival. Not at all . . . *Hmmm* . . .

He sits down next to Amy. "Can I hope to be invited to dinner, Miss Trevelyne, since I came all the way here?"

"You may, Mr. Pickering," she says.

But I take it further. "You have news, Ezra, else you would not be here."

"That is true, Miss Faber," he says, dusting some chaff off his perfectly tailored sleeve. "HMS *Dolphin* has docked at Long Wharf and your presence there tomorrow has been . . . how shall we say . . . 'requested.'"

# Chapter 12

It was Solomon Freeman who brought Ezra Pickering over to Dovecote in the *Morning Star* yesterday, and it is he who brings me back in her today.

"I am honored that the great Lord Othello deigns to convey my poor self back to Boston," I tease, leaning back against the gunwale, watching him trim the sail and tend the tiller. I note that he has become quite expert in small-boat handling since last I saw him, and I compliment him on it. "How good of His Lordship to come all the way across Massachusetts Bay just for me."

Solomon laughs and adjusts the sail a bit, steering a course for the Boston docks. "Well, I may play the warrior Othello on the stage, but you, Miss Faber, are still the boss of Faber Shipping here in the real world, and so I will come pick you up anytime you want me to."

Higgins and I had taken in the play several nights ago and Solomon was magnificent—every inch the victorious general in the beginning, every bit the broken man brought down by treachery and his own jealousy at the end. Mr. Bean plays Iago, and for the duration of their play, I hate him.

It caused a bit of a scandal in Boston, of course, but it shouldn't have—a black actor playing a black character, what could be more natural?

After the final curtain, I joined the cast for a bit of carousing at the Pig and Whistle and got in quite late, but it was good to see Messrs. Fennel and Bean again, as well as Chloe Cantrell, my friend and Faber Shipping's part-time secretary.

Yesterday, in a little side office at Dovecote, Ezra and I had some time to go over the affairs of Faber Shipping Worldwide, he being the Clerk of the Corporation and all. We went over money on hand (not much); the state of our equipment—boats, traps, lines, et cetera; rates of pay for employees—Solomon had to hire several wharf rats to help with the trap hauling, me having most of the able-bodied men with me across the sea; the going price on lobsters, clams, and fish; profit and loss, profit and loss, till my head spun. But Higgins did sell off that china at a good price, so, at the end of it all, we get to meet the payroll and go on.

"Maybe this new expedition will yield something for us," I said, putting my hand on his arm. "Maybe some crumbs will fall through the cracks. Never can tell. We'll see . . ."

"Well, if anyone can nudge those crumbs toward those cracks," Ezra said, chuckling and gathering up his papers and stuffing them back in his valise, "it is you, Madame President. And now I believe we are being called to dinner."

That evening, Colonel and Mrs. Trevelyne received me most cordially at their table, even though I know they do not entirely approve of me as a suitable companion for their daughter, Amy, or, God forbid, a suitable match for their son, Randall. Of course they were overjoyed to hear my news of their hotheaded son, who had disappeared in late summer after an argument with the Colonel over Randall's performance, or lack of it, at college. *I'll wager he'll come back with his head a good deal less hot after having seen that awful slaughter at Jena-Auerstadt,* I'm thinking.

Having stormed out of Dovecote, Randall had wrangled a letter of introduction to an important general in Napoleon's army out of Lissette's father, le Comte de Lise, and so ended up as a light horseman on the march to Germany. With me. Pressed for details, I recount how shocked Randall and I were to meet each other that day in Marshal Murat's tent and how, some days later, we both rode in Murat's cavalry charge on the Prussian lines at Jena. I told them of Randall's bravery and how he saved my very life. I know Colonel Trevelyne was pleased to hear that. I also told them of my last meeting with Randall and of his stated intention to resign his commission and return to Dovecote. I know Mrs. Trevelyne was pleased to hear *that*.

Right now I am at sea and bundled up against the cold—it is early December, after all—a beautiful day with clear skies and just the right amount of following wind to speed us on our way across the bay. Aye, it's a bit chilly, but I still prefer this to a tooth-rattling ride in a coach, which is how Amy and Ezra are returning to Boston at this very moment. I smile to think of the two of them there in the cramped interior of the carriage . . . *How cozy* . . . I know Ezra's having a good time of it and I believe Amy is, too, though she won't show it, the fool.

"There she is," says Solomon, heading straight for the side of the *Nancy B.* lying dead ahead, now tied up outboard of the newly arrived *Dolphin*. "The captain of that ship ordered us to bring her alongside, so we did it. We moved her yesterday. Hope that was all right with you."

I nod. *Aye, I'm certainly not the one calling the shots now, Solly, not even on my own boat.*

"Yes, you did right, Mr. Freeman. The men on that ship are my friends." *Most of them, anyway.*

We are close enough now that I can make out John Tinker and John Thomas and Smasher McGee standing on the deck of my schooner and young Daniel Prescott and Joannie together up in the rigging. Jim Tanner and Davy Jones are, of course, nowhere to be seen. And on the *Dolphin* I believe I spy . . . aye, that's him . . . Captain Hannibal Hudson on his quarterdeck, hands clasped behind him and deep in conversation with another, younger officer and . . . Is it? . . . *Yes! It's Jaimy!*

I jump to my feet and shout, "Hullo, Jaimy Fletcher!" waving my arms wildly about in my joy at seeing him safely delivered from across the sea.

Hearing my call, he bows to Captain Hudson—no doubt begging his pardon for the sudden, female intrusion—and then turns and brings his hand to his hat in salute to me. *Oh, Jaimy, I am so glad.* I can see the white gleam of his teeth as he gestures over the side to the brow that has been set up alongside the *Dolphin*.

"I see it, Cap'n," says Solomon, anticipating my order, his grin huge in seeing the complete happiness writ all over my face. "We'll be right there. Steady, now, Missy."

He brings the *Morning Star* about, drops the sail, and steers her expertly in. I doff my cloak, leap over onto the platform, up the stairs, and onto the deck of the *Dolphin*. In spite of my excitement and my urge to leap upon Jaimy, I know that courtesies must be paid, so I go up before Captain Hudson, and the officers who stand beside him, and dip down into a deep curtsy.

"So good to see you again, Captain," I murmur, as I come up from the curtsy and give him my hand and look into his merry eyes.

Captain Hudson bows. "And good to see you again, Miss Faber," he says with a smile. "It is not often we welcome a French officer onboard one of His Majesty's ships. You shall have to tell us the tale of that sometime."

I expected a comment like that, for I am wearing my French Hussar's jacket, all blue, with gold frogging across the front, and strapped down nice and tight, just the way I like it. It is the one I wore as a messenger in Napoleon's army, and it matches the blue skirt I have on. I knew I could not get away with the trousers I actually wore during that campaign, so I made do with the skirt. Likewise, I do not wear my old shako but instead have perched on my head a bonnet to match. I do, however, wear the five-pointed star of the Legion of Honor on the left side of my chest, just like *l'empereur* wears his. Let them think what they like. I had thought of wearing my Trafalgar medal, too, but it ain't that formal an occasion, so I don't. And it might be a bit much, even for me.

"I shall, with great pleasure, Captain Hudson," I purr. "And Mr. Bennett, I am pleased to see you once again onboard a Royal Navy ship." And indeed I am pleased—the last time I saw him we were both in a foul French prison.

"And Mr. Flashby, my Second Mate."

I lock the frostiest of my Lawson Peabody Looks in place—back straight, eyes hooded, lips together, teeth apart—and dip down ever so slightly before the cur. "Sir," is all I say in greeting.

"We meet again, Miss Faber," he says, smiling and bowing just as slightly in return. "It is to be hoped that this time things will be more . . . cordial . . . between us?" This exchange is *not* missed by Captain Hudson.

I don't answer the bastard, but turn my face to the next man in line, and, *Oh, Jaimy, it is so good to see you!*

"And my Third Mate, Mr. Fletcher, with whom I believe you are already acquainted."

*Oh, very well acquainted, indeed!*

I dip down in my best curtsy, swirling my skirt so that it describes a perfect circle on the deck, and then I rise up and take Jaimy's hand in mine and look into those beautiful slate blue eyes and—

"Ahem!" says Captain Hudson. "Time for that later. Maybe. Ha-ha. Now we must go below and gaze upon the wonderful scientific device that has just been brought aboard. I think you will be most interested. Dr. Sebastian is already below with the scientist who designed the thing. If you will follow me?"

I give Jaimy a nudge and one of my foxy grins and plant a quick kiss on his lovely cheek and allow him to lead me toward Three Hatch. As we pass it, I see that the hatch is uncovered and a very stout line runs taut from a crane above and disappears into the gloom below. As it sways slowly back and forth, I assume something very heavy is suspended from it.

I find I am not wrong in that assumption. As we descend the ladder and my eyes become used to the gloom, I am able to make out a large, bell-like thing made, it seems, of iron and brass. It is about six feet across and about eight feet high and has a window of very thick glass, fitted and dogged down with brass toggles. The bottom of it has what appears to be lead weights attached to it by short thick chain, and all are suspended about three feet off the deck. Out of the bottom of it also sticks two pairs of trousered legs and I hear excited talk coming from within what I shall now, and probably always will, call the Damned Bell.

". . . and you see, Doctor, the construction is such that when lowered into the water, it is kept upright so that atmospheric pressure keeps the air trapped within, so that the occupant can easily and freely breathe while observing all about him," says the owner of one of the pairs of legs. The voice sounds somewhat familiar, and for some reason I feel a sense of dread and impending catastrophe come over me. "It's good, I am quite sure, to withstand the pressures down to at least two hundred and fifty feet below."

"But how does that occupant get out should he . . . or, in this case, she . . . wish to get out?"

I feel Jaimy tighten up beside me.

"Why, my good fellow, the bell will be suspended a few feet off the bottom of the sea and she will be able to just duck under the edge and be off to do his . . . or her . . . work and come back every minute or so to sit on that bench there for a refreshing breath of air. Oh, what a brave new world, to have such wonders in it!"

"Ahem," says the Doctor. "Yes, brave and all, but I must point out that many of us have a certain affection for said . . . occupant . . . and we do not wish to see her hurt."

"Now, now, my good Doctor, put your mind at rest. My diving machine is perfectly safe and thoroughly tested . . ."

*Where have I heard that voice saying exactly that before?*

And it hits me—*"My flying machine is perfectly safe and thoroughly tested."*

I am astounded. *Tilly? Oh no!*

Oh yes. I drop Jaimy's arm and duck under the edge of the dreadful Thing and stand up inside. Before me I see Dr. Stephen Sebastian holding up a lamp and beside him, none other than Professor Phineas Tilden, our old schoolmaster.

*Aw, Tilly, you tried to kill me with your damned kite, and now you've come back to finish me off with this! Oh Lord, please, no!*

I feel Jaimy slip up beside me and take my hand.

"I don't like this," he mutters, tightening his grip. Then loud enough for all to hear, he says, "I don't like this at all."

"Ah. What have we here? Why, it is our little Jacky Faber," says Tilly, ignoring Jaimy's concerns. He peers out at me through his tiny spectacles, as fat, unworldly, and befuddled as ever. "I see by your dress and your manner that you have benefited from your time at Miranda Pimm's school and I am glad that I was able to place you there. And is it James Fletcher that I see standing there beside you? Well, good . . . good to see that two of my former students have profited by my early tutelage and have come up somewhat in the world as a result. Ahem, yes . . . Now, Jacky . . . er . . . Miss Faber . . ."

Tilly has never, it seems, gotten over the fact that Jacky Faber, the ship's boy he once tutored—and used in his experiments—turned out to be a girl.

"Professor Tilden," I say, "I think—"

*I think you are quite mad* is what I start to blurt out. *Two hundred and fifty feet in this iron coffin!* But I don't get to.

"And I think it's getting rather stuffy in here," says Dr. Sebastian before I can say anything. "I rather think the four of us and this lamp have used up most of the available oxygen in this thing"—the lamp indeed does start to sputter—"and we had best step out before we all pass out in a heap."

We do it and it is a relief to suck in a lungful of fresh air—or as fresh as air exists down here in Three Hatch, which ain't very fresh at all, considering we ain't very far from the bilges. Still, it's better than being inside that thing.

I am surprised to find myself somewhat woozy and I lean against Jaimy sayin', "Oi'm sorry, Jaimy luv, but I seems to be a bit unsteady on me pins, I am."

He puts his arm around me and holds me up. "Sir," he says to Captain Hudson, "I must protest. You see how frail she is. How can she possibly be sent to the bottom of the ocean in that thing?"

Captain Hudson casts a jaundiced eye upon my frail self, thinking, no doubt, of the many reports of my distinctly non-frail behavior in the past.

"Now, Jacky," says Tilly, "we will take things very gradually, only going down, say, six fathoms on the first descent."

I fake a slight faint.

"I insist, Sir, that I be allowed to take her place," says Jaimy.

I straighten up upon hearing that—I cannot let *that* happen.

"You are too big, James," says Tilly, shaking his head. "Look at the size of her—she would require very little air at all, while you would require much."

"Plus, it is reported that she can swim like a fish," says Captain Hudson. "Which you, sir, cannot."

"And just think of the specimens we shall collect from down there," says Dr. Sebastian. "Just think of the glorious specimens!"

And with that I know I am doomed.

"Well, now," says the Captain. "Now that we have seen this wonderful device"—and he gives it a rap with his knuckles—"let us go topside and prepare for dinner."

As we emerge back into the light, the Captain says, "Mr. Fletcher, you and your lady have a bit of time before dinner . . . enough time for, say . . . a ten-minute promenade about the deck." Unable to restrain himself, he then chortles, "And remember always, Lieutenant, to keep your pistol on half cock, for safety's sake." Exit the Captain, laughing over his own joke.

Jaimy's face turns a surprising shade of red. "The Captain is apprised of the . . . agreement by which you and I are bound and finds it most hilarious," he says through clenched teeth. "I have been the butt of many jokes by those officers senior to me. The junior ones dare not, but I know what they are thinking, the dogs."

"Ah, let it go, Jaimy. We must enjoy the moment," I say,

linking my arm in his and leading him off to what I hope will be a more private place.

"I like and respect the Captain and the Doctor, but I hate the fact that Naval Intelligence seems to feel that they . . . own you."

"Well, maybe this mission will clear that up."

"A scientific expedition is going to clear your name so they will bother you no more?"

"Well, maybe there's more to it than that." *And more than that I cannot tell you just yet.* "Now, come around here behind this bulkhead and give your lady a bit of a kiss."

When we separate from that kiss—a particularly good one, involving wet lips, open mouths, and some gentle panting, at least on my part—I say to him, "It was most noble of you, James Emerson Fletcher, to volunteer to go into the bell in my place when you cannot even, as far as I know, swim." I brush back a lock of hair from his forehead.

"Ah, but I can swim, Jacky," he says, pulling me tighter to him. "I taught myself when I was on the river. Since I was navigating a sometimes very rough stream in a very unstable Indian canoe, I thought I should be able to swim should I capsize."

"Ah, so you taught yourself, then?"

"Aye. You see, Jacky, you were not the only one to . . . enjoy . . . the waters of the Mississippi."

I put my hands on his chest and push him a bit away. I know he is referring to the time he came upon myself and a certain Captain Richard Allen enjoying a bit of a skinny-dip in a tranquil pool on that same river.

"That was explained, Jaimy," I say, frowning and putting my full gaze upon him. I want to say, *Perhaps in return, James Emerson Fletcher, you'd like to explain a certain Missus Clementine Fletcher, hmmmm?* But I don't. Why wreck the moment? Boys, after all, will be boys, and as such, they generally require a good deal of forgiving on the part of us girls. And hey, I take some forgiving, too.

*Ummm,* I breathe, moving myself against him. "Just kiss me again, Jaimy, and we will forget about everything else in this world and—"

"Mr. Fletcher," says a very young and very red-faced midshipman, who is suddenly standing next to us. "Beggin' your pardon, Sir, but you—you and the la-lady—are called to dinner in the Captain's cabin. Sir."

Jaimy drops his hands from my waist, takes a deep breath, and sighs. "Thank you, Mr. Thorpe. We will be right there."

The thoroughly embarrassed middie salutes, does an about-face, and quickly leaves.

"One more, Jaimy, and then we shall go, and then later we'll go off to the Pig and Whistle and, oh Jaimy, it'll be such fun, and I'll get to show off my fine young sailor boy lieutenant to all my friends."

"Yes, we shall," he says, taking my arm and leading me aft to the Captain's cabin. I see that Three Hatch is now closed, the line suspending the bell gone, leaving that *thing* below to rest in darkness. I suppress a chill as we pass.

I enter the cabin and find the table set and five men standing about in conversation—Captain Hudson, Mr. Bennett, Dr. Sebastian, Professor Tilden, and that Flashby—all those, I presume, who are privy to the real mission of this expedition.

I am given my place next to Jaimy, and I silently thank the Captain for that. Mr. Bennett is asked to give us the King, and he does, and we all repeat, *The King!* at the end of his toast. Then we sit down and dig in. I am quizzed about my recent experiences in France and Germany, my meeting up with Napoleon and my Legion of Honor medal. I throw in the bit about me falling asleep in Bonaparte's lap and then delivering the letter to Empress Josephine, and I sparkle in the telling of it all—I do love being the center of attention.

I notice that Flashby is also doing his best to be a hail-fellow-well-met, and he seems to be good at it. The other officers, Jaimy excepted, seem glad of his company. I am not, however, and never will be.

The dinner being over, we get down to business.

"Mr. Thorpe, if you will wait outside," orders the Captain, and the midshipman bows and leaves. The Captain's stewards as well are ordered out.

*Hmmm* . . . Since they're not asking Jaimy to leave, I guess they're going to let him in on the plot. Probably they figure I would tell him, anyway, being a stupid blabber-mouth girl.

"Now then, Doctor, will you please tell us of the *Santa Magdalena*?"

Dr. Sebastian reaches inside his coat to bring out a folded paper, but before he can answer the Captain's request, I pipe up with, "Do you think we might be overheard, Sir?," pointedly looking up at the windows that encircle the cabin, several of which are open. "We all know there are no secrets on a ship."

"There will be on this ship, Miss, you can depend on

that," says the Captain firmly. "Rest assured, all is quite secure."

*Right,* I'm thinking. I had seen sailors out on deck who were plainly from many different nationalities. Wouldn't be too hard to believe that there might be some Spaniards—or even some former pirates—among them.

I nod, but reserve judgment on that score.

"This is a translation of a letter that has come into the hands of Naval Intelligence," says Dr. Sebastian, passing the letter to me. "It was written by a Carlos Juarez, a young officer who was one of the few survivors of the wreck of the *Santa Magdalena* in 1733."

I take it up and read it to myself. After introducing himself, Juarez goes on to describe the terrible storm and the noble but fruitless efforts of him and his shipmates to save the vessel. Then, as the ship foundered and was clearly headed down, the young man had the presence of mind to try to mark the spot. He goes on:

> I looked across the face of our compass to the end of the Key of Bones and saw that it bore away at about 010 degrees—that was the best reading I could get, as our poor ship was listing so badly. Then I took a bearing on a house that was built on the shore some distance to the east and that bearing was about 075 degrees.

Below that he had drawn a crude map showing the south coast of Key West, two lines of bearing—one from the tip of the island and the other farther up—and where the lines crossed, he had penned a large X marking the grave of the *Santa Magdalena.*

By my reckoning we were about two miles from the shore, but I cannot be sure, as the storm was so fierce.
I thank the Good God for my deliverance and I pray daily for the souls of my lost comrades.

Carlos Maria Santana Juarez
Lieutenant
His Most Catholic Majesty's Navy
December 10, 1733

I hand the letter to Jaimy, figuring he's the only one here who hasn't read it.

"And this ship was carrying . . . ?" asks Jaimy after he reads it.

"Several million pounds' worth of silver and gold. Some in coin, most in ingots."

Jaimy's eyebrows go up.

"Will this count as prize money?" asks the ever-greedy me.

"Afraid not. There's just too much money," says Captain Hudson. "Besides, you would not have a share in it, anyway. But I have been assured that all involved will profit handsomely from it."

"*If* we find it," says Mr. Bennett.

*If I find it, you mean,* thinks I, picturing myself, the one without a share, stuffed in that bell, two hundred and fifty feet down in the murky depths. I suppress yet another shudder.

"Yes," says the Captain. "Find it we will, but we will not find it sitting here. We must get moving. I have more than a few courtesy calls to make in the town, and Professor Tilden tells me he has to tweak some things in his diving machine before it is fully ready to go. We figure we will be able to leave in a week's time."

*That sounds good to me—a week on the town with Jaimy, hoo-ray!*

"But as for you, Miss Faber, I suggest you leave soon."

*What?*

"You will have the wind and the tide in the morning. Your getting to Key West early will enable you and Dr. Sebastian to set up the scientific part of this mission—the cover, as it were. You'll be sailing under your American colors and should have no problem with the Spanish authorities in Florida. *And* you'll have time to acclimate yourself to the water."

With a heavy sigh, I look over at Jaimy, and he does not look happy, for he knows as well as I do that if "I suggest" comes from the mouth of the commanding officer, then it means *I so order,* and "soon" means *now.*

I pat Jaimy's arm and say to the Captain, "Captain Hudson, would you be so good as to call in Mr. Thorpe and ask him to get my First Officer, Mr. Higgins?"

It is done, and soon Higgins stands before me.

"Mr. Higgins, we are leaving for the Caribbean tomorrow morning on the outgoing tide. As final preparations need to be made, please send Daniel and Joannie to fetch Jim Tanner and David Jones . . . No, no, belay that. Send seamen Thomas and McGee instead. Jim and Davy will be at the Pig and Whistle with their wives."

*And they will not be at all happy.* Which is why I'm sending my two biggest seamen to get them—they might resist most vigorously being torn so abruptly from their connubial bliss.

Higgins replies that he will attend to things, then leaves, and as he does, the Captain rises, as do we all.

"A toast," he says, lifting his glass to me. "To success . . . and to our pretty little mermaid!"

"Hear, hear!" from all assembled.

And from the mermaid, herself, another deep and heart-felt sigh . . . *Oh Lord, send me where you will, and I will go . . .*

# Chapter 13

We had been steadily bringing supplies aboard since our arrival, so there really was not all that much more needed to get under way. Yes, there was the running gear to be oiled and laid out, the rigging to be checked for the hundredth time, but we got that done early on in the evening of the same day and I pronounced the *Nancy B.* to be in good order for departure in the morn.

Davy and Tim had been brought back in the foulest of tempers, having been rudely jerked from their very warm matrimonial beds by the very rough hands of John Thomas and Smasher McGee, but they were somewhat mollified by my announcement that, when the work was all done, we would all repair to the Pig and Whistle for a last dinner. Since the *Nancy B.* was moored outboard of the *Dolphin* and was therefore perfectly safe, there was no need to post a guard, and the entire crew could attend. And so the call went out to friends, wives, and sweethearts to gather at the Pig to celebrate our last night ashore.

After a good deal of big-eyed pleading on my part,

Captain Hudson did allow Jaimy to accompany me this evening—with the admonition to remember our promise of chastity and for him to be back by midnight—and so on the arm of Lieutenant James Emerson Fletcher, I did proudly arrive at the tavern. There I found Davy and Annie Jones, Betsey and Ephraim Fyffe, Daniel and Joannie, already getting into everything and makin' pests of themselves, with Maudie swattin' at 'em and tellin' 'em to be good and finally puttin' 'em to work swabbin' tables, which stopped their foolishness. And there was Ezra Pickering, who had somehow managed to pry Miss Amy Trevelyne out of the Lawson Peabody School for Young Girls, and Miss Chloe Cantrell and Mr. Solomon Freeman, and Sylvie and Henry Hoffman, she now big with child, and on and on—all my dearest friends in this world . . .

. . . and there was Clementine and Jim Tanner. I knew that Jaimy had not seen her close up since they had parted in Pittsburgh last year, but he did know that she was in Boston and married to Jim. Ever the gent, Jaimy handles it well. As he and I enter the tavern, there is a cheer from those already assembled, and Jaimy shakes hands with those men he knows from that time when they kept vigil for us lost captives on the vile *Bloodhound*. He embraces the girls he knew from that time, too.

Then he extends his hand to Clementine Tanner and bows. She manages an acceptable curtsy, her eyes cast down, her flaxen hair in ringlets about her face.

"Dear Clementine. It is so good to see you again, the dear girl who saved my body from death and my soul from deep despair in the wilderness. I can never hope to repay you. Are you happy now?"

"Yes, Jaimy, I am very happy, and I hope you are the same."

*Grrrr . . .* I growl to myself. *I'm sure you were both very happy back there rollin' around on the grassy banks of the Allegheny, you . . .* Then I control myself. *Stop it, Jacky. Let it go. Get back to the party.*

And so I do. I sparkle and I am gay. The food and drinks are brought on and we all fall to. Higgins leans over and whispers in my ear, "This will definitely empty the coffers of Faber Shipping, Miss, I regret to inform you."

But I say, "What of it. Tomorrow is another day, and fortune will surely shine on us, Higgins, it always does."

I perceive there is some sadness amongst some of us, since in the morning we will cast off our lines and leave on what might well prove to be a long cruise, so I take out fiddle and pennywhistle and get up on the stage and do a short set, which revives the spirits of all in the room. I do "The Rocky Road to Dublin" and "The Rakes of Mallow," tell a few stories, some funny poems, and then end up with my specialty, playing "Dicey Riley" on the fiddle and dancing the Irish jig at the same time. Not many can do it, but I can.

I reflect that, while I have given hundreds of shows, on two continents and in many countries, this is actually the very first time that Jaimy has seen me in full performance. I do hope he liked it, but I don't know. He did clap enthusiastically. Because he was here, I resolved to restrain myself a bit in the dancing and to not tell some of the more racy jokes, but the resolve did not last long. I still don't know . . . *Alas, poor Jaimy . . . you who are so upright and noble, could you have picked a more unsuitable girl to stand by your side than me?*

But the ale and the rum and the wine did flow and warm fellowship did spread throughout the party. Concerns of rank and status and class fell away from Jaimy, Tink, Davy, and me, and we were, at the end, still just fellow members of the Dread Brotherhood of the Ship's Boys of HMS *Dolphin*.

Throughout the night, I noticed Amy and Ezra getting a bit closer than Amy usually allowed—even to the extent of a bit of handholding. *Hmmm . . .* And, of course, both Annie and Clementine were making the most of their last evening with their boys, as I was making the most of my last evening with Jaimy—'cept that, unlike them, I did expect to see him, however distant, in a week or so. Once, when Davy had to go off for a bit, my dear friend Annie comes up and says in my ear, "Oooh, Jacky, he's a pretty one, he is!" And I, grasping Jaimy's hand and nestling into his side, have to agree.

But it did have to end, after all, as morning comes early and the party has to break up. Embraces are exchanged, goodbyes are said, and we leave the Pig. Some of us, anyway—I relented in my order for Jim and Davy to spend the night aboard so's I could be sure we'd be ready to go in the morning, and let them spend this last night with their wives. *You're not so far away that you won't be able to hear the* Nancy B.*'s bell ringin' at five in the mornin', and you'd better be runnin' on down to her right quick or you'll pay for it! You hear me? Good. Now off with you.*

Jaimy and I walk slowly back to our ships, arm in arm.

"It's a lovely night, Jaimy," I say, the gentle breeze from the sea wrapping around us.

"Yes, it is, Jacky. I can scarce believe we are here, after all that has happened."

I give him a poke in the ribs. "Hey. Maybe star-crossed lovers no more, eh, Jay-mee?"

He laughs. "I hope so. But this coming expedition does worry me some."

"Don't let it, love. Live in the moment as I do. And in this particular moment, I am standing by the side of my own true love under a star-spangled sky, and nothing could be finer."

We arrive at the silent *Dolphin* and walk aboard, saluted by the Officer of the Deck, Mr. Ropp. We cross the deck and stand by the brow that leads down to my schooner, lying below. I can hear Joannie and Daniel chattering below, and I see that John Thomas, Finn McGee, and John Tinker have strung their hammocks on the deck, in the cool night air, and are already in them.

Jaimy and I come together, and after our lips part I put my mouth to his ear and softly whisper, "Can you hear my heart beating, Jaimy?" I breathe, taking his hand and placing it flat on my heaving chest. "Can you?"

I hear him take a deep breath.

"If you can, Jaimy, I want you to know that it is beating for love of you."

"Yes, Jacky," he says. "I can feel your dear heart . . ."

"Good. Now hold me to you, Jaimy, and give me a last kiss, and then fare-thee-well for a time. I'll see you in the Caribbean, and then we shall be together again."

One last kiss, we part, and I turn and go down into my ship.

.  .  .

The *Nancy B.*'s bell is rung at five in the morning, and twenty minutes later, Davy and Jim come down to the ship, arm in arm with their wives. A last embrace and the lads come onboard, leaving Annie and Clementine on the dock.

Same as it ever was, the boys sail off and the girls are left to weep.

The sails are raised, the lines thrown off, a final wave, and we are bound for the Caribbean Sea.

# PART III

# Chapter 14

On our way to Key West it was ever so good feeling the world warm up with each degree of latitude that we crossed on our way south, shedding layer after layer of clothing as we went. I really don't like cold-weather sailing much—having to go around bundled up and all—and knowing that it's instant death if you happen to fall into the water ain't at all restful to the mind.

Davy and Jim were mighty grumpy for the first few days after being so untimely ripped from the beds of their respective brides, but they soon cheered up. After all, what else could they do—moan the whole voyage? The rest of the crew—Tink and John Thomas, Smasher, and the kids—seemed content, as well, and all looked forward to the Caribbean.

Dr. Sebastian was a little unsteady when we first got under way—the *Nancy B.* rockin' and rollin' a bit more than the *Dolphin*—but he did become used to the increased pitch and yaw and soon was pottering happily in his new laboratory. He had brought along several specimens of his precious butterflies, and I painted them up for him as we sailed. Back in London he had purchased the very finest paper and colors, and it was a pleasure to work with them and with him.

Daniel and Joannie are quite tight now, he even allowing that she is all right . . . for a girl; and she admits in return that he doesn't stink too bad . . . for a boy. At first, of course, they were standoffish with each other, but they soon got together, and now I see their legs hanging side by side off the edge of the crow's-nest, which on the *Nancy B.* passes for a foretop. They are about the same size and the same age, so they have each other for companionship, and that is a good thing.

Sailors have a lot of time to think when they are off on the bounding main, and this particular sailor did some of her own, and what I was thinking about was what we lacked. During that summer cruising the Caribbean on my *Emerald,* and looking for any profitable mischief I might get in to, I noticed that the sponge divers in the area, if they were diving off a large boat, would have a small raft tied alongside for ease of getting in and out of the water, and I resolved to have one of my own. Climbing a loose and twisty rope ladder up and down the side of a ship ain't all that much fun after you've done it seven or eight times of a morning.

*Hmmm.* Yes, and some good, thick, supple leather for the making of the eye goggles I'd seen other divers wearing, like those boys that time off the coast of Sardinia. Considering the speed with which they retrieved the pennies thrown into the water by my crew, the goggles must have been quite useful to them. And I suspect that they will be very useful to me, as well. And I'll need glass and cutters and a trident would be handy, too, and . . .

That settles it. I need to get into a ship's chandlery. We must be supplied.

I go into my cabin to check the chart, then meet with Dr. Sebastian and tell him of my intentions, and he agrees with my plans. Then I go out on the quarterdeck and say to the helmsman loud enough for all on deck to hear, "Put your rudder right, Jim. Steer 270 degrees."

He does it and, without being told, Davy, Tink, John Thomas, and Finn McGee leap up to trim the sails consistent with the new heading. *Good boys. That's the way I like it.*

"Make ready, lads," I sing out. "We're goin' into Charleston, in the State of South Car-o-li-na. We need to take on some supplies." I pause for theatrical effect, and then I say, "There will be short-time shore leave for all."

At *that* there is a cheer.

*Jack-the-Sailor loves the sea,*
*But he also loves his lib-er-ty.*

# Chapter 15

We slip into Charleston Harbor on the morning tide, with a following wind, and find a cozy berth. There are many other ships in the harbor, mostly American, but some Spanish and Dutch, and others flying flags I don't recognize. There are American sailors all over the place, and that's fine—hey, the *Nancy B.* is American, too, even if I ain't.

Pay is issued to everybody, and I get ship's money from Higgins and stuff it into my purse. Davy and Tink join me, and Daniel and Joannie tag along, too, in a high state of excitement.

Business first: Higgins takes John Thomas, Finn McGee, and Jim Tanner to see about the logs and planks for the raft and we hie off to a ship's chandlery to purchase the stuff I need—the leather, the glass, the trident—and have it all sent back to the ship, and then we head off into the town.

Daniel and Joannie skip alongside, soaking in the sights of the new city—well, new to them, anyway, but then, everything's new to them. We round a corner and come on to a big open square, and the two take off. *Hmmmm.* "You two be back to the ship at four o'clock, or we'll warm up your britches for you!" I shout after them. "I mean it, too!"

There are not many people in this square, but there is a stage in the center of it and I think, *Ah, maybe there'll be a show later on . . . music and such . . .*

Watching the younger ones go, I take Tink's arm and say, "Ah, lads, ain't this just like the old days? Like in Palma, all those years ago, us mates rolling down the street on our first liberty call, hey?" Davy is close enough to me that I can give him a poke in the ribs. "Hey?"

"Right, 'cept then you was a scrawny little runt of a boy I could kick around and now you's the Captain of the ship that has me poor arse on it," grumbles Davy. "Don't seem right, somehow."

"Aw, give it a rest, Davy," says Tink, patting my hand that rests on his arm. "Least you ain't got some brutal Bo'sun's Mate layin' his knobby over yer back anytime yer a bit too slow to do his biddin'. You gotta admit this is better than that. And our Jacky was a bossy one even back then. You gotta remember that. So you should be used to it."

"That's true," allows Davy, "but—"

"And you'd never have met your lovely Annie if not for me," I say, hooking my other arm in his and squeezing it against me. "Admit it, you."

"All right," he says, and laughs. "I'll own up to that. And I'll also own that there's a likely lookin' tavern right there and my throat is powerful dry."

The sign over the place says The Swamp Fox, and there is a crude painting of a grinning fox under the words.

"Looks like just the place," says I, grinning my foxy grin. "Let's go, lads. The Brotherhood forever!"

We come out somewhat later, considerably refreshed, and head back toward the docks. The ale was cool and plentiful and the wine was good and so was the food. We link arms and start singing some of our old songs, and on the way, we meet John Thomas and Finn McGee, who report that the logs and planks are onboard. I know they have money in their pockets and are looking to spend it, so I point out The Swamp Fox and give it a good report and warn them to be back to the *Nancy B.* by six in the morning 'cause we will be sailing then and will leave them here if they don't make it back. I don't mean it, but I must make the threat. The two roughnecks grin and knuckle their brows and are gone. As they go, I see that Daniel and Joannie have come back to join us from wherever they had got off to. They both wear new straw hats as well as sheepish grins. I can only imagine what mischief they have been up to, but I don't ask. They run ahead, holding hands and laughing as they go.

I reflect that it has been a very good day.

The now very jolly Brotherhood passes an alley, and we are not at all surprised to see that from the end of it protrudes a pair of tarpaulin-trousered legs topped with a striped shirt. The owner of both the legs and the shirt is plainly a poor seaman who has had a bit too much to drink. We recognize him as one we had seen earlier in The Swamp Fox, and he was well into his cups then, even before he staggered out the door.

Davy heaves a theatrical sigh, shakes his head, and says, "Alas, another poor innocent sailorman brought low by wild women, conniving landlubbers, and strong drink. It has ever been so." Davy, the hypocrite, had certainly downed his share of ale during our time in The Fox, that's for sure. The dog clears his throat and begins to sing "The Drunken Sailor," a chantey sung by sailors when they haul on the buntlines to raise a ship's heavy sails:

> *What shall we do with a drunken sailor,*
> *What shall we do with a drunken sailor,*
> *What shall we do with a drunken sailor,*
> *Earl-lie in the morn-ing!*

Then all three of us join in bellowing out the chorus:

> *Way, hey, and up she rises,*
> *Way, hey, and up she rises,*
> *Way, hey, and up she rises,*
> *Earl-lie in the morn-ing!*

Then Tink chimes in with one of the many, many verses that deal with what to do with the unfortunate swab:

> *Put him in the scuppers with a hose pipe on him,*
> *Take him and shake him and try to wake him,*
> *Give him a dose of salt and water,*
> *Earl-lie in the morn-ing!*

Another round of the chorus and I come in with my favorite verse. I like it for its simplicity and the image it brings to me . . . er . . . my . . . mind:

*Shave his belly with a rusty razor,*
*Shave his belly with a rusty razor,*
*Shave his belly with a rusty razor,*
*Earl-lie in the morn-ing!*

Back to the chorus again and I throw my arms around each of my brothers' necks and plant a kiss on each of their cheeks, and yes, the wine was very good and plentiful. And hey, it's been a while since I've had a roarin' good time.

Davy is of the opinion that next we should do "Bully in the Alley," 'cause it's a similar tune, like, and I agree, and Davy starts it off with:

*Well, Annie is the girl that I love dearly.*
*Way, hey, bully in the alley!*
*Annie is the girl that I spliced nearly.*
*Bully down in Shinbone Alley!*

"Bully" in this song means like one of your mates what had too much to drink and ended up face-down in an alley like that poor gob we spotted a while ago. We swing into the chorus:

*Help me, Bob, I'm bully in the alley,*
*Way, hey, bully in the alley!*
*Help me, Bob, I'm bully in the alley,*
*Bully down in Shinbone Alley!*

But we don't do any more verses or any more songs, 'cause all the high spirits and hilarity are very quickly knocked out of us when we get to the end of the street and come upon that square we had crossed before, a square that is no longer empty of people. There is now quite a crowd grouped about that stage I had noticed earlier and had thought might be set up for a musical or theatrical performance. But I was wrong in thinking that, as I soon find out.

A man in a dark suit and broad-brimmed hat now stands upon it. He carries a cane and holds a megaphone to his lips. "Gentlemen," he calls out. "And ladies. Welcome to all. Today we have twenty-five prime Negroes, both male and female, for sale, all certified to be docile, healthy, and free of any disease. My name is Silas Meade, and many of you know me to be a man of honor in my business dealings, and I believe you will be pleased with today's offerings."

All joy is gone from me now. I can see that the slaves to be sold are grouped around the back, guarded by men with whips and guns. I begin to shake with fury.

"Let's get out of here, Jacky," urges Tink. "This is dirty business."

I've seen slaves working the fields under the blazing sun. I've sailed on a slaver and observed the horrible conditions on it close up. I've met slaves and freed some. Yes, I know all about slavery—but I've never before seen this part of it. I am stunned and rooted to the spot.

"Don't do it, Jacky," warns Davy, looking at the tight expression on my face. "You're gonna do somethin' stupid, you know you will, and you're gonna get in trouble. This ain't your fight. You can't save them, any of them; you haven't got enough money."

"I ain't gonna do nothin' stupid," I hiss, shaking with rage. "I know how things lie. Only the very rich can afford to buy other human beings. Go back to the ship, both of you, if you can't bear to watch." I stand, rigid, watching, bearing witness.

*Oh, God, how can You let this go on?*

My brothers do not go back to the ship, no. I feel them still standing by my side.

A young black man has been brought up on the stage, and Mr. Silas Meade begins the sale.

"What am I bid for this fine young buck? Only seventeen years old and already strong as an ox! Just look at those muscles!" The young man, whose wrists are bound, has been stripped of his shirt and he is, indeed, well muscled. The auctioneer has a cane and he taps it on the boy's chest. "Shall we start the bidding at one thousand dollars?"

"One thousand!" shouts a rather fat but prosperous-looking gentleman, waving a card with a number on it. He has a woman with him, finely dressed—she leans on his arm, smiling broadly and waving at friends across the square. Such a lark, *such fun,* to be here laughing gaily as human beings are being auctioned off like animals.

Another man, dressed much like the other, jumps up on the platform to examine the slave more closely. He puts his hand on the Negro's face and uses his thumb to lift the man's upper lip to examine his teeth. "Eleven hundred!" he says, leaving the stage.

"Twelve hundred!"

"Thirteen!" calls out another man.

"Thirteen-fifty!" cries the fat man, and then there is silence.

"Gentlemen, I have one thousand three hundred and fifty dollars!" says the auctioneer. "Do I hear fourteen? No? Going once . . . Going twice . . . Sold! To Mr. Wilkes!"

Next a plainly terrified girl is pulled to the platform by a rope that is tied around her neck. Because she is young and pretty, she is stripped down to her skin and made to stand naked before the crowd. She tries to cover herself with her hands, but those hands are roughly pushed down by one of the slave handlers.

She is sold for sixteen hundred and fifty dollars, again to Mr. Wilkes, the fat man.

Another woman, this one heavy with child, is now brought up. There is a boy of about seven years old clinging to her side. He is crying. The auctioneer pushes the boy aside and uses his cane to lift up the front of the mother's simple white shift to show her belly. "Look at that!" he exclaims. "A proven breeder! How can you go wrong? Three for the price of one! Let's start at twelve hundred dollars for the lot! Who will give me twelve hundred?"

Someone does, and so the bidding goes on until—*Sold! To Mr. O'Hara!*—she, and her son, too, have been bought and are led off.

"Haven't you seen enough?" asks Davy, sounding thoroughly disgusted. "Do you want to stay to see them whipped?"

"I suppose I have been made sick enough," I say, hardened in my resolve to fight this evil whenever and however I can. "Let's leave the scum to their vile business and may they rot in— Hold on, what's this?"

As we are turning to leave, I notice that an older woman is now being shoved onto the stage, to much laughter from the crowd. True, compared to the young blacks who had been displayed before, she is a pitiful sight—heavy of body, a shawl around her shoulders and faded skirts hanging about her hips, an old rag tied around her graying hair.

She stands, head up, eyes looking straight ahead, with her hands clasped before her.

"Hey, Silas! You gonna pay someone to haul that away? Hey?" shouts out some wit in the crowd, and there is laughter all around.

"Now, boys," says the auctioneer, signaling with his hands for silence. "This here Negress has been a house Nigra for forty-odd years now, and she can clean and she can sew and she can cook."

"Cook?" cries the wit again. "Hell, I reckon! And I reckon she been into the lard real good, from the looks of her!" More laughter.

I look over at the man who has been saying these things. He is thin, stooped, wearing a floppy black hat and smoking a thin cheroot.

"So what am I bid? Shall we start at five hundred dollars? Do I hear five hundred?"

No, he does not.

"One hundred dollars!" calls out the man with the cigar. "Hell, if I get her for that I can put her to chopping cotton till she drops dead. Still be worth it." He doesn't get as big a laugh on that one. It seems that not everyone here is quite as cruel as he.

"Come, Colonel Tarleton, surely you can do better than that?"

"Surely, I cannot, Suh!" responds this Tarleton. "Hell, she could die tomorrow, and then where would I be? Out one hundred dollars, and with one fat dead Nigra on my hands, that's where."

"I have one hundred dollars, then," says the auctioneer, looking out over the crowd. "Do I hear two hundred?"

Silence. Then . . .

"One hundred and fifty dollars!" I sing out. I have reached down and felt the gold coins in my money belt, as well as the money in my purse, and I think I have that amount.

"What the hell are you doin'?" demands Davy. Tink, beside him, looks shocked.

I grab each of the lads by the forearm and hiss, "Davy . . . Tink . . . Pretend to smile and laugh like all of this is nothing to you. If they see I want her too bad, they'll bid me up! And I ain't got no more money. Now, do it!"

And they play along, pretending they have absolutely no interest in what is going on in this slave market. I put on the Lawson Peabody Look, and wait.

"I have one hundred and fifty dollars!" says the auctioneer through his megaphone. "Do I have two hundred? Colonel Tarleton?"

Colonel Tarleton looks over at me. "Why you want this old Negress?" He takes the cigar from his mouth, throws it on the ground, and grinds it out with the heel of his boot.

"I need someone to look after my baby girl, Suh, as I am sickly and can no longer do it fo' m'self." I put the back of my hand to my forehead and affect a bit of a swoon.

"Hah! You shall have her, then. Never let it be said that Colonel Ashley Tarleton kept a flower of southern womanhood from having a proper mammy fo' her baby!" He takes off his hat and bows low.

I simper and curtsy to his bow.

"One hundred and fifty," says the auctioneer, impatient to get past this very unprofitable transaction. "Once, twice, gone! To the lady in the black dress! Now next we have a fine . . ."

I go around to the back of the stage, where I find a man seated at a table collecting the money and writing out the Bills of Sale. I tell him my name and pay him his money and he gives me the paper.

# Bill of Sale
## For the Negro Woman known as Jemimah. Formerly owned by Asa Hamilton. Sold in as-is condition to J. M. Faber.

### Attested Herewith
### William Meade, Esq.

Just as simple as that—the ownership of a person is passed from one to the next. I fold the paper and put it in my purse.

"Thank you for your purchase," says this Mr. Meade with a smirk. He has to be the brother of the auctioneer. "We do hope you will be pleased." I am handed the end of a rope, the other end of which is attached to the neck of . . . Who? . . . Oh, yes . . . Jemimah.

She picks up a bundle, which I suspect holds all her earthly goods, and she looks at me and then gazes off, her eyes revealing nothing.

"You are crazy," says Davy. "You know that, don't you?"

"Yes, I do," I answer, my nose in the air, as we all head back to the *Nancy B.*

# Chapter 16

Higgins, Dr. Sebastian, and I are going off to see a musical revue this evening at Tagliaferro Hall in Charleston and will join the others later at The Fox. Higgins is giving me a bit of a brush-up. I sense that he is not entirely pleased with me. It doesn't take him long to get down to it.

"So, now you own a slave, Miss?"

"Yes, I do, Higgins. We needed a cook, and now we've got one." We have been getting along with Tink as cook, but I know it hurts his sailor pride, me and his brother Davy being onboard and all. Plus he's not really very good at it. And Higgins, though he will cook for me, doesn't like cooking for a crowd. Hey, he's second in command of Faber Shipping, not Ship's Cook.

"I see," says Higgins. His touch is not quite so gentle as usual. "We needed a cook, so you just went out and bought one."

"Ouch! Come on, Higgins, you know I'm going to set her free."

"Oh? And when will that happen? When we are done with this voyage? How convenient."

"As soon as we throw off the lines, clear the harbor, and leave this town. If she wants to get off in our next port, she can."

"Well, that eases my mind somewhat. Still, I shall have to ponder the morality of all this. By that transaction you have, you must know, participated in the slave trade. Every dollar made by the traders furthers the evil."

"I don't have to ponder anything, my dear and ever-present conscience, because I know that had I not bought her, she would have been put into the fields to pick cotton till she died. That's what I know."

Higgins does not reply to that but goes on silently brushing. Eventually he asks, "What will you wear tonight?"

I think for a moment and then decide. "The French one. Direct from Paris. That oughta set the Charleston ladies back on their heels."

Earlier, when Jemimah had been brought onboard, I straight-away led her down into the hold and showed her the galley and where she was to sleep, which was the bunk closest to the stove, just as Crow Jane once had done back on the *Belle of the Golden West*. Joannie and Daniel hung about close by, eyes wide, curious.

"They said you are a cook, Jemimah. Are you?" I asked.

"Yes, Ma'am," she said, those being the first words she had spoken. I know that she was startled when we had come down the wharf and she had gotten a look at what was to be her new home. But she said nothing then, and she is of very few words now.

"Well, then, your duties shall be cooking for the crew and some light housekeeping. Can you do that?"

"Yes, Ma'am."

"Good. Take some time now to settle in. Check out our cooking utensils and see what we've got in the way of stores. Most of us are going off the ship tonight, so you will not have to make dinner. Just put something together for yourself and these two kids here and the man on watch. This is Daniel, and that's Joannie. They are your helpers. Make them mind and don't take any back talk."

She nodded and I continued.

"We are leaving on the outgoing tide at six in the morning. We'll expect breakfast for the crew at eight." Then I raised my finger in the air and said as sternly as I could, "The one thing we fear most on a ship is fire, so you must be very, *very* careful with the galley stove. Do you understand that?"

"Yes, Ma'am. How many?"

"How many what?"

"How many for breakf'st?"

"Oh." Feeling foolish, I mentally counted up my crew. "Eleven. Including you."

She nodded again and I said briskly, "Very well, then. Joannie, Daniel, show Jemimah around the ship. Carry on."

I then left the galley and went back to my cabin, feeling not foolish now, but decidedly uncomfortable.

The musical revue at Tagliaferro Hall was great fun, the production having very professional singers, musicians, and dancers, and wildly funny skits.

And, curiously, in the middle of it all, the theatrical company performed a little playlet, which was very much like the thing I had written and that we had performed on the *Belle of the Golden West* when we were on the Mississippi. *Very* much like mine. Mine was called *The Villain Pursues Constant Maiden, or Fair Virtue in Peril,* while this production was titled simply *The Villain Pursues Her.* Hmmm.

Higgins, who was seated next to me, leaned over and whispered in my ear, "Could it be, Miss, that your rights to that little gem of deathless literature have been violated?" I gave him an elbow for his cheek, and then I thought about it and shrugged—no matter, for it is nice to know that one's literary efforts have been noticed and appreciated even if copied for someone else's profit. We joined the rest of the audience heartily booing and hissing the villain, and, yes, the heroine's tear-away dress did come off just like mine did all those times.

We topped off the evening at The Swamp Fox, eating and drinking our fill, and got back to the ship, the whole lot of us, arms about each other's necks, singing and carousing, at about midnight.

As I snugged down into my bed and prepared for sleep, my thoughts, after a prayer for Jaimy's health and safety, turned to Jemimah, who was lying down below.

*What must she think of us? She has only seen us at our brawling worst. What must it be like for her, to come on this little ship, not knowing who we are and where we are going?*

Ah, well, I'll clear that up for her tomorrow.

*G'night, Jaimy. I behaved pretty good today, I think, I . . . I . . .*

# Chapter 17

Morning came early, *very* early, but the grumbly group of us managed to struggle up and get the *Nancy B.* unmoored and under way on the morning tide—Davy on helm, me on the con, and the rest tending the sails. We had done this many times before, taking her out after a night of excess, but this leave-taking was a little different. As we stood blearily on deck, silently promising ourselves never to do it again and knowing that we would break that promise, Daniel and Joannie brought up trays of steaming mugs of coffee. *Very* good mugs of coffee, thick and sweet, that did much to restore our usual high spirits. That, and the good smells wafting up from the galley.

After getting her well out of the harbor and into the open sea, and putting her on a course due south, we left the watch to Davy and McGee and went down to breakfast.

On the mess deck we have a long wooden table made of two-inch-thick maple bolted to the deck and big enough to seat fourteen, one at the head, one at the foot, and six down each side. While on most ships of this type, the sailors eat out of metal mess kits, I insist on proper china. And since

Faber Shipping has hauled a lot of it around, we have some of the best. Never let it be said that we suffer anything but first class. When first I got the *Nancy B.* into port in Boston, I contracted with my dear friend Ephraim Fyffe, Master Carpenter and husband to the former Betsey Byrnes, to come aboard with his carpentry tools to exercise his skill. First I had him rout out circular depressions at each place setting into which would fit the feet of the plates, and then in the center of each of those, another deeper one to hold a bowl when we are having chowder or burgoo. Then, within easy reach of a sailor's hand, a hole to hold his glass or cup. Pretty crafty, I thought. This all was done, of course, to keep the settings from sliding off the table when the *Nancy B.* is rolling around in heavy seas, which she's doing a pretty good job of right now.

Jemimah is standing at the stove, at the end of the long room, putting her spatula to the bacon that sits sizzling on the griddle, and Daniel and Joannie are carrying plates of hotcakes and putting them at each place.

I take my seat at the head of the gleaming table— Ephraim had put six coats of good spar varnish on it when he was done with the routing, and it glows like a wooden jewel—and the others take their places, as well. I stick my coffee mug in its slot and lean back as Joannie puts my plate in front of me.

"Thank you, dear," I say, and dig into the beautifully browned pancakes adorned with melted butter and maple syrup with crispy bacon on the side. *Mmmmmm . . .*

After I get a few more delightful mouthfuls down, I look over at Tink and say, "Mr. Tinker, I am afraid I must dismiss you as ship's cook."

"That's just fine with me, Jacky," says Tink, and there is laughter and mumbled murmurs of assent around the table as all heartily wolf down their food.

Finishing up, I wipe my mouth, stick my napkin back in its ring, and sip at a second cup of excellent coffee while I make plans with Dr. Sebastian for the day's drawings. Then there is some small talk concerning last night's activities, and those of us who were at Tagliaferro's recount some of the better japes and jokes for those who were not.

At last I say to Higgins, who has been sitting, mostly silent, on my right, "Please have Jemimah report to me as soon as breakfast is cleared away, so I can do what needs to be done."

I rise, and so does he, and I go back to my cabin.

My cabin on the *Nancy B.*, current flagship of Faber Shipping Worldwide, is tiny compared to other captain's cabins I have occupied, but it is quite cozy. There is a bank of narrow windows around the curved aft wall that opens to let in a breeze. There is, of course, a bedstead built into the starboard wall, and in addition, there is a small desk that I had Ephraim Fyffe make and install for me. It is beautifully done—and I still cannot believe such fine things are made with simple hand tools—and it converts, with a simple flip of its lid, to a small table should I want to entertain someone privately in my cabin.

It is at that desk that I sit, ink bottle open and quill in hand, when I hear a knock at the door.

"Come in," I say, and the door opens and Jemimah ducks her head under the narrow hatchway and enters to stand before me.

"Yes, Ma'am. You wanted to see me. Here I am."

I regard her for a moment and then say, "The breakfast was very good, Jemimah."

"Thank you, Ma'am."

"I am happy that you did not get seasick. Many do, you know."

"I didn't get sick on the way over here, and don't 'spect to get sick now."

*Hmmm . . .*

"Have Joannie and Daniel been good?"

"Yes'm. They washin' up the dishes right now."

"You seem to be good with children."

"I raised Mastah Hamilton's four children and then his ten gran'children. Six of my own, too. I knows how to handle 'em. If'n a sharp word don't do, then a switch will."

"Where are your children now?"

"Don't know. Sold off."

There is an eternity of suffering in her eyes, but she does not lower her head, just stares straight at the wall behind me.

"What happened?"

"Mastah Hamilton died and soon after Missus Hamilton did, too. And then their children got to squabblin' over the property, and the people they owed money to came after 'em an' so the place was broke up. All the Nigras was sold and here I am."

I consider all this for a while and then say, "Jemimah, I have here your permanent indenture papers before me. I have written on them words to the effect that, when I sign it, you shall be freed of servitude. You shall be free."

The dark eyes now come down upon mine. "What? You can do that? But you . . . you a girl and hardly more than a child."

"That may be true, but I do own this boat, and until I put this pen to that paper, I do own *you*."

A chuckle rumbles deep in her throat. "Free? Huh! How 'bout that?"

"You'll need a last name, Jemimah," I say, my pen poised over the paper. "What will it be?"

She thinks for a moment and then says, "Moses. Jemimah Moses," and I write it down. At the time, I thought she was naming herself after the prophet who led the Hebrew children out of slavery in Egypt, but I find out much later that I was wrong in thinking that.

She looks off into the shadowy corners of my cabin. "Free at last. My, my, I'm free at last."

I take the pen and scribble my name on the paper. "Yes, you are, Jemimah Moses. As of this moment you are free."

Somehow I expected more joy, more gratitude, but I don't get it.

"So I'm free. Free to jump over the side of this boat if'n I want to, that kind of free?"

"Whatever you want to do, Jemimah, do it . . . But listen to this, first. From now on, and for however long you wish to remain in that position, you are an employee of Faber Shipping Worldwide and will receive pay of ten dollars a month, five dollars of which will be withheld to eventually pay back the one hundred and fifty dollars I have invested in you. And you will receive a half of one share of whatever we make on this voyage. Do you understand that?"

"Yes, Ma'am."

"And if you want to leave us at our next port call, you may. Here's the papers sayin' that you are now a free person of color. Keep them with you and don't lose them. They are very important."

I hand her the folded papers and she takes them.

"And you've got to stop callin' me Ma'am. You may choose from Jacky, Missy, Skipper, Captain, or Boss, or Miss, all names my crew use for me."

"Yes, Miss Jacky," she says, choosing a name not on the list.

*Hmmmm . . .*

# Chapter 18

As for what I did on the rest of that journey south-ward, well, I spent my idle time in several pursuits. The first was to take cloth and needle and make a replica of my old pirate flag, the one that I had lost when I was taken by Captain Trumbull of HMS *Wolverine*. That particular flag now rests at the bottom of the sea off Cape Trafalgar with that same *Wolverine* and many others. *Many* others, I think with sorrow, some made of iron and wood, and some made of skin and bone. But I let that go.

Members of the Piratical Brotherhood design and fly their own flags, not only so they can strike terror into the prey they are pursuing, but also so they'll be able to recognize one another so as not to blow one another out of the water upon an unfortunate chance meeting. In my travels, I have found that there is some honor among thieves. Not much, but a bit. Some of the flags are red while others are black, but almost all have some version of a skull, however crudely done, upon them. My own Jolly Roger has a white skull on a black background, with two crossed bones below. A pretty common design, except that my skull wears a huge, open-mouthed grin. There were many stitches in the making of it, but Joannie helped me sew a lot of them as we sat cross-legged on the deck of my cabin, needles and thread in hand, giggling over the evilness in what we were doing. They taught her well at the Home, I see.

Second, I set about, with the help of Tink—who has shown himself to be very good with his hands and has become our ship's carpenter, ship fitter, and all-around handyman—to fashion a pair of those goggles I had mentioned before so that I will be able to see better when I am underwater. I want some like the ones I had seen on those Arab coin divers when I was in the Mediterranean on the *Emerald* in '04.

We make my pair using thick leather into which are set two round disks of glass like those used for circular miniature portraits. Cutting the leather to fit both the glass and my eye sockets was difficult, but by trial and error, we got it done. There are two straps of lighter leather that tie behind my head to hold the goggles tight to my face. When I am ready to go down, we'll seal the eyeglass edges with pine pitch to make them watertight, I hope.

Third, I plan to train certain members in a particular skill . . .

As we pass Key Largo, the first of the Upper Keys of Florida, and observing that it is a very mild day with little wind, the water being warm and getting quite clear, I decide to accomplish some of that training.

The day also being a Sunday, I call the crew to Church, something I seldom do—well, actually *never* have done before—and after they line up, slightly mystified, before me as I stand on the quarterdeck, I read a few verses from the Bible, those that speak to our condition. Then I lead them in a few hymns, all of which they musically butcher. When we finish that last atonal atrocity, I offer up a prayer for our safety and the health of those we love who are not here with us today.

Then I lift my voice and say, "Instead of a sermon today, I shall read from the Cor-po-rate By-Laws of Faber Shipping Worldwide." I think of Captain Locke reading out the Articles of War back on the *Dolphin,* outlining all the crimes we poor sailors might be guilty of, all of which were punishable by death, as I pull out a sheaf of papers that actually have no words written on them, just sketches of butterflies, and begin to recite.

"Ahem! Section Two, Article One. All members of this Corporation shall present a Clean and Orderly Appearance consistent with the Usual Standards of Nautical Dress . . ."

That gets a few snickers since I myself am dressed in my usual warm-weather nautical gear of loose white shirt, short buckskin skirt, and bare legs and feet.

"Article Two. All members shall learn to read and write in an acceptable manner." Groans from Daniel and Joannie on this.

"Article Three. All members shall demonstrate an ability to swim."

Here I fold up the papers and put them under my arm before concluding. "Mr. Thomas and Mr. McGee, if you will please grasp Seaman Jones by the arms and hold him fast, I would be most grateful."

Davy, who has been standing with his arms folded, looking up at me with an air of complete and contemptuous indifference to what I have been saying, now stares with concern at the two huge, grinning seamen who stand by his side, holding him tightly. Then he looks back at me and glowers. Davy, though he has gotten over being torn so abruptly from his dear Annie's side, does still chafe somewhat on being under my command. Well, we'll see about *that,* boyo . . .

"We shall commence your swimming lesson right now, Seaman Jones. You should not fear for your life as you have just been to church and washed clean of your sins, many though I suspect those sins to be. Washed in the Blood of the Lamb, as it were. Well, now you shall be washed in God's own great salt sea, as well, and I am sure you will profit by it," I say grandly, still in church mode. "Mr. Tanner, if you will please affix that line around Seaman Jones's waist. Thank you, Jim."

Earlier, seeing that we were in very light winds and were scarcely making two knots, the pace of a leisurely walk on land, I figured this was a good time to begin Davy's swimming lessons—and maybe bring him down a peg as well. I had Jim attach a stout pulley to the end of the main yard and run a line through it—that same line that now tightly encircles Davy's waist.

Davy struggles but to no avail. "Now, Mate, it won't be so bad, you'll see," says Smasher McGee. "She had me and John Thomas do the same thing when last we was down here, and now we can swim like any fishes and don't fear a dip in the old salt, not no more we don't."

There is an air of barely suppressed hilarity on the *Nancy B.* All the rest of the able-bodied men have previously passed the swimming test and know that they shall not be subjected to this. Jim Tanner learned to swim when we were on the Mississippi, and Daniel Prescott, being a river rat since birth, already knew how, and my good John Higgins spent many happy hours as a youth with other young lads in a deep millpond near where he grew up in Colchester.

Nay, all of the other men are qualified and now it is Davy's turn, and he accepts his fate. He looks at me with a grim smile that says, *I'll get you for this, Jacky.*

Ignoring the look, I ask, "Now, Davy, would you like to shed any of your clothes? We are not shy in that way here on the *Nancy B.,* and I remember that you were not at all shy in dropping your drawers when we all went into the *Dolphin*'s bowsprit netting back when we were children."

He toes off his shoes and then pulls his red and white striped shirt off over his head. I notice he has grown more hair on his chest since last I saw it bared. Then he undoes the drawstring of his white trousers and lets them drop, leaving him standing there only in his drawers.

"Whyn't you drop the drawers, too, Davy?" giggles Joannie, who has all along been convulsed with laughter over the proceedings.

I ignore her, too, and go up nose to nose with Davy. "Remember, Brother, that time back on the *Dolphin,* when you called me *the little fairy* and then the rest of the Brotherhood picked it up and called me that, too? Hmmm?"

He sets his jaw, stares straight ahead, and does not reply.

I turn away and say, "Throw him over," and they do it.

He sinks straight down when he hits the water. "Take up the slack, Tink," I say, giving the thumbs-up signal. The rope tightens and Davy is hauled, sputtering, back to the surface.

"Stroke with your arms, Davy. Kick with your legs. When you can keep up with the ship, we'll bring you back aboard."

We all lean over the rail and shout encouragement. Joannie stands beside me, laughing and fairly jumping up and down in her glee over poor Davy's watery struggles.

Davy thrashes about, but he does not seem to be getting it.

I step back from the rail and unfasten the drawstring of my buckskin skirt, slide it off, and hand it to Higgins.

All of my crew have seen me do this many times and are quite used to it. Dr. Sebastian, however, has not, and I see his eyebrows go up in mild surprise. I tuck the loose shirt into the waistband of my short underdrawers, hop up on the rail, and dive in.

I resurface close to Davy—close, but just out of his reach, as I know he'd risk punishment for the chance to give me a bit of a strangle.

"Watch me, Brother," I say, beginning to swim. "Like this, see? Nice and easy now, arm over arm, kick your feet. Turn your face to take a breath with each stroke. That's it, keep it going."

He does, and eventually he is able to do it to my satisfaction and is hauled back up, to the cheers of his shipmates. Jim tosses me down a rope, but I do not climb up it, not yet, anyway.

I do hang on to the line to rest for a moment, and say, "Mr. Tanner, will you please divest Seaman Apprentice Joan

Nichols of her shirt and trousers, affix the rope about her, and send her down here?"

Joannie's eyes—which had been watching me down here below—pop wide open, no longer with the delight of watching someone else's troubles, oh no, but now with fear for her own. Then her face disappears from the rail as she turns to flee. To no avail, of course. There is the sound of some struggle, accompanied by squeals from her and laughter from the crew, but eventually she comes flying over the side.

Shrieking, she splashes into the water next to me, eyes squeezed tightly shut, arms and legs flailing about. I start swimming slowly beside her.

"Now, Joannie, no reason to be afraid . . . Here, like this . . . Stroke . . . Stroke . . . Open your eyes. Yes, that's it . . ."

And so, all in all, we had a very good trip down, and on Christmas Day, 1806, we dropped anchor two miles off Key West, Florida, and, being only ninety-some miles from Cuba, it's very much in the Spanish Main.

# Chapter 19

Sunlight filters down through the clear, blue-green water, dappling the coral reef below me. It is not deep, only about twenty feet down, and I give my feet a kick and swim down to it. Ah, there are some nice sponges over there. I pull my shiv from my forearm sheath and go collect them, sawing off their stems and stuffing them into the net bag that hangs by my side. Pretty little fish come around to peer at me, all brightly colored and curious. There are some bigger fish down there, too, lurking in the crevices of the coral, but I shan't mess with them—not now, anyway. Later I'll dive down with my trident and see what I can do about dinner.

Another kick and I glide over the reef and look down into the abyss that lies on the seaward side of the reef. I cannot see to the bottom of it, and that is a pity, for I know that somewhere down there is where the Santa Magdalena rests, where she lies silent with her dead . . . and with all her gold.

Ship's Log: The schooner *Nancy B. Alsop.* December 28, 1806. Anchored in five fathoms of water, two miles off Key West, Spanish Territory of Florida. Bottom sand

**and coral. Taking on sponges and scientific specimens. Weather calm. No other vessels in sight.**

"Look, Jacky!" cries Dr. Sebastian. "Right down there! Do you see it? Right next to that fan coral!"

I see it, all right—a particularly disgusting-looking creature with a slug's body and yellow tentacles sticking out of what I suppose is its back.

"I believe it is what is called a Spanish Shawl, a member of the Nudibranch family of Gastropods, *Flabellina iodinea!*" exults the Doctor. "Oh, Miss, we simply must have it!"

We are both lying belly down on the raft that is tied beside the *Nancy B.,* peering through the glass-bottomed buckets we have designed for scanning the sea floor for specimens and possible treasure. We took Spanish Lieutenant Carlos Maria Santana Juarez at his word concerning the approximate location of the *Santa Magdalena,* but we have found nothing yet in that regard, which is not surprising. We know she is deep, and probably rotted away by now, and I can only dive down so far. Still, we hope.

I sigh and pull on my goggles, which have been resting on my forehead, and press them to my face to seal them around my eyes. "Does it bite or sting?"

"No, my dear, it is perfectly harmless. It is merely a clam without a shell. Oh, look at it! It is beautiful!"

I do not don the heavy leather gloves I had made for picking up the things that *do* bite and sting—once burned, twice learned—so I just roll over the side of the raft and slip into the water.

My loose shirt swirls about me as I prepare to go down.

It had been decided that I would dive in my undershirt and long drawers for the sake of modesty—decided not by me, though. As for me, I had asked them why couldn't they all just face away when I go into the water and I'd dive starkers, but Higgins and Dr. Sebastian would have none of that, so I must put up with all this cloth billowing around me.

I thrust my head under, put rump and legs in the air, and surface dive on down to the reef.

It is not deep here, only about twenty feet down, and I give my feet a kick and swim over to the coral reef.

Ah, there are some nice sponges there . . . I shall have to come collect them later. I had decided early on that I would harvest the plentiful sponges I found in these waters, as it would be an excellent cover for our other activities. *Hey, señores, we're just some simple sponge divers trying to make an honest living from the sea, so just leave us alone.* The *Nancy B.*'s rigging is now adorned with fifty, maybe sixty, fine sponges drying in the tropical sun, which I'll be able to sell as soon as I find a market. Never let it be said that Jacky Faber ever passed up a chance for profit when one presented itself.

I grab the unfortunate slug and kick back to the surface and slap the thing onto the raft.

"Wonderful!" exclaims Dr. Sebastian, who has a bucket of seawater ready to plunge the creature into, prolonging its life a bit. I know that I will soon be drawing, painting, and labeling it, and then it will go into a jar of alcohol.

Since I'm already in the water, I decide to go down and take another quick look around.

This time I glide beyond the reef and hang motionless over the abyss that lies on the seaward side of the reef. I cannot see to the bottom of it, and that is a pity, for I know that somewhere down there lies that death-doomed Spanish ship.

*Enough daydreaming, girl. Back to work.* I twist around to head back over the reef and I'm about ready to head up for another breath when . . . *There!* Sticking out from under a clump of seaweed are the telltale whiskers of a good-sized lobster. *Ha, you rascal, you shall grace our table tonight! Come here, now . . .*

I reach out to grab his antennae and whisk him out of there, but then . . . Oh God, then . . . something grabs on to *me*. Something green and hideous—the head of a huge snakelike thing. When its jaws clamp down, it just misses the skin of my arm but has me by the shirt and is dragging me down toward its den and I am helpless to stop it. While the head looks at me with baleful eyes, the tail of the hideous thing remains anchored in its burrow and holds tight against all my struggles to free myself from it.

I start to panic.

*Oh God, am I to drown in sight of my friends? Is this the end of me, finally?* The sunlight and sweet air are right up there, but I can't . . . I can't . . . get loose from the thing. My lungs cry out for some of that sweet air and my fingers seek the drawstring of my shirt so that I might loosen it and slip it off and let the fiend have it, but I can't, it's tied too tight, I can't, I can't . . . *I'm gonna drown . . . I'm gonna drown right here . . .*

The serpent gives another constriction while drawing back even further into its hole, draggin' me with it. Playin' my last desperate card, I reach up my sleeve and pull out me shiv and stab it at the snake's face, but it doesn't let go. No, it doesn't, and I do it again. But still it won't let go. No, it won't. Now I start sawing through its neck right behind its head, but it still won't let go. Then I feel my knife cut through till it hits the bone and grinds against it and then it's through, and finally . . . finally I am released.

I push off the wall of coral with my feet and lunge toward the surface and I wanna suck in a breath so bad. *But wait, no not yet, one more second, 'cause if I suck in the water I'll be dead.* Just two more feet and . . . *Now!*

I burst through the surface and suck in a great lungful of the blessed air. *Oh Lord, how good is your blessed clean air and more valuable than any gold.* I lean gasping against the side of the raft, my chest heaving.

My distress below did not go unnoticed. Both Joannie and Davy now stand on the raft with Dr. Sebastian, all looking very concerned.

"A monster . . . it almost killed me . . . a horrible snake . . . I . . ."

Davy leans over and puts a hand into each of my armpits and pulls me aboard the platform.

"It wouldn't! It didn't let go . . . it . . ." I gasp.

"Damn," says Davy, staring down at my middle, amazed at what he sees.

*What? Oh my God!*

I scramble to my feet, shrieking, for there on my shirt, dangling between my knees, is the head of the snake, clamped on tight. It never did let go, even in death.

"*Get it off me!*" I scream, and take my shiv, which I still have clutched in my hand, and slash through that traitorous waist cord of my shirt and then rip off the shirt and fling it to the deck of the raft. That hateful thing is still attached, its implacable eyes still staring into mine.

"Ah, a moray eel," says Dr. Sebastian, leaning down to examine the head. "*Gymnothorax miliaris.* Such luck. I'd been hoping that we'd get an example of the Family Muraenidae on this expedition, and now we have one. Part of one, at least."

Aghast and shaking with disgust, I cross my arms over my chest and snarl through my clenched teeth, "No, Doctor, no! Family Monster, Genus *Monster,* Species *monster.* I will not dive again this day, and I will never on any other day go down there dressed as I was. Know that. That shirt almost got me killed. Propriety be damned."

I turn to climb up the short ladder to the deck of my ship. Higgins is there with a towel, which he throws around my shoulders. I call back to Joannie, "Go down to the stores and get a bolt of light canvas. Then ask Jemimah to meet me in my cabin. Tell her to bring her sewing kit."

"Girl, you nothin' but skin and bones. We've got to get some flesh on you, that's for damned sure."

After that day when Jemimah had been given her freedom papers, she had called me Miss Jacky for a while, but that didn't last. As soon as she got used to the idea that she was really free, I very quickly became just "girl," which is all right with me.

"It ain't for lack of tryin' on your part, Jemimah," I say, finally calm now after my encounter with the fiend. I think back to last night's dinner—fish fried in batter, beans baked in molasses, and fluffy buttered biscuits on the side. Lord, it was so good.

"I mean, how you 'spect to feed babies on them little titties?"

I consider this and then say, "Maybe they'll get bigger when the time comes that I'm actually growin' a baby in my belly."

"Nope. Can't wait till then. Gotta get some meat on your bones. The men, they likes a little jiggle here and there."

*Well...*

"I'll have you know, Jemimah, that I do have a young man, who says he wants to marry me." I sniff, all prim and proper. "And he seems to like me just as I am. Says he does, anyway."

"Huh! He lyin', then. He'd like you a whole lot better if your skinny hipbones ain't grindin' into his when you two into makin' them babies."

I'm looking over to see how Joannie's taking all this talk. Doesn't seem to interest her much. She doesn't let on that she's even heard.

I had told Jemimah what I wanted in the way of this new diving outfit. *Make the bottom snug, Jemimah, with only two- or three-inch legs that I can roll up tight, and don't make it come up too high—just below my belly button. Don't want one loose bit of cloth, nothing for those monsters down there to latch on to. And make me a small top, just big enough to cover my chest. Then sew on some thin shoulder straps to hold it up and put buttons in back to keep it snug.* She had nodded and allowed that she could do that, though it did not seem to her to be at all respectable.

"Can you make one for me, too, Auntie?" Joannie asks of Jemimah. Ever since Joannie got the swimming lesson, we've had a hard time keeping her out of the water.

"Huh! Suppose I can. Gettin' tired of dryin' out your

clothes over my stove. All right, girl, you done," she says, and I step down. "Little girl, you get up here now."

Joannie sheds her clothes and hops up on the chair. I look her over.

*Hmmm . . .*

Nothing yet, but I know it won't be long.

Jemimah runs her tape over her thin form and makes more marks on the light canvas cloth.

As I climb back into my own regular underway rig, I ask, watching her face, "Joannie, where have you been sleepin' at night?"

She flushes, looks down, then says, "With Danny. Me and him took one of those little rooms down there. Hope you don't mind, Jacky." She gives me the big eyes.

*We'll see what I mind, Joannie Nichols, and don't try to pull that look on me 'cause I know all about that.*

There are six tiny staterooms on the mess deck, three on either side of the long table. Higgins has one, and so does Dr. Sebastian, and Professor Tilly will have one when he comes aboard. Jim Tanner could have one, too, but he perfers to sling his hammock with the rest of the men in the fo'c's'le, where it's cooler. Or out on deck now that it's getting really warm. Jemimah's is one of the rooms, too. The one closest to her galley.

So the two little rascals are all snugged up. Didn't waste much time.

*Hmmmm . . .*

# Chapter 20

I gaze over at the island and try to put myself in the place of that Spanish lieutenant who stood on the deck of his sinking ship and tried to mark the spot where she was going down. I picture him as young, idealistic, trying to do his duty to his ship and to his men as best he could. I think on the words he later wrote:

*I looked across the face of our compass to the end of the Key of Bones and saw that it bore away at about 010 degrees . . .*

I look across my own compass to the western tip of Key West and see that it does indeed bear north, northeast at 010 degrees, just like Spanish Lieutenant Carlos Maria Santana Juarez marked it. Or marked it as well as he could, seeing that his ship was foundering at the time he took the bearing and he would have been rather rushed.

*Then I took a bearing on a house that was built on the shore some distance to the east and that bearing was about 075 degrees . . .*

*That* is the problem. When I squint across my compass rose on that bearing, I see nothing—just a long line of mangroves and, behind them, some scrubby trees, so I cannot get that second and very crucial cross-bearing that would give us a better idea of where the treasure ship lies. The house, or more likely an Indian thatch-roofed hut, that Juarez saw is long gone, no doubt wiped out by a storm. Probably a hundred hurricanes have hit here since the one that took the *Santa Magdalena* down.

I sigh for lost bearings and look out over the activity on my ship. It is morning and we have had breakfast but haven't started the day's exploratory dives. Jim Tanner has manned the helm and my crew is getting ready to move the ship another fifty yards up the reef. That's the routine we've worked out: Move to a different spot each day, then I go down and look around. If I find nothing—and I have found nothing but many members of the local slug and bug population, to the great delight of the Doctor but to the joy of no one else—then we move on, and so inch our way along the coast. I have seen nothing that looks like the remains of a wrecked ship. 'Course the *Santa Magdalena* has been down there for seventy-odd years and there might not be much left of her.

This day, I do not give the order to move. Not yet, anyway. Instead, I call out, "Davy . . . Tink . . . Get the *Star* down and ready. I want to have a close look around that shore. Take rifles."

Dr. Sebastian comes up next to me and lifts his eyebrows in question.

"I'm going over to look for any sign of habitation on that shore. We need that other bearing, Doctor, else we'll be scouring the sea floor forever."

"Which would be all right with me," replies our avid natural scientist, looking over at the key. "I believe I shall accompany you on this little expedition. I must get my equipment." He scurries off to gather his specimen jars, magnifying glass, and, I am sure, his butterfly net.

The *Star* is lowered over the side, to bob in the water next to the raft, and as the sail is being rigged, Joannie comes up and gives me the big eyes. She already has her swimming suit on—she fairly lives in the thing—but I have not yet donned mine today.

"The galley all cleaned up?" I ask and she nods. "Did Jemimah say you were done?" Another nod. "All right, Joannie, get in. You, too, Daniel." They both *whoop* as they head for the boat. Not to be outdone by Joannie, Daniel now has a pair of canvas shorts of his own, and goes about virtually shirtless, tanned brown as a nut.

"Wait jes' a minute," says Jemimah, who has just come on deck to take up her usual after-breakfast post—a chair she has set up just after the forward mast where she sits and watches the ship's doings or gazes serenely out to sea. "Since you goin' over there, each of you take a pail and bring back a mess of them coon oysters. Full pails now, y'hear?"

"Yes, Auntie, we do," chorus the pair, as each grabs one of the buckets used for swabbing the deck and clambers onto the lifeboat. I guess they both have been instructed by Jemimah as to how to address her.

"And you, girl, you oughta look out for some fresh water . . . See if there's any over there," she says to me as she settles into her chair. "We're gettin' low, mighty low. Only two barrels left."

*Hmmm* . . . That is a problem. We've got all our catch

basins out, ready to collect the rain when it falls, but the trouble is, it hasn't. In the tropics, the rains come nearly every day in the summer, but this ain't summer, and I myself need at least three bucketsful a day to rinse off the salt after a day's diving. *Damn.*

"Yes, Jemimah, I will look, but I have my doubts. When we were over there before, it seemed to be just a low, dry sandbar with those mangrove trees around the edges."

We had, some days ago, taken the *Star* and sailed around Key West, hoping to find some sort of settlement where we could resupply and I could maybe sell my sponges. But after landing on a likely looking beach at the western tip of the island, we found nothing except some evidence of earlier rude encampments—whether Spanish, Indian, or pirate, we could not tell. The Spanish named the island Cayo Hueso, or "Bone Key," because of the piles of human bones they found there, remnants of some ancient Indian massacre, and there still are some of those bones around. It's got a nice little harbor, though, and I decide that we will pull the *Nancy B.* in there in the event of a storm.

"Well, you got to fix it somehow, what with you and the girl child takin' all them baths," Jemimah goes on. "And I can't make biscuits and soups and such without water." She has a basket of potatoes next to her on the deck and reaches down for one and begins to peel it.

"I know, Jemimah," I say, then sigh, as I turn to go down into my cabin. "Don't worry, we'll fix it."

When I get there, I doff my clothes and reach for my swimming suit, which had been hung up to dry from yesterday's diving, and climb into the bottom part.

The suit has worked out beautifully. When first I got it

wet, it shrank up most admirably, molding itself to my form perfectly and I was no more bothered with loose cloth swirling about me underwater. Plus, it doesn't go all transparent when wet like my shirt and drawers did, so I don't have to be constantly pulling it away from myself. The only thing the bottom of the suit does do that's a little annoying is ride up over my butt cheeks a bit, but, again, who cares about that?

The first time I appeared on deck in it, the day after the encounter with that horrid eel, I heard some sharp intakes of breath from certain members of my crew, but they all got over it right quick. After all, it's just me in all my scrawniness, so who could possibly care? Well, Higgins does, for one, as he is right there with a towel to wrap around me every time I step back on the deck after a day's diving. Davy just laughed and said, "And what would Jaimy say about his blushing bride-to-be if he saw her prancin' about like that?" And I shot back, "Just you mind your work, Seaman Jones, and don't worry about what your betters are thinkin'. Remember, Davy, who's the Captain of this here barky."

I'm slipping the straps of my suit top over my shoulders as I hear a light knock on the door—two raps, a pause, then another two.

"Come in, Higgins, and do me up." In a moment I feel his hands at my shoulder blades, fastening the buttons. There, all nice and snug now.

Higgins goes to the drawer where I keep my pistols, takes them out, and commences loading them.

"I don't think I'll need those today. The place looks to be deserted." I reach into my seabag and pull out a red bandanna, which I tie around my neck to keep off the sun.

"Still, Miss, there's no sense in taking chances." Unless we are in some nice, safe town, Higgins doesn't like to let me out of his sight without my being armed.

I roll up the short legs of the suit as far as they will go and then put my right foot up on my chair. Taking my shiv in its sheath from the desktop, I strap it around my right calf—I had altered the sheath's harness to fit there where it is out of the way yet still very convenient to my hand when needed underwater—and then stand with my fists on my hips, grin, and say, "So, Higgins, how do I look?"

"Perfectly barbarous." He sighs, with one of his deep whatever-is-to-be-done-with-her sighs. "However, let's get these on you to complete the travesty."

He straps on my pistols and I am out the hatch, over the deck, and into the *Star*.

"All right, lads, let's go."

It takes us about a half hour to get to the western tip of the key, then we start to work our way eastward close to shore, peering into the wall of mangroves for any sign of an opening. The bottom, about four feet down, is mostly sandy with occasional large patches of waving sea grass. I'm standing at the mast, Davy's in the bow, Tink's tending the sail, while Daniel's on the tiller. I wanted to give Daniel some experience in small-boat handling, plus let him show off to Joannie what a fine young sailor lad he is. She is seated beside him, feigning disinterest in his manly display.

The Doctor has a long glass with him and scans the treetops for any species of bird he might not yet have seen and recorded. We see a flock of pink things flying overhead, which gets him most agitated. "Roseate spoonbills! If I could just get one to have stuffed and taken back to London! Jones, shoot one!"

Davy lifts the rifle and looks to me and I shake my head and say, "Nay, Doctor, if it please you, they are much too high. And we wouldn't want to alert any wild savages that might be lurking about to our presence, now would we?" Davy lowers the rifle. Dr. Sebastian may be in charge of the expedition, but *I* run the ship. "There will be other opportunities, Doctor, I assure you."

There was actually a good chance Davy might have brought down one of the birds. The old smooth-bore muskets of twenty years ago have no place on my ship. No, now we have fine rifles with grooved barrels to give the bullets a spin on their way to the target, making them much more deadly accurate. Plus, these rifles use percussion caps instead of flintlocks. They cost Faber Shipping a bundle, but, hey, while the *Nancy B. Alsop* may be small compared to a man-o'-war, all her gear is the very finest. On the way down from Boston, I had the crew practice with the weapons, blasting countless bottles off the fantail, and Davy and Tink in particular have grown into superior marksmen. Looking at the rifle in Davy's hands, I reflect that science marches ever onward and advances us in many, many ways—the ways of war and killing not being the least of them.

"Whole bunch of the same damn thing," grumbles Davy as we glide along the featureless shore. We are about a mile from the western tip now and have seen nothing. Everybody on the *Nancy B.* has known for a long time that what we are seeking is not just scientific specimens but rather Spanish gold, and they are growing impatient.

"Hey. Wait a minute."

This from Joannie, who, having grown bored by the never-ending mangroves, has taken to leaning over the side, rump in the air, looking at the bottom scudding by.

"There's a bunch of shells or something down there."

"Bring her about, Daniel," I order, so he puts the tiller over and we circle around the spot. Sure enough, there seems to be a pile of discarded shells leading from the shore into the deeper water.

"Hmmm," says the Doctor, peering down. "It could be what's called a midden, a native shell mound."

I immediately look to the shore. Could that be a slight opening there? Would that be where the Indians came through to launch their boats and dump their shells?

"Tink. Strike the sail." The sail comes down. "Everyone grab an oar and let's try to shove her through right there." There are four oars onboard and Davy and Tink sling their rifles over their shoulders and each grabs one. I take one, too, as does Dr. Sebastian, and we point the *Star*'s nose to the opening and strain to pole her through. Joannie jumps up forward to push the branches aside as we slide in.

Yes. We are in. There is a low body of dark water on the other side of the mangroves, and then the land comes up to a low plain. We pull the boat up and look about. It is a desert area, with a large lagoon in the middle of it.

"Daniel. Joannie. Take your buckets and fill them up, like Jemimah told you, while we explore."

The kids groan and wade in the water and begin pulling the plentiful oysters off the exposed mangrove roots and dropping them into the pails. They're called coon oysters because, I suppose, the local raccoons like them as much as we do. Davy and Tink and I go looking around, while the

Doctor noses about in the brush. I go to the lagoon and dip my hand down into the water and bring it up to taste it. Then I quickly spit it out again. Salt. No fresh water here, that's for sure.

Davy and Tink unshoulder their rifles, looking, no doubt, for some poor innocent creature to shoot—*boys, I swear*—while I look about the land close to the shore.

*Hmmmm* . . . Close to the path we came in on is a curiously flattened-out spot. It is rectangular and seems to have some vestiges of postholes. I could be wrong—trees could have fallen in that particular pattern naturally, but somehow I don't think so. I walk to the center of the place and fall to my knees and begin to dig in the soft sand. I don't have to dig long before my hand hits a hard thing, and I pull it up and look at it. It is a bone and has teeth on it and it seems to be a jawbone of some sort.

"Doctor," I call. "Could you come here a second?"

He ceases his relentless pursuit of the local insect population and comes over near me. Taking the jawbone from my hand, he weighs it and remarks, "Probably the jaw of one of those tiny deer we spotted on these keys." He looks about him. "This could be a homestead. That might have been a fire pit right there." I look over and see a depression in the ground that I had not noticed before.

"I believe you are right, Doctor. This could have been a large thatched hut on a cleared shore back in 1733. Just what Carlos Juarez could have seen as the *Santa Magdalena* was going down."

"Could very well be, Miss," he says, plainly anxious to get back to his scientific explorations.

"Well, I am going to mark this spot," I say, and wade

back through the opening we had come through. Taking the red scarf from my neck, I tie it to a branch where it should be plainly visible from the *Nancy B.* and then I head back to the interior.

"Doctor! Doctor! Come look at this!" I hear both Joannie and Daniel call out. They are close to the edge of the quiet lagoon, pointing down. Dr. Sebastian goes over to see what they are on about, and so do I.

There, covering the shore, are hundreds of tiny crabs, each holding up an outsized claw to fend off intruders. I reach down and scoop one up and look at the brightly colored little beast in my palm. While it is only about a half inch across and I could easily crush it by simply closing my fist, it holds its claw up in my face, challenging me to do it.

"Ah," says Dr. Sebastian, "they are called fiddler crabs, because they look like they are fiddling when they brandish their claws. *Uca pugnax.*" He scoops up a few unlucky ones, which I will draw and which will ultimately take a dip in pure alcohol. I put my own feisty warrior back on the ground, allowing him to scurry back to his hole. Courage is not always a function of size.

Daniel and Joannie have made a game of herding the swarm of fiddler crabs as they course back and forth across the mucky sand next to the lagoon.

"Head 'em off, Danny!" shouts Joannie. "They're gonna . . . they're gonna . . . *Oh my God!*"

I jerk my head around and see that a monstrous form has surged out of the quiet lagoon and is running straight for the kids.

"*Run!*" I shriek. "*It's a gator! Run!*"

They try to run, but the footing is bad, and the gator

rushes on, bellowing. Joannie slips in the loose sand and falls down. The gator keeps coming on, so Danny grabs Joannie by her arm and tries to haul her forward, but the gator is too fast. It keeps rushing toward them, and its jaws open and then clamp down on Joannie's middle. The gator gives her a violent shake, and her eyes, which had been wild with fear, now roll back in her head, and she falls limp in the monster's jaws.

The alligator then turns to drag his prey into the water.

Daniel takes his knife from his side and leaps on the gator's back and begins stabbing at it, but I know it ain't doin' no good. The hide is just too thick. *Oh God, Joannie, no!*

I pound over, pulling out my pistols as I go. "Davy! Tink! To me! To me!" I point the barrel of the gun in my right hand point-blank at the creature's forehead and fire.

It doesn't even flinch.

"Boys! Fire just behind its front leg!" *Maybe we can find its heart! Oh God, please!*

Tink and Davy fire and two holes appear in the gator's side, but still it moves inexorably onward. In a few feet it'll be in the water and Joannie will be lost forever.

Desperate, I leap up on the monster's back and aim my remaining pistol at the monster's left eye and pull the trigger.

*That* gets its attention. It opens its mouth to bellow out its pain and anger and Joannie flops out.

"Davy! Pick her up and get her back to the boat!" I yell. "Watch out for its tail! And its teeth!"

Davy nimbly jumps out of the way of the thrashing tail and tosses his rifle to Daniel. Careful of the snapping jaws, he picks up Joannie's limp form and cradles her in his arms.

Spots of blood are appearing and beginning to spread on her once white swimsuit.

As Davy starts his run with his pitiful burden, we hear a loud roiling of the water behind us. *What . . . ?*

"Good God, there's more of 'em!" I shout, as what looks to be dozens of the huge creatures come roaring out of the water. They gaze balefully at us and then begin to move forward. "Run!"

We run for all we're worth, through the mangroves and back to the boat. Whether the alligators are slower than we are, or they pause to devour their wounded comrade, I do not know. Or care. All I know is we make it back to the boat and push off, raise the sail, and head back to the *Nancy B.* as fast as we can go.

"Put her on the transom and let's have a look," orders Dr. Sebastian, and Davy puts her down on the thwart—where the rowers normally sit. I kneel down beside her on the left and the Doctor kneels down on the right. Joannie lies motionless, unconscious . . . or maybe . . .

"Is she dead, Doctor?"

He leans over and presses his ear to her chest.

"No. Not yet. I can hear her heart . . ."

*Hang on, Joannie, hang on . . .*

". . . but her breathing is not right. I hear wheezing. I hope the lung was not punctured," he says, "because if it has been . . ."

He does not have to say it.

"Take off that halter," is what he does say, and I reach back and undo the buttons and pull it away from her. There are teeth marks all over her chest, and the right half of it looks sickeningly deflated.

"Yes, I see. The beast broke her ribs on that side. We've got to get more air into her."

Taking my cue, I lean over, suck in a deep breath, put my mouth on hers, and blow. But all that happens is the air comes pouring out her nose to brush against my cheek. I try again. This time I hook my thumb in the corner of her mouth to make a tighter seal with my lips, and hold her nostrils shut with my other thumb and forefinger. This time her chest rises.

"Good," says the Doctor. "Do it again."

I do it again . . . and again . . . and again.

"Let me listen. Everyone quiet."

A hush falls over the boat as Dr. Sebastian puts his ear over each of the chest wounds as I keep Joannie's chest inflated.

"Good," he says. "You can stop now. I hear no aspiration, no sucking wounds. The lung is sound, I think. Flip her over."

Davy and I turn her on her stomach. There are bleeding teeth marks on her back, but they do not appear deep, thank God.

"But wh-wh-why is she still not awake?" asks a very stricken Daniel from back on the tiller.

"Three possibilities, boy," says the Doctor. "One, the beast broke her back when he shook her. That is how many carnivores kill their prey, you know. Let us see." The Doctor splays out the fore and middle fingers of his right hand and, starting high on the back of Joannie's neck, runs those two fingers slowly down on either side of her spine all the way down to her tailbone. "Hmmm . . . seems all right. Can't feel any break. But I can't be positive. Turn her over again."

We do it.

"Another possibility is that she fainted from terror, which would certainly be understandable. But knowing this girl, I do not think that is the case. Plus, she would have revived by now."

"Then what?" I ask. Now that she's face-up again, I give her another puff of air, but it seems that her own thin chest is now doing that job on its own.

"Her head could have been slammed against the ground in her struggle with the alligator, giving her a concussion of the brain and rendering the girl unconscious," says the Doctor. He runs his fingers up the side of Joannie's head, feeling for any wound.

"Ah," he says, "there is a swelling here. On her left temple. And it looks like it is starting to discolor. A good sign. But we can't be sure. There could still be internal bleeding. We don't know. Time will tell."

We have a kind, following wind on the way back, and soon the masts of the *Nancy B.* loom over us.

As we approach, we shout out the nature of our distress, and as we pull in next to the raft, John Thomas is there to gather up Joannie and hand her to Higgins on the deck.

"Put her on the mess table, Higgins, and bring up my medical kit, if you would."

I hop over the rail and head down to the mess deck, where I find Joannie already stretched out, with the Doctor beginning to thread his stitching needles.

Jemimah is there and lightly smoothes the hair away from Joannie's forehead, and, without being told, holds a cool compress to the bruise on the side of her face.

"Poor baby," she croons as she does it. "Poor little child, poor little thing."

Higgins, knowing my mind, has opened my medical kit and poured some of the pure alcohol into the shallow little basin. I thread my own needle and dip both needle and thread into the liquid.

"Doctor," I say, as I get ready to start sewing, "if you will humor me, please put your own surgical tools in the alcohol bath before you apply them to the patient. I have found that it decreases the chances of infection."

Dr. Sebastian shrugs. "It can't hurt, so why not?" He does it and we get to work sewing her up.

I start sewing up a nasty rip on her belly after pouring some pure alcohol on the wound. She jerks when I lay it on, which, I find, is a good sign—*hey, if it hurts, it's gotta be good* is what I figure.

"There are some cuts down below. Get the pants off her," orders the Doctor.

I pull off the suit and get to work on what I find down there.

"I worry about that one there," he says, pointing to one particularly deep puncture. "If it penetrated the peristaltic sac, then she's in serious trouble. We shall see. Let's get on with it."

Before he can sew the lips of the gaping wound shut, I pour some pure spirits of alcohol down on it, and Joannie's eyes fly open. She screams and starts to cry and struggle and twist about.

"Hold her down," orders Dr. Sebastian. "We're almost done."

"There, there, baby," says Jemimah softly. "Hush, now. You're gonna be all right. Jus' be still."

"Here, Joannie," I say, shoving a plug of leather between her teeth. "Bite down on this. Be brave. It'll all be over soon."

She subsides to an agonized groan and the Doctor finishes up his stitching.

He then takes a roll of wide bandage. "We've got to wrap those ribs. Sit her up," and he starts rolling the cloth around her thin chest. "All right, that's it. Time will tell. Clean her up and put her to bed."

The Doctor puts his tools away as Jemimah and I take wet cloths and begin cleaning the bloody smears from Joannie's body. When we are done, I ask of Higgins, who has been standing by, "Please take her up and put her in my bed. The air is better in there than down here, and it might do her some good."

He picks up the now quietly weeping girl and goes out the hatch, past a very distressed Daniel Prescott, who has been waiting anxiously there. Jemimah and I follow him out and into my cabin. I pull back the sheets from my bed and Joannie is placed upon it, while Jemimah sits down next to her and tries to calm the plainly still terrified girl. It's clear that I will not be the only one suffering from nightmares.

There's a bottle containing a special liquid in the cabinet where I keep my medical supplies. It's got lots of names—paregoric, laudanum, tincture of opium—but I call it Jacky's Little Helper 'cause it's gotten me out of many a scrape, and now it's going to help Joannie get through her horrors. I take up the bottle and pour a dollop into a small glass and then lift Joannie's head and hold it to her lips.

"Here, Joannie. Drink this. It will make you feel better."

She manages to swallow it, and I let her sink back into the pillow. Jemimah takes up her hand and says, "Now, child, you just rest now. Ain't nothin' can harm you here." Then she begins to sing a lullaby.

> *Hush-a-bye, don't you cry,*
> *Go to sleepy, little baby.*
> *When you wake, you'll have cake,*
> *And all the pretty little horses.*
>
> *Blacks and bays, dapples and grays,*
> *All the pretty little horses.*
> *Hush-a-bye, don't you cry,*
> *Go to sleepy, little baby.*

The terror in Joannie's eyes slowly fades, and she sleeps.

Later, before the fall of evening, I go out on deck. I take my long glass and look over at the key to see if I can locate the red scarf that I had tied to that mangrove. Yes, there it is, plain as day. I lower the glass.

*Well, we got the bearing,* I think with a deep sigh, but if Joannie dies, we will have paid very dearly for it.

# Chapter 21

*. . . By my reckoning we were about two miles from the shore, but I cannot be sure, as the storm was so fierce.*

*I thank the Good God for my deliverance and I pray daily for the souls of my lost comrades.*

You were off by a good mile, Lieutenant Carlos Maria Santana Juarez, but that is understandable, given your circumstances, and so we forgive you.

Yesterday, using the newly acquired cross-bearing, we maneuvered to our new position and dropped the hook. We found ourselves in somewhat deeper water, about three miles offshore. Probably five fathoms down. Still, when I looked over the side of the raft, I could see clear to the bottom and should be able to reach it.

I went into my cabin to suit up and to get ready to dive.

And I did dive, and many times, too, but yesterday's diving yielded nothing except more sponges to decorate our rigging, which now sags with over a hundred of the things.

However, today is bright with promise and, ever optimistic, especially when it comes to possible gold, I slip over the side and slide into the water. I know it's down there and I know we're getting close. I can just smell it.

I swim down, planning to explore a bit more to the west. We had moved the *Nancy B.* in that direction yesterday before securing for the day. A quick scan of the sandy, coral-dotted bottom shows nothing but the usual flora and fauna; and as I work my way down to the deeper depth, I reflect that I am using up too much of my air in just getting to the bottom, leaving very little time for looking around before I have to go up for a breath. I have an idea and kick back to the surface and hang on to the side of the raft.

After I've gulped in a lungful of air, I call out, "John Thomas, take the lifeboat's anchor and tie a long line to it. Put a knot in the rope every three feet. And then drop it over the side right there. Straight up and down. Nice and taut."

"Aye, Cap'n," says John Thomas as he goes to do it.

Since I know it'll take him a while to rig that up, I pull myself onto the raft. The Doctor, who has been looking through his glass-bottomed bucket, gives me a questioning look.

"I'll be able to climb down the rope hand over hand and so get to the bottom quicker. It's much deeper here, you know."

He nods as I stand and then go up the ladder and to the deck of the *Nancy B.* As always, Higgins is there with a towel to dry me. Then I pop down into my cabin to see how Joannie is doing.

Quite well, it seems, and she is chafing at being kept abed.

"I'm ready to get up now, I am," she declares.

"You'll get up when the Doctor says you're ready to get up," I say, "and not before." I go to my bookshelf and pull out a book. "Here, read this. Since you cannot perform your usual duties, you might as well study."

She sticks out her lower lip in a fine pout, then says, "Wasn't my fault that thing tried to eat me." She picks up the book and opens it. "Looks like it's for babies."

"It is *McFeeney's Eclectic Reader,* Volume One," I reply in my best schoolmarmish voice. "A very respected school-book, it is. It will teach you grammar and moral lessons on behavior. When you are done with it, I will test you, and if you pass, I shall give you some more grown-up things to read."

The lower lip comes out even further as I leave. Outside my door I see Daniel Prescott hunkered down beside the bulkhead. I heave a great sigh and say, "All right, you little rascal, get in there. But be good. She needs her rest."

He is in there in an instant. I don't know what good my warning will do, but, hey, I ain't their mother.

Going below and thinking to grab a bite, I hear Jemimah up forward, feeding the chickens, and I go to join her, where I hear the hens clucking and her singing.

> *Cluck old hen, cluck and sing,*
> *Ain't laid an egg since way last spring.*
> *Cluck old hen, cluck and squall,*
> *Ain't laid an egg since way last fall.*

I hear the seed corn hitting the deck as Jemimah scatters it, and I hear the hens scratching about. Higgins had brought several crates of chickens onboard back in Boston, but he didn't know quite what to do with them, 'cept to chop their heads off and have 'em for dinner. For the ones that managed to survive until she came onboard, Jemimah had a better idea. She set up an area forward, where they could get some sunlight, and made up some nests for them so they would be comfortable and maybe lay more eggs.

> *My old hen, she's a good old hen,*
> *She lays eggs for the workin' men.*
> *Sometimes two, sometimes ten,*
> *That's enough for the workin' men.*

I know that Jemimah likes her chickens, but I also know what happens to a hen what won't lay, as we have seen several of them on our plates on the mess deck, and very tasty they were, poor things.

> *Cluck old hen, cluck in the lot,*
> *Next time you cackle, you'll cackle in the pot.*

Ah, well, it's a hard life for both chicken and person, and what can you say about it all? I dunno.

Jemimah sees me watching her feed the chickens and says, "Come over here, girl, and learn somethin' that you don't know."

I obediently walk over, where I see a nest that a large brown hen has just left so she can eat some of the seeds that Jemimah has been spreading around.

"What we got here is a broody hen. See, the other girls

let me take the eggs they lay, but this one, uh-uh, she means to hatch these ones out. Musta got with a rooster."

I nod and continue to absorb all this chicken lore as Jemimah goes on.

"Y'see, those round eggs is gonna be hens, and those two more pointy ones is gonna be roosters. And that one there, that tiny one is gonna be a banty—a real small little rooster, what ain't good for nothin' 'cept struttin' around all proud and causin' trouble. Jus' like that one over there."

The broody hen hops back up on the eggs and settles in, eyeing us suspiciously. I look over into the gaggle of chickens and see a very small black-and-white rooster. He walks about with an air of absolute authority, flipping his cockscomb back and forth over his head and keeping his beady black eye on us and on the only other rooster left in the flock—a big red fellow twice the size of the banty. Uh-oh. Apparently the red rooster gets a little too close to a plump and comely white hen and the banty flies into a rage. Giving out a wild *cock-a-doodle-doo,* he leaps at the other suitor and brings the spurs he carries on the back of his feet down on the unfortunate red and fiercely pecks at him, the banty's head hammering back and forth. The bigger rooster runs off, wings out and squawking.

"All right, that's it for you," says Jemimah, reaching out and snatching up the little rooster by his neck. With her other hand she grabs the small hatchet she keeps next to the stove. "You ain't much, but you'll sweeten the pot tonight, you will."

The banty fixes his eye on Jemimah, as if daring her to do it.

"Stay your hand, Jemimah, if you would," I say. "Let him live a while longer."

She casts an eye on me and says, "If you don't lay, you don't stay."

"I just want to give him a sporting chance, Jemimah. You'll see." *And a sporting chance is exactly what I have in mind.*

"All right, girl." Jemimah sighs. "You just do what you wanna do."

She releases the banty, who shakes his feathers and gives a look as if to say that all this was a serious affront to his dignity and he is not pleased. Jemimah then grabs the much gentler big red rooster by his neck and pulls him flapping and fluttering from the coop. It will do him no good. As I leave the hold, I hear a *thunk!* and reflect on the qualities of a warlike nature and those of meek nature, and I can draw no conclusions.

I go back on deck, where I find that things are ready for me to take my deepest dive yet.

I adjust my goggles, hop down to the raft, and put my hand on the anchor rope that John Thomas has set up.

"Be careful, Miss," says Dr. Sebastian. "There are things that happen to people in the depths and science knows little about them."

I nod and take three great gulps of air, hold the last one, and drop into the water. *This is much easier,* I think, pulling myself hand over hand down the rope, glad of the knots. In no time, and at the expense of very little air, I am at the bottom, thirty feet below.

I look around. While there are some very interesting corals and the usual brilliantly colored fishes milling about my face, they are not what I am here for. A kick and I am into the deeper water that lies to seaward and . . . *What's that?*

There, half buried in the sand that slopes into the depths, is something that looks out of place . . . A roundish, white thing . . . Not a clam shell, not a piece of coral . . . *What is it?*

I've still got some breath left, so I leave my anchor rope and swim over to the object. There is not much silt down below here in the Keys, but there is some, and what there is obscures the thing I am studying. *Hmmmm . . .*

*Out of my way, little ones,* I say to the brightly colored fish that always gather in front of my face when I'm down here. *Scat, you. I've got work to do.*

It looks like a pot of some sort. I wave my hand in front of it to remove the silt, and as it flies off, I find myself looking into the empty eye sockets of a human skull. *Oh my God!*

Shocked, I grab the anchor rope and fly back up and gasp when I break the surface.

*Calm down, girl. The dead cannot hurt you.*

"What?" asks Dr. Sebastian. "What did you find?"

"Something . . . Maybe," I say, panting. All the rest of the crew is hanging on the rail looking down at me. "I'm goin' down again."

Another three big breaths and then under.

This time I am more calm. I see that the skeleton lies with his head down the slope. The rib cage is still there, but the legs are gone. With one arm left, its boney hand seems to be pointing down into the depths below. *Pointing down to a lost ship? Could it be?* I brush the dust from the face of the skull and see a gleam next to the right side of it. I reach for it because I know instantly what it is—a golden hoop, a sailor's earring.

I put it between my teeth and go back to the surface to hold up the piece of gold before the crew. There is a common intake of breath.

"I have found a skeleton down there. Give me the net bag," I say. "We must bring him up."

The Doctor looks mystified, but the sailors—each of whom, like me, wears an identical hoop in his ear—are not. It is a fellow seaman down below, and he must be brought back up.

The bag is delivered and I put rump up to make a surface dive and head back down. When I get to the drowned sailor, I carefully drop his bones into the bag. There is not much of him left—just the skull with some backbone attached, ribs, hipbone, arm and fingers—but what there is, I handle carefully, as I would want my own bones handled when the time comes.

I grab the anchor line and shoot back up into the air. The net bag is taken from me as I pull myself onto the raft and sprawl on my back to regain my breath. I reflect that sometimes I push myself to the limit and maybe I shouldn't do that all the time.

My chest eventually stops heaving and I sit back up, to find Dr. Sebastian going over the bones. "So what do you think, Doctor?" I ask, kneeling next to him.

"Well, from the condition of his teeth, I'd say he was young and in good health. Since you found neither sword belt nor sword around him, I assume he was a common seaman. But nothing singles him out as Spanish, or as belonging to the *Santa Magdalena*. He could have been any poor seaman lost overboard in these waters."

"I have the feeling that he was a member of that crew," I say. "The way he lay down there, the way—"

"Wait a moment," says the Doctor. "What's this?"

Just below the skull and wrapped around the backbone is what appears to be a thin strand of seaweed with a lump at the end of it. Dr. Sebastian takes up the lump and rubs it between thumb and forefinger. It is not seaweed. The black tarnish comes off and what rests in his hand is a piece of silver, a piece of silver in the form of a crucifix.

"Well, he was Spanish all right," says Dr. Sebastian. "But what that means, I don't know."

"I know what it means," I say, getting up and climbing back onto the *Nancy B.* "It means the *Santa Magdalena* with all her gold is right down there beneath us and I'm gonna prove it right now. Finn McGee, please pull up the anchor rope."

He nods and starts hauling in the small lifeboat anchor, coiling the knotted rope on the deck. When the anchor comes onboard, I ask him to take it to the other side of the ship and just lay it there, which he does.

I tighten my goggles and start to take my usual deep breaths before diving, when Higgins asks me, "What do you intend to do?"

"It's simple. Instead of climbing down the anchor rope, I will just grab hold of the anchor and jump over so I'll get to the bottom that much quicker. And going over this side of the ship will put me a good thirty feet farther out into the deep water. I want to look around."

Davy and Tink overhear this, and Davy says, "That's the stupidest thing I've ever heard. Do you really want to drown? Do you want yours to be just another skull down there? Yours would be thicker than most, but it would still be just an empty skull."

"I absolutely agree," says Higgins, looking at me severely. "What you have been doing has been dangerous enough. I have always tried to avoid comment on your personal conduct, but jumping overboard in deep water holding an anchor is just too much."

"Look, I'll ride the anchor down as far as I can for a good look, and when it gets chancy, I'll just let go of it and come back up. What could be safer?"

"A lot of things could be safer, Jackass," says Davy, fixing his eye upon me. "You know what I think? I think you've got too fierce a lust for the gold that's down there. Prolly 'cause you was poor like the rest of us when we was growin' up and you don't wanna be poor no more. But you gotta know that even if you find all the gold in the world, if'n you're dead, it don't mean a goddamn thing. What did it mean to that sailor you just brought up?"

*Is this mutiny? If so, by God, it must be nipped in the bud.*

"I'm the Captain of this ship, Seaman Jones, and I'll do—"

"What you are is a royal pain in the ass, Jacky, but we still don't want to see you dead. We—"

"Here's what we'll do, *Captain*," says Tink, who takes the end of a long coil of rope and ties it around my waist. "We'll give a long count of twenty and then we'll haul you back up, whether you want to come or not. When you feel the tug, drop the anchor. It'll still be attached to the knotted line, so we won't lose it."

*Ah, John Tinker, the soul of reason.*

"Anybody else got a damned opinion?" I ask, miffed, to the ship at large. "Daniel? Jim? John Thomas? Finn? Jemimah?"

"I think you crazy to git in the water at all, crazy to prance aroun' half bare like that," says Jemimah from her chair, "so this is jes' more of yo' craziness."

Dr. Sebastian speaks up. "While it is true that you are the commander of this ship, I am the leader of the expedition, and I order that you go down with the rope about your waist, or you do not go down at all. You are too valuable to this project to be lost this early."

"All right," I say, tired of all this. I hop up onto the rail. "Let's get on with it. Give me the anchor."

It is put in my hands, and my arms strain to hold its fifty heavy pounds. One deep breath . . . another deep breath . . . and a third, *really* deep breath and hold . . . and I am over and into the water.

I plummet like a stone, past the shadow of the *Nancy B.*'s hull, past her keel, past her anchor chain leading down, then past the big anchor itself imbedded in the bottom, past the slope where I found the Spanish sailor, past all that and down into the abyss.

It is still clear here, but the light is now far overhead and the bottom of the chasm is dim and I can't see . . . My ears start to hurt and I'm gonna have to let go soon and I . . . I . . . One more moment . . . just one more . . . and . . . *There!* Coming up at me like a spear from out of the depths—

unmistakable—the mainmast of a sunken ship, scraps of canvas still clinging to the topgallant spar.

I drop the lifeboat's anchor and, at the same time, feel the tug of the lifeline at my middle, towing me swiftly back to the surface.

When my head breaks through, I gasp, then say, "I've found her! She's right down there! I saw her masts! Don't take up the little anchor. Attach a buoy or something to mark this spot. Oh lads, we have found the *Magdalena*!"

# Chapter 22

The elation we feel upon finding what has to be the treasure ship is immediately dashed by a shout from the lookout.

"Skipper! Ship ahoy! Due south! Two points abaft the port beam!" shouts Daniel in the crow's-nest.

I rush to my quarterdeck to grab my long glass, then train it on the approaching ship.

"What is she?" asks Higgins.

"Don't know yet, but she's big and she's headin' straight for us." I keep my eye pressed to the glass, trying to make out her colors. Then I don't have to look for her flag anymore, 'cause I see something attached to the foot of her mainmast—it is a six-foot-tall golden crucifix.

*Damn!*

"It's a Spanish man-of-war," I say, snapping the glass shut. "And it looks like he means to board us. Everyone take your places. Remember, we are all Americans here. We are a sponge boat with a naturalist aboard and that is all. Doctor, take the skeleton down into your lab. It will not look out of place there. Me, I shall get back in the water and start col-

177

lecting sponges. Everybody be calm, maybe this is nothing to worry about."

Saying that, I hurry back down to the diving raft and, with goggles on, slip into the water.

I pause for a moment to collect my thoughts. *What is he doing here? Could word of our doings have leaked out somehow? I don't know, just collect your sponges, girl, and let things play out as they will.*

Looking down, I see a likely looking batch of sponges on the bottom and dive down to collect them. It's a little deeper here, but I still have no trouble getting to them, then cutting their tough stalks with my shiv, hauling them back to the surface, and slapping them on the raft, water oozing out of their pores. It'd be nice to have Joannie help me with this, but she's still laid up, and will be for a while yet. But she is getting better, which is good.

I sneak a peek at the rapidly closing-in Spaniard, and then nip back down. As I harvest this newest batch of unfortunate sponge, again I marvel at the ease with which the little fishies that gather about me flit through the water with simple flicks of their tails, while I have to struggle to do the same. And then I see what looks to be a huge ray at the bottom, leisurely flying along as if he were an albatross riding a rising wind. *Hmmm* . . . More study is required on that . . . But later—time now to deal with the Dons above.

A massive shadow moves overhead and I know it is the hull of the Spanish man-of-war. I swim back up, deposit my sponges, and putting my elbows on the raft, I look at the thing looming over me.

It is a First-Rate Ship-of-the-Line-of-Battle, a huge

fighting machine carrying at least eighty guns, six hundred men, and enough firepower to reduce something like us to splinters in a matter of seconds . . . And I notice the gun ports are open and the gun barrels sticking out. A worm of worry works its way into my mind, not for the *Nancy B.*— as we are insignificant next to this floating instrument of death and destruction—but for the *Dolphin*, due here in a few days, and for my friends who are upon her. If she encounters this ship, she will be honor bound to fight, though she is half its size. *Oh Lord, please* . . .

The ship is called the *San Cristobal*, I see from the name painted in gilt on the stern, and a boat is being loaded, and ten men and an officer are in it.

I nip back under again, go to the bottom, and hack off a few more sponges. As I head back up, I see the hull bottom of the small boat making its way overhead to the raft of the *Nancy B.* I wait a bit, till I'm reasonably sure the occupants are out of the boat, then I resurface and place my arms on the raft and lie still to listen.

"Who are you and what are you doing here in Spanish waters?" the officer demands of John Higgins, who stands onboard as Captain. I observe that the young man is quite handsome—dark hair, noble nose—and is resplendent in a blue, yellow, and gold uniform. From the amount of gold braid on him, he looks to be a Senior Lieutenant.

"We are the *Nancy B. Alsop*, out of Boston, Massachusetts, United States, engaged in the harvesting of sponges. We also have a naturalist aboard who is studying the local flora and fauna—may I present Dr. Stephen Sebastian, here?"

The young officer does not seem particularly interested

in who we are and what we are doing. He ignores the Doctor and directs his men to search our ship, and so they plunge down into our inner spaces.

"I will point out to you, Señor," says Higgins, "that we are five miles from shore and are, therefore, in international waters."

The officer slowly turns himself to bring his gaze upon Higgins.

"We will decide whose waters you are in, Señor, and not you."

An uneasy silence falls over the ship. Presently Higgins, who believes there is never an excuse for bad manners, says, "May we offer you something to eat or drink, Señor, while your men conduct their search?"

"If you have any decent rum aboard, you may give me a cup."

Higgins nods to Daniel, who goes below to get it. He comes back carefully balancing a tumbler of the amber liquor.

The Spaniard takes it and knocks back half of it. A disagreeable look comes over his face. "Swill," he says with a sneer, then flings the rest of the rum in Daniel's face. Shocked, the boy cries out and wipes at his eyes.

"You would serve that to a Castellano?" the Lieutenant asks, as he flings the cup over his shoulder. It hits the deck and shatters.

"And you will spurn our hospitality and cause distress to a small boy?" asks Higgins, unable to let the insult pass. I know that Higgins stocks only the finest of whiskeys and rums, and it is not good to question his taste.

The officer puts his hand on the hilt of his sword, his

dark eyes hard. "Be careful of your tongue, *Yanqui,* else you might lose it."

Higgins is about to reply, when the Spanish sailors return to the deck, the lead man saying, *"Nada, Teniente."* They found nothing, just as we had thought.

"Very well. *Vamos, hombres!"* The Lieutenant spins on his heel and leads his men back toward their boat. I figure this would be a good time for me to go back down for more sponges and so stay out of the Castilian gentleman's notice.

It doesn't work out that way.

When I come back up, figuring the Spaniards would already be back in their boat, I fling my catch onto the raft like any good sponge diver—which would be fine if the Lieutenant had left the platform, which he had not. He was still very much there, and I see with a certain amount of horror that I have sprayed water from the dripping sponges all over his shiny black boots.

*Uh-oh . . .*

*"Madre de Dios!"* he yells. "Look what you've done, you miserable *perro!"*

"I am sorry, Sir," I say, thinking about swimming away to escape his wrath.

I don't get the chance.

"Bring him up here!" he roars to his men, and strong hands grab me under the arms to haul me up on the raft and then fling me all sprawled out down upon it.

He gives me a kick and says, "You piece of—" His eyes widen as he takes in my costume . . . and me. "What? A *girl?* Get up, you!"

I get to my feet, my rump smarting from his boot.

His gaze sweeps over me and a smile comes to his

thin lips. "*Bueno*. A welcome little diversion, eh, *chica*? Turn around." He pushes my right shoulder and I reluctantly turn around, slipping my forefingers under the bottom of my suit to tug it down to cover my bum.

"Very nice," he says. I endure his gaze, knowing that the *San Cristobal* could send us straight to the bottom with no questions asked if we dare to cross the Spaniards. I have heard sounds of my crewmen up on deck being restrained by both Higgins and Dr. Sebastian from pulling their knives and jumping down to my aid, which is good. *Steady boys, steady . . .*

The officer, who has not removed his hand, then calls up to Higgins, "Why do you have girls diving for your sponges, man?"

Higgins, staying in character, replies, "Good seamen are hard to replace. Girls we can get anywhere. Plus they can stay down longer than men because they do not smoke tobacco."

"So you consider them expendable? Very good. And we know there are other uses for them as well, do we not? Dry this one off and she would warm a bed quite nicely."

Higgins does not reply, and the Spanish Lieutenant says, "Ah well, this has been most amusing, but now I must be off." I heave a sigh of relief. A little too soon, it turns out.

"There is still the matter of my boots," he goes on. "You sullied them. You shall kneel and clean them," and he shoves me down to my knees. I look at the tops of his boots and the sprinkles of seawater that glisten there. It is all I can do not to push this insufferable so-called gentleman over the side of the raft and then dive down to watch his face as he drowns.

But I stifle my rage—there is too much at stake for me to give in to it.

When I am diving, Higgins always makes sure a folded towel is placed on the raft for me to dry off with when I am done, so now I reach for it and wipe the offending droplets from the blackguard's boots.

Apparently I have done it to his satisfaction, for, after snarling, "I should have had you lick it off, girl," he reaches down and grabs a fistful of my hair and yanks me to my feet, his face in mine. "Next time I will."

Done with me, I am flung aside as he addresses Higgins. "We have heard rumors . . . and there is much irregular here." He looks at me. "I have my suspicions. We will be watching you and we shall see."

He climbs into his boat, and says, *"Vamos!"* and the Spaniards pull away. The Lieutenant's last glance is at me, and though the day is warm, I give a bit of a shiver, then I dive back into the warm, cleansing waters of the Caribbean Sea.

# Chapter 23

Later that day, we put the seaman's bones into a canvas sack and sew it up. We let him keep his crucifix about his neck, but we do take his earring. The *Star* is rigged for a short sail and we put the bag in the lifeboat and prepare to cast off. As we are climbing in, I inform Dr. Sebastian of our intention to cross over to the Key to bury the remains.

"But why?" asks the Doctor. "They are just bones."

"It's an age-old tradition, Dr. Sebastian, a bargain, really, between those who sail the sea and those who live on land—between the living and the dead," I explain to the landsman. "You see that all of us seamen wear a single gold hoop in our ears? Well, if a sailor meets his end at sea and later washes up on shore, the person who finds him must give his body a proper burial, and is then allowed to take the gold ring for his payment. We took his gold ring, so now we've got to bury him. Simple as that." I reach up to touch my own earring.

"I see," says the practical surgeon, who has undoubtedly cut up more bodies and thrown away more bones than he could possibly count. "More nautical foolishness."

"Just so, Doctor. Sailors are very superstitious as a rule, and one of the things they don't like is being buried at sea." I motion for Davy to hoist the *Star*'s sail, and Tink takes his place on the tiller as I call up to my First Mate, "Mr. Tanner, make all preparations for getting under way. When we come back aboard, we'll pull the hook and head over to Cuba to take on fresh water and sell our sponges. The *Dolphin* is not due to rendezvous for five more days, and we can't do anything till we get that diving bell. All right, shove off."

"He could have been a real rotter, you know, this man we are burying," says Tink. He turns the last shovelful of Key West dirt over the grave of the Spanish sailor and tamps it down.

Since we did not know his name, we made up a crude wooden cross with just the words *Vaya con Dios, Marinero,* "Go with God, Mariner," written in ship's ink thereon, and we stuck it in the sand above his head. We are at the western tip of Key West, having had no intention of getting anywhere near that alligator pit.

"Right," says Davy. "Or a real son of a bitch of a Bosun's Mate."

"Myself," I say, "I want to believe that he was a nice young man who loved the girl he left behind with a heartfelt promise of a quick return, and she, in turn, mourned his loss when he did not come back, not ever." It's the romantic in my nature.

"Of course," says Davy, with a heavy sigh.

By common consent, we have given the Spanish sailor's earring to Davy, who had none, since he had placed his on the finger of Annie Byrnes when he married her. He now has another hanging on his ear, one that is certainly salty, having lain below all these years.

"Whoever and whatever he was, he showed us the way to the *Santa Magdalena,* and for that I am grateful," I go on. "And I think he is glad to be buried at last on Spanish soil, and he will, perhaps, bless our expedition for our doing it."

"It's gonna be dark soon, Jacky, we'd best be getting back," warns Tink.

I look up into the reddening sky and realize that Tink is right. We'll want to get the *Nancy B.* headed south before true night sets in.

"We did what we came to do. Let's get back," I order, and we return to the boat. "Rest in peace, sailor," I say as we push off.

We reach the *Nancy B.,* lift the anchor, raise the sails, get her on course, set the watch, and as she surges toward Cuba, we go down for dinner. We have an excellent soup featuring, I believe, the parts of a certain unfortunate red rooster, as well as biscuits, potatoes, ham, and redeye gravy.

After I have eaten my fill, I lean back in my chair, place the back of my fist against my mouth to stifle a discreet burp, and lift my glass to my crew, to announce, "It will take us eighteen to twenty hours to get to Cuba, if the current wind holds, and the same sailing time to get us back to our rendezvous with the *Dolphin* on Friday. That means three days of sweet liberty in one of the finest ports in the Caribbean. Do I hear a cheer?"

"*Hear, hear!*" shouts my parcel of rogues.

*On to Havana and all her charms.*

# Chapter 24

"So, Jemimah. We are nearing Havana. Will you leave us there, or will you stay? Now that you're free and all."

We have seen the land looming before us and are working our way up the coast, to the city. Breakfast has been served and cleared away, and I am gazing down at the new chicks, which the broody hen just hatched.

"Don't know," she says, tossing out the grain to the clucking chickens. "What's there for me?"

"Oh, about seventy thousand people. Lots of big buildings and forts. Biggest town north of Peru, and that includes Boston, New York, and Charleston. New Orleans, too." I got this information from Dr. Sebastian, who, aside from being an avid naturalist, is also an agent of British Intelligence. "I'll give you what you've earned so far if you want to go. You shouldn't have any trouble finding work, 'cause you're one fine cook."

"Hmmm . . . Suppose someone come up and try to put me back as a slave. Wouldn't be no trouble for them to do it—I'm black, they white."

"Dr. Sebastian tells me there's over fifteen thousand free blacks on the island. You wouldn't stand out."

"Ummm . . ."

"Don't want you to go, Jemimah, but it's up to you."

"Well, we'll see."

I let it go at that and reach down to scoop up one of the peeps. While the rest of the chicks are a fuzz of bright yellow, this one is white with streaks of black.

"Hmmm . . . Ain't too tough to figure out who this one's dad is," I say, looking over at the banty, who seems to be glad to be the only rooster still standing. The chick fixes me with his bright little eye and then pecks my thumb. "Nope, not hard at all."

I put the feisty little thing back with his nest mates and go out the hatchway. I hop up on my quarterdeck to watch our approach to Havana.

I have dressed in my serving-girl rig—loose white blouse, tight black vest, black skirt, black stockings, black shoes—figuring it more appropriate for a visit to a Catholic port than my usual attire. After all, the Spanish Inquisition still does exist and I'd hate to end up on the rack. Or at the stake, for that matter, ready to be roasted for my many misdeeds. I suspect that my tombstone shall someday read *She sure had it comin'*.

I'm also wearing my curly black wig, and with my deep tan, I become Jacky Bouvier, Creole girl and Sponge Diver. *Huh!* Jemimah had said upon first seeing me in this costume, *Least you fin'ly got some clothes on you, gal. But what you doin', tryin' to pass?* and I fluffed up and retorted that I had indeed passed for a high yellow before, like that time in New Orleans with Mam'selle Claudelle, so there. *Wouldna fooled none of my kinfolk, not with that skinny little nose. Huh! Mebbe they thought you was Ethiopian or sumthin'.*

Both Higgins and Dr. Sebastian are on the quarterdeck when I arrive and Jim is on the helm. Davy and the other lads handle the sails, and Joannie has been allowed topside to sit in Jemimah's chair. I think the child's wounds were more to her mind than to her body. Higgins, I know, has the fake papers for the *Nancy B.* tucked in his jacket that designate him as Captain of my schooner. It wouldn't serve for me to be seen as such in these parts, as I did prey on Spanish shipping during that summer on my *Emerald* with my wild Irish crew. So I'd best lie low. Just a simple sponge diver and servant to Dr. Sebastian, that's all this poor girl is.

The mouth of the harbor opens up before us as we head in.

Yes, we could have taken on water in many a small Cuban port on our way here, but Dr. Sebastian wanted to check in with his contacts in Havana, and as for me, hey, I wanna go where the action is. And the action is certainly in this city, the biggest city in North, Central, and most of South America. Plus the ever-mercantile J. M. Faber wants to sell her sponges. And have a little fun.

"Yes," says Dr. Sebastian, echoing my thoughts, "Havana! Crossroads of the great treasure fleets of the Spanish Empire. The most heavily fortified port in the New World. Look over there—Castillo de los Tres Reyes del Morro!"

I follow his point and see the turreted fortress of Morro Castle now looming above us. Guns stick out from every opening.

"There used to be a submerged chain strung across the harbor to keep out pirates, but that is no longer needed be-

189

cause, as you will see, the Fortaleza de San Carlos de la Cabaña guards the city from the north and Castillo de la Real Fuerza does the same to the south. Protecting the shipyard is the Castillo de Atares. And there is the Castillo del Principe. And observe all the heavy batteries all along this canal. Five mighty forts protecting this harbor. Now the chains are in place only at the sides of the channel, to direct all traffic down the middle and so into the range of the guns. Nothing gets in or out without the permission of the Spanish governor."

"You certainly could not pull your Harwich trick here, Miss," says Higgins. "There are just too many guns for you to spike, even if you had Mairead Delaney by your side."

I have to nod and agree with that. "But then I was a bold privateer and now I am but a simple sponge merchant and have nothing to fear from any government."

I get a few snorts on that.

"And speaking of the government, there it sits."

There she sits, indeed. As we slide into the harbor, we see the formidable *San Cristobal* moored in the middle of the channel, her eighty-eight guns providing even further protection for the harbor. Beyond her I see the city's waterfront, and tied up there is probably the largest number of ships I have ever seen in one single port. It is a veritable forest of masts and spars.

"Daniel, run up and dip the colors," I call, and the boy leaps up from Joannie's side and into the rigging to where the Stars and Stripes is flying, unties a line, and lowers the flag halfway in salute, and then returns it to its two-blocked position.

The Spanish man-of-war does not return the salute, of

course—I mean, why would a proud thirty-five-hundred-ton, more than two-hundred-foot, double-decker First-Rate return the salute of a puny little schooner—but we *are* noticed, for a small boat is quickly launched and heads straight for us. A man stands at the bow and signals for us to stop. It is the same insufferably arrogant lieutenant who yanked me aboard the *Nancy B.*'s raft that day. *Hmmmm . . . .*

"Heave to, lads," I say, with a sigh. "Let's see what he's about." Davy and the others jump to it and our sails go slack, and we wallow there and wait, till the boat comes alongside.

"Put down the ladder, McGee," I say. "I think he wants to come aboard. Be careful, everyone—remember, we are all Americans. No Brits here. This is enemy territory."

Indeed, the Lieutenant does want to come aboard. He climbs our ladder and swaggers up to me. No courtly bow, no pleasantries, no manners, just—

"More clothes now, *muchacha*? Too bad. I must pronounce that I liked you better before."

I note that I am not given even the minor honor of being called *señorita*, but am named instead by the word for *girl . . . little girl.*

"Why could you possibly care about what I wear, *Teniente*? I am just a simple sponge diver, not worthy of your attention, merely coming into your city to sell my sponges."

"*Sí*," he says, and comes over to me and puts his fingers under my chin and lifts my face to his. "But maybe there is more to you than sponges, eh, *muchacha*?"

"Señor, I must protest!" says Higgins, stepping between us.

The Lieutenant turns to Higgins. "What? You are now

protective of your girl divers? How benevolent of you. When we met before, I thought you said they were . . . expendable." His eyes are hooded as he looks about our deck. "But no matter. I am here to tell you that my Captain will expect 15 percent of whatever amount you sell your cargo for. I will direct you into the market area, where you will dispose of the sponges, and I will keep an eye on the proceeding and then will expect immediate payment. Otherwise, you will not leave this harbor."

"Ah," I say, unable to resist, "*la mordida*, the bribe, the *little bite*, as we who know Spanish ways call it."

"Or you could call it port fees. Call it what you want, *chica*. You there, get your men into a boat and start rowing this ship over to that dock right there."

Higgins nods to John Thomas and our lifeboat is put in. A bowline is fastened to the bowsprit of the *Nancy B.*, and the oars are manned.

I suspect that this man resents being sent to do this trifling little job and he is smarting under the indignity of it all. *Males and their sense of worth and honor, I swear.* I decide to play upon that.

"You serve your master well . . . *muchacho*," I say, putting on the Lawson Peabody Look and bringing the full force of it to bear upon him.

He stiffens. Stung by my calling him "boy," and by the snickers of his men who have overheard this little exchange, he whirls around and puts his face in mine. I keep the Look in place and hold his gaze as he hisses at me, "My name is Juan Carlos Cisneros y Siquieros, Lieutenant in His Most Catholic Majesty's Royal Navy. You will address me as such in the future, unless you wish to have this filthy boat impounded. *Comprende, puta?*"

"Does your mother know how you treat helpless *muchachas,* Juan Carlos?" I puff up and ask. "And how you call them foul names? Does she?"

"You dare to stain the name of my sainted mother with your whore's tongue?" he replies, taken aback by the turn in the exchange.

"Does she? I should think she would be a little ashamed of you, Juan Carlos," I say. Well steamed now, I poke my finger in his chest. "She would, if she thought she had raised you right."

He makes a choking sound and lifts his hand as if to strike me across the face for my impudence, and I, not taking my eyes off his for even an instant, put my chin in the air and get ready for the blow.

But it does not come. Instead, Dr. Sebastian speaks up. "Do not strike her, Señor. I will lodge a protest with the United States consul. I am a well-known and respected scientist and my words carry weight and there will be some degree of trouble for you."

Juan Carlos glowers and looks over at the Doctor.

"And in return, I will give my assistant a sound beating and advise her to watch her tongue when she is speaking to a Spanish gentleman."

That defuses the situation. Male honor is served. Lieutenant Cisneros lowers his hand, but I can tell he is still furious.

"I am done with this! Tell your *peones* to put their backs into it. Get this stinking boat over to that dock. Now!"

"*Por supuesto, Teniente Cisneros,*" I purr with a slight, mocking curtsy. "*Sin duda.*"

He turns abruptly away, to supervise getting us into port.

Davy, Tink, John Thomas, and McGee bend to their task and the *Nancy B.* is towed into her berth and tied up. We find ourselves moored next to a huge market plaza. *Very convenient,* I'm thinking, and almost worth the 15 percent gouge.

"There is the sponge exchange. You will sell yours there," says the Spanish officer. "Make it quick. I grow quickly bored with the small doings of common tradesmen. I have better things to do."

I nod to Higgins and he bounds over to deal with the sponge factotum. The Lieutenant goes with him, and after speaking to the sponge merchant, no doubt to make sure he gets his proper cut, he then ducks into a nearby tavern.

*Ah-ha.*


After my rigging has been stripped clean of dried-out sponge, which is delivered to market and sold, Higgins returns with the money the sponges brought. Not much— three hundred and fifty pesos—but not too bad. It will pay for several nights on the town for me and my crew.

"Best count out the bribe money, Higgins, for I see our taxman is returning," I say. Lieutenant Cisneros has left the tavern and, after checking with the sponge merchant on how much he paid us, is heading back to the wharf. "Put it in my hand. I want to be the one to give it to him."

When his boots again thump on my deck, I see that Juan Carlos has recovered his male pride, his precious *machismo.* Nothing like a few slugs of rum to restore your manhood, *eh, hombre*?

"Give me Captain Morello's money and I will leave this dirty scow," he says, his hand out.

I dump the coins into his palm, being very careful not to touch him. *"La mordida, muchacho del marinero,"* I say. "Take it on your knees to *la rata gorda,* who is so much, much bigger than you, *el ratón chico."*

The little mouse does not take the bait. Instead he picks a small gold piece from the pile in his hand and holds it before my face. "You got the price for your sponges, but what is the price for you, *chiquita*? Hmmm? Ten pesos for an hour, down below, hey?"

"Were I for sale, it would certainly not be for ten pesos, Señor," I reply, nose in air. "Is our business concluded? If so, please leave my ship."

"Your ship? Ah . . . and I thought you were a simple sponge diver."

*Damn,* I think, instantly regretting my words, *I'm risking our cover.*

"It is my only home, which is why I refer to it so," I say, and cast down the eyes.

"Ha!" he says, apparently satisfied with that and pleased with the sight of my bowed head. "But we shall see about you later, believe me. You have not seen the last of me yet."

We watch him go off in the *San Cristobal's* boat, to return to his ship.

"Well, that was intense," observes Dr. Sebastian. "Perhaps you should not have baited him so. He could cause us trouble."

"I couldn't help myself, he was so insufferably arrogant," I say in my defense. "But then, I have met much worse . . . and he *is* very good-looking."

"You've got to get over that someday, Miss," says Higgins, "equating good looks with good character."

"Oh, I know, Higgins," I say, with a heavy sigh. "I have only to look at Flashby—handsome as a god but rotten to the core. So I know, but still . . . Enough of Lieutenant Cisneros and all his ilk. Get everyone paid up and then let's hit this town."

Higgins sets up at the mess table and doles out the coins from our sponge sale. John Thomas and Smasher McGee scoop up their pay and head off to Havana's lower depths. "Back in two days, you swabs!" I shout after their rapidly retreating forms. "Or I'll leave you here and I mean it!"

Jim Tanner lost the draw and so will remain with the ship this day and night. Due to health, Joannie is confined to quarters against all her protests, and Daniel has elected to stay with her. *Good lad,* I'm thinking. And Jemimah has appeared on deck with the bag of her possessions over her shoulder.

I had directed Higgins to give her not only her share of the sponge take, but also her regular pay for the time she had spent with us, without deductions.

"So, Jemimah," I say, as she goes to the gangway, "if you do not come back to us, enjoy your freedom. I know it was late in coming, but it should still be sweet."

She puts her dark gaze upon me. "I thank you, girl, for what you done for me. I will now go see what I will see." Joannie and Daniel stand next to her, pouting. She reaches out her hand and ruffles both of their heads. "You two be good, now, y'hear?"

"But you ain't told us what all happened to Brother Rabbit and Brother Fox and Brother Bear, Jemimah," wails

Joannie. "Brother Fox had Brother Rabbit in the cook pot and . . . and you just can't leave him there. You can't just go and not come back!"

"Oh, child, someone else'll tell you them old stories. Your Aunt Jemimah's gotta go now. Gotta go and see what's out there."

She turns and steps off the *Nancy B.* and disappears into the marketplace crowd.

I shoo the kids back into my cabin. "You two, clean up this room. Dust every surface. I'll inspect with a white glove when I get back, and woe to your backsides should I find any smudge. Tomorrow you may be allowed off if I find all well."

I know they did not want to see Jemimah going away forever, so it's best their bodies and minds are occupied.

Dr. Sebastian has dressed and gone off to meet with both his scientific and his intelligence contacts.

Davy and Tink are spruced up and ready to go.

I stick my finger into Davy's chest and say, "You're a married man now, Davy, and you've got to be good, for Annie's sake."

"But *I* ain't a married man, Jacky," says Tink, grinning. "And I mean to have some fun."

"We'll see about that." I sniff. "But for now, let us go off together and see what this city has to offer what's left of the Dread Brotherhood of HMS *Dolphin*."

And away we go into *Ciudad de la Habana*.


We sample the fare at a few small taverns near the docks—and since neither Tink nor Davy have been in a Spanish port before, I get to introduce the *tapas*, small, bite-sized bits of food laid out on the bar. And we enjoy them all—

well, almost all—they both proclaim themselves disgusted when they see me chew up the little baby octopus, pickled and laced with olive oil and spices. *Hey, Dr. Sebastian says they're just clams with legs, so there.*

After leaving the last tavern, we find a great arena with many flags all about it and discover that it will host a bull-fight, and we decide to attend. Though the boys enjoy it, I don't really. My sympathies lie entirely with the poor bull, who I know ain't got a chance. And the matadors remind me too much of that strutting Lieutenant Juan Carlos Cisneros y Siquieros. The pageant starts off with the bull being let into the ring. What he finds there, aside from a crowd screaming for his blood, are two picadors, brightly costumed men holding sharp lances, astride horses specially padded to protect them from the bull's horns—the horses that is. The picadors' legs are left unprotected, I suppose for the element of danger. As the bull, already enraged from the beating he has taken in the stall, trots around the ring, the picadors ride up next to him and prick his back with their spears. Blood flows, the bull is sufficently angered, and the matador, bearing his red cape, enters the ring.

I heave a great sigh. It all takes me back to my youth in Cheapside, when the Rooster Charlie Gang and I would go to bull baitings, to work the crowds gathered there. Those proceedings didn't even have a trace of the bloody elegance of this Spanish bullfight where there is a chance that the bull out there could get lucky and the matador could get himself gored right proper and good for him. No, in London the poor bull was just tied to a stake and dogs—big bulldogs and mastiffs and such—were sent in to rip the poor beast apart. Never saw the sport in that, no I didn't. I mean, at the end, the poor helpless bull could only fall to his knees and bawl out his anguish as the dogs ripped out his throat. No, no sport at all—it was all just blood lust. But the crowds did drink a lot of gin and got worked up, so we were sometimes able to beg some tips for running betting slips, and maybe manage to pick a few pockets, too.

I have often wondered how people, even educated, highborn people, could excuse that kind of cruelty to animals. Maybe it goes back to that thing in the Bible where God gave man dominion over the beasts of the field—I remember Pap Beam reciting that one to me when he and his boys had a rope around my neck and were preparing to string me up—and how the Church holds that animals ain't got souls, which I believe is wrong. I think animals got souls just like us . . . and better ones than the ones we got, generally.

I shake myself out of that reverie and return myself to the present. Back here in Cuba, blood is spilled and the bull at last lies dead on the ground, gaily be-ribboned *banderillas* sticking out of his back. Trumpets blare, the matador parades around twitching his bum, and the ears and tail of the vanquished bull are cut off and presented to some simpering mantilla-clad señorita in the bleachers, and that is that. End of bull, end of contest. *Come on, lads, let's get out of here.*

We leave the arena and get back out into the plaza and cast about for the next thing to do. There are crowds in the town square and the mood is most festive. I like it. I like it a lot.

"Hey, how 'bout that over there?" asks Davy. I look and see from its sign over the door that it is a tavern called Café Americano, and I see many men going in and some coming out. *Hmmmm . . .* I had overheard talk of this place in the last tavern. Apparently it is a very popular spot.

"Later, lads. We'll come back with my fiddle and whistle and maybe give 'em a few tunes, but right now, let's soak up some more of the local color. The Spanish lands do have their charms, you know. Ah! What's that?"

*That* is a large building at the side of the square, with many people pouring into it, mostly men. There are posters to either side of the doorway and they proclaim that a certain event is going to take place there.

"C'mon, let's go!" I crow to my mates and lead them into the place. *Ah, yes, there's nothing I like better than goin' into a likely spot with my bully boys at my back!*

It's a big circular room with a fenced-in pit area. There are tiers of seats all around. Most of the seats are taken, but I manage to elbow my way to the front. *Hey, I'm a girl and that gives me some privileges.* Davy and Tink worm their way in to stand beside me. I see that the sand in the pit has been raked clean of yesterday's blood and smoothed out. We settle in and wait for the main events. Small girls and boys come bearing trays of wine, rum, and *tapas,* and we take some and flip coins onto the trays in payment.

At the end of the pit are two closed doors, and a man with a sash across his chest stands in front of them, his arms crossed. Two men sit at a table next to the ring, with an hourglass between them—they will be the judges of the matches. It seems everything is in readiness.

"Did you lads ever go to the cockfights at MacMillan's back in Cheapside, when you were kids?" I ask.

Now, I had seen lots of cockfights back in London when I was runnin' with the Rooster Charlie Gang, and I

gotta say they didn't bother me as much as the bull baiting . . . or the bear baiting. After all, they were just chickens
and doomed for the pot anyway and sometimes us orphans
were able to pick up the bodies of the defeated birds. We
would take them and wrap them in discarded clay from the
potters and then roast them next to the blacksmith's fires till
they were done. The clay took the feathers off and then we
could pick at the bits of meat, which were wondrous good.
*Hey, I wasn't raised up proper, so sod off.*

"Ah, yes," says Tink, and Davy nods in agreement.
"Good pickin's there. Well worth the trouble of sneakin'
through the Shankys' turf to get in."

The Shanky Boys were the biggest, meanest gang of
street urchins in London, and we generally tried to stay well
out of their way. I was glad to find, early in my days as a ship's
boy on the *Dolphin,* that neither Tink nor Davy had been a
Shanky, 'cause they were a nasty bunch. Tink, it turned out,
had belonged to the Royal Street Rounders, and Davy to the
King's Own Cavaliers. We all gave our gangs rough and glorious names, I guess to give us a bit of pride, knowin' that to
the good people of London the whole lot of us weren't
worth a handful of dirt. But once inside MacMillan's, it was
neutral territory, with truce 'tween the gangs, like, 'cause if
we got in a fight and raised a ruckus, we'd all get tossed out,
and where would the profit be in that for any of us?

"Then we prolly saw each other there, sometimes, me
bein' wi' the Rooster Charlie bunch," I says, fallin' back into
the old Cockney way o' talkin', as I always do when I'm wi'
me mates, or really scared or excited about somethin'.

"Aye," says Davy. "I knew Charlie, but I wouldna noticed you, being a stupid little rag of a girl like you was."

I give him an elbow and I'm about to frost him with a Lawson Peabody Look and comment on how I might've been little, but I warn't stupid, and ain't it strange how things work out sometimes, Common Seaman Jones, when—

"Hey," says Tink. "Looks like it's gonna start."

Sure enough, a trumpet blares a short trill and the doors behind the red-sashed man swing open and two men walk out, each clasping a gamecock to his chest. When the men get out into the open, one walks clockwise around the edge of the pit, while the other walks in the other direction.

The man in the red sash speaks up and points to one of the chickens. "Behold . . . El Conquistador!" The man holding that particular fighter lifts him up for the scrutiny of the crowd and there are great cheers. El Conquistador has had both his cockscomb and his wattles cut off, making him more fit for battle. He also wears silver spurs over his natural ones—the ones he was born with are a scant half-inch long, while the silver ones are a full two inches and are razor sharp, with needle points. This cock is mainly black with some streaks of white, while the other has streaks of red in his feathers.

Red Sash points to the contender and says, "El Caballero!" and there are cheers for The Cowboy, as well. He, too, is in fighting trim—no cockscomb, no wattles.

"Engage!" The handlers stand facing each other, and holding their gamecocks tightly, they shove them together to get them really mad and in a mood to fight. It works. The cocks crow out their battle cries and struggle to get at each other. Then the men kneel down and wait for the call. There is a rush to get in last-minute bets, and I spot a man nearby naming the odds and taking bets. It seems El Conquistador is the heavy favorite. I hold up two fingers and cry out, *"Dos pesos al Conquistador!"*

I do like to be part of the action wherever I find myself.

The oddsmaker nods and writes a note on a tiny piece of paper and hands it to me. I give him my two coins and wait for the battle to begin.

"Fight!" shouts Red Sash. The judges turn over the sand glass and the handlers release their birds and step back.

The cocks fly at each other, wings wildly beating, necks stretched out and reaching for the other's throat, while their legs pump furiously trying to plunge their silver spurs into any part of their adversary. Neither succeeds right off, so they step back and strut for a moment, sizing up the enemy, and then they're back at it in a flurry of feathers and cackles. The crowd roars, and so do I. *Come on, Conquistador, get him!*

I can see why the birds' combs and wattles have been trimmed—if an opponent managed to get a spur through either of those things, then the fighter's head could be held to the ground and he would be finished.

When they part again, blood is beginning to show on the feathers of El Caballero. His step is not so sure and he shows signs of weakening. The sand is not halfway down the neck of the hourglass when El Conquistador, seeing an opening, leaps high in the air and brings his spurs straight down into the back of El Caballero.

The Cowboy is done. He staggers, croaks out a last crow of defiance, and then topples over. He tries to rise, but he cannot. He lowers his head and dies. There is a great roar from the crowd. *Olé! El Conquistador! Olé!*

The victorious cock is held aloft and paraded around the ring.

"It was a good, clean kill," says a man near to me, plainly an *aficionado* of this sport. He is well dressed in a white linen suit and matching hat. "It was a thing of beauty."

"Yes," says another. "And El Caballero, he fought well, and died well."

However well he died, the fallen warrior's dead and bloody body is picked up by his owner with, I think, a certain amount of tenderness and taken back through those same doors he had come through alive not ten minutes ago. I go to collect my winnings.

I hand over my chit and I get back my original two pesos and a peso and a half to boot. *Hmmmm.* Not so much as even money and not very good odds. El Conquistador is quite the formidable chicken, it seems. We shall see.

As the next match is being set up, I cast my eyes about the place. The swells seem to prefer the balcony—there are several small groups of women seated there, their dark eyes looking out over the tops of veils—and many well-dressed men, some of whom are soldiers and some of whom are naval officers. I do not see Juan Carlos Cisneros, which is good.

Down here below, however, I see a much more diverse mix of people. Many men, of course, in various kinds of dress—planters, laborers, and free blacks, too—but many women as well. Some are with husbands and family, but some are plainly working girls. I also see a bunch of Spanish sailors leaning over the edge of the pit, and plainly well into their cups. They wear caps that have a headband that stretches across their foreheads, and stitched on that headband are the words *San Cristobal.*

How convenient. Well, I'm supposed to be a spy, so I might as well get to it.

"Lads," I say to my mates, "I'm going to sit out the next match and go over to talk to those sailors. Keep an eye on me, and if I draw my mantilla back up about my head, come and claim me. All right?"

"But why?" asks Tink.

"Because, Seaman Tinker, it might be handy to know when the *San Cristobal* will sail again and maybe cause us trouble. I'm sure those on the *Dolphin* will want to know, as they might have to fight that ship soon."

"Ah," says Tink, nodding. I pull my mantilla from my head and let it fall on my shoulders, thereby branding myself as a bad girl, and then I head off. I wriggle through the crowd and plant myself in the middle of the Spanish sailors, and with my palm modestly to my lips, I pretend to be surprised at finding myself in their manly midst.

I put the big eyes on the one who seems to be the leader of the group and say, "*Cuánto lo siento, señores*, but I seem to have lost my way."

"Do not be sorry, señorita," he says, glancing at my uncovered head and winking broadly at his comrades. "Your way is not lost. You have come to just the right place. I have money and I have time and I have . . . desires."

For a common seaman, this one is pretty smooth.

"Oh?" I purr in return. "And what brings you brave sailor boys to shore?"

They glance at one another, sly grins all around. The glib one puts his arm around my waist and says, "We came here to see you, *mi querida*. You and your many sisters."

That bit of wit is met with snorts of laughter. *Men, I swear,* no matter what the country, no matter what the culture.

"But I do not often take up with sailor men, as they are never here for very long and they break my poor heart when they leave."

"Do not worry, little one. We have plenty of time to attend to matters of love. My name is Eduardo Santoro and I have knowledge that the great and glorious ship *San Cristobal* will not move its fat ass for at least two weeks. There are repairs to be made and the Captain must tend to his mistress." More snickers. These lads have had quite a bit to drink.

*Well, that was easy enough,* I'm thinking. I must be becoming quite the spy. Mr. Peel would be proud, I think. *But, time to go now, girl.* I flip my mantilla back up on my head and say, "I regret that I am here with others, Eduardo, and so I must—"

"No, no, *mi corazón,* you are now with me," he says, not taking his arm from my waist nor his hot eyes from mine. Actually, he is not bad-looking . . .

Davy and Tink appear at my side, looking hard at the Spanish sailors.

"Come on, Jacky, let's go," urges Davy, grabbing my arm and pulling me away. I'm a little amazed at just how hard he can look.

Suspecting that knives will soon be drawn, I pull the fuse on the situation by laying my hand on Eduardo's arm and saying, "I will be at Café Americano tonight. I've heard that everyone in Havana goes to Ric's. Will I see you there as well?"

Eduardo relaxes, taking his arm from my waist and casting an equally hard look at Davy. "You will," he answers, and turns away.

Davy, Tink, and I go back to our former spot at the rail to watch the final matches. Davy says, "Why'd you tell him that? You lookin' for more trouble?"

I sigh and say, "Davy, the *San Cristobal* is a great danger to us. The more we know about her, the better. These men can tell us. That is why. Now, let's watch."

The next fight is between two novice birds who fight to a draw. When the hourglass sand runs out, Red Sash calls out, "Fight over!" so the handlers rush to collect their birds, both bloody but still living. One is declared the winner, but both will live to fight another day. I lost money on that one.

The last battle is a mismatch. The first bird, El Matador, is big, strong, and plainly the veteran of many a fight. The crowd roars at the sound of his name. *El Matador! El Matador!* The other bird is named Pepino, and he does not last for even a minute before he lies dead on the sand with El Matador strutting around his body.

The crowd pours out of the place and it is soon empty. I linger by the ring as the handler of Pepino picks up his dead warrior and heads for the door.

"Señor!" I call out, pointing to the fallen gladiator. "*Cuánto para el pollo?*"

He looks at me and then down at the cock in his hand. "How much for a dead chicken? You can have him."

"But with the spurs, Señor?"

"Ah," he says. "*Un peso,* then."

"Done," I say, and fish out the coin and give it to him.

He hands me the corpse of the gamecock and I take it by the neck. The silver spurs jingle about the bird's limp ankles.

"Let's go, lads," I say. "Back to the *Nancy B.*"

"You are one weird bint, Jacky," says Tink, shaking his head.

"We shall rest up, and tonight we shall go to Ric's Café Americano," I say, unperturbed. "They say that everyone goes there."

# Chapter 25

It is the morning of the second day of our Havana visit. I am in the chicken coop area, attended by a very curious Joannie and Daniel. I have taken two short pieces of batten and fastened them together in the shape of a cross and nailed it to the tip of a yard-long, cut-off broomstick. To it I will now tie the body of the recently deceased gamecock Pepino.

Higgins looks on, not at all in approval. I sense his disdain and say, "Hey, the renowned and very beloved General George Washington liked his cockfights. I hear he even bred a line of gamecocks on his farm."

"A true Southern gentleman."

"And President Jefferson enjoys the sport, too, so there."

"I hear there are many things President Jefferson enjoys," sniffs Higgins.

"Don't believe everything you read in the papers, Higgins," I sniff back at him. Thomas Jefferson has been accused of fathering some children with one of his slaves. I don't believe it, but many do. Amy Trevelyne for one, but then she's always been ready to believe the worst of anyone, especially me. Plus, she's a Federalist in her political thinking, and Mr. Jefferson sure ain't one of those.

"There, that's done," I say with some satisfaction. I have tied the dead bird to the cross such that his wings are outspread and his head is held up by a piece of string around his neck. His legs swing free, but no longer wear the sharp silver spurs. "Let's get on with it. Joannie, Daniel, shoo the hens and peeps back into their coop and close the door. Leave El Gringo Furioso out here."

They do it and soon my fighter is alone in the pen, strutting about and cocking an eye at me—an eye that I swear has a question in it: *What is going on here, foolish but big, featherless thing?*

"That is what you have given him as a nom de guerre?" says Higgins, more a statement than a question.

"Yes. I thought it had a nice fierce ring to it. And being he was from Boston and all—remember, it was you who bought him when you were bringing on supplies for our voyage—I felt he should have a North American touch to his name. Yanqui Doodle didn't have quite the right fearsome threat in it, nor did Boston Blackie."

"I can imagine what Mistress Pimm would say about all this. The word *unseemly* comes readily to mind."

"Just about everything I do Mistress finds unseemly."

"I cannot imagine why."

"And look, Higgins, this chicken has a choice—the fight ring or the pot. I know what I'd say were I in his place. Plus, there are some pretty sweet prizes for the winners. El Matador won a purse of one hundred and fifty pesos yesterday. That's not chicken feed, pardon the pun."

"There is no pardon for puns."

"We've got payrolls to meet. I played a short set at Ricardo's Café Americano last night and got some good tips, and Ric liked my act, so I'm gonna do a full concert tonight. It'll help, but it won't be enough," I say, and ready my chicken-on-a-cross, which I've kept out of El Gringo's sight up to now. "So if my little gladiator here can add something to our coffers, then I will bless him for it."

"And if not?"

"Then he will die an honorable death. So be it."

I bring my decoy around and put it full in Gringo's face. I shake the broomstick back and forth, making the dead chicken's feet, legs, and head fly about in a very realistic way. Visibly shocked, Gringo squawks and takes a few steps back. Then he goes completely berserk.

He flies up in the air as far as his wings will take him and comes down on the intruder with beak, spurs, and claws, shrieking out his fury.

"Whoa!" says Daniel. "He's a fighter, he is."

"I'll say!" echoes Joannie. "Go get him, Gringo!"

I withdraw the stick and Gringo struts around the ring, looking very, very pleased with himself. I give him a few moments of sinful pride at the retreat of his enemy and then shove the decoy against him again, and again he rises in anger and attacks, crowing for all he is worth, his neck feathers fully lifted in don't-mess-with-me-'cause-I'm-one-big-bad-rooster fighting fashion.

"Now let's try it with the spurs," I say, and pull the decoy out and hide it behind the stove. "Come here, you." I reach in and scoop up the banty.

"Ouch. Daniel, hold his head." I'm sure those pecks on

my wrist are affectionate, but I want them to stop, anyway. "Joannie, hand me those scissors."

Daniel's hands gently envelop Gringo's head, rendering him sightless, which is good 'cause he ain't gonna want to watch this. Taking the scissors, I quickly snip off his natural spurs from the backs of his legs.

*Squawk!*

"I know you didn't like that, Gringo," I say by way of apology. I tie the shiny and very sharp spurs on to his legs where the old ones had been. "But I think you'll like these much better. Besides, you oughta be glad I ain't gonna cut off your comb and wattles . . ." I decided to let him fight in all his manly glory, not having the heart—or the stomach—to do that particular job. And I don't think it really makes all that much difference. "There. All done. Now let's get you back in the pen. So, how do they feel, boyo? Pretty good, eh?"

Grudgingly forgiving the indignity he has just suffered at the hands of the big, featherless things, he tries an experimental strut. Then he bends his head down, sees the spur bindings, and begins pecking at them.

"Quick. Give me the decoy. Let's show El Gringo just what he can do with those new spurs, before he takes 'em off."

Daniel hands me the stick and I shove poor limp Pepino back into the fray and El Gringo Furioso comes on furiously in a black blur of slashing spurs, ripping claws, and stabbing beak.

"Whoa!" says Daniel. "I think he gets it!"

"I'll say," says Joannie.

"And I believe I shall leave you to your . . . sport," says Higgins. "After supervising the loading of the water and other supplies, I shall see you later for a tour of the city, Miss? You did request that, I recall."

"Yes, Higgins, and thank you," I say, turning my attention back to the matter at hand.

El Gringo attacks again, and bloody streaks begin to appear on the decoy's breast, then more on its wings. One slash of Gringo's spurs cuts through the string holding the right wing of the dead bird to the cross and it flops down in seeming defeat. I decide to end it there for today and allow Pepino, now doubly dead, to lie down before the triumphant Gringo. Gringo himself casts a contemptuous eye at his fallen foe and strides off. I take the opportunity to pull the shredded decoy rooster from the pen and stand up.

"Auntie!" cries Joannie, and she and Daniel rise from the coop and run to the door. "You came back!"

I look up and see Jemimah entering the galley. She wears a new dress and kerchief and carries the largest frying pan I think I've ever seen.

"You two get away and let Jemimah walk," she says. "Dan'l, I see a chicken there that needs guttin' and cleanin'. Save the heart and liver and get it in the gumbo pot. Joannie, put on a pot to boil so's you can pluck him." She gets to the stove and lays the pan upon it.

Then she looks over at me, and I say, "I'm glad you're back, Jemimah."

"Huh! They got ten t'ousand Nigras over there and they don't need another old black woman, no, they don't."

I had a suspicion Jemimah would be back, 'cause I had noticed she'd left her apron hanging on a hook next to the stove, which apron she now takes down and wraps around herself. I had the feeling that she went off just to prove it to herself that she actually could. And now she knows.

"Also I gotta keep an eye on these two young'uns else they gonna go bad, you know they will," she continues. "And you, girl, you could stand some watchin', too. Here I come back and find you crucifyin' chickens. What's with that?"

I still have Pepino-on-a-stick in my hand.

"This look like some of that hoodoo—that conjure stuff. Shouldn't be messin' with that, you."

I hand the dead chicken off to Daniel, who unfastens the strings, takes a kitchen knife from the rack, and begins dressing the bird. Joannie shoves a few more sticks of wood into the stove to get it going good and puts the kettle of water on top.

Jemimah steps away from the stove and goes to the other end of the mess table. I get the feeling she wants to talk with me out of the kids' hearing, so I follow her.

"Nice dress," I say.

"Yup. Bought me some nice stuff, stayed in a good hotel, had me a fine bath with perfumed soap, and ate some good food that was cooked by someone other than me for a change."

"So you like the high life, Jemimah? So do I. Stick with us and maybe you'll enjoy some more of it."

She considers for a moment and then says, "Right, it's fine. But that ain't it, girl. That ain't it at all." She pauses. "I know you lookin' for gold down there under that water."

"That's right, Jemimah. I hope you didn't say anything about that when you were ashore."

"One t'ing a slave knows is when to keep that slave's mouth shut. I ain't said nothin' to nobody."

"That's good, Jemimah, 'cause there're ears everywhere and some people around are suspicious about us and what we're doin'."

"You find that gold, what I get? 'Fore you said somethin' about shares . . ."

"Right. Here's how it works: After a voyage, we total up what we have made and split it up this way—Faber Shipping, which is me, gets half right off the top. I gotta pay for the upkeep of the boat and buying supplies and meet the payroll for the crew's regular pay. Plus I gotta pay my lawyer who, because of my ways, is generally kept pretty busy. The other half of the take is divided up into shares. Mr. Higgins gets three shares and Mr. Tanner two. One share for each for the seamen, a quarter share for each of the kids, and a half share for you. After you've been with us for a while, you'll be moved up to a full share."

"So if the boat get a t'ousand, I get . . ."

"At a half share . . ." I say, calculating in my head, "about thirty dollars, above your usual pay."

"Umm . . . And how much you t'ink is down there?"

"A lot more than a thousand, Jemimah," I say. "A lot more . . . 'Course King George gets first dibs 'cause his men is sorta in charge of this expedition. But there should be enough to go around."

"Umm. Why this King git *you* to do all this—a little scrap of a girl like you what should be fussin' about in crinolines and tryin' to git herself married off?"

" 'Cause he'll hang me and cause trouble for my friends if I don't do it."

"Huh! Caught 'tween the Devil and the whippin' post, you."

"Just so, Jemimah."

"All right," she says, turning to go back to the stove. "I'll go with that. Let's see what happens."

"You want the money to buy other fine things, Jemimah?" I don't blame her for that. I like fine things, too.

She pauses on her way back to her duties. "No, that ain't it," she says. "If I get enough money put t'gether I want to buy back my kids. As many of 'em as I can find. And the only way I see to do that is t'rough you."

*Oh.*

"All right, you two," Jemimah says, back at her station in front of the stove, "you got that chicken ready?"

"Oh, yes, Auntie, now tell us how Brother Rabbit got out of that pot!" demands Joannie.

The warrior Pepino has been stripped of his worldly raiment and has been cut up and put in the gumbo pot. Least he didn't suffer the indignity of having his lifeless corpse dragged three times around the walls of Troy behind the chariot of his killer, Achilles, like poor Hector. But in the way of indignities, it was close. *Sic transit gloria mundi.*

"All right, children, listen close," says Jemimah. "Now ol' Brother Rabbit, he be sittin' in that pot and it be gettin' warmer and warmer such that he can't touch the bottom of the pot with his foot no more, so he got to be thinkin' about what he got to do to get out of this fix he in."

She gives the gumbo pot a stir with her long spoon. She says nothing for a while, then Daniel pops up with: "Auntie, how come Brother Fox and Brother Bear didn't gut and skin Brother Rabbit before they put him in the pot, like I just done with that chicken?"

"'Cause that ain't how the story goes, boy," retorts Jemimah. "Don't you know nothin' about stories?" Daniel sits back, abashed.

After a decent interval to build up the tension, Jemimah goes on.

"Brother Fox, he be dicin' up some carrots and yams and tossin' the pieces in the broth around Brother Rabbit and the rabbit he be eatin' 'em up just as fast as the fox be t'rowin' 'em in.

"'You stop dat,' says Brother Fox. 'Them ain't fer you. Them is for de broth.'

"'You gonna get 'em one way or t'other,' says Brother Rabbit, 'whether in my belly or in the stew.'

"'Dat's true,' says Brother Bear, who's leanin' his nose over the pot to breathe in the smell of hot rabbit and yams. '*Ummm, uh!* Smells mighty fine t'me! Gonna be a fine, *fine* day!'"

Jemimah gives the pot another stir. She calls it the gumbo pot. Up in Boston, we called it hunter's stew, and in France it's called pot-au-feu. Every culture's got a version and they're all the same—a pot that's kept simmering on the stovetop, and anything that comes along that's at all edible goes into it.

I hear Higgins calling me from above and I prepare to go, but I do linger a bit as Jemimah goes on . . .

"'Brother Rabbit, things gettin' a bit warm for you in dere?' asks Brother Fox, shaking some salt and pepper over Brother Rabbit's head and dancing around the cauldron.

"'No, Brother Fox, it's jes' fine . . . 'cept fo' one thing . . .'

"'And what's dat, Brother Rabbit?'"

Another pause on Jemimah's part. Silence from the kids.

"'Brother Fox, you gone hafta change this here broth,' says the rabbit.

"'Why dat? Getting too hot for you? Hee-hee.'

"'No, Brother Fox . . . It's 'cause I just peed in it.'"

Daniel and Joannie fall to the deck, convulsed with laughter as I leave the galley. I shall have to find out later just how the wily Brother Rabbit got out of that one. He seems to be a kindred spirit.

Higgins is already dressed in a lightweight white linen suit, and he gets me quickly into my white Paris Empire dress. We picked it 'cause it seems to fit in better in this place, where the women wear similar long, flowing dresses, full on the bottom and low-cut up topside. I put on one of my more modest hairpieces and, with the mantilla over it, I become a proper Spanish lady, or as close to proper as I can get.

That done, we go out onto the dock, where Higgins hands me up into an open coach that stands waiting for us. Good old Higgins. The driver clucks at the horses and we are off into the city of Havana.

Daniel and Joannie have been given some pay and will be allowed off the ship this afternoon, after Jemimah is satisfied they have done all their chores. They have been told to be good and they had better be. I am severe in my warning, but secretly I am so glad that Joannie is going to survive her wounds that I really don't care whether or not she behaves. The Doctor says the bindings on her rib cage can come off tomorrow and I know she'll be grateful for that.

As for John Thomas and Smasher McGee, they disappeared shortly after seeing all the stores brought aboard.

I don't expect to see them till the day after tomorrow, when we sail to rendezvous with the *Dolphin,* but they have never yet missed a sailing, so I shan't worry about them. Not much, anyway.

The Doctor is still off visiting his scientific cronies. He took with him the leather portfolio of my latest drawings and I allow myself a little whiff of the sin of pride.

Jim Tanner, Davy, and Tink have been given sufficient money so as to be fitted for proper suits of clothes. Though I think all three look ever so cute in their striped shirts and tight-across-the-butt white canvas pants, there are times when one should dress up . . . like tonight, at Ric's. Plus I know both Clementine and Annie will be very pleased to see their lads lookin' like fine gentlemen.

*Hmmm,* on that score I am reminded that I must do something in the way of finding female companionship for Tink, of which he has none now. A good girl, it must be, before he falls in with some slattern of low character who would take advantage of his good nature. He is a good-looking lad, with his curly black hair and easy smile, and could easily fall prey to somesuch. I know he's shy about his leg, but it has been getting better. He no longer uses the crutch and now walks with only a slight limp. Dr. Sebastian is of the opinion that other muscles in that leg have taken up the functions that the destroyed muscles formerly performed. We will hope and we shall see.

Yes, the three of them are off for new clothes. 'Course, I shall dock their pay for the cost of all that, but I think they shall thank me for it. Well, maybe, someday they will . . . But right now, Higgins and I are off on our jaunt.

We clatter down the street and along the docks and

past many vast shipyards. We had no trouble resupplying our stove wood because of leavings from Havana's mighty shipbuilding industry—the largest in the New World. In fact, the world's biggest warship, the *Santisima Trinidad,* was built here. Right over there, probably. She was about two hundred and fifty feet long, had four decks and one hundred forty-four cannons. *One hundred and forty-four!* The *Dolphin,* which is a pretty fearsome ship, carries only forty-four, and the *Wolverine* a scant twenty-six. Yes, the *Santisima* was a glorious sight, all right, when I saw her from the deck of that same *Wolverine* at Trafalgar, and I saw her go down, too, with many men aboard, sunk by ships much less glorious than she. Again, *sic transit gloria* comes to mind, a phrase I should remember when I get above myself, which happens sometimes.

We leave the docks and head through the market area and come out into a large open plaza at the end of which sits a large church.

"That is the Catedral de la Habana," points out Higgins. "Is it not magnificent?"

"Yes, it is quite grand," I agree. "Well, sort of grand. After all, I have stood in the nave of the Cathedral Notre Dame de Paris, and all pales next to that. Saint Paul's in London ain't no small potatoes, neither."

"Well," sniffs Higgins. "Did our blasé world traveler know that the bones of Christopher Columbus rest right there in that very church?"

I express mild surprise.

"Yes, some of us have been improving our minds and acquainting ourselves with the works and wonders of other cultures, while others have been frequenting cockfights and low dives."

"Ric's ain't a low dive. It's quite elegant. Come with us tonight and you'll see."

"Very well, I will."

"And by going to that cockfight, I met some Spanish sailors and found out that the *San Cristobal,* which you must admit is a clear and very present danger to us, will not sail for at least two weeks. So there," I say, fluffing up. "Have I not been a good spy, Mr. Special Intelligence Agent John Higgins?"

"Um," says Higgins, considering. "Yes, that is good to know."

"And later last night, when we were all at Ric's and I had finished my set and they were all well into their cups, they confided in me that they consider their Captain Morello to be a tyrant as well as a coward and that they hate their gunnery division officer, Lieutenant Juan Carlos Cisneros y Siquieros, with a deep and abiding passion."

"And *they* are?"

"Eduardo, Jesus, Manuelo, and Mateo. Pretty good coves, actually, even though they are the enemy. They've gotten used to treating me as an entertainer, rather than as *una puta.*"

"That is good," says my friend and protector, whom I know I should never, ever get miffed at. "Now, let us have a look at the rest of this fine city. Driver, push on!"

We visit a tobacco plantation, where Higgins buys several boxes of the vile things—*They are the very finest, Miss. None can compare.* I do not protest, as we all have our vices.

Then Los Baños de San Diego, a fine beach where small thatched huts are built out into the water such that the fine ladies of Havana can bathe in privacy. Me, I'm thinkin' about rentin' out one of those *baños* should Jaimy and I ever get shore leave in Havana. We could have some fun, we could. Ain't bloody likely, but still ... heh-heh ... but never mind. Mostly what we look at are the formidable fortifications that encircle the city.

"This city has always feared attack from all sides," says Higgins. "And well they should—the place has been captured by pirates, and by us British not too long ago."

"Yes, I know about that," I say. My belly gives out with a little growl and I'm thinking that maybe we should be getting back to the *Nancy B.* for a bit of a snack before we head out to Ric's for the evening. I have been promised a full set tonight and must prepare.

"What you perhaps do not know is that this city very much fears a slave rebellion above all things," says Higgins.

"Oh?"

"There are at least two thousand escaped slaves in those hills over there." I look over the green and peaceful-seeming country. "They have been joined by many free men of color as well. They have been gathering arms and are ... waiting ... waiting for their chance. They are led by a black man who calls himself Emperor León de Cuba, the Lion of Cuba."

"And how do you know this, Friend and Conscience Higgins?" I ask.

"I have been spending my time at the local university, reading and immersing myself in the culture of Cuba."

"Uh-huh," I say, giving him a poke in the ribs. "And what else have you been doing?"

"Well, ahem, I have made . . . friends . . . with some of the scholars there, young hidalgos, aristocratic young men of pure Castilian extraction. They know much of what is going on."

"Well, Higgins, I think we both have been doing our jobs. I am good at chatting up the low types, and you are very good at doing the same with the nobs. Is that not right?"

"Yes, Miss," Higgins says with his secret smile. "You are very right."

And back we go to the *Nancy B.*

# Chapter 26

We're all onboard and suiting up for tonight's performance at Ric's. I had expected Jim, Davy, and Tink to come back dressed in the loose linen suits favored by the local gentry, but no, they all had bought short, tight, heavily brocaded jackets that come down only to the waist, with gold trimmed tails behind, tight white trousers below, in short, exactly what young Spanish naval officers would have chosen. Seems the lads have given themselves promotions. Oh, well . . . They do look good, I must say.

Joannie and Daniel returned as Higgins and I arrived, and then went rather quickly down below—rather *too* quickly, I'm thinking—and I waste no time in plunging down after them to find out what mischief the two little rotters have been up to.

The kids are standing by the stove, facing away. "All right, out with it," I demand. "What did you do?" I take Joannie by the shoulders and spin her around.

There, hanging from her left earlobe is a bright gold ring. A quick glance at Daniel proves that he wears one, too.

They both try weak, anxious smiles. "The Sailor's Bargain, remember?" says Joannie.

I do not smile. "Both of you. In my cabin. *Now!*"

Their smiles disappear as they dash toward my cabin and to what they must assume will be certain doom. The two miscreants are standing nervously next to my table when I get there. I say nothing as I go to my medicine cabinet and pull out the bottle of pure alcohol.

"All right. Across the table, both of you. Earring up."

They do it and I am reminded of the many times I myself was spread out across Mistress Pimm's desk at the Lawson Peabody School for Young Girls in Boston, my skirts up, my bottom ready to receive the rod.

Instead of the whip, I have something better in mind for these two. I start with Daniel. I soak a clean piece of cloth in the spirits of wine, peer at his swollen red earlobe, and then place the alcohol directly upon the wound. He flinches, but does not cry out; he merely lets out a long *eeeeeeee!* I flip his earlobe over and hit it from the back. Another *eeeeeee!* I hit the lobe with a healthy dab of my healing salve, and that's it.

"All right, you. You're done, but we will do this every day till your ear heals up . . . or turns black and falls off. Do you understand, Daniel Prescott? Good. Now stand up."

Now for Joannie. Her ear is more swollen and inflamed than Daniel's. *Damn!* I put the alcohol to it and she, too, jerks, but she makes not a sound. I clean out the blood that has gathered about the hoop on both sides, give the ring a quarter turn to make sure the alcohol gets right in there, and she squirms and writhes on the tabletop. *I know it hurts, but it's good for you.* Then it's the salve, then up on her feet.

I confront her. "I can't believe it. You're just recovering from a serious injury, and yet you go out and inflict another one on yourself," I say, an accusing finger in her face. "What about the danger of infection? Well? What about that?" She hangs her head.

"Prescott! Did you put her up to this?"

"N-no, Jacky. It was my idea," whispers Joannie.

"Well, I ain't your mother, but . . ."

Joannie's head jerks back up.

"That's right, you're not," she snaps, her eyes on mine. "So why don't you stop acting like you are?"

"Don't you speak to me like that, young lady!" I hiss, and, without thinking, reach out and slap her across the face.

I instantly regret it.

Her eyes fill with tears. "You were s-s-supposed to be my friend . . . But now you . . . hit me."

I throw my arms around her. She stands stiff in my embrace. "I am so sorry, Joannie," I wail. "It's just that I worry about you so much!"

She remains rigid. The tears that were in her eyes now run down her cheeks.

I drop my arms to my sides. "Here, Joannie. Slap me back, then we'll be even," I say, holding out my chin, hoping she'll take me up on it.

She doesn't.

"I love you, Jacky. I could never hit you."

*Could I feel any more rotten and ashamed? Oh, I am such a hypocrite!*

226

I put my arms around her again. "I love you, too, and I promise never to do it again. Never again. Do you forgive me? Say you will, Joannie. Please."

I feel her relax and nod her head.

"Thank you, Sister," I say, and plant a kiss on her forehead. "Now, out, the both of you, and put your best clothes on. Tonight we're all going to Ric's."

With whoops of delight, they charge out the door, the tensions of the last few minutes forgotten as they anticipate a night out on the town. As they leave, Higgins appears and watches them go.

"You seem flushed, Miss," he says. "May I inquire as to the matter?"

"Oh, it's nothing, Higgins. I was just taught a lesson in love and trust by a twelve-year-old, is all."

"Ah," says Higgins, withholding comment on that. "And what will you wear tonight?"

"Oh, the blue! Definitely the blue! With the red wig!"

Heavy sigh from Higgins, as he sets to work making me look presentable, which ain't an easy task.


Ricardo Mendoza is a small, dapper gent, who wears perfectly tailored suits and rules over his establishment with a quiet but iron hand. Break one of his rules and you will never again step into Café Americano, which is a *very* popular spot. The rules are:

**Do not ever provoke a fight.**
**Do not ever become a nasty or sloppy drunk.**
**Do not ever force your attentions on any of the
    women and girls in the place.**

**Do not ever cheat at the gaming tables (that one
could get you killed as well).**

**Do conduct yourselves, always, as ladies and gentle-
men.**

Yes, Ric runs a classy joint, and I like it and feel right at
home. There is a long, curving bar at the end of the large
room, with many brightly colored liquors displayed and
softly lit with lamps hidden behind the rows of bottles.
There are tables all about that seat anywhere from two to
ten people, and food, good food, is served by smiling young
girls, modestly dressed.

The gaming tables are off to the left, the stage is in the
center, and there are private rooms off a hallway that goes
back to the privy.

In the center of it all stands Ricardo Mendoza, ramrod
straight, greeting his customers with a quiet dignity.

*"Buenas noches, Señorita Bouvier,"* he says, bowing. "It
is very good to see you again. We very much enjoyed your
performance last night."

"Good evening, Señor Ric," say I, dipping down into a
medium curtsy. "I hope tonight will be as successful." He
then leads me and my entourage to a fine table. The kids are
beside me—carrying my guitar, fiddle, and concertina—
and they are followed by Tink, Davy, and Higgins, all looking fine. I have my pennywhistle up one sleeve and my shiv
up the other.

It's a good hour before the performance, so we order
food and drink—delicious, spicy Cuban dishes, fine wine
for me, rum punches for the lads, and straight rum, carefully sipped, for Higgins. Joannie and Daniel delight in the

piles of sweetened tropical fruit placed on the table—oranges, grapefruit, pomegranates, passion fruit, bananas—and the drinks made from them, as well as a rice water and sugar mixture that they especially like.

At the end of the dinner, I lift my glass and say, "A toast to the Brotherhood . . . and the Sisterhood of the *Nancy B. Alsop*. Long may all sail."

*Hear, hear!*

The toast is drunk and I look across all the riches laid on the table and say to Joannie, "A far cry from the old kip in Cheapside, eh girl?"

She nods, putting another breaded shrimp in her mouth, grinding it up, and washing it down with a slug of lemonade.

"But not too much, Sister, or you'll get sick," I say, dispatching a last shrimp of my own. "I know I ain't your mother"—and here I give her a big wink—"but we do have to sing for our supper soon." We have been practicing a few numbers together, and tonight will be the first time she performs in public. I know she is a little nervous about it.

She nods again, and slacks off a bit.

I pat my lips with my napkin and rise. "Come, Joannie, time to continue your education," I say, and head for the gambling tables, with her following behind.

I lose a little money at the chuck-a-luck wheel, explain the bad odds to Joannie, and then sit at a table where a version of poker is being played. I quickly pick up the rules, and even though I'm playing it straight, I manage to end up winning some. Joannie stands behind me, taking it all in.

It is a pleasant interlude, and I know it keeps Joannie's mind off the coming show. Or, rather, it is pleasant until an empty chair is pulled back and a certain Spanish naval officer sits down in it and fixes his mocking gaze upon me.

"Ah. It is Lieutenant Juan Carlos Cisneros, the pride of the Spanish Navy," I say in my coldest voice. "How good to see you."

"So. The *muchacha* Bouvier, simple sponge diver, is now found to be an acclaimed café singer, as well," he says, signaling for the deck of cards to be given to him. "And now I find her simple self sitting at a table with the quality of Cuba. How interesting."

The other men at the table begin to look concerned when I rise, throw down my cards, take up my cash, and say, "I may not be of the quality, Señor, but all the same, I am not so low as to sit at the same table with a man who has abused me, who has put his unwanted hand upon me, and who has forced me to kneel to clean his boots!" At that they look downright shocked.

I spin around to head back into the main room, and to our table, with Joannie following. "It's time for me to get up on the stage. I'll take the guitar to start. Joannie, I'll call you up later." I put the guitar strap around my neck and lift my eyebrows to Señor Ric. He nods and mounts the stage, and the place falls silent.

"*Señoritas y señores.* Ladies and gentlemen," he calls out, acknowledging the international character of his clientele. "Fresh from the United States, England, and France, may I present Mademoiselle Jacqueline Bouvier!"

There is applause and I mount the platform, strum a chord, then go right into a Spanish love song "Sólo Tú," which means "Only You," which I guess sums up the sentiments of most love songs in only two words.

I always figure it's best to start out slow and then get wilder. That song gets a very good response, and I pick up the fiddle and rip into "Spanish Fandango," and that gets 'em where they live. Hispanics are a much less reserved people than us English. They hear a tune they like and they are up on their feet, clicking castanets and swirling skirts and shouting *Olé!*

I like this kind of audience—they certainly don't sit on their hands.

After that I do a few Anglo American fiddle tunes— "Billy in the Low Ground," then "Rabbit in the Pea Patch," and then I have a trembling Joannie come up and together we do a medley of "Sail Away Ladies" and "Old Molly Hare." She does well and gathers confidence with each sung note and, at the end, is glowing under the applause.

As she leaves the stage, I notice that Eduardo Santoro and his mates have come in and seated themselves near the front. I assume they came in with that damned Cisneros. I catch Eduardo's eye and nod, letting him know that I will be joining them at the break.

After that, I recite the poem "La Boca Dulce," "The Sweet Mouth," followed by some Galician tunes on the concertina. Then I end the set with "The Rocky Road to Dublin," a great Irish tune that seems to travel well across national borders.

I curtsy and leave the stage to resounding applause, which warms me to my soul, and I go over to the Spanish sailors' table and sit down next to Eduardo.

"So how are my fine and gallant Spanish sailors this lovely Caribbean evening?" I purr, settling in. I pat the hand of Mateo, the youngest of them, and he blushes quite pink.

I don't think he has had his first shave yet, and I find him very . . . well . . . cute.

They inform me that they are in the finest of fettle, and I can tell that they are delighted to be seen having drinks with the star entertainer.

"Tell me, *hermanos,* what exactly is it that you do on the great and glorious *San Cristobal,*" I ask by way of innocent conversation. "Are you cooks? Stewards? Carpenters?"

Jesus looks at me with great disdain. "No, *mi corazón,* we are gunners . . . great and magnificent gunners!" Jesus has had a few, I can tell.

"It is true," says Eduardo. "We can aim, fire, and reload our cannon in under ninety seconds. I should like to see the English match—"

All four of them suddenly shoot to their feet as I sense a presence behind me.

"So," says Lieutenant Juan Carlos Cisneros y Siquieros, in a low and sinister tone, "you are telling everything you know about the *San Cristobal* to this girl?"

"No, *Teniente,* your pardon," pleads a very white-faced Eduardo. "She is only a common *cantante.* What could be the harm?"

"She is not a common anything, fool. She has been pumping you idiots for information. Mondragon!"

There is another sailor behind Cisneros, probably a bosun's mate. He steps forward and says, "*Sí, Teniente?*"

"They are all under arrest. Take them back to the ship."

"*Sí, Teniente,*" says Mondragon. "*Vamos, hombres,*" and he leads the very chastened and unhappy four Spanish sailors out of the Café Americano. *Poor lads, what started out as a fine evening for you turned into something very dif-*

*ferent. Looks like a long stretch of no shore leave for you fellows. Oh well, you're all good Catholic boys, so just offer it up—it will reduce your time in Purgatory, or so they say . . .*

"As for you," says Cisneros, grasping me by the arm, "you will come with me. I have a room nearby and we will—"

I shake his hand off my arm. "We will do nothing, *perro*," I say. "Look around you." He does and sees my lads standing up and staring hard at him. He knows there are weapons under those suits. Señor Ric, also, has noticed and is headed this way. *The Rules, Cisneros—surely you remember?*

"You have sent away your men, Lieutenant, but mine are still here. Do you see? Good. Now get yourself gone, you."

His face turns a dangerous shade of red. Then he hits a brace, clicks his heels, bows slightly, and says, "I will take you. Count on that. I swear it."

He turns and leaves the place, his heels clicking on the hardwood floor.

I look over at my boys and see that they are sinking back into their chairs. I give them a nod and slight smile of thanks, and then remount the stage for the second set.

As I am putting my bow to the Lady Gay, a group of masked revelers, mostly men, but some women, too, enter and are seated. The one who sits at the head of the table wears a white half mask with red tassels to either side, and he seems to have taken a keen interest in me. But I am the leading entertainer, so why should he not? The masks are not unusual—it is Carnival, after all, and, besides, there are many times a gent likes to be anonymous, especially when he is out on the town and with a woman who is *not* his wife.

They call for drinks and I welcome them, and then I lower the bow and take off into the opening number.

After all is said and sung, I bow and take the applause, then head for the hallway that leads to the back rooms, as if I were going to my dressing room. I do like to keep up the illusion that I am a class act. Actually, I'm going back to the privy.

On my way, I notice that the group of revelers who had come in during the break had left. Too bad. They seemed most appreciative of my performance and I expected some good tips from them. *Oh, well, stiffed again, girl.*

My violin case is left open on the stage, and people are tossing coins into it. From the corner of my greedy eye I can see that, while most of the coins are silver, some are gold. *Ah yes, how I love it—loud applause and gold to boot.* Joannie has instructions to close the case and bring it back to our table after the last coin falls.

I nip into the hall and go past the closed doors to the private rooms, and into the privy. In there I find an old attendant, who hands me a damp cloth and opens the inner door for me. The latrine consists of a hole in the floor, at the bottom of a shallow masonry funnel. On either side are flat places to put your feet as you squat down over it to answer Nature's call. I drop drawers, hike skirts, and do it, put the damp cloth to good use, and then toss it in a nearby receptacle. Pretty neat, I'm thinking. Least I didn't have to sit down on something nasty. Up drawers, down skirts, and back out to the anteroom to check my face in the mirror while the attendant whisks any dust off my shoulders with her brush. Satisfied that all is as well as it could be with my appearance, I give her a good tip—*Muchas gracias, Señora*—and go back out to rejoin my mates.

I don't get there.

As I stride by the second door on the left, it opens and a hand snakes out to grab me by the neck and pull me in.

A strong hand is clapped over my mouth, and I am unable to cry out for help. My arms are pinned to my sides, preventing me from drawing my shiv. *If this your work, Cisneros, you will pay for it!* I squirm and kick, but it avails me nothing. As I am carried across the room, I can see that I have been taken by that bunch of masked revelers.

"*Aquí, Capitán*. Take her!" says the brute who has me by the neck and who flings me now into the lap of the man seated at the head of the table. "*Mucho gusto!*"

There is laughter all around. Well, let 'em laugh at *this*.

I whip out my shiv and put it to the throat of the white-masked man.

He merely chuckles and reaches up to pull off his mask.

"It is good to see you again, my sweet little English pirate. Let us have a kiss."

I sit astounded.

*Flaco!*

# Chapter 27

"Flaco!" I cry, and fling my arms around his neck. "Flaco Jimenez! You devil! Well met, oh, so very well met!" Once again I gaze fondly upon my old comrade-in-piratical-arms. Same long black hair braided in thin strands that end in brightly colored beads and ribbons, same thin mustache and pointed chin beard, teeth gleaming white in his tanned face as he smiles upon me. The very picture of a dashing buccaneer.

"So good to see you again, Jacky Faber, my little English pirate. Let us have a kiss."

I look around the table at the various scarred and furrowed faces, some grinning, some not, and cry out, "Jorge! Moto! Not yet hanged, you jolly banditos! I am so very glad! And there's Serpiente and Coyote, and young Perrito, too! Lift your glasses!" A serving girl goes by with a tray of wine goblets and I snag one and hold it up. "To the waves and to the foam and to the Red Brotherhood. Let us always stand onboard as brothers! *Salud, dinero, y amor!*"

There is a roar of *Salud!* and the toast is drunk. Pirates will always drink to money and love. I notice that while many of the faces are familiar, many are not, and then I look for a face that is not there. I sit up straight.

"Where is Chucho? Oh my God, he wasn't . . . ?" Chucho was Flaco's First Mate, and I liked him very much.

"No, my sweet, he was not killed or hanged," says Flaco, shaking his head, his braids flying about his face. "No, it was far worse than that."

I steel myself for the worst. Chucho was a good friend to me.

"No, the Grand Chucho, his sword feared from Martinique to Saint Martin, from Saint Thomas to Puerto Rico, has fallen . . . and fallen to a woman, at that. A hostage we took in a raid on Puerto Gordo. While she was aboard and waiting to be ransomed, poor Chucho fell under her spell. He and the woman now have a farm and raise sugar cane and a horde of brats on Santo Domingo." Again Jimenez shakes his head at the ways of the world. "No proper end for a pirate, no." That sentiment is echoed around the table. "El Feo there has been elected First Mate." I look over to see a large, scowling, and very unpleasant-looking cove. *El Feo* means "the ugly one," and it seems to fit. I take an instant dislike to him, and I have a suspicion that he feels the same way about the bit of *inglesa* fluff that has just landed in his captain's lap.

"But enough of the henpecked and disgraced Chucho, *chiquita,* time now for that kiss."

I lift my face and give it to the rascal, and there are cheers all around—*Olé, Capitán!* Yes, I have always been free with my kisses, but then, I wasn't raised up proper. I say, what's the harm?

As I take my lips from his, he says, "That was lovely, *mi*

*corazón,* and we must have another. But if you would put that blade away, I would be even more appreciative of your very obvious charms." He glances nervously at my shiv, which is still in my hand, the razor-sharp edge of which rests not very far from his right ear.

Leaving my left arm about his neck, I bring the knife around and put the point of it to his chin and gently tickle his beard with it. "*No hay rosas sin espinas,* eh, Flaco? You taught me that one—'No roses without thorns.' True, *cómo no?*"

"*Es la verdad, mi querida,* and especially in your case, my British *rosa,* but if you would just . . ."

I whip my knife back into my forearm sheath, and as soon as I do, he clasps me to him.

"You have become even more beautiful, my quivering little bowl of jalapeño jelly," he says, his nose a bare inch from the top of my bodice. The danger from my shiv now past, he leans in and plunges his face in the cleft between my breasts, then gives his chin a bit of a shake back and forth. I yelp and grasp his hair and jerk his head back up and out of there. I hear a faint tinkle, and see that at the ends of several of the braids now dangle tiny chimes.

"Bells, is it now? The beads and ribbons were not enough? Are you now a horse and carriage, Flaco?"

"Our captives and hostages seem to demand something colorful in the way of fierce pirate captains. I only seek to oblige them, my dear. And now for the second kiss, which I trust will be even sweeter than the first."

His arm goes about my waist, and as he draws me even closer to him, I take a deep breath and muse about the past.

· · ·

*I must admit, Jaimy, that I have sat in this very same lap be-fore—yes, I have. It was during that summer on the* Emerald *when I thought you were out of my life for good and ever. I met Flaco Jimenez, Captain of* El Diablo Rojo, *in a smoke-filled tavern in Fort-de-France on Martinique, right after the lot of us, sailing in consort, had sacked and pillaged that very town. It was, after all, a French town, and being an English priva-teer, that's what I was supposed to do, wasn't it? Parts of the town were burning right merrily when my Irish crew and I piled into that tavern and, after many a drink, formed sort of an alliance with the crew of* El Diablo Rojo, *and I formed more than a bit of an alliance with her Captain, Flaco Maria Castro de Jimenez.*

*Anyway, I don't think very many people got hurt in that raid. Most of the smart ones, including the local police, headed for the hills as soon as they spotted our ships coming into their harbor, each bearing a version of the skull-and-crossed-bones flags flying at our mastheads as we charged in. I hope not, anyway.*

*It turned out that Flaco was a decent sort, for a Spanish pirate. He had a sense of honor in that he did not abuse his captives, and he did not push me any further than I wanted to go with him . . . which was far enough, but never mind.*

"Things have changed, my gallant buccaneer," I say, my mind and body back in Havana and still in Flaco's lap. "I am now promised in marriage to Lieutenant James Emerson Fletcher, an officer in His Majesty's Royal Navy."

Flaco affects shock. "What a silliness—*pirata bonita muchacha* is going to wed an *inglés* pig of a Royal Navy offi-cer? No, it cannot be—it is a crime against nature."

I laugh. Flaco always did have a poetic way about him.

I decide to give him a bit of fun and squirm my bottom around and say, for the benefit of his mates, "Do you have a jackknife in your pocket, Flaco, or are you just glad to see me?"

Roars of laughter and poundings of the table.

"I am *most* glad to see you, Jacky," he says.

More hilarity all around, and Flaco presses his advantage, again clutching me to him. "That next kiss, my little chili pepper, will you give it?"

*Why not,* think I. *I could scream for help if I need it.*

I wrap my arms about his neck and lift my face to his and our lips meet . . . *uummmm* . . . and a part of my mind—the sane part, which is admittedly a very small part of that mind—says to me, *Isn't this the part when James Emerson Fletcher comes bursting onto the scene?*

Sure enough, there is a kick and the door flies open, and there, holding two pistols before him, is . . . not Jaimy Fletcher . . . but, rather, Higgins, with Davy and Tink to either side, knives drawn and about to do damage. Beside them I see, all big-eyed, Daniel and Joannie.

Taking my mouth off Flaco's I cry, "Higgins! It is our old friend Flaco!"

Higgins thumbs the pistols back on half cock and says to Davy and Tink, "It's all right, lads. Stand down." He puts the pistols into the vest holsters, where they habitually reside.

Davy's and Tink's knives were not the only ones drawn upon Higgins's entrance—pirates do not live to old age by allowing themselves to be caught unawares—but eventually all blades go back into their sheaths. I notice that El Feo's is the last one to disappear.

"The worthy Señor Higgins! Come in!" says Flaco. "Enrique, get up, and let the man sit down! We must talk business!"

The man next to Flaco vacates the chair and Higgins seats himself. Davy and Tink, and now Jim Tanner, stand around him, hard-eyed and very vigilant. Since there are no more open chairs, I figure I'll stay where I am.

"We are all friends here, mates," I say, and nod to the serving girl such that drinks are placed in my lads' hands. *Everybody be calm, please.*

"*Buenas noches,* Captain Jimenez," says Higgins, picking up his glass and taking a sip. "It is good to see you again."

*When we had been sailing in company with Flaco and El Diablo Rojo, we had fallen upon a merchant ship that had a good, fat cargo, and several hostages as well—a Spanish girl, Rosalita, and her brother Alfonso, she being eighteen and bound for an arranged marriage in Puerto Rico, he being ten and going into apprenticeship with a distant uncle in cotton trading. He was told that he would not be forced to walk the plank if he succeeded in teaching me Spanish within two months. Although he realized very shortly that we had no intention of drowning him, he was relentless in his instruction, and soon I was quite good in conversational Spanish. Higgins, also, decided to avail himself of this chance to learn another language, and that is why he is able to converse so easily with Flaco.*

*After several months with us, Alfonso didn't want to be ransomed, but, alas, it had to be so. His sister, however, was another story—she fell in love with one of my crew, Sean Mc-Murphy, and they were married in San Juan and are now in Ireland. She preferred the man she knew to the one she did not, and who am I to stand in the way of true love? Flaco was angry with me over the loss of the ransom, but he soon got over it.*

"So, Captain Jimenez," says Higgins, beginning the sparring that I know is coming. "How do you come to be here in the heart of the Spanish Empire? Why do you take the chance?"

"Ha!" laughs Flaco. "I am here at Ric's, and Señor Ricardo Mendoza very much appreciates the goods that I bring to him from my various . . . uh . . . forays. The rum, the spices, the women . . ."

"But where is *El Diablo Rojo,* Flaco?" I ask from my perch. "Are you not afraid the *San Cristobal* might take you?"

"Pah! That fat hog of a boat cannot sail out of its own way. I spit on the name of *San Cristobal.*"

"Still, she carries a lot of iron."

"Well, no matter. Our ship is up the coast at Bahia Honda."

"But still, we wonder at your presence here," persists Higgins.

"And we, in turn, wonder at yours," says Flaco. He picks up a shrimp from the platter in front of him and places it between my lips.

I chew it, then swallow, and say, "I am no longer a pirate, Flaco. I am now a simple sponge diver. We are here in Havana merely to sell our catch."

Flaco laughs out loud. "You. Jacky Faber. A simple sponge diver. Ha! That shall never be!"

"It is true, my friend. We also have a naturalist aboard and are doing scientific research," I say, running my finger down the side of his face and smiling upon him with my best open-mouthed grin.

"Jacky, you were always the greatest liar," says Flaco, suddenly standing up and pitching me to the floor. "We know you are after gold, and we want to know what will be our cut."

*What?*

"We have absolutely no idea what you are talking about," says Higgins.

"Oh, please, Señor Higgins," says Flaco, reseating himself without me. "Do you see that man over there? Yes? Well, he was onboard a ship called the *Dolphin* in Boston and he overheard some very interesting things. And when that vessel docked in Savannah, he jumped ship and got on a fast mail cutter and came straight to me. So, what do you say to that?"

*Damn! I warned Captain Hudson about that! And here we are in deep trouble . . . and if Flaco knows, who else knows?*

I pick myself up off the floor and poke my finger in Flaco's face.

"There is no gold. None that you're gonna get your hands on, anyway, Flaco!"

"We shall see, Jacky. Bahia Honda is not very far from Cayo Hueso."

"Right, Flaco," hiss I. "And in the future, be careful just who you throw on the floor. Come on, mates, let's get out of this place."

I leave to the sound of laughing pirates.

I'm seething on the way back to the *Nancy B*. The whole thing is blown wide open!

"Were those really pirates?" asks Joannie, tugging at my sleeve.

"Yes, dear, they were. Now hush," says I, irritated.

"Coo," she says in wonder.

"You have interesting friends, Jacky," comments Davy, his view not asked for but offered, anyway.

"What you saw back there was not necessarily the truth, Davy, so button your lip."

"Hey." He shrugs. "You're Jaimy's problem, not mine. I've got a good girl."

*Grrrrrrrr . . .*

# Chapter 28

The next day we ready ourselves for departure. All the stores and supplies are in, and we are due to rendezvous with the *Dolphin* within a few days. Everybody is back, including John Thomas and Smasher McGee, who return leaning on each other, both of them stone broke. I suppose it has always been thus with sailors, all the way back to Jason and the Argonauts. In fact, I bet ol' Jason had to comb the bars for an errant Argonaut or two when it came time for him to sail from the Isle of Lemnos or Colchis, Golden Fleece in hand or not.

Yes, 'tis time to leave the charms of Havana behind, which the *Nancy B.* will do—right after the noon cockfights, that is.

Dr. Sebastian, too, has returned from his pursuits ashore, so he escorts me to the arena. On the way, I fill him in on the events of the past two days, little of which pleases him.

"So, it seems the entire Hispanic world knows of our intentions. That is not good, not good at all," he grumbles, lost in thought.

"I did warn our good Captain Hudson of the ears that wag on a ship," I say.

I've got El Gringo in a little canvas pouch held at my side, his head sticking out of the top of it, peering avidly about. I figure this is better than a chicken cage—better for his *machismo*.

The Doctor sighs. "Captain Hannibal Hudson is my dearest friend, and he has no equal as to bravery in battle or in knowledge of things nautical. But I am afraid that he is a complete fool when it comes to intelligence. Ah, well, we shall deal with this when we rendezvous. Ah, here we are."

We stand before the great hall of cockfighting and take in the flags whipping about, along with the colorful posters advertising the gladiatorial combat that will soon take place inside. The crowd pours in. Dr. Sebastian takes his leave of me and goes in the front entrance, while I am directed to a side door where the combatants enter. Inside I find a room filled with caged cocks and their handlers. At the other end of the room are the big doors that I know open out into the ring, through which Gringo and I will go when it is time. Meanwhile, back here there is a great deal of cackling and crowing, with challenges thrown back and forth between the birds. I can feel Gringo quivering with rage beneath my hand. He works himself up into a mighty crow and delivers it with a certain kiss-my-feathered-ass-and-stay-away-from-my-hens-all-you-pretenders-to-my-throne sort of quality. *Be patient,* mi amigo, *you'll get your chance.*

The man in the red sash is there and I go up to him to register as well as to pay my entrance fee—the prize money for the winners has to come from somewhere, doesn't it? He writes Gringo's name on a slip of paper and drops it into a basket. I am the only female in the place, but that's nothing new to me. The men don't seem to mind, either. Here, it's all about the fighters and everyone pays very little attention to me.

Eventually the ringmaster goes to the doors that open on to the ring and announces, "The first contest, El Demonio against El Gordo." Two men stand up, take their birds from out of their cages, and hold them to their chests. "The second will be El Asesino versus El Rey." More preparations are made. "The third match shall be El Matador"—and here he pauses to snicker—"in mortal combat with . . . El Gringo Furioso!"

There is laughter all around.

I puff up and say, "But El Matador is the champion and this is El Gringo's first battle! That cannot be fair!"

Red Sash shrugs and says, "The luck of the draw, Señorita. Either your fighter goes through those doors in honor"—here he points to doors leading to the ring—"or out those, in disgrace." He points again, this time to the back doors. "And there will be no return of the entrance fee. *Comprende?*"

*Grrrr . . .*

We sit back to wait our turn.

There is a roar as the doors are opened and Red Sash makes his announcements and El Demonio and El Gordo, along with their handlers, advance to the center.

The battle is joined and soon El Gordo lies dead in the dust. Then it is El Asesino and El Rey's turn.

As I sit and wait for the outcome of that battle, I think back to last night and wonder how Cisneros knew that Eduardo and the others had been keeping company with me—probably the lads were bragging about it back on their ship. *Stupid men, I swear . . .*

I am jolted out of my reverie by the announcement, "And now El Matador versus El Gringo Furioso!"

I remove Gringo from his bag and head out into the ring. There is a roar, but I know it is not for me and my bird—it is for the champion, El Matador. For us there is laughter.

*El Gringo Furioso? No, El Gringo Lamentable! Ha! Ha!*

*Look at that! Just the kind of bird a stupid girl would bring to the ring!*

*El Gringo Loco! El Gringo Soon-to-Be-Dead!*

I flush and try to keep my mind on the business at hand. I see the reason for their laughter—El Matador is half again the size of Gringo, and a good two pounds heavier. El Matador's handler gazes upon me and my bird with great contempt—*This will not take long,* I know he is thinking.

"Engage!" shouts Red Sash and we shove our cocks together to get them in fighting spirit.

The neck feathers of both birds stand straight out as they struggle to get at each other. Gringo fixes his eye straight on El Matador and he flips his cockscomb back and forth as if to say, *Where is your comb,* maricón, *where are your wattles? Did they cut off your* cojones *as well?*

"Ready!" cries Red Sash, and I crouch down with Gringo quivering in my grasp. Both birds are insane with rage.

"Fight!"

The hourglass at the judges' table is turned upside down, so I release Gringo and step back to the rail as the birds fly at each other, wings beating, spurs up, each beak seeking out the eyes of the other.

After the initial contact, they step back and seemingly size up their opponent, then they are at it again. This time Gringo manages to flap his wings enough to rise above El Matador so that he can bring down his spurs upon the other fighter's back, but they cause little effect. The other bird is just too big, I am coming to realize with a sinking feeling. *Just hang on, Gringo. He is bigger, but you are faster. Hang on. Live to fight another day.*

The birds separate again, and once more appear to be looking for signs of weakness in each other. I lean against the rail and a very familiar head covered with beaded braids appears next to me.

"*Buenos días,* my sweet little English cupcake."

"*Bese mi culo,* Flaco," I say. "I am mad at you, and besides, I am busy. Go away."

"I would gladly kiss your perfect bottom, Jacky," he says, grinning his avaricious grin. "But you cannot be mad at your Flaco, as we are going to be very rich together, no? Shall we not bathe together in silver tubs full of golden doubloons? Shall we not—"

"No. I don't know what you are talking about, Flaco. Leave me alone." Flaco's crew is gathered about him, and I spot El Feo, his ugly First Mate. He has his eye upon me, and I don't like the way he looks at me.

The birds are at it again, and I leave the rail. Streaks of blood have appeared on the wings of both gladiators. The audience is appreciative.

*The little one, he is small. But he fights well, no?*

*Sí, he is fast. There is no disgrace here.*

*But El Matador, he is so much stronger. The end must be near for El Gringo Furioso.*

I look over at the hourglass—there are many grains of sand left. The birds engage again and El Matador, with his superior strength, forces Gringo up against the rail, and though Gringo tries with all his might, he cannot get away. El Matador raises his left spur and brings it down on Gringo's breast, and then he does it again. Blood appears, and Gringo staggers. El Matador steps away and then heads in for the kill.

"Time! Fight over!" cries the judge, and I leap over to pick up my fallen fighter and cradle him in my arms. He tries to raise his head, but he cannot.

"Hang on, Gringo," I say, "hang on."

As I leave the ring, there is applause, but I am sure Gringo does not hear it. There is also Flaco calling after me, "Soon, heart of my heart, we shall meet again."

Back at the *Nancy B.*, I lay Gringo on a bed of soft straw. I have put healing salve on all his wounds, and I hope for the best.

As I leave him there, I hear Jemimah wrapping up her last Brother Rabbit tale with Daniel and Joannie in rapt attendance. The rest of my crew is topside, preparing to get under way.

" . . . so Brother Fox, mad as hell at Brother Rabbit for foulin' up the stew in which he was the main ingredient, pulls him out of the pot, but Brother Rabbit's big fat ol' rabbit foot catches on the edge of the pot and pulls it over so that the broth runs over the feet of Brother Fox and Brother Bear and they howls with the pain of it and it snuffs out the fire, and Brother Rabbit hops away, singin' a song. End of story."

I go to the stove and pick up a bit of bacon that's grilling off to the side and stick it in my mouth. Then I ask, "How come Brother Rabbit always ends up in that pot, him being so fast and all?"

Jemimah considers and then says, "Well, there are lot o' traps in the world, child, not all of 'em made outta wire and wood and other hardware."

Jemimah is involved in baking bread, and she's kneading dough and has flour up to her elbows. Then she starts . . .

"Now there was this one bunny, she bein' called Sister Rabbit, and she was of a mind to marry up with Brother Rabbit, and she was a pretty little thing wi' a nice fluffy chest, carried high, and her little white cottontail sittin' up all fine on top o' her behind. Brother Rabbit like her a lot, but he fancy himself a free-travelin' man and didn't want to mess with any of that marryin' stuff, no, he didn't. He want his lovin' fun for free like all the men do. You mind that, Sister Joan," she says, waving a floury finger in Joannie's face.

"That's true. I've met many like Brother Rabbit," I say, putting my two cents in and thinking rather fondly of that rogue Randall . . . and Captain Lord Richard Allen . . . and Joseph Jared . . . and maybe a couple dozen others.

"You hush. You a bad influence on this girl. She want to be just like you, and as far as I can see, that cain't be any good."

I cast eyes heavenward and hush up, as she goes on.

"Now Brother Fox and Brother Bear know that they can't get Brother Rabbit on the level, he bein' much too fast with his two big back feet, so they gets to thinkin' as to how they can ketch 'im.

"'Hmmmm . . . we cain't catch him,' says Brother Fox, 'but we can get him to come to us. Look over dere, Brother Bear.'

"Brother Bear looks out t'rough the bushes and sees the churchyard, where Sister Rabbit is holdin' Sunday school—Raccoon Child and Possum Boy and Muskrat Girl is sittin' there in front o' her on little benches, holdin' on to their prayer books.

"'We cain't grab her in church, Brother Fox,' says Brother Bear. 'We go to Hell for dat.'

"Brother Fox cuts his eyes over to Brother Bear, thinkin' maybe Brother Bear ain't quite as bright as he need to be.

"'We wait till she done, fool.'

"An' Sister Rabbit teaches 'em the Parable of the Ten Talents, and then she say, 'Now chil'ren, 'fore we all go away and spread the word of the Lord, we goin' t' sing a fine ol' gospel song.'"

And Jemimah lifts her voice and sings.

> *O Come along, Moses, you'll not get lost,*
> *Let my people go,*
> *Stretch out your rod and come across,*
> *Let my people go.*

Then she swings into the chorus:

*Go down, Moses,*
*Way down in Egypt's land.*
*Tell ol' Pharoah,*
*Let my people go.*

I speak up and say, "For a little bitty bunny, Sister Rabbit sure got a fine, deep voice." I am once again shushed and Jemimah goes on.

"So then the meetin' breaks up and all the chil'ren run off, and Sister Rabbit is collectin' the hymn books when the fox and the bear come up and grab that poor sister and take her back to their lair and get ready for some fun.

"By and by, Brother Rabbit come hoppin' along the road, whistlin' a tune, and Brother Fox call out to him, 'Hey, Brother Rabbit, look what we got chere!' And he lift Sister Rabbit up by her ears and holds her over the boilin' oil. 'We about to have us a snack! Hee-hee!'

"Sister Rabbit, she got her front paws put t'gether, her eyes on Heaven, mumblin' a prayer and gettin' ready to meet her Lord, and Brother Rabbit see her there and say, 'Brother Fox, now you know that ain't nice. You let her go now, y'hear?'

"But Brother Fox, he shake his head and say, 'I'll be lettin' her go, Brother Rabbit, when you come over chere and take her place.'

"And Sister Rabbit, she wail, 'Oh, don't do it, Brother Rabbit! Run, and save yo'self! I done made my peace with the Lord!'

"But Brother Rabbit, he got a noble streak in him, and so he go over to Brother Fox and lets him grab him by the ears, and the fox say, 'Ha! Got you now, you slipp'ry rascal!' Brother Fox flip Sister Rabbit away and she run off cryin'."

Jemimah pauses to shape the loaf on the breadboard, which gives Daniel a chance to jump in with a question. "Why didn't they just eat Sister Rabbit and forget about Brother Rabbit?" asks Daniel. "I figure a rabbit in the hand is worth—"

"Because Brother Rabbit got a lot more meat on him, is why, Brother Boy. Plus they got a lot of scores to settle with him. And don't interrup' your Aunt Jemimah when she in a story."

Daniel clams up, and she continues.

"So Brother Fox picks up Brother Rabbit and holds him over the bubblin' pot. And Brother Bear ties his napkin round his neck and picks up his knife and fo'k as Fox slowly lowers Rabbit down—"

Just then Davy pops his head in the hatchway and says, "Sorry to break up story hour, Jacky, but we're ready to get under way. Danny, get up on lookout. Joannie, to the land lines."

The story will have to wait for another time as we all go to our stations.


I blink in the bright light on the quarterdeck. When my eyes adjust I see that all is well. We have the tide and the breeze behind us and will not have to tow ourselves out.

"All right," I call. "Raise the Main, Fore, and Spanker. We'll go with those on the port tack till we clear the harbor. Throw off the lines." Joannie removes the land lines, and they are hauled aboard as she scampers onboard after them.

"Jim, steer to the left of the channel. I'd like to stay as

far away from the *San Cristobal* as possible. Maybe she won't notice us leaving."

"Aye, Missy."

But she notices, all right. As we approach the big ship, a boat is lowered and pulls straight for us.

*Uh-oh . . .*

When it draws abreast, a young Spanish midshipman standing in the bow calls out, "You there! Americano! You are commanded to take your ship portside of the *San Cristobal*. There you will slack your sails and stop to wait until you are given permission to proceed. If you fail to do this, you will be destroyed."

*Lord, what now?*

I find out soon enough. As we pull alongside, I see Lieutenant Cisneros standing at the rail. Then I realize with horror that four gratings have been set up next to him and on them four men are bound, face-first and spread-eagled—Eduardo, Jesus, Manuelo, and Mateo. They have been stripped of all clothing, and next to each stands a sailor with a whip.

When we have stopped, Cisneros raises his hand and then drops it. The seamen wind up and bring their whips down on the bare backs of my poor Spanish sailors.

*One . . . two . . . three . . . four . . . five . . .*

Eduardo, Jesus, and Manuelo writhe and groan, but the young boy Mateo does not.

No, he *screams.*

# Chapter 29

The *Nancy B.* is anchored off Key West once again, and I am back to diving. 'Course we ain't divin' on *that* spot—don't want to give that away should anyone come along. No, we're just diving for sponges and scientific specimens, innocent as can be, and about a half mile from where the *Santa Magdalena* lies.

We've been here for two days, waiting for the *Dolphin,* which hasn't showed up yet, and I'm starting to worry a bit.

*Jaimy, where are you?*

We've finished up with breakfast and I'm about to go to my cabin to change into my swimsuit to begin the day's work, when Daniel, who has been stacking firewood next to the stove, pipes up with, "Auntie, I ain't stackin' no more wood till you tell us how Brother Rabbit got out of that fix he was in."

Jemimah, who is washing the morning's dishes, with Joannie beside her drying them and putting them away, looks at him and says, "How you know he got outta that trouble, boy? How you know they didn't just pop him right inta that hot oil and then cut him up and eat him right on the spot and then lean back and suck on his bones? How you know that? Hmmmm? Happened to a lot o' rabbits, you know . . . a whole *lot* o' rabbits. Oh, yes it did."

"Oh, come on, Auntie," pleads Joannie. "Tell us what happened to *that* rabbit . . . *Please.*"

Jemimah sighs a theatrical sigh and begins. "Well, you recollect that Brother Fox had got Brother Rabbit by his ears and was holdin' him above that pot of boilin' lard, ready to fry him up good?"

"Yes, we do," chorus all three of us together, eagerly anticipating the rest of the story.

Jemimah hangs her huge skillet on its nail and goes on.

"'So,' says Brother Fox, relishin' the moment. 'You got any last words, Rabbit, 'fore your delicious self takes a real hot dip?'

"Brother Rabbit, he cut his eyes over to Brother Bear, who's sharpenin' up his knives on a rock and grinnin' a big toothy hungry grin, and Brother Rabbit figures his time on this earth is finally up, so he stretches out his arms in prayer and lifts his face to Heaven.

"'Lord, this poor little ol' no-account rabbit is comin' home to you, and I thanks you for the life you give me so far,' says Brother Rabbit, and though he cain't perk up his ears, 'cause they both in Brother Fox's fist, he does hear a sound from not far off, which give him some hope.

"'*Ooooooooo . . . oooooooo . . . ahooooooooo . . .*'

"And he decide to keep talking as long as he can.

"'Lord, don't be too hard on Brother Fox and Brother

Bear for murderin' me—don't send 'em to Hell for too long—maybe only an eternity or two. After all, it's just in their natures and they too dumb to know any better.'

"'Oooo . . . ahooooooo . . . ahooooooo . . .'

"'Brother Fox, whyn't you just dunk him on down dere and shut up dat rabbit's wise mouth for good and ever?' asks Brother Bear, gettin' impatient and beginnin' to drool a bit, which ain't a pretty sight, no. He uses one of his knives to slice up some 'taters and tosses 'em into the pot, where they sizzles up real good.

"'Ooooooooo . . . oooooOOOOO . . . AHOOO . . . HOOOO . . .'

"'What dat sound?' say Brother Fox, cockin' his head. He don't have long to wonder, as the sound gets louder and louder and then . . .'"

". . . and then . . . ?" breathe Joannie and Daniel, leaning forward together. ". . . and then . . . ?"

". . . and then . . . there's a big fuss in the bushes and all of a sudden Sister Rabbit come burstin' into the camp, winded but still runnin' for all she worth. Brother Rabbit see what she been up to, and it warms him to his manly core. Right behind her are 'bout a dozen dogs. She must've gone down to the plantation and showed herself to the master's foxhounds, and they, bayin' and hallooin' all the way, take off after Sister Rabbit, and she leads 'em straight into Brother Fox's camp."

Jemimah indulges in some more rattling of pots and pans as she's putting them away, and then she finishes up.

"Now, when them dogs see what's goin' on, they forgit all about Sister Rabbit and head right off for Brother Fox, 'cause they's foxhounds, y'see, and don't care nothin' 'bout no silly rabbits when there's foxes around to be chased. Brother Fox flings Brother Rabbit aside, and he take off as fast as he can, with those hounds right on his red bushy tail, and Brother Bear runs bawlin' into the woods with a few of those dogs on his brown stumpy tail, as well.

"And that's the story of how Sister Rabbit saved Brother Rabbit's little white tail after he had put his life on the line for her. Not only were them two bunnies safe and sound, but they also happily had lunch t'gether on Brother Bear's crispy fried potatoes. End of that Rabbit Tale."

As the last pot is hung on its hook, Jemimah sings:

> *Little piece o' cornbread, sitting on a shelf,*
> *You want any more, yo' can sing it yo'self.*

"Now get off, all of yous," she orders. "Ain'cha got no work to do?"

Daniel and Joannie scamper off topside, but I linger a bit before going to change into my swimsuit. I check in with Gringo, who seems to be recovering well, and then turn back to Jemimah.

"Jemimah," I say, "I've noticed something about you."

"And what's that, girl?"

"You got two ways of talking. One slavey, and one . . . well, *regular,* like."

"Huh!" She laughs. "I spent forty years waitin' on white folks' tables—of course, I can talk just like them . . . When I want to. But I think the darky way fits better with the Rabbit Tales, don't you?"

*Can't argue wi' dat.*

. . .

It's just after two in the afternoon, and Joannie—she being healed up enough to dive with me again—and I are on the raft, lying back amid all the sponges we have harvested this day, soaking up the sun and talking.

"Joannie, you see how fast those little fishies down there can move with just a flick of their tails? I wish we could move through the water like that."

"Uh-huh . . . me too, Jacky, but we ain't got tails. Not like they got, anyway."

"Hmmm . . . But maybe we could work something out," I say, putting my arms behind my head and stretching out all lazy, like a wet seal drying off in the sun. "You know how my very good friend Amy Trevelyne back in Boston goes on and on about the American scientist Benjamin Franklin . . . No? Well, she does, believe me, and one of the things she tells me about him is that he was a devoted swimmer, telling all the people about the benefits of that particular exercise for one's health and all that, and in connection with that, he invented some paddles that you strapped on your hands to make you move faster through the water."

I pause to watch some fluffy white clouds scud across the sky. Then I continue.

"But I don't think those hand things is gonna get it—it'd be like trying to claw your way through the water, and I figure you gotta sorta wiggle through it. Like the fishies do." I think further on this and then say, "Maybe if we put those things on our feet and made them all loose and whippy, like the fishies' tail fins . . ."

"That might work," says Joannie, doubtfully.

"I'll get Ship's Engineer John Tinker on it right away. And speakin' of makin' things, I'd like you to take some light canvas and make a little bitsy vestlike thing with tiny pockets in it for Gringo, if he gets better."

She looks at me curiously. "For sure . . . but why?"

"I figure he lost the last fight 'cause he wasn't strong enough, especially in the legs. Oh, he was faster than the other bird, but El Matador was just too big and too well trained. It was my fault. I started him too early. But I plan on fixing that. Once he's back on his feet, we'll start putting lead slugs in the pockets of that vest, just a few and then a lot, till his drumsticks are just like iron. Then we shall see, El Matador— Hey, look there, Joannie, there's a flock of those pink things."

I reach over and thump on the side of the *Nancy B.* "On deck there! Tell Dr. Sebastian there are birds of interest out here!"

In response to my call, Davy appears at the rail with a long glass to his eye, but he ain't lookin' at birds.

"He knows, Jacky, but we got somethin' else here," he says. "A small boat, headin' straight for us. No markings. Don't know what . . ."

Now, we've had lots of small shipping pass us here in the Florida Straits, and none of them has paid us any notice or given us any trouble, but no sense in taking chances. We must play our role.

"Come, Sister," I say, giving Joannie a nudge. "Back in the water for us."

And like any two seals rolling off slippery, seaweed-covered rocks, we slide back into the sea.

Under the surface we kick down to the bottom and start sawing at sponge stalks. When we have enough, we head back up, where we see above us the hull of a small boat

261

slip in overhead. It appears that it has tied up to our raft. Joannie and I give each other questioning looks with our eyebrows, then go up, and as our heads break the surface, we suck in air.

I am shocked to see a man in the uniform of a British Navy coxswain standing at the bow of the mystery boat. And then two other men, both standing on our raft, advance into my field of vision. My jaw drops open when I see that one of them is Captain Hannibal Hudson of HMS *Dolphin,* and next to him is Professor Tilden, and the other is . . .

*Jaimy!*

I leap out of the water and onto the raft and then jump up in front of Jaimy and open my arms. "Oh, Jaimy, love, it is so good to see you!"

"Your fiancée, I presume, Mr. Fletcher," says Captain Hudson, unable to suppress a grin.

"Yes, Sir," says Jaimy, his face reddening. "It is definitely she."

And then Higgins is there to wrap me in the big towel and hustle me down to my cabin.

"We shall get you dressed, Miss, and then you shall await a visit from Captain Hudson and Mr. Fletcher."

"But Higgins . . ."

"*But* nothing. We must get you decent."

We will have dinner on the mess deck, my cabin being much too small for the number of people that need to be at the table. As Higgins was getting me rigged out in something presentable, I sent for Jemimah and said, "Dinner for six. Put out some wine for them till I get there. Pull out all the stops. Send out something for the men in the *Dolphin*'s boat. Food for our crew later. Do what you can. And thanks."

She smiles and nods. "We'll do that, girl. Don't you worry. You just talk your talk." She leaves to get it done.

Higgins stuffs me into my Lawson Peabody dress, does what he can with my hair, and then we both go down to the mess deck to take our places at the table.

Captain Hudson has graciously left the place at the head of the table for me. I protest, but he insists that I take it, so I do. Seated around me are Dr. Sebastian, John Higgins, Tilly, with Captain Hudson on my left, and, on my right, Lieutenant James Emerson Fletcher.

There is a glass in front of each of us, and arranged on the table are bottles of good wine and plates of crab cakes and hush puppies—*Thanks, Jemimah.*

I apologize for the cramped quarters, but Captain Hudson recalls that his first command was a sloop of war and that this is quite luxurious in comparison. He then compliments me on the shipshape condition of my ship, which warms me. We toast the King, but before we fall to the main course, we have a Council of War.

"I think Agent Faber should bring us all up to date, as she is the one who has garnered the most information," says Dr. Sebastian. He pops a hush puppy—a fried cornbread biscuit—into his mouth. Joannie and Daniel, dressed in their best, hover about to refill glasses when they are emptied.

I take a sip of my wine and begin. "The good news is that we believe we have found the final resting place of the *Santa Magdalena.* I have seen the tops of her masts. She lies in about one hundred and fifty feet of water, well out of reach of a free dive."

There are murmurs of approval from Captain Hudson and Tilly, but then I say, "As to bad news, I regret to say that our activities here have not gone unnoticed." I look to Dr. Sebastian and he shrugs and nods ruefully. I don't want to insult Captain Hudson, but I must go on. "The conversations we had onboard the *Dolphin* when we were in Boston were overheard by a Spanish sailor who later jumped ship in Savannah and then made his way down to Havana and reported all to the pirate Flaco Jimenez."

Captain Hudson's face darkens, recalling his words that all was secure on his ship, and he asks, "And how do you know this?"

"I am acquainted with Captain Jimenez and met with him at Ric's Café Americano in Havana last week." Jaimy's hand has been on mine, and I feel it tighten. *It's all right, Jaimy, I'll explain.*

"Ummmm . . ." says the Captain.

"And that is not the worst of it, Captain," I say, pushing on. "A Spanish warship, the *San Cristobal,* patrols these waters. She is a First-Rate with three gun decks and eighty-eight guns. An officer aboard her, Lieutenant Juan Carlos Cisneros y Siquieros, is certain that we are up to something. On the *San Cristobal*'s last patrol, she boarded us, and we were searched. Many questions were asked. She is now anchored in Havana Harbor, and I have learned from some Spanish sailors"—I feel another tightening of Jaimy's hand—"that the *San Cristobal* will not sail again for some time. The sailors consider her captain a coward and a wastrel, but still . . . all those guns. And the Spanish sailors I met are proud of their gunnery."

Silence around the table.

I take another sip and continue. "This Lieutenant Cisneros is a cruel man. He debased me upon our first meeting, and . . . and when we were leaving the harbor two days ago, he forced me to stop my ship and made me watch as he had the sailors who had talked to me at Ric's whipped into insensibility. Fifty lashes each. They were all unconscious at the end. And one was no more than a boy."

Silence again.

Then the Captain speaks up. "What shall we do? I'll tell you what. My plan is to charge into Havana and blow that *San Cristobal* into splinters. Then we shall not be bothered. And to hell with some pissant pirate."

Dr. Sebastian nods and says, "I am sure you could accomplish that, Brother, but I believe Mr. Higgins has something to say on that matter."

Higgins then recounts the armaments in the various battlement arrayed about the harbor. "I'm afraid you would not get by Morro Castle before you were sunk. Since we British took the port in 1762, the Spanish have increased the fortifications tenfold."

"What's to be done then?" asks the Captain.

"I say I dive on the wreck, with the *Dolphin* lying nearby to protect us should Flaco or the *San Cristobal* come out to bother us. I think we've got at least a week and a half. With luck we can get the gold up by then and be gone."

Captain Hudson nods and says, "Good. And should that Spanish bastard come out, he'll see what for!"

*Hear, hear!* is the cheer, and dinner is served by Daniel and Joannie—great platters of Florida lobster and deep-fried grouper, a large fish speared by me that very morning, and perfectly fresh I assure Captain Hudson, who had an unfortunate experience with bad fish last year.

When all is eaten and drunk, Captain Hudson prepares to take his party back to the *Dolphin,* and I put my hand on his arm and say, "Could I ask that Mr. Fletcher be allowed to stay here with me this night?"

He looks from Jaimy to me and says, "You both remember your solemn vows in this respect?"

We both nod. "Very well, but just for tonight."

Later, in my cabin, Higgins serves us a late-night apéritif, and Jaimy and I talk far into the night, with much being said, and then we undress and go to bed. I think of our hammock back on the *Dolphin* as I lay my head on Jaimy's chest and slip off into blissful sleep.

*Tomorrow I will dive into the depths in that horrid bell, but tonight I am supremely happy.*

# Chapter 30

I wake before Jaimy does, take a deep breath, then bury my face in his hair spread out on the pillow. *Ahhhh . . . how fine is this . . .* He lies on his back so that his face is in profile, and for a while, I revel in just looking at him. His lips are slightly parted in sleep and I rise up and gently kiss them. He stirs a bit, but stays asleep. With my fingertip I trace from his forehead down over his nose and then to those lips and then to his chin and along his throat and then down onto his chest. *He is just the most beautiful boy.*

I run my hand across his chest, but he still does not awaken, so I stick my tongue in his ear. *That* pops those lovely eyes wide open.

His senses return to him as he turns his head and smiles upon me.

"I cannot believe that I am really here," he says.

"Me either." I snuggle in a little closer.

"The last time we woke up in the morning together was back in our hammock on the *Dolphin.* Do you remember?"

"Of course, I do. It was right after we ran the ship aground on that island. I have thought about that time every day since with great yearning . . . longing that we should be that way again. And here we are, love."

"Yes, indeed, we are, and I am glad."

Jaimy puts his arm around me and I lay my head on his shoulder and bury my nose in the tousled black hair behind his ear.

After a few more delicious moments, I rise up on an elbow and run my fingers through that thick dark hair. Well, almost all dark—there is now a streak that runs through it, and I know it comes from the head wound he suffered last year during a battle with a French squadron in the Mediterranean. The hair above the scar has grown in pure white.

"Your slash of silver hair looks quite dashing, Jaimy. It matches my eyebrow."

"Well, since I have no choice, I shall wear it. Now lie you back down."

I lay my head back down again and press myself against him. "Pet me, Jaimy."

And he does, and I purr . . . *Ummmmm* . . .

*Ding, ding . . . Ding, ding . . . Ding . . .* The quarterdeck bell is tolling Six Bells in the Morning Watch, telling us that it is six thirty and breakfast is about to be served.

"We must get up soon, Jaimy."

"I want to lie here next to you forever."

"Me, too, but duty calls. If I know the Royal Navy, the *Dolphin* will be alongside within the hour, ready to start the day's work. So you must get up and go off, dear, for I have to get dressed and make myself presentable, which is something, believe me, that you do not want to witness."

He plants a kiss at the base of my throat, then rolls out of bed and begins pulling on his clothes. I cannot help but watch and admire the breadth of his shoulders, the narrowness of his hips, the length of his legs. Oh, yes.

"Please come back at Seven Bells, Jaimy. I've arranged for us to have a private breakfast."

After he is dressed once again in his trousers and shirt, he reaches for his uniform jacket, but I say, "Don't bother with that, Jaimy, not just yet. It's too warm. We don't stand on ceremony here." He nods, throws the coat over the back of a chair, then comes back to stand next to me. He strips off the sheet that covers me, leans down to place a kiss on my tattoo, and says, "The Dread Brotherhood of the *Dolphin* forever!" He then tousles my hair and strides out the door.

*Hear, hear.*

I get up, go to my washstand, do the necessaries, wash parts, dry myself, and dress. I just throw on one of my simple dresses, 'cause I figure I'll be in my swimsuit before noon.

As I am pulling the frock over my head, there is a knock on the door, and after I say, "Come in," Joannie enters, bearing a tray with silverware, two cups, and a steaming pot of coffee. She also wears a huge smirk on her face.

"What's with the look?" I ask, thinking perhaps that Jemimah has been regaling the kids with another Rabbit Tale. But, no, that is not it.

She glances over at the rumpled bed and giggles.

*Hmmmm . . .*

"Never mind that, you," I say, sternly, "just set the table. Keep your mind on your job and out of other people's business, you hear?"

Just then Jaimy comes back to my cabin, looking grand in his tight pants, boots, and open white shirt.

Joannie looks at him and turns bright red, snorting with the effort to keep from laughing out loud with delight. She manages to get the small table set and then leaves.

*I shall have to talk to that girl . . . Grrrrr . . .*

Jaimy seats himself, and I get up to pour him a cup. I am not used to doing this sort of thing, but I know it is expected, so I do it.

"Who is the girl?" asks Jaimy, plopping a few lumps of sugar into his coffee.

"Her name is Joan Nichols, and she is my . . . responsibility. And if she thinks she is too big to be spanked, she is sadly mistaken."

Jaimy laughs. "You always did want things your own way, didn't you? I certainly recall your bullying the rest of us into submission on the *Dolphin.*"

"Well, all of you were certainly in need of correction, that's for sure," I answer primly. "And I think you all were the better for it, so there."

There is a discreet knock, so I know it is not Joannie. The door opens and Higgins enters, bearing yet another tray.

"Good morning, Miss . . . Lieutenant Fletcher . . . I hope you slept well."

"Yes, we did, Higgins, and thank you," say I, seating myself at the table. Higgins does not have to do this, as he is the Chief Executive Officer of Faber Shipping Worldwide, but still I appreciate it.

He removes the covers of the dishes, revealing eggs with bright yellow yolks, bacon, sausage, fried potatoes, and buttered toast, and we fall to as Higgins takes his leave.

"This is really quite good, Jacky."

"Yes, Jemimah is a fine cook."

"Is she your slave?"

"No, she is not. Like everyone else of my crew, she is an employee of Faber Shipping and shares in all of our profits. When we have any."

"It was good seeing Davy and Tink again. Hard to believe so many of us are once again on the same ship. We lack only Benjy and Willie."

I imagine that all was easy between the lads when Jaimy appeared on deck this morning. I suspect there was a lot of male braying and punching and back thumping—anything to conceal the real affection between them. 'Course, as soon as the *Dolphin* gets here, his uniform jacket goes back on, and then it'll be *Mr.* Fletcher again and not their old mate Jaimy. That is exactly why I had asked him to leave it off, at least for now.

"We shall forever lack Benjy, at least till we go to our reward, but Willie we may someday see."

"And here you are with your own ship," he says, looking around at my neat little cabin. "Just like you always wanted."

"And there you are, a fine young Lieutenant in the Royal Navy. Something you always wanted."

"I have, however, not gotten everything I wanted, though." He looks at me with real heat in his gaze.

"Me either, Jaimy. Not yet, I haven't." I put down my fork and put my hand on his. "But we must be patient and hope for the future."

He nods. "I worry about that diving bell, though. It has to be dangerous."

*I worry about it, too,* I want to say, but I don't. There's no sense upsetting the boy any more than he is. "Tilly says we'll take it easy at first. I'll go down only five or ten fathoms," is what I do say. "You'll be standing by. You'll see. It'll be all right."

Again he nods, but he appears unconvinced. I try another tack.

"You should come down with me. Oh, just for a shallow dive. Tink is very good at making the goggles, and he could fit you with a pair. You'll find it is very beautiful down there, with fishes like little jewels, forests of waving ferns, sunlight streaming down. What do you say? It'd be fun."

His fork stops on the way to his mouth. It is plain that he would not find it fun at all. I have found that sailors would much rather be on top of the water than under it. And while I know that Jaimy would die for me—he has already proven that—he is more than a little afraid to dive down deep.

"Um . . . yes . . . ahem. Well, we shall see."

*Poor Jaimy. I'll let you off the hook.* "Well, perhaps we won't have the time."

His fork stays suspended in midair. "And speaking of swimming . . . that . . . costume . . . you were wearing yesterday . . ."

"My swimming suit, you mean?"

"Yes," he says, reddening. "You have to wear that?"

"Yes, dear, I must." I put my hand on his, give him the big eyes, and recount for him the moray eel incident.

"Um."

"Don't worry, dear, my crew is well used to my eccentric ways."

"Yes, but the crew of the *Dolphin* is not."

*No, but they will be soon, count on it.*

"Please, Jaimy, I really don't mind."

"I believe I shall be confiscating telescopes," he says, cracking a slight smile.

I smile back at him, pat his hand, and go back to my breakfast.

"I think you ought to suggest to the Captain that a lifeboat be stationed several miles to the east, between here and Havana, in case the *San Cristobal* does come out. Then we would not be surprised and could get in fighting trim before she came upon us. We'd get the weather gauge and sail up wind of him and all."

"Um. Yes. Good idea."

I spear another fat sausage, and as I chew it, I ruminate. "Maybe the fact that you are out here will keep him in port, which would be good."

"How's that?"

"He might be afraid to come out. And believe me, he will know very shortly that the *Dolphin* is on station here." Many small fishing boats have gone past us on the way to Cuba, and they will tell of a British ship lying not far offshore.

"Hmmm . . . I'm afraid Captain Hudson may send in a personal challenge."

"That would not be a wise thing to do. The *San Cristobal* is not the only Spanish warship in Havana Harbor. Captain Morello could bring out a fleet."

Finally, we finish up, pat our lips with our napkins— fine white ones with Faber Shipping's blue anchor logo stitched in the corner—and lean back to enjoy a second cup of coffee, and each other's dear company.

But such is not to be.

There is a knock on the door, and Jim Tanner's voice calls out, "The *Dolphin* is coming alongside, Missy."

I rise and take Jaimy's jacket and hold it open for him. "Come, love, you must dress, and then so must I."

He dons the coat, which I button up for him and smooth over his chest with my fingertips, and then I hold my face up to his.

"Now give your salty sea sailor lass a kiss, Jaimy, then off with you. It is time for each of us to turn out and tend to our duties."

# Chapter 31

After I have put on my swimming suit and strapped my shiv to my calf, I pick up my goggles and head out onto the deck. I have a towel thrown over my shoulder, but I do not wrap it around me. They are just going to have to get used to it.

The raft is tied to the starboard side of the *Nancy B.*, and the *Dolphin* looms over our port side. The great metal diving bell squats on the bigger ship's main hatch top and preparations are being made to hoist it up and swing it over to our deck.

I go to the raft, where I see that Joannie is already suited up and on it.

"Jacky! Look!" she cries, holding something up. "Tink has made these swim-finny things for us! Come on, let's try them out!"

Tossing my towel and goggles down to her, I step up on the *Nancy B.*'s starboard rail and get ready to dive off.

Once again I reach back with my forefingers to pull the back of my traitorous suit down over my cheeks—I've got to get that fixed—and lift my arms over my head.

*"Eyes on your job, you dogs!"* shouts someone on the *Dolphin,* someone who might well be Jaimy, *"or your backs will pay, by God!"*

I dive, and hit the water cleanly, swim a few strokes underwater, and then surface next to the raft and clamber on. I am now out of sight of those on the *Dolphin,* except for anyone who might be in the top rigging, above the Royal spars. The Top, however, does seem to be unusually well staffed today.

Am I showing off? Of course I am. It's in my nature, and besides, this is my ship, so I'll act as I please.

"Here, Jacky, look how cunning these are made," says Joannie. "Here's how they fit on."

The fins are each made of a wood shingle to which is attached a leather saddlelike thing that your foot fits in, with a strap across the instep to hold everything snug. Out by the toes, the thin end of the shingle has three very whippy pieces of leather affixed. I wave one of the shoelike things around in the air. It sure looks like a fish's fin.

*Yes! Let's try 'em!*

I lift my knees to my chest and strap on the fins. Joannie already has hers on.

We adjust our goggles, and I say *"Let's go!"* and we both roll over the side of the raft and into the water.

It takes a little getting used to, but as soon as we learn to wiggle our legs just right, we swim at least twice as fast through the water as we could before. We gambol about down there within the space of our two chestfuls of air and then joyously burst through the surface, side by side, rejoicing in our new agility.

"We have become true mermaids, Sister!" I exult,

clasping her slippery form to me, and we both laugh and sing out our joy.

But then we stop, for over us falls a shadow. The bell has been hoisted and it is now right above us.

"It's too heavy for the raft!" I shout. "Put it on the deck!"

John Thomas and Finn McGee put their shoulders to the capstan wheel, winch the bell higher, and swing it back over the deck. Then they throw the ratchet bar and winch it down till it rests on the deck.

I jump out of the water and crawl over the rail, to stand next to the thing. I see that there have been some changes made in it. When I had last seen it, the lead weights keeping the bell upright and the air trapped within had been held by short lengths of chain. Now they are at the ends of six stiff legs, four feet in length. Plenty of room for the diver to get out beneath . . . I hope.

I nip underneath and see the same thick wood bench for the diver to sit on . . . and there are small viewing windows at either end of the bench. Some iron handles have been added to the inside, should things start to get rough, though I really don't know what help they would be if this thing were to tip over at two hundred feet below.

I duck my head and come back out and find Professor Tilden rubbing his hands in anticipation of a test dive of his wonderful diving bell.

"My dear, this is going to be such a marvelous thing!"

I stand there, the water still streaming off me, and say, "I hope so, Professor. The bottom is flat and sandy and only sixty feet below. It should be a good place to test this thing."

"Oh, yes, oh, yes!" he exclaims. "Let us get on with it!"

Tilly is a dear man, but sometimes I wish he did not treat me as one of his laboratory rats.

He contains himself and says, "Now, dear, there are several things to remember. There will be an assortment of ropes inside the bell connected to those of us above by a system of pulleys—two tugs on the rope that ends with one monkey-fist knot means come down gradually till you tug again. There will also be a rope ending in two monkey-fist knots." I can see the various ropes laid out next to the bell. "One sharp pull signals stop, two tugs on that means come up slowly till you tug again. Four tugs means bring it up all the way. The rope with three knots will have a net bag at the end of it to bring up whatever you find. Do you understand?"

I nod and ready myself to get in. I put my goggles on my forehead. I still have my feet fins on and feel that I must look like the perfect frog.

"And one other thing," continues Tilly. "If you go down in the bell, you must come up in the bell."

"All right," I say, "but why?"

"There are scientific considerations," Tilly says, then sniffs. "Never you mind. Just remember."

There are some thumps on the deck, and I see that both Captain Hudson and Jaimy have joined us, as well as Dr. Sebastian. Jaimy looks worried and Dr. Sebastian glances over dubiously at Professor Tilden, I believe for the first time questioning his scientific credentials.

"All right, in you go, Jacky," says Tilly. "Let us go for twenty minutes on the first descent, shall we."

Dr. Sebastian looks pained. "Perhaps, Professor, we

should start with ten minutes. After all, we do not know how long the air trapped in the bell will last her. In addition, she will be going through extreme exertions in swimming in and out of the device, and in the process using up a lot of oxygen. Hmmm . . . ?"

"Very well," says Tilly, slightly miffed. "Ten minutes it is. Are you ready, girl?"

"Yes," I say, and instead of giving Jaimy the big-eyed worried look that I want to give, I toss him a wink and a carefree grin, and duck under the lower edge of the bell.

Inside, I climb up the ladder attached to the inside and seat myself on the bench and wait.

Soon I feel a jerk as the winch engages, and I feel myself and the bell lifted. Looking down, I see the deck fall away, then I see the *Nancy B.*'s rail go by, and then, under me, there is nothing but water. I hear the ratchet thrown again as the winch turns in the other direction and the water comes up toward me.

When the lower edge of the bell breaks through the surface, the water beneath my feet immediately flattens out and it is like looking down through a big version of our glass-bottomed buckets. I can see perfectly, all the way to the bottom, which is good, as I'll be able to see what I'm coming down on. It looks like a clear stretch of sand below, which is also good. There'll be no stand of coral to catch one leg of the bell and tip it over and me out.

There is a good deal of light coming in through the viewing windows and the open bottom, so I check out the knotted ropes hanging next to me. All seems in order. I peek out the windows, but all I see is blueness there, for the real show is below. A large skate flies lazily across my field of vision, as I am down far enough now to make out smaller fishes grazing amongst patches of seaweed.

The surface of the water has come up some and my ears are starting to hurt, both caused, as I was told by Tilly, by the compression of the air inside the bell. As instructed, I swallow a few times and hold my nose shut and blow, and I hear a little *pop . . . fizzz* and the ears don't hurt anymore. Good.

I'm about twenty feet from the bottom and decide to test the rope signals. I reach out to give a yank to the line knotted with the two monkey fists, which goes through a pulley above me and then snakes down and out the bottom of the bell. It stops its descent.

*Well, good. At least that works. Let's see if this does.*

I bring my goggles down over my eyes, make them snug, take three deep breaths, hold the last, slide my bottom off the bench, and plunge feet-first into the water below me.

I take a moment to get my bearings, then with a flick of my feet fins, I glide out from under the bell.

*This is really not so bad, not so bad at all.* I'm down forty feet, and I didn't have to swim for it; all I had to do was sit there and then pop out from under. *Pretty neat.*

I twist and look up to the surface shining above me. The dark hulls of the *Nancy B.* and the *Dolphin* loom above, with their anchor lines trailing down—there's the *Dolphin*'s big hook right over there, half buried in the sand and holding well. That is good, for I don't want my bell dragged all over the bottom of the sea.

I see also the raft at the *Nancy B.*'s side, and what appear to be two people leaning over the side and peering down through the glass-bottomed buckets. There is also a white-suited form, which I know to be Joannie, floating out to the side. I wave to all, and Joannie waves back as I head under the bell to resurface inside. Then it's up the ladder and back on the bench to give the one-knotted rope two quick tugs.

The bell starts down again, and this time I let it go all the way to the bottom. Twenty more feet and it comes to rest on the sand, almost level.

Once again I drop down off of the bench, this time to stand with my feet on the sandy bottom. *Amazing,* I think, *I'm standing on the bottom of the sea, the water to my chest, but with my head in the air. What a brave new world this is, indeed.*

Another big gulp of breath, then I duck under, between the legs of the bell, and come up outside. This time, being on the bottom, I take up the green net bag and hunt for sponges and specimens—hey, the ever practical Jacky Faber. Waste not, want not.

Some things try to scurry away from me, but they don't quite make it, so they get stuffed into the bag. When all of the other creatures of the bottom have safely fled from my grasp, I jerk the three-knotted rope twice, and the bag with its contents flies up out of sight. I hope Dr. Sebastian will be pleased.

A final scan of this piece of the bottom yields nothing else, so it's back under and into the bell, as I think the ten minutes are about up.

Sure enough, as soon as I am seated on the bench and

pull on the proper rope, I feel myself and the bell being hauled slowly to the surface.

There will be more test dives done today, I know, but tomorrow the Belle of the Caribbean Sea will dive on the wreck of the *Santa Magdalena,* and then we shall see what we shall see.

# Chapter 32

Yesterday, after that first descent, when the bell was brought up and put back on my deck and I had crawled out from under it, a great cheer went up from the men on both ships. It surprised me, but hey, I like attention, so I took a little bow. Then we got back to work.

We ungrappled the two ships and moved the *Nancy B.* a few hundred yards farther out and reanchored, this time with four hooks to hold us steady in the wind, current, and tide.

The next dive was a little deeper, and this time I took a very excited Joannie with me, partly because she wanted to so much, and partly because we wanted to see how the air in the bell would hold up with two people in it. We harvested some sponges, and caught two lobsters, which we presented to Captain Hudson for his dinner—we're somewhat sick of lobster, ourselves. The third time that we ducked back into the bell, we found that the air within was becoming somewhat stuffy, so I yanked on the rope with the one big knot and up we went.

I reported on the lack of decent air to Tilly and Dr. Sebastian, and they decided that only one person (me) should go down for longer periods at great depths.

On the last dive before lunch, we swung the bell to the other, seaward side of the ship, and this time I went down a good hundred feet and all went well. I didn't take any specimens this time, instead just making sure that I could get about easily at this new depth—and it turned out that I could.

When I stepped out on the deck again, water streaming off me, Higgins was waiting with a big towel.

"We must get us one of these, Higgins!" I exclaimed. "Can you imagine the salvage possibilities? Why in Boston Harbor alone—"

"Yes, Miss, perhaps we shall recover the tea from the great Boston Tea Party. But for now, let us get you into something dry," replied Higgins as he hustled me into my cabin.

I reflected that it had been a most wondrous morning.

That afternoon, we took the *Nancy B.* in closer to land, where the water depth was only about thirty feet, and found a spot between two big coral heads where we could lower the marvelous bell between them and take our people down on excursions to see the beauty of the undersea world—any of them brave enough to go, that is.

It was a rare day for this sort of thing, and all who went down gasped in wonder at the beauty below. There was not a cloud in the sky, and the sun was almost directly overhead, sending shafts of light streaming through the clear, blue-green water and lighting the multicolored coral and its attendant plants most beautifully.

I went down with each to calm their nerves with my chatter, and when we reached the bottom, I slipped outside to swim about, to show them how easy it was—yes, and maybe to show off a bit. Perhaps I didn't have to do the somersaults . . . oh, well . . .

Dr. Sebastian was the first to go down. "I cannot believe this!" said the good Doctor, entranced by the bright little fish who swam up to his window to peer in. "We must have a drawing of this entire expedition for presentation to the Academy! Oh, what a sensation it will be!"

Later Tink and Davy went down, each having dared the other so they both had to do it. When I was down with Davy, I made sure to swim outside the window, stick my thumbs in my ears, wiggle my fingers, and make faces at him. Tink, charmed by it all, declared his intention of making fins and goggles for himself.

Then I let Joannie take Daniel down, but kept a good eye on the proceedings below. When they reached the bottom, Joannie came out and cavorted about as much as I had; but then, instead of going back under, she wiggled her feet fins and shot straight to the surface, to play a bit of a trick on Daniel, I suppose.

The trick turned out to be on her, however. As soon as her head broke the surface, Tilly was leaning over the rail, pointing his finger at her face.

"If you go *down* in the bell, girl, you must come *up* in the bell!" he roared.

Joannie looked at me, mystified. *Haven't we free-dived to that shallow depth a hundred times already?* she seemed to ask.

I shrugged and pointed down. If Tilly doesn't see fit to explain, well, so be it.

She flipped over, stuck her little rump in the air, wiggled back down to the bell, and got in, and we hauled it up. She emerged very abashed, poor thing. Nobody likes to be yelled at, especially my crew, who ain't used to it.

I then took Jim Tanner down. When we came back up, Captain Hudson was standing on our deck, his shirt off and with a big grin on his face.

"Take me down, Miss," he ordered. "And let's see what the fuss is all about."

We did it and he was suitably impressed. I pointed out many things of interest and then slipped out to do my underwater ballet act.

"You really are a piece of work, Jacky Faber," said Captain Hudson, on our way back up, looking as much at me as at the panorama of nature outside. *Hmmmm.*

Yes, many took the little trip down that day—including the Brotherhood, except for Jaimy. He did not. He just went a little pale when I held out my hand to him and shook his head. I regret the offering, because he was so plainly distressed, and I shan't do it again.

*Too bad, Jaimy. We could have had a little bit of naughty fun down there.*

# Chapter 33

Having once again taken our bearings on the western tip of Key West, and on the red rag still hanging in the mangrove bush that marks the old Indian campground and alligator pit, we maneuver the *Nancy B.* into position, fish out our marker buoy, and I get ready to dive.

We figured the first time we'd dive on the *Magdalena* would be to the depth I had previously gone when I first spotted her—about a hundred and fifty feet, I reckon. Tink measures out that distance on the bell's winch line and attaches a marker.

"Ready to go, Jacky."

I put my goggles on my forehead and prepare to duck under.

"Be careful, Miss," warns Dr. Sebastian. "This is the farthest you've gone down in the bell, so far." Professor Tilly and Captain Hudson are also in attendance.

"As far down as the *Dolphin* is high," mutters Jaimy, who also stands by, looking into the mainmast rigging of the *Dolphin* and imagining the depth to which I will go. He looks rather sickish.

I put my hand on his arm and look up into his eyes. "Don't worry, Jaimy. It's just a lot of water, and you must admit I have a way of always bobbing back up." Big grin and big eyes. "You'll see, we'll have dinner together tonight and everything will be fine."

"Nothing to it, eh, what?" That's from Lieutenant Flashby, who has graced us with his presence on my deck today, there being no danger of his being invited to go below. He swaggers about in full uniform, tapping the bell with his knuckles and pronouncing it a fine thing. I suspect he is here because he thinks the gold might be brought up soon. And maybe because he likes looking at me in my diving gear. I do not mind the others looking at me, but I do mind it when he looks at me, because he makes it very plain what he is thinking. Which to me, ain't a pretty sight . . . or a pretty thought.

"All right, let's do it," I say, as I duck under the bell and climb onto the bench. In a moment John Thomas and Finn McGee begin to turn the capstan and I am lifted up and swung over the side. Then once again I see the waves of the water beneath me flatten out as the bell heads down.

And down and down and down . . . The surface of the water within the bell inches higher with each fathom lower—soon it almost touches the tips of my swim fins. The air in the bell is getting mightily compressed; I can tell, 'cause I keep having to swallow to clear my ears.

Finally the bell stops, and I hang there for a while, looking down. It's like looking into the depths of an emerald . . . No, more blue than that . . . More like a sapphire, actually . . . But I see no sign of the *Magdalena*.

*Ah, well, best get out and have a bit of a look around.*

I adjust my goggles and slip out the bottom, curious to see if this greater depth has any effect on me.

I swim out, and it seems that everything is as it was before—'cept that when I turn around to look up, the hulls of the *Nancy B.* and the much bigger *Dolphin* look really tiny way up there.

Twisting around again, I peer into the azure watery mist all around me. I head off in a direction to the east and find nothing, except to note that the ocean bottom slopes off sharply, into the lower depths. There are sparse stands of coral down here, and various large rays and fishes. And, yes, sharks drift by—but they pay me no mind—and so I search on.

I pop back into the bell, rest for a moment, take a breath, and then head out in the other direction. This bottom, too, has outcroppings of coral, and there seem to be rocky ledges with caves and crevices carved into them—better watch out for the big eels if I venture close to that . . . and . . .

. . . *and there she is, once again!*

My greedy heart beats ever faster. *There she is!*

I float over the *Santa Magdalena,* her spectral masts and spars to either side of me, her hull lying spread out below. I want to go to her now, but no, I must be deeper before I do that.

I fly back to the bell, slide inside, take a big breath, and pull the rope. I am drawn up slowly, too slowly by my way of thinkin'.

When at last I am brought back onboard, I spill out of

the bottom of the bell and say, "We are on her. We've got to move a hundred yards in that direction. Get out as many anchors as you can to hold us steady. Tink, I'll go another fifty feet down." I take off my goggles and lay them aside. "And this time I shall lay my hand upon her."

I know it will take some time to affect this change of position, so I grab Jaimy's wrist and head for my cabin for a bit of . . . well . . . rest . . . when I hear the call from Daniel, high in our crow's-nest.

"Missy! Sail off to the south! She flies the red colors!"

Jim Tanner slaps my long glass into my hand as I run by him, put my feet on the rail, and jump over onto the *Dolphin*, then run up the ratlines to the foretop, where I train the glass on the intruder. I feel a presence behind me and then two hands on my waist.

"What is he?" asks Jaimy.

I continue to squint at the ship that seems intent at lying just out of cannon range. From the mainmast flies a very familiar flag—a red-horned skull on a field of black, with two crossed cannons below. *Flaco, you dog, we meet on the sea once again.* I smile and bring down the glass.

"It is only Flaco Jimenez. Don't worry, he won't close with us," I call down to those below. "The *Dolphin* is just too formidable." I turn to Jaimy. "Plus, we are friends, sort of."

"We are?" asks Jaimy, looking off into the rigging. I give him a poke in the ribs.

"Come on, Jaimy, be happy. Look where we are—on the foretop of the dear old *Dolphin*, where first we started out as kids. No one can see us, so give me a kiss."

I throw my arms around his neck and present my face, lips pursed, and he obliges me . . . *oh, yes!* A kiss *and* a pet.

"Missy! What to do?" comes the call from Jim Tanner below.

I break away from Jaimy and lean over the edge of the foretop and say, "It's nothing, Jim. Prepare for the next dive. I'll be down in a minute."

I turn back to Jaimy, determined to enjoy this little bit of time, but then I see something on the foremast that brings tears to my eyes. Carved in the thick wood is **JF+JF** with a circle about the initials.

I run my fingers over the rough letters and say, "Oh, Jaimy, that is so sweet."

He reddens and looks away. "I . . . I carved it on the day we left you in that school in Boston . . . I . . . I . . ."

"I know, Jaimy. I was at a window and watched you sail away, and it was all so sad. I just could not hold back the tears. I could hardly stand it."

He nods and says nothing.

"But no sadness, Jaimy. Let us just live in the moment. Now give me another kiss . . . That's it . . . Oh, so good, Jaimy . . ."

"Miss Faber?" calls Dr. Sebastian from the main deck, and I know I must go.

"Later, Jaimy," I say, pulling away from him and giving him a peck on the cheek. He sighs and lets his hand fall from the small of my back, where it had been resting, and I put my own hand on the ratlines. "I've got to go under again."

And I swing back down to the deck, pick up my goggles, and get back in the bell.

"Let's go."

. . .

This time the bell comes down to rest well below the tops of the masts of the *Santa Magdalena,* and I get myself ready to go out for a look. I had kept my hand on the panic rope the whole way down in case the bell got hung up on one of the wreck's masts, but I ended up about ten yards to the left of the hull and only about fifteen feet higher than the deck, with plenty of room for the bell to swing around. *Perfect.*

I slip out and swim over to the *Santa Magdalena* and lay my hand upon her, the first living hand to touch her in over seventy years. I give a thought to the lost Spanish sailors—whether seamen be enemy or friend, English, Spanish, American, or French, all sailors die the same hard death when a ship goes down.

Proper reverence being paid, I then kick and glide over the main hatch to the foot of the mainmast. All the rope rigging, except for a few threads hanging here and there, is long gone. But there is something large and covered with silt attached to the foot of the mast, and I think I know what it is. I take my hand to brush off the sea dust and find myself staring into the face of Jesus.

Yes, it is the golden crucifix that all Spanish warships carry fixed to their main! And this one is a good five feet high.

Back to the bell for a breath and then out for a check of the *Magdalena*'s hull. It is generally intact, which is not all to the good, since it doesn't give me a way in. Well, I guess I shouldn't expect the gold cargo to be just lying there waiting for me to pick it up.

Another wiggle of my swimming fins as I scan the various hatchways that lead down into the ship. All the hatchway covers are off, their hinges having rotted away long ago. I go to peer into one, but all is darkness in there, and I cannot go in. Prolly monsters in there, too. Not only would I not be able to see, but the deck could fall in, trapping me beyond all hope of rescue, and I've no wish to lie down here in the deep alongside these unfortunate Spanish sailors for all eternity. While I am sure they would be good company, I have other things to do.

I pull my shiv from its sheath and poke about the wreck's wood in various places. It generally goes in easily, right to the hilt. Sheathing the knife, I go back to the bell, yank the rope, and we start our slow ascent. As I go up, I think on the problem of just how to retrieve that gold.

Eight Bells rings out just as I step on deck. *Good. I'm getting hungry.* "Captain Hudson, Lieutenant Fletcher, will you join us for lunch on my mess deck?" I ask as I towel off. "As you know, we do not stand on ceremony and we all eat at the same table, but, I'll wager our cook is better than yours."

"By God, I accept," says Captain Hudson. "Lead on!"

"Dr. Sebastian, if you will show the gentlemen to their places while I change? Thank you, Sir. Joannie, run down and tell Jemimah that two more will be joining us. Higgins, some of our better wine, perhaps?"

I leave Flashby to find his own lunch back on the *Dolphin,* while I pop down into my cabin to shed my swimsuit and toss on a light cotton dress. I'll be damned if I'll feed that man.

Entering the mess deck, I see that all are standing by

their chairs, even my own uncouth *Nancy* boys. I go to my place at the head of the table—and thank you, Captain Hudson, for again being gracious about that—raise the glass that has been placed there for me, and say, "Gentlemen . . . to our mutual enterprise."

*Hear, hear!* is heard and all sit down.

I place my now-dry, cotton-clad bottom in my chair as Joannie places my plate in its slot in front of me and I fall to. Nothing like a morning spent two hundred feet beneath the sea to whet the appetite, I say. Today Jemimah has prepared *arroz con pollo,* with side dishes of conch chowder and a corn pudding. It is all wondrous good.

For a while, all that is heard is the crunching of bones, the slurping of wine, and the smacking of lips. "My word, this is uncommon good!" the Captain cries, and looks over covetously at Jemimah, who stands at her station down in front of the stove.

A little later, as all of the food has been served, Jemimah herself eases into her chair at the foot of the table, and as has been our custom, Joannie and Daniel place her dish and cup in front of her, and she eats.

I cut a sly look at Captain Hudson, absolutely sure that he has never sat at a table with a black person before. To his credit, he merely smiles and says nothing.

I, however, do lean back and say something.

"I have placed my hand on the *Santa Magdalena* today, but I cannot get inside her." I tell them of my explorations. "Does anyone have any ideas?"

Silence.

"We could place a charge," says Tink, far down on the table.

"Hmm," says Dr. Sebastian. "There is a problem with that—how to keep the fuse dry on the way down."

"And we could just blow everything all over the place and then not find anything," I answer.

"There's no way to rig an underwater lantern so she could see her way into the hull?" asks Tilly.

"No, there is not."

"You said the wood was soft, Jacky," says Davy. "Perhaps we could go at her that way."

"Yes," I say, grasping on to the thread of his idea. "Maybe we can peel her like an orange."

"Hmmm . . ." muses Captain Hudson. "Yes. We could rig up a grappling hook on a very stout line, then lower it down, and our intrepid mermaid here could attach the hook to various parts of the wreck and we could take a strain on the rope and pull the sunken ship apart—exposing its innards, as it were."

"And the very much stronger capstan on the *Dolphin* will serve much better than our puny winch," says Davy, and all concur. I think Davy secretly enjoys having a familiar conversation with a Post Captain of His Majesty's Royal Navy.

*Careful, Davy, remember you are still a member of that service.*

"What about that pirate Jimenez hanging about?" says Jaimy.

"Ah, well, he already knows what we are up to, so no sense in hiding," I say. "But if we ever start bringing up anything of value, we might try to keep that out of his sight."

Agreement all around.

And so it is decided. That is what we shall do. Of course, I had already come up with this idea, on the way up in the bell's last dive, but sometimes it's best that you let the males think it was their plan from the start. It's easier that way.

Back into my clammy swimsuit—note to self: Get another one of these made, and one that doesn't crawl up the crack of my bum—then it's back on deck and into the bell. Before I duck under, I notice a coil of thick rope on the *Dolphin*'s deck, rope that ends in a three-pronged grappling hook. All right, down we go again.

Reaching the bottom, I see the grappling hook has come down with me, lying off to the left, waiting. Well, it will not have to wait long, for I know exactly what I am going to do—which is to give those above a taste of gold.

I slip out of the bell and take the grappling rope in hand. There is not enough slack in it for my purpose, so I give it a sharp tug and more line comes slowly tumbling down. I pick up the grappling hook and clasp it to my chest, to head off for the mainmast. The hook does not weigh nearly as much down here as it does in the air, which is good, else I would not be able to do this.

Back to the bell for a breath—'cause this is hard work—then it's back out again. This time I take up the hook and wrap the line three or four times around the base of the mast—*sorry, Jesus*—and then fasten the hook to its own lead line. There. All secure. Let's go up.

When the bell breaks the surface, I am out in an instant and over to the deck of the *Dolphin*. There are twelve men standing at their posts around the capstan wheel, each with a thick wooden spar in their hand, which is inserted into a slot on the head of the capstan winch. This capstan is capable of lifting a very stubborn five-hundred-pound anchor off the bottom of the sea; let's see what it can do here.

"All right, lads, put your backs to it!"

And they do, trudging around in a circle till the slack is taken up, and then they are brought to a stop.

Grunting, they put more force into it, but the capstan still does not turn.

I run over and get next to a likely cove and lend my puny strength to his, and I lift my voice.

> *As I was a-goin' round Cape Horn,*
> *GO DOWN, you blood-red roses, GO DOWN!*
> *I wished to the Lord, I'd never been born!*
> *GO DOWN, you blood-red roses, GO DOWN!*

It's an old capstan chantey, designed to make the grueling work of lifting anchors and raising heavy sails go easier, and the men immediately take it up, coming down hard on the *GO DOWN!* parts with both voice and muscles.

> *Oh, you pinks and posies,*
> *GO DOWN, you blood-red roses, GO DOWN!*

I push hard on the oaken bar, next to the rough seaman, who I am sure will recount this to his children should he survive to have any. "Push, Jacky," he says, then laughs, and we push with all our might. *Push!*

*Just one more pull and that'll do, boys,*
*GO DOWN, you blood-red roses, GO DOWN!*
*And we're just the boys to pull her through!*
*GO DOWN, you blood-red roses, GO DOWN!*

I lean on the damned stick, pushing with all my might, and then, suddenly, I feel it let go. There is a shout from the sailors on the wheel as they run around the capstan. I let go and run to the side.

The taut line comes streaming out of the water, all eyes fastened upon it, fathom after fathom, and then, suddenly, the mainmast of the *Santa Magdalena* comes breaking through the surface, and there, with the silt of the sea washed off . . . is Jesus, glowing in agony on the cross. A roar goes out from all of the throats on both the ships.

*Gold!*

# Chapter 34

After the joy of seeing the golden crucifix come up into the air, we settle into the serious business of salvage. I go back down and so does the grappling hook.

I swim over to the *Santa Magdalena* and ask for forgiveness for the ripping out of her mainmast, which left a gaping hole in her deck but still gives no access to her lower spaces. None that I could use, anyway. However, I do see where I must hook the grapples for the next pull—the edge of the main cargo hatch—and it is there that I attach it. Giving the hook line several jerks, I dart back out of the way as the slack is taken up and the hook takes hold.

I get back into the bell and watch from a window. The grappling rope quivers with the tension of the pull, but finally the hatch top lifts and falls over the side of the ship, neatly out of the way.

Big breath, slip out, and swim over the now-open hatch.

*That's more like it.*

The *Magdalena*'s gun deck lies beneath me. Plainly, it was the officers' mess. There is a long table, over on its side, and ghostly chairs scattered about. *My poor* Emerald *must look a lot like this, lying as she does on the bottom of the Atlantic,* I think sadly. But enough of that—*push on, girl.*

There are the butt ends of the big cannons and more hatchways leading down into darkness. *Hmmmmm . . .* That would be the Captain's cabin right there. It makes sense that he would keep his precious cargo near him and all in one place, so it could be easily guarded against pilferage. It would be a powerful temptation, as I imagine the common Spanish seaman is no better paid than ours.

Let's see what that holds. I put the hook to the upper edge of the Captain's hatchway and give the signal. The boys upstairs do their work and the whole front of the cabin comes off, as well as the roof. The rotten wood hangs in the hooks for a moment and then falls apart.

Back for a breath to let the dust settle and then back to the Captain's cabin. There is a table, chairs, a bed with the springs rotted out, crumbling shelves, spilled plates. I pick one up and look at it—it is gold but it is not the treasure.

I return to the bell and give the return rope a tug and settle in—got to go back up to get some more fresh air. What a bother . . .

"Well, there's proof we're in the right spot," says Dr. Sebastian, who is examining the plate I had brought up. "Look at this."

I've got a towel around me and am slurping from the hot mug of tea that Higgins has kindly brought me, and I look at where the Doctor is pointing. Around the outer edge of the plate is inscribed *La Santa Magdalena, Siempre lista.*

*Well, almost always prepared,* I think.

Much jubilation all around.

Well, that proves it to them, but I already knew, deep in my soul, that it was she we were diving on, so I turn to more practical matters.

"John Thomas. Finn. This time let's lower the net swag bag as well. One tug on that line will mean take a tension on the grappling line and pull for all you're worth. Two tugs will mean slack off. Three tugs will mean pull up the swag bag. Everybody got that? Good. Let's go back down."

With the new signals I am better able to control the tearing apart of the *Magdalena*. Now I put the hooks to the underdeck of the Captain's cabin, and give a tug on the line, and the deck is lifted off. This yields nothing but an empty storeroom below—probably the Captain's own stores, the victuals long ago devoured by the denizens of the deep. I slack off the hooks and wait for the dust to settle. When it does, I see some bottles and I take two and put them in the net bag—maybe the wine'll still be good. Worth a try. Some four-decades-old fine Spanish amontillado? Yum. Back for a good, deep breath.

And so it goes—put the hooks on, tear away at the wreck, slack the hooks, wait for the silt to settle, check on the progress, and it's back into the bell for another breath. Repeat the process, then make the trip back up every half hour or so, and then head back down again. I like working on the *Magdalena* because the possibility of success is wildly exciting, but the trips back up in the bell are becoming tedious.

I'm three decks down in the after section of the ship when I see it—a heavy door studded with metal bolts, with a thick chain drawn across it and secured with a large padlock. On the deck in front are two skulls and the remnants of weaponry—guards, perhaps, who stayed at their post till the end? We shall see.

I give two tugs on the net bag line to get some slack in the hook's line and then slip the grapples under the chain. One tug to signal those above to take a strain and then back to the bell to catch a breath.

From inside the bell, I see the door being lifted up and away. I nip back out to give the bag line a tug so that they'll let the door sink to the ocean floor—no sense hauling up a useless slab of wood and chain. Then I float back over the wreck, and . . .

*Oh, my God . . .*

I gasp and get a mouthful of salt for my astonishment. There is so much gold that it spills out the now open doorway. I kick down and peer into the vault—there are casks upon casks of golden coins, some of which have fallen apart, their contents spilling onto the deck. There are chests that contain who knows what splendor. There are golden crosses and chalices and stacks and stacks of ingots and . . . oh, Lord, riches untold!

*I have found the treasure of the* Santa Magdalena*!*

I must go tell them! I dart down and pick up a gold coin for proof and stuff it down the front of my suit top and race back to the bell. I'm about to go under, but I'm so excited that I just can't do it, I just can't! Not the slow old bell, not now!

I look up at the hulls of the ships hanging above me and think, *It ain't so far, girl, and it'll be a helluva lot quicker! Go!*

And I do it.

I give my fins a flip and race for the surface, my legs pumping as fast as I can. *Oh, wait till they hear!*

*It's funny,* I'm thinkin' as I go up, *air keeps bubbling out of my lungs.* I let out a lungful and then clamp my lips shut, but my chest just fills back up again and I let that out and it happens again. No, it's not just funny, it's hilarious! *It's magic!*

*That's it! I must have been turned into a real mermaid! Oh, this is just like flying! I don't need any stupid bell. I could live down here forever! Go up? Nay, I think I'll go right back down to the bottom and play with the cute little fishies . . . no, wait . . . I'll go get Jaimy, and we'll both go down together and live happily ever after in that beautiful place with the waving fans and . . . Oh, this is all just so glorious! Ha-ha! I could just burst with happiness! I feel so good all over, every inch of me tingles with utter joy!*

*Wheeeeeeeeeeeee!*

Then my head breaks the surface and hands are put on me, and a part of my reeling mind notices that I have been pulled onto the deck of my dear little ship—*Hello,* Nancy!— and I see Jaimy, and I stagger toward him. I pull at my swimming suit, trying to get the coin out of it to show them but I can't. So I try to pull my top off, and I think I succeed, 'cause I hear the coin hit the deck—*giggle!*—I think, but I don't know. All I know is that I say to Jaimy, *Come Jaimy, let us go to bed, down below, on the sea-bed! Get it? On the sea-BED! Ha-ha. Let's do it!* Jaimy holds me, and I nuzzle my giggling face into his shirtfront. *You smell so good, Jaimy . . .* I hear a tumble of voices, but they don't mean anythin' to me, nothin' at all.

*What's the matter with her?*

*Get that goddamn bell back up here and put her in it!
Quickly! There's another side to this!*

*To what?*

*It's the Rapture of the Deep, you fool! Nitrogen narcosis!
Why didn't you warn her about it, Tilden?*

*I did, but she just wouldn't listen! She came up outside
the bell!*

Rapture? What Rapture? I'm beginning to calm down a
bit . . . and then I feel it—first in my elbows, then my knees.
A little shot of pain . . . and then, in my knees . . . then a *lot* of
pain, shooting like needles into every one of my joints. I let
loose of Jaimy and fall to the deck, twisting and screaming.

*We've got to get her back down to equalize the pressure.
She's got the bends! It could kill her! Here it is! Put her on the
bench! Tie her down!*

*No time! I'll . . . I'll . . . hold her on. Look out.*

In my agony, I feel myself lifted up and taken into
the bell.

*Down!*


"It is awful brave of you to come down in the bell, Jaimy. I
know you didn't want to . . ."

He sits rigid, ashen faced.

We have come to the bottom of our journey down and
the pain had gradually lessened the farther down we got.

". . . but you'll see, it's not so bad, is it? Look out the
window there, Jaimy. See, there's the *Santa Magdalena*. Isn't
she beautiful? And look at the pretty little fishes, too. Oh,
and there's a ray flying by. Isn't it magical, Jaimy?"

I reverse myself on the bench such that I can wrap my

arms about him and bury my face in his shirtfront. I discovered early in our descent that I had, indeed, been successful in taking off my top on the deck of the *Nancy B*. Oh, well, what's the harm. I squeeze him tighter and feel him relax.

"You can kiss me, Jaimy. Please?"

And before we are brought to the surface, we use up all the air in the bell.

*Oh, yes, we do.*

# Chapter 35

We start bringing up the gold in earnest now. I go down, fill up the swag bag, give three tugs on the line, and the bag whips up out of sight. I go back to the bell, and in a few minutes, the hungry bag comes down again.

Yesterday, when the bell containing me and Jaimy was brought back up and we were deposited onto the deck, we couldn't help but hear the hot words being exchanged twixt Dr. Sebastian and Professor Tilden.

"I simply cannot understand why you didn't inform her of the effects of coming up on her own, without the diving bell. Didn't you warn her about the danger of nitrogen bubbling through her system if she were to come to the surface without proper decompression?"

"But she is just a girl! I felt she would not understand the science . . ."

As Jaimy and I tumbled from the bell, Higgins was waiting with a towel and immediately wrapped me in it and was leading me off to my cabin, when we were stopped by Dr. Sebastian, who took me by the shoulder and pointed his finger at my temple. Me, I'm still dizzy from the Rapture, the bends, *and* my time with Jaimy in the bell.

"You see this, *Professor*?" he hissed. "Behind that girl's skull is a brain, and one that is just as good as mine and most certainly as good as yours! Do not forget that!"

Poor red-faced Tilly puffed up like a toad.

"You didn't explain because you thought she was just a stupid girl! I assure you she is *not* stupid, and if she had been told of the dangers, she would not have done what she did!" snaps Dr. Sebastian, in a fine froth. He turned to us. "No more diving today! Get her into bed! She will need rest!"

Higgins hustled me below, and I heard no more of the . . . discussion.

In my cabin, a nice hot bath was arranged, and I and my still-sore joints sank gratefully into it.

*Thank you, Higgins, you are just the best. Ahhhh . . .*

But that was yesterday, and this is today. Back to work. Pick up the gold and stick it in the basket, pick up the gold and stick it in the basket, a tisket, a tasket, a green and yellow basket . . .

*Hey, keep your mind on the job, girl.*

I pick up a golden goblet encrusted with jewels and am about to shove it into the plunder bag when I hear her voice.

*Jacky . . .*

I cock my head to listen. *Is this more of that Rapture of the Deep stuff?* No, somehow I don't think so.

*Jacky. It's me. Little Mary Faber from the Rooster Charlie Gang. Do you 'member me?*

*Of course, I remember you, Mary. You're never far from me, you know that.* I pick up an ingot and thrust it into the bag with the rest. That's enough for this load, I'm thinking, so I give the line three sharp tugs. The net bag and its contents whisk up out of sight. I know it will return shortly, empty and waiting.

*There's a lot of gold down 'ere, Jacky. Look at it all. Just lyin' there.*

*I know, Mary.*

*We should 'ave some of it, too. For ourselves, like. You know we should.*

I give a kick and pop back under the bell for a breath. As I gulp it and several others, I'm thinking, *No, it's not the Rapture, girl. It's my own greed talking to me, and she is very persuasive.*

I duck back out to resume the work, but I find my inner imp out there is still waiting for me.

*They took our ship, Jacky. They took the* Nancy B. *They took our little schooner that we named after our mother. They think they own us, but they don't. They do owe us, Jacky, they do.*

*I know, Mary, I know, but how—*

*See that bunch of fan coral there? Behind it is a little cave in the rocks. You spotted it before; you can't deny it. It'd be ever so easy to put some there. Just a bit. No one would ever know. But you would know, wouldn't you? And so would I, and we could find our way back sometime later.*

*But—*

*But, nothin'. This is the biggest stand of coral down here. It stands out like a sore thumb—how could you miss it? And up top you took the compass bearings from the land points, so you know where we are. You could get back here, you know you could.*

I don't say anythin' to that. I just float there . . . thinking.

*Jacky,* entices the little temptress, *remember the* Emerald, *our fine, fine brigantine bark and how much you loved her? Ah, Jacky, you could have another just like her, you could. You could . . . You could gather the lads again—Liam, Padraic, Arthur McBride, John Reilly, and all the rest and sail off again to far ports of call to see all the wonders of this world, you could . . . You could . . . You could . . .*

That cuts it.

I take my spear stick, swim over behind the fans, and poke it around in the shallow cave to roust out any creatures that might be dwelling within. Several things skitter out, but nothing large nor poisonous enough to do me damage, so I head back and look down at the pile of gold that glows beneath me. I pick up an ingot and carry it to the undersea safe hold of Faber Shipping Worldwide, and I put it in.

*Good girl, Jacky. Good girl.*

*I don't know just how good I'm being, but they did sink my* Emerald, *they did.*

*After all, this gold doesn't belong to King Georgie. It belongs to the Spanish, so the King is stealing, too, Jacky. That's the way I sees it.*

*All right, Mary, now get lost and let me get this done.*

*Goodbye, Jacky . . .*

Back for a breath, and then I get on with it. No rest for the weary . . .

. . . nor for the wicked.

# Chapter 36

Little Mary had a good idea, but I've got a lot better one.

We completed that day's morning dives and had lunch on the mess deck, and when we were finished, I arose from the table and asked Tink and Davy to go with me down into the bilges, while preparations for the afternoon dives were being made. I said that I thought I had noticed a seam opening up next to the *Nancy*'s keel on my last dive, though I had noticed no such thing, of course. I just needed to get the lads down somewhere private so we could talk. The fewer people who know about this the better—as Ben Franklin once said, "Three men can keep a secret, if two of them are dead."

I got a lantern and led the way down into the bowels of my little schooner. When we got down to the absolute bottom, where the heavy lead ingots of our lead ballast lay, I stopped and put the lantern down.

"I don't see no leak," says Davy, casting his eyes about in the gloom. "Looks tight as a drum t'me."

"Davy. Tink. Put your fists on your tattoos. I did not bring you down here to talk of leaks. Swear you will say nothing of this."

"So sworn," says Tink, putting his hand on his hip. "What are you up to, Jacky?"

I lean into the glow of the lantern. "What do you think I'm up to, mates? Gold, that's what. We have been bringin' up a lot of it, and there's lots more down there, ready to be grabbed."

"So?" asks Davy. "What are we poor seamen to think of that?"

"You should think that maybe it shouldn't all go to good King George. It's Spanish gold. It ain't his. Right? A good part should go to him, for Merrie Olde England and all that, but some should come to us, too!"

"To us?" asks Davy.

"Right. To Faber Shipping and—"

"How sick I am of hearing that name pronounced."

". . . and you'll all get your proper share," I say, getting steamed. "Have I not been generous in all of my dealings with you?"

I know Tink agrees, having been down and out very recently, but Davy, as always, is a lot more stubborn. I press on.

"Wouldn't you and Annie like to buy a nice little cottage to raise your children in? Wouldn't you?" I say. "And Tink, what do you want out of this world? A life at sea? The respect of your comrades? A tidy wife, maybe?"

"All right, Jacky-O," says Davy, hunkering down. "What's the scam, then?"

"This is it," I say, hunkering down myself. "Tink, inside

the bell is a heavy wood bench, as you know since you have both sat upon it. It is a single plank, going from one side to the other. About two inches thick. I want you to put in another thick board below it—to make it look like it was put there to lend strength to the top plank. Add stain and varnish so no one will notice the change. Nobody but me goes in there, anyway, so who's gonna notice?"

"That's easy enough," says Tink. "But what good—"

"I'll tell you what good. Around the back of that seemingly innocent board, you're going to hollow out a slot that you will make with your chisels and gouges. And then I'm going to slide in ingots of gold—cobs, they are called—each one ten pounds of pure gold and each one enough to keep you in fish, chips, and ale for a hundred years."

There are two sharp intakes of breath.

"Make it so that I will be able to fit in ten cobs a day. Davy, you and Tink will be able to retrieve them in the dark of night, when the bell is stowed down in the fore hatch. King George will be getting five to any one of ours, but so it goes. There's a lot down there. I'll put most of the flashier stuff, like the crosses and the goblets, into the King's stash, but a good number of the ingots will come to us."

I turn again to Tink.

"You've got to use your brace and bits, augers, screws, whatever you've got, but no hammers—we can't have any noise. Tilly or the Doctor might wake up and find you messin' with the bell."

"They could hang us for this. You're already in some trouble with the Crown," says Davy.

"I don't see us gettin' caught for this. And as for me, might as well be hanged for a wolf as for a lamb, I always say."

"What do we do with the gold when we get it up?"

"Well, you, Davy, will disguise the cobs, then we will hide them in plain sight. We have both white and black paint on the ship, so after you mix up a lead color and paint them, you'll stash them under here. They'll look just like the lead ingots we're already using as ballast."

Davy gives out a low chuckle. "Very crafty, Jack-O."

"I hope so, Davy."

"I'll have the shelf in tonight, Jacky, count on it," says Tink, smiling, the white of his teeth gleaming in the light of the lantern. "Looks like old King George might be givin' poor John Tinker his rightful pension after all."

"So we are agreed, then? So say ye one. So say we all."

"Yes," says Tink.

"Yes," adds Davy.

"Good lads," say I. "Then it is done."

# Chapter 37

The plan is going well.

Over the past week, we have hauled up a king's ransom in gold and jewels, which will swell the coffers of King George III most admirably . . . and fifty fat gold ingots now lie nestled safely with the lead ingots in the hold of the *Nancy B. Alsop*. Life is good, and the future looks even better.

I did not completely empty out my underwater stash. In fact, I added to it—twenty more golden ingots and several likely looking small chests were put into the little watery cave. I mean, suppose, God forbid, that the *Nancy B.* should be lost—to a storm or to pirates—where would we be then? Broke is where, with no ship and no gold. Nay, best to leave a nice cache here. I could always find the spot again, should the need arise.

Ten more gold cobs are stashed in the bench of the bell for Davy and Tink to put away in the dead of night, and I ride up from the last dive of the day.

Earlier, I was not pleased to find that Lieutenant

Flashby had been assigned to supervise today's take. I assigned Joannie to keep an eye on him, to make sure he didn't pocket any of the booty. It turns out that he had the very same suspicions of me.

I take the towel to dry off and am ready to go into my cabin when Flashby speaks up.

"How do we know she is not squirreling away coins and jewels in her . . . garb?" He looks me over. "She does have a history of chicanery. I think she needs to be thoroughly searched."

"What? How could I possibly hide anything under this suit?"

"Small but very valuable things such as gold coins and precious jewels are easily concealed on the female form, as I am sure you realize," he says with the slightest hint of a leer.

"Sir, I must protest most vigorously!" says Dr. Sebastian, outraged.

"I am merely exercising caution, Doctor. She does have a checkered past."

I go at Flashby claws extended, but a calmer head intervenes.

Higgins steps between us and says, "Surely you cannot be serious, Sir. Miss Faber is a fellow member of our Service and a person of honor. If she swears that she has no purloined gold on her person, then we must believe her."

I know that ain't gonna be enough for the vile Flashby, so I fluff up, put on the Lawson Peabody Look, glare at the villain, and say, "I swear that I have no purloined gold or jewels or anything of value upon my person. To set your mind at ease, I will ask Mr. John Higgins, who is also a member of our fine Service and a man of impeccable honor, to help me dress for dinner. Are your fears now at rest, *Sir*?"

Flashby just barely nods his head.

"Very well, then," I say coldly, turning abruptly away from him and heading for my cabin. "Mr. Higgins, if you would assist me?"

"Damn that Flashby!" I strip off my suit and fling it aside. "See, Mr. Intelligence Agent—no gold, no jewels, just me. All right?"

"Of course, Miss, I expected no other, and, yes, Mr. Flashby can be an annoyance. If you will get into the tub?"

I slide gratefully into my little metal tub . . . *Ahhhhh* . . . and lean back and close my eyes. It's been a long day.

"I should've just killed him when I had the chance, and I would have been done with it."

"I know that you are not by nature a murderess, Miss. Please duck your head under."

I stick my head between my knees and come up with water streaming over my face. Higgins puts the soap to my hair and massages it in with his strong fingers.

*Ahhhhh* . . .

"Do not ever think that Mr. Flashby has forgotten that time on the *Belle of the Golden West*," Higgins continues, "when you made him walk the plank, he soiling his pants in the certainty of his coming death while you prodded him along at sword point."

"I don't care. He had it coming. Buying the scalps of innocent men, women, and children. It makes me sick to even think of it."

"Rinse, please."

I duck my head under again and ruffle my hair with my fingers to free it of the suds.

I emerge and am handed the soap and a washcloth and proceed to wash my arms, legs, feet, and various parts, and then I lean forward for Higgins to scrub my back, a luxury I particularly enjoy.

I cannot stop breathing out luxurious *ahhhh*s.

There's a knock on the door and I call out, "Who?"

"It's me," answers Joannie.

"Come in, then."

Joannie enters, bearing a large kettle of hot water. She glances at Higgins and then pours the water between my feet, which are sticking out of the end of the tub.

Yet another *ahhhhh*.

Bathing in the early evening has become a common practice with us, the expedition's two divers. Joannie also had spent a good deal of time in the water today, as she and Daniel had taken the lifeboat and sailed in close to shore to gather shellfish, and now she needs the salt rinsed off her. Her hair is as stiff with salt as mine had been. She peers doubtfully down at the soapy water. "You didn't let loose in there with that Brother Rabbit trick, did you?"

I reach out to swat her with the wet washcloth, but she is too agile and I miss.

"No, I did not, because I am a lady, which you ain't, not by a long shot. Now get your tail in this tub."

Saying that, I stand up, take the towel that Higgins holds up, and step out of the bath.

As I dry off, Joannie, by now well used to Higgins's presence at times like these, doffs her suit and climbs into the tub.

I find I am not the only who can sigh *ahhhhh*.

"And what will you wear tonight, Miss?" Higgins asks.

I think for a moment and then say, "I believe I'll wear my uniform—*with* the trousers. Every man on both these ships has seen enough of my scrawny self, so that my wearing pants should no longer be a scandal."

"Very well, Miss."

As Higgins gets my stuff together, I pull up a chair next to the tub and unloosen Joannie's long hair from its braids and proceed to wash it.

A boat was sent over to get us at Two Bells into the Second Dog Watch. Since it's just Higgins, the Doctor, and me, I suspect this will be a strategy meeting, the Professor not being invited.

As I step onboard the dear old *Dolphin*, I am pleased to see that we are received by Captain Hudson, Lieutenant Bennett, and Lieutenant Fletcher. I am not pleased to see Lieutenant Flashby there, too, but let that go.

Then I hear a familiar refrain whispered low from up in the rigging:

*Puss ... Puss ... Puss-in-Boots!*

Unlike the cat in the old French tale, I do not carry a sword, not now, anyway. But I am wearing my lieutenant's blue jacket with its gold lace threaded through the lapels, and tight white breeches tucked into my shiny black riding boots, so I guess that's close enough.

In response to the cheer, I hit a brace, give a quick bow to fo'c's'le, main deck, and fantail, and then follow the Captain to his cabin.

We are quickly seated and wineglasses are put in our hands. The King's health—and new wealth—are toasted and drunk to, and food is served and eaten. It's good, but not as good as what Jemimah dishes out, I note with some satisfaction.

And then we get down to business.

Captain Hudson stands at his chair and lifts his glass. "To our little mermaid, who has added considerable wealth to our beleaguered nation."

*Hear, hear!*

I affect modesty and acknowledge the toast by saying, "We are all but simple foot soldiers in our march toward freedom and security for our blessed isle." I swear I hear Flashby choke at that, and, for once, I don't blame him.

The Captain leans back, relaxes, and says, "We have a considerable fortune in gold in our hold, and I am not easy with that. Not easy at all. Though I challenge any enemy to come before us and taste the mettle of our courage, I know that we could be taken by a superior force and the treasure would be lost to our cause."

Captain Hudson pauses to take a draught of his wine, and then he continues. "The fight against Napoleon Bonaparte is on in earnest, and that takes treasure—much treasure to pay soldiers, much treasure to mount an army. Much treasure like we now have lying in our hold."

I agree. "Ah, yes. I heard the First Lord speak of the campaign along with the need for more funds when I was last in his office."

A low hum on that. Most of the officers at this table could not hope to be in the same room with the First Lord.

*Come up in the world a bit, have you, Jacky Faber?* I pat my lips with my napkin, then sit back and listen. My hand searches out Jaimy's under the table and finds it.

"Therefore," continues the Captain, "I have decided to take what treasure we now have to our base in Jamaica, place it in safekeeping, and then, after we have come back for the rest of it, we will mount up a well-armored squadron to get it all safely back to England."

I consider this and then say, "That sounds like a good plan to me, Captain. However, I do not want my ship floating out here like a sitting duck without your kind protection. Therefore, I'd like to take her back into Havana to reprovision while you are gone. We could arrange to rendezvous again in what . . . a week? In this same spot."

The Captain nods, plainly thinking this over.

"We might pick up more information on the *San Cristobal* when we are in port as well," adds Dr. Sebastian. "It would be good for us to know when that behemoth plans to sail."

"Right," says Captain Hudson, coming to a decision. "We will leave in the morning and will escort you as far as the mouth of Havana Harbor. Mr. Bennett, make all preparations."

"Aye, Sir," says Mr. Bennett.

That business done, the party turns to the wine in earnest. Glasses are filled and emptied and songs are proposed and sung. Eventually I make so bold as to ask, "Perhaps, Captain, you would be so good as to allow Mr. Fletcher to stay again with me for the night, as it would give me great comfort?"

Captain Hudson looks at me through lowered eyelids and says, "It wouldn't give *me* any great comfort." Then he looks at Jaimy. "If I were about twenty years younger, Mr. Fletcher, you would have a problem on your hands . . . Oh, never mind. Do the same conditions on your behavior apply?"

Both Jaimy and I nod, neither one of us very enthusiastically.

"Very well, then, but you will be back onboard at five thirty in the morning, or you will be put on report," he says to Jaimy. "And you, Miss, will behave yourself. I do believe you have this officer in the palm of your little hand to do with him as you will."

The wine works on me, too, and I enter into the exchange.

"Mr. Fletcher is the captain of his own fate, Sir. As for behaving myself, I believe I have always done that," I say, speaking the first outright lie I have said this night. "Perhaps Intelligence should have fitted me for a chastity belt before we embarked on this mission."

Laughter all around—except from Jaimy. I give his hand an extra squeeze.

"Ah, if those medieval devices actually worked, I'm sure the Service would have put one on you!" says Dr. Sebastian. "Except that we know you to be an expert lock picker and would have the thing off in an instant."

"I'm sure it would have been deucedly uncomfortable," I retort, moving my bottom around a bit on the chair. "And totally unnecessary . . . I think." I give Jaimy a hot look on that one.

*Har-har!*

*These men have been at sea too long.*

Much later I am locked in my lover's arms onboard the *Nancy B.*, and that's the way the world's supposed to be as I figure it.

*Oh, Jaimy, this is just so fine . . .*

# PART IV

# Chapter 38

*Booooooommmm . . .*

The sound of the cannon rolls out across the water, the signal from the *Dolphin* that she is turning west for Kingston and leaving us to our own devices. We are on course, 110 degrees south southeast and bound for Havana.

I knew the salute was coming and had decided to return it. My nine-pound guns, called that because of the size of shot that they throw, are puny next to the massive twenty-four-pounders of the *Dolphin,* but they still give out with a satisfying sound and can do much damage when called upon to do so.

"Fire, Mr. Thomas," I say, and John Thomas jerks the lanyard on gun number one, portside forward.

*Crrrack!*

I give it a moment and then say, "Fire, Mr. McGee."

*Crrrack!*

The powder smoke drifts away and I order, "Reload, lads. Davy, Tink, check the charges on the other guns, but leave the canvas covers on. I have a feeling we're going to have a visitor."

We have two nine-pound guns on each side of the *Nancy,* as well as a three-pound swivel gun mounted both fore and aft. The sailors tend to the cannons and then shortly give the thumbs-up signal. I nod and wait.

Dr. Sebastian comes up next to me on my quarterdeck. "You are expecting company?"

Professor Tilly had left us and gone aboard the *Dolphin* last night, there being no diving or other scientific research being done now, and relations still being rather cool between the two men of science since the near killing of me. Dr. Sebastian cannot forgive Tilly's failure to warn me about the Rapture of the Deep . . . and the bends. The bell has been left in the *Nancy*'s forward hold, which is good for three reasons. Number one, I think Tilly has lost interest in it and is ready to pursue his next foolish fancy. Number two, we'll need it to bring up the rest of the gold when we rendezvous in a week. The third is that I intend to keep it when all is said and done.

"Yes, Doctor," I answer, and before I can even scan the horizon, there is a call from Daniel Prescott on lookout above.

"On deck there! Ship to the east!"

Sure enough, the *Dolphin* was hardly out of sight when Flaco Jimenez's ship heaves into sight. I lift my long glass and see his colors flying at the masthead—a red devil's skull with the two crossed cannons below. *El Diablo Rojo.*

"Who is it?" asks the Doctor.

Dr. Sebastian could have gone off with Tilly, but he did not. I suspect our good Doctor, in hanging around with me, has gotten a bit of a taste for the high life—or the low life, depending on how you look at it. Plus, I'm sure he wants to get some more drawings out of me. We have done quite a lot already, including depictions of diving in the bell, but if a few more go into his leather portfolio, well, all the better, as he sees it.

"It's only Flaco," I say, snapping my long glass shut. "On the *Red Devil*."

"The pirate Jimenez? But—"

"Don't worry, Flaco won't hurt us," I say, trying unsuccessfully not to smile. "We were once members of the same . . . fraternity. Plus, I have nothing onboard worth stealing" . . . *fingers crossed behind my back* . . . "But still . . ."

I do trust Flaco—up to a point. He is a pirate after all. But I do not trust that El Feo, not a bit. So I lift my voice.

"Battle stations everyone! Clear for action! Let's show him we have teeth!" My crew springs to their stations—Tink, Davy, McGee, and John Thomas to the port and starboard nine-pounders, Jim Tanner on helm, Joannie and Daniel to the hatch, standing by as powder monkeys. Higgins and I will handle the bow and stern swivel guns should the need arise. "Let's show him we are still in the game. Joannie, put up our black colors. Dr. Sebastian, best get below."

The girl gives an excited whoop, dives down into my cabin, and pops back out with my pirate flag. Then she whips down our American colors and hoists our Jolly Roger. I know what she is thinking—*Look at that! A real pirate ship!*

"Highly irregular," murmurs Dr. Sebastian, looking up at the grinning skull and crossed bones waving in the breeze.

"It's necessary, you'll see," I reply. "I will have to draw on some old friendships to keep us safe. Otherwise, we will have to fight."

"Trust her, Doctor," urges Higgins. Since "Battle Stations" has been called, he has brought up my sword and pistols and he straps them on me. The grips of his own two pistols stick out of his waistcoat, primed and ready. "She has a certain way with these brigands." *Being one herself, Higgins is thinking, I'm sure.*

The Doctor goes below to his lab, which I hope will not very shortly be turning into a bloody surgery.

The *Red Devil is* a fast little brig—I know because I had raced her many times on my sweet *Emerald* and almost lost a few times—with six twenty-four-pounders on either side. There are two chasers—nine-pound Long Toms mounted forward, 'cause that's what a pirate does, chase its prey, unlike an honest merchantman like the *Nancy B.* 'Course everything's a mess, with ropes hanging everywhere, stained sails, unkempt men lazing about the rigging and staring down at us—all things that offend the Royal Navy sailor in me.

Flaco swoops down upon us and pulls his ship alongside. Some good seamanship is shown as he matches his vessel's speed with ours so that he can call over from his quarterdeck.

"*Hola, Jacquelina! Qué pasa, muchacha?*"

I go over to my rail and Flaco goes to his so that we are face to face.

"*Nada, Flaco,*" I call back. "We are nothing but simple sponge divers going in to Havana to sell our catch."

He looks up at the sponges drying on our rigging. Joannie has been diligent in collecting them in the shallows while I was below, collecting gold, but we do not have nearly the number that we had on our last trip into Havana.

"We know you are anything but simple, Jacky, my heart. We have been watching you, going up and down in that thing that looks like a cathedral bell. We are not stupid, nor are we overly greedy. Come, dear one, share with us. It will benefit us both. You give us half the gold, and we'll give you and your ship safe passage to wherever you want to go. What do you say?"

I say, "Get yourself off, Flaco. If you are good, I will let you buy me a drink at Señor Ric's when we get to Havana."

The rascal grins back at me. "Surely not a proper welcome for your once and future lover, Captain Flaco Jimenez."

"You flatter yourself, Flaco. I was never your lover, and you know it."

"*Sí*. But it was a close thing, *querida mía*, and you know it was," he says. "So let us take up where we left off and let me board you now."

"You may board my ship, but as for me, you will board *nada*."

He motions to his man on the helm, and the ships come together. Then he hops aboard, flamboyant as usual—cocked hat on head, braided hair ending in ribbons, beads, and tinkly bells, teeth gleaming in his tanned face. He wears loose pantaloons tucked into heavy boots, a frilly white shirt open at the neck, and a brocaded waistcoat over that.

"You treated me badly when last we met, Flaco." I stick out my lower lip and put on a pout.

"I am sorry, my heart, but my *machismo* got the best of me." He grins, making a mock bow and putting one knee to the deck. "It always happens when I get close to my sweet little *Inglesa*."

"I don't like being dumped on the floor," I say, with a sniff, "by some second-rate pirate, like you did to me at Ric's."

"I do not mind being called a pirate, my soul, but I am wounded by being called a second-rate one by the very love of my life." He puts on a hurt look. I try to suppress a smile but am not successful. I find it very hard to stay mad at this jolly rogue.

"And now you will demand to search my poor little boat for this supposed gold?" I ask. "That is so rude and unkind of you, but go ahead. We have nothing to hide."

"The fact that you, my devious little rabbit, would allow us to do so assures me that we would find nothing, so we shall not look."

From the corner of my eye, I notice something that Flaco does not. His ship has drawn away from us, perhaps a little farther away than he would like. Then there are sounds that Flaco *does* notice—cries of alarm from his ship, the crack of shots being fired.

*Uh-oh . . .*

Flaco's head snaps up. His ship is pulling away from our side. "What? What is . . . ?" And then he realizes—it's *mutiny*! He has been betrayed!

"Feo, you bastard son of a whore!" he shouts, shaking his fist. "Bring the ship back here!"

"Lick her boots, weakling!" shouts El Feo, now astride the quarterdeck in full captain rig, complete with feathered turban. The distance between us is closing again. "We just had an election, and you lost. *El Diablo Rojo* now has a real Captain!"

Flaco Jimenez stands straight and tall, glaring at his mutinous former First Mate.

"You go over and ask the girl, oh so polite," continues El Feo. "'Oh, please tell me where is the gold?' like a *maricón*, a fancy boy. What happened to your *cojones*, Flaco? When did you lose them? I do not know, but I think you lost them today for good! No ship, no famous pirate Jimenez!" Much laughter from the pirate ship, where stand many men with muskets aimed at us. I recognize none of them—Flaco's loyal men must be locked below, or else dead.

Grinning pirates holding cutlasses line the lee side of the *Red Devil* and they beat the hilts of those swords against the rail and shout out insults and curses. *Muerte! Muerte! Muerte! Death! Death! Death to the gringos! Death to Jimenez! Death to the English girl! Muerte!* They mime drawing their swords across their throats and point at us. *Muerte!*

Well, we'll see about *that!*

"I will now come over and show you how a man asks a stupid girl a simple question," El Feo says, coming over to the rail and pulling out a long thin knife from his broad leather belt. "*Compadres*. Shoot the old woman Jimenez." All the muskets are then trained on Flaco's chest.

I take a step away from Flaco and say, "Davy . . . Tink . . . ready . . . *FIRE!*"

Both of my lads jerk their lanyards at the same instant. *Crrraaack!*

Flaco has wisely hit the deck, as bullets fly over his head and splinters fly from the side of the *Red Devil.*

El Feo bellows out, *"Tiren los cañónes,"* and his six twenty-four-pound portside guns roar out.

*Craaack! Craack! Craaack! Craaash!*

But the *Red Devil* is so much higher than the *Nancy* that the balls sail through our rigging and not through our hull. We lose some lines, and the foresail spar, but that's it, thank God!

"Reload, lads! Daniel, Joannie! Powder, grape! Hard Left your helm, Jim!" I shriek. The kids scurry below and return lugging bags of powder and canisters of grapeshot.

The *Nancy* turns and presents a much more narrow target for El Feo's guns. I note with some satisfaction that it takes his men a lot longer to reload than it does mine.

"Ready, Jacky!" shouts Davy and Tink.

"Hard Right!" I shout. "Fire when they bear!"

The *Nancy* turns to starboard and my lads lean over their cannons and . . .

*Crrraaack!*

Davy shoots and then Tink jerks his lanyard and . . .

*Crrraaack!*

The grapeshot rakes the deck of the *Red Devil,* and there are screams from the other ship—a bee is small but she may still sting a bull—and many men lie still, but not El Feo. He has taken refuge behind his cabin during this exchange of fire.

"John! Finn! Take over the guns!" I shout. "Brothers, take up your rifles!" John Thomas and McGee rush to reload the cannons while Tink and Davy pick up their rifles and fire. Two men on the other ship pitch over and fall. Too bad neither of them is El Feo—he now comes back to stand on what is now his quarterdeck, confident that we have done our worst.

*Not yet, Feo . . .*

Flaco, in his rage, hurls down curses so obscene that

even I haven't heard them before. El Feo's mother is especially featured in many colorful ways, I note, even though my mind is fully occupied with the fight.

On my order, Davy and Tink climb up to the crow's-nest with their long rifles and powder horns slung over their shoulders, cartridges in their belts. Once there, they commence to rain bullets down on *El Diablo Rojo,* and more men fall victim to their marksmanship.

"*Pistola!*" pleads Flaco, holding out his hands to me. I pull out my pistols and flip one to him. He catches it, then leaps onto the ratlines, yelling, "Show yourself, Feo, you miserable dog! Show yourself, coward!"

El Feo, for an instant out in the open, looks up at Flaco, raises his own pistol, and fires and shouts, "*Tenga su madre, maricón!*" but misses. Then Flaco fires, but he, too, misses, clipping only the tip of one of the feathers in El Feo's headdress. Feo takes that as a sign to once again duck behind his cabin.

"That's it, hide yourself, you cowardly bastard," shouts Flaco. He, himself, is not cowering but instead hangs there in full view of the musketeers on the other ship, and I worry for his safety. Bullets buzz and snap all around us. Although none have yet hit flesh, as far as I can tell, they are bound to get lucky soon, lousy shots or not. We've got to get out of here.

"Another pistol, Jacky, *por favor!*" yells Flaco, but I do not give it to him.

Instead, I say to faithful Higgins, who has stood by my side during all this hurly-burly, "Higgins, with our pistols, let us take down their helmsman."

He draws his two handguns and aims, as do I with my remaining one.

"On the count of three, we will fire. One . . . two . . . three!"

Our pistols bark out and the man at the wheel grabs his chest and falls. I don't know which of us got him, but one certainly did . . . and I don't want to know.

"That'll slow him down," I say as we see *El Diablo Rojo* suddenly yaw to the right, being deprived of its helm.

Then I shout, "Left Full Rudder! Let's show him her tail! Go!"

We leap away from the pirate—*Good girl,* Nancy!—and though he chases us for a while, he cannot close the distance. And as night falls, he turns away, his nose well bloodied.

I let out the breath I have been holding for a long time and say, "Good work, all. Secure from Battle Stations. Let's have dinner."

Flaco stands desolate at the rail, watching the ship that once was his disappear into the dark. I know the terrible crushing feeling of losing one's ship and put my arm around him. "Come, amigo, you shall have dinner with me tonight in my cabin, and we shall talk of old times and maybe plot for the future. There will be another day." I give him a squeeze. "Hey?"

He looks down at me and nods. *"Gracias, mi corazón."*

We repair the damage, bind up any wounds, and set sail for Cuba.

# Chapter 39

*Lieutenant James Emerson Fletcher*
*Onboard HMS* Dolphin
*En route to Kingston, Jamaica*

*Jacky Faber*
*Onboard the* Nancy B. Alsop
*En route to Havana, Cuba*

*My dearest Jacky,*

*For once I am actually penning this letter instead of just making it up in my mind, for there is the very good chance, God willing, that I will see you again in a week and you might actually read it, unlike those many others I have written and sent out on the winds of chance.*

This will *not* be one for our children to read . . .

I have the midwatch tonight, and so I must turn in early to my lonely bunk. But I know that sleep will not come easy for me tonight, for I will be again reliving our last night together in your cabin.

"Turn around, Jaimy, please," you had said after we had finished our dinner and were preparing for bed. I did so, thinking it uncommon shyness on your part. I heard a whisper of cloth, then . . .

"All right, Jaimy."

I turned around and beheld you and understood.

"And what do you think of your saucy sailor girl now?"

I was astounded to see you wearing the same impossibly light, filmy little dress you wore on that glorious day in Jamaica three years ago.

You lowered your eyelashes in the way that you have and whispered, "It's my Kingston dress, Jaimy, the one I wore on that happy day in Jamaica. Do you remember?"

Ah, yes, well I remember.

"I had it in my chest in Boston and brought it with me, in case we should, by some impossible chance, be married—you did say you wanted me to wear it on our wedding day, didn't you?"

I rejoiced to see you in that dear relic, but I liked it even better when it floated to the floor and I beheld you in your natural state. You stood in the soft glow of the lamplight, your skin impossibly bronzed in some places, the purest white in others. Then, smiling, you came to me and put your arms about me, but . . . I must stop thinking of that, else I drive myself mad.

I have taken to washing in *very* cold water each night before turning in to my solitary bunk, but I comfort myself with the possibility that you and I might very soon lie together again.

*The midwatch comes in three hours. I shall try to sleep; but when I close my eyes, there you are again.*

*Good night, Jacky. With all my affection, I remain*

*Yours,*

*Jaimy*

# Chapter 40

Breakfast is over and cleaned up after, and I'm checking out the condition of my fighter in the coop behind the stove. I lift El Gringo to feel his drumsticks. *Hmmmm . . . much, much stronger now,* I think with some satisfaction. The ever increasing lead weights that have been tucked into his vest have been good for him. He should be very light on his feet now when the vest comes off. *Beware, El Matador.*

Daniel and Joannie sit in front of Jemimah and listen like mindful students. Would that the scamps paid as close attention to the studies I assign them. *Grrrr . . .*

Jemimah clatters some pans and starts in . . .

"So it happen that one fine day Brother Rabbit was hoppin' along a path that a lot of the animals used, goin' about their business, him singin' a happy song, and glad to be off by himself for a spell. Y'see, Sister Rabbit did have her way with that man, and now there's a whole bunch of baby bunnies all over the rabbit shack, gettin' underfoot all the time and settin' up a fuss just like you two, and sometimes a daddy just gotta go off by hisself for a bit and pretend he still be a free-rambling man.

"By 'n' by Brother Rabbit come to a bend in the road and he perks up them big ears o' his 'cause he hears somethin' goin' on up ahead. When he rounds the bend, he sees a bunch of men diggin' a hole right in the middle of the path and he duck back in the bushes and lays back his big ol' ears to watch what they doin,' him bein' a curious sort of rabbit.

"He watches 'em for a while and he's thinkin', 'They's diggin' a mighty deep hole there and it's gotta be some kinda trap for us pore animals, but they dug it so deep wit' the sides so steep that they must have the big critters in mind.' The rabbit puts his front paws to his chin and thinks on it some more as he watch the men come out of the hole and lay light branches across it and then scatter some leafs over that so it look all natural. 'Nope, that trap ain't for us rabbits and possums and 'coons and such. No, dey lookin' for somethin' else . . . sumthin' like dat big ol' brown bear dat's been lately tearin' up the Man's beehives down at the plantation and stealin' all his honey . . . hmm . . . ? Or mebbe it's dat ol' red fox what's been down in the Man's henhouse, pluckin' out some o' his fine hens and leavin' only the feathers behind . . . hmmm?'

"The men take up their shovels and pickaxes and head on off, back to the Man's plantation down in the valley, leavin' the place all quiet. Brother Rabbit sits up, grins him an evil grin, and heads off back down the road, lookin' for a certain pair of rascals."

Jemimah pauses to clean an imaginary spot from her big skillet and then hangs it on its hook on the side of the stove. She is well aware of the effect this pause has on her impatient audience. When she figures the kids have squirmed enough, she goes on.

"Soon Brother Rabbit spots Brother Fox and Brother Bear lyin' under a persimmon tree, asleep and snorin' away. The rabbit figures he'll get behind a bush and wake 'em up with a song, pretendin' he don't know they're there. He opens his mouth and sings.

> *'Oh, de Squirrel he got a bushy tail,*
> *Possum's tail is bare.*
> *Raccoon's tail is ringed all 'round,*
> *And stumpy goes de Bear.*
> *Stumpy goes dat ooooold*
> *Brown bear.'*

"The fox's ears perk up and he cracks open an eyelid. He nudges the bear, who grunts and keeps on sleepin'. Sleepin' is one thing bears is really good at.

"'Wake up, Brother,' says the fox. 'I think I hears dat rabbit comin' along.'

"Well, that gets up the bear. He wake up droolin', cause he been dreamin' of some nice rabbit stew and now the main ingredient in that kinda stew was comin' near.

"Brother Fox and Brother Bear get to their feet and listen as Brother Rabbit puff out his chest and sing up another verse.

> *'Brother Fox he got a bushy tail,*
> *Muskrat's tail is bare.*
> *Rabbit got no tail at all,*

> *Just a little tuft of hair.*
> *Just a little tuft of hair*
> *Back there.'*

"Then he burst right into the clearin' where the fox and bear is waitin'.

"'Grab him, Brother!' shouts the fox.

"'Feets, do yo' stuff!' shouts the rabbit, and he spin about and he dash off down the road with Brother Fox and Brother Bear right behind him. They can run fast, but the rabbit be little bit faster. Still, he don't get too far ahead of them, no, he just wave his little cottontail in front of their noses and they keep on pantin' after him.

"Soon Brother Rabbit see the trap up ahead and as he get close to it, he gather up all the strength in his hind legs, and when he get to the edge, he springs and leaps clean over it and lands on the other side.

"Then he hear *crash* and he turn and look and, sure enough, the fox and the bear have fallen right into the trap. The rabbit creep up to the edge and look down. 'My, my,' he thinks, 'the mens sure dug this hole deep, yessuh! Ain't no way them two is gettin' outta dere, nossuh! Even if the fox get on the bear's shoulder, he still won't be able to jump out.'

"Brother Rabbit got a big toothy grin on his face. 'My, my, ain't life just fine, sometimes? Two o' de baddest Brothers in de woods stuck in a hole wit' no way out! Oooooowee!'"

"And ain't Brother Rabbit just the smartest rabbit ever?" I tease from my perch next to the coop.

"Hush, you," says Jemimah.

I hush myself and reach down to stroke Gringo behind his head. He seems to like it.

Earlier, we made landfall at a spot close to Bahia Honda and put a very resolute Flaco Jimenez ashore there with my warning not to do anything rash. He didn't say anything to that, but instead bent me over backward and planted a good one on my mouth and then leaped into the waiting boat before I could swat him. As Thomas and McGee rowed him away, he stood and took off his hat and waved it, calling out, "*Adiós, Jacquelina!* We shall sail together again! I swear it!"

*I hope so, Flaco . . . I really do.*

Jemimah rattles some of the breakfast pots and skillets as she's hanging them back on their hooks and resumes her story.

"The fox and the bear, they still be stunned from the fall, but Brother Fox, he recovers some and commences growlin' and leapin' up the sides of the trap, tryin' to get out, but it don't do him no good, no. He just fall back down on top of Brother Bear.

"'What is all dis?' ask the bear, shakin' his big ol' head, all confused.

"'Dis a trap, fool,' says the rabbit, 'what de men dug to catch de bear what's been eatin' up dere honey and de fox dat's been eatin' up dere chickens. Dat's what it is. And you know what, Brother Bear?'

"The bear look up at the rabbit. 'What?'

"'By 'n' by, the mens is gwine come back up here wit' dere guns and dey's gwine shoot you both full o' holes and den haul yo' dead butts away. Hee-hee, oh glory!'

"At this, the fox starts snarlin' and pacin' about, but the bear just sits down and starts in moanin' and cryin'. Brother Rabbit, he roll over laughin' and kickin' all four of his feet in the air in joyful appreciation of the moment. Then he roll back over and lie himself down next to the edge of the hole and he rest his chin on his forepaws.

"'And you know what else, Brothers?'

"'What?' says the fox, barin' his teeth and wishin' to God he could sink them teeth in Brother Rabbit's neck and grind 'em real hard.

"'Well, let's us speculate on what's gonna happen to yo' sorry selves real soon. First you, Brother Fox: The mens gonna take sharp knives and skin you and tan yo' red hide and they gonna make you into one o' them fancy fur pieces the men's ladies wear to church—you seen 'em—de ones where the fox fur loops 'round the lady's neck and the skinners leave the head on and make it look like the pore dead fox is bitin' his own tail. Hee-hee! You finally get to be a regular churchgoer, Fox.'

"Brother Fox make one more try at leapin' off the bear's back at the rabbit, but all he can do is snap his teeth in front of the grinnin' rabbit's nose.

"'You'll finally be a churchgoin' brother, 'cept you won't know it, 'cause you'll be dead.'

"'And as for you, Brother Bear, oh, dey gots lots o' uses for yore pore body,' Brother Rabbit goes on, while Brother Bear whimpers and rubs his cryin' eyes. 'First they gwine take your skin, and then make a big ol' rug outta it and put it in front o' dere fireplace so they young'uns kin sit there all cozy. Don't dat make a nice, warm picture in yore mind, Brother Bear? Then they gone cut up the rest o' you and roast you up and eat up anything you got on you worth eatin'. Den dey throw yo' bones to dere dogs. And then, dat ain't de end of it, oh, no, then they render down yo' fat, yo' very *considerable* fat, and dat dey uses to rub all over dem-selves to keep the mosskeeters off, 'cause yo' fat stink so bad even the skeeters can't stand it and they flies away to go bite someone else.'

"'Oh, oh, oh, we's done for, fo' sure! Oh, what will my pore Mama Bear say,' moans Brother Bear, 'when she hear her li'l baby boy is gone?'

"'She'll prolly say she wish she had birthed a brighter cub,' says the rabbit, showin' no mercy at all to the poor blubbering bear. 'One what wasn't fooled by a little rabbit and ended up as a rug.'"

Jemimah wipes her hands on a dishrag and sits heavily down, ignoring the kids' pleas to keep going with the tale.

"Later, children. Let your auntie catch her breath. Go do your chores now."

As I stand there and flick choice seeds to Gringo, I think back to last night and to my dinner with poor Flaco.

A nod and a few words to Higgins and he sets the finest table the *Nancy B.* is capable of, which ain't too shabby, con-siderin' we always go first class whenever we can. And now, with Jemimah's help, we have gumbos thick with shrimp and okra, gently roasted meats covered with delicate mush-room sauces, bread as light as air, and potatoes baked and garnished with butter and cheese. It's served with the best of our clarets and topped off with the finest port wine.

It cheers Flaco considerably—hell, that dinner would cheer a condemned heretic on his way to the stake—and he sits back after all is done and pats his belly. Then he voices his opinion, looking pointedly at my sleeping accommodations off to the side of my cabin, that there is one further thing that I might do that would cheer him greatly and restore him to his former confidence, if I would so agree.

*Alas, Flaco, I cannot agree to that—my lusting heart tells me "yes," but my better self tells me "no"—as I have given my word before God that I am promised to a fine young man, and I cannot break that vow.* That vow, *and* the one I made to the Admiralty concerning my chastity on this voyage. Things sure do get complicated with all these vows—I mean, who could possibly care about the rag of skin, bone, and hair that is me? Beats me. It's strange, but it seems that some do. Ah, well . . .

And so ex-Captain Flaco Jimenez slung his hammock that night out on the deck with the rest of my crew, and I kept my solitary vigil in my own bed, knees pulled up to chin, saying prayers for all my mates, whether they be Royal Navy, Faber Shipping, charming pirates, or ladies of the Lawson Peabody . . . and a special goodnight, love, to one James Emerson Fletcher, ah, yes . . .

*And you'd better be good in Kingston, Jaimy! And I mean it!*

"Dan'l. You think you got enough wood in this pile?" asks Jemimah. She arranges herself on a chair with a big bowl and commences shelling peas.

"Yes, Ma'am," says Daniel Prescott.

"Well, you wrong, boy. Go fetch some more. Joannie, get us a bucket of fresh water, and then sit down and help me with these peas. Mebbe then we'll see what happened to them critters."

The kids shoot off down below to do her bidding. I ruefully wish I could have that same sort of enthusiastic response to orders on my ship. Maybe I should tell more stories. Oh, well, when it comes down to the real business, my men are just as sharp.

With the wood in the bin and the water in the bucket, the tale resumes.

"As you know, Brother Fox was still stuck down in that hole with Brother Bear where we last left 'em, and he be glarin' up at the grinnin' rabbit lookin' down on him, 'You know dis ain't right, Brother Rabbit,' says the fox, lookin' the rabbit in the eye, 'it just ain't the natch'rul way of things in the woods. You gotta get us outta here.'

"'Get you out? Har, har! Get you out?' The rabbit laugh and laugh. 'Oh, Brother Fox, I ain't gonna do dat at all. Hain't y'all bin gnawin' on the bones o' my pore rabbit brethren and sistern all these years? Yes, you have. Been trying to eat me, too, but you ain't had much luck in dat, have you? Hee-hee!'

"The fox growl and the bear whines and then . . . the rabbit about jump outta his skin when he hear behind him, 'What'cha doin,' Daddy?'

"Brother Rabbit whip around and see that one of his young'uns had followed him up here and is standin' next to him.

"'Boy,' he say, 'don't yo' *never* sneak up on yo' pappy like dat again. *Wooo!* You almost made me fall in de hole wi' dem two. Sho'nuff woulda hated endin' up as dere last meal on God's green earth! C'mere. Look down dere and tell me what you see.'

"Rabbit Child creeps over and looks down the hole.

"'Whoa!' he say in wonderment. 'Dat Brother Fox and Brother Bear down dere. What they doing dere, Daddy?'

"'Fixing to die is what dey doin' and . . . hmmm . . . ,' say Brother Rabbit, thinkin' to himself. 'These ol' boys'll gonna wanna be gettin' right wi' the Lord 'fore they goes off. Prolly want some words said over 'em . . . hmmm . . . and yore mama, she bein' a church woman, know how to do dat. Make yo'self useful, son, and go git her and tell her to bring her Bible.'

"Rabbit Child hurry on off down the hill and Brother Rabbit get to his feet and shade his brow and look off into the distance.

"'Uh-oh,' he say to the prisoners in the hole. 'Dis don't look good for y'all. Appears de mens is startin' up de valley to check on dere trap. *Ooooweee*, what they gonna find! Won't be long now, Brothers, yessuh! When de time comes, I'm gonna tuck myself back in de bushes and watch dem mens fill you boys full o' holes!'

"'Course the rabbit don't see nothin' of the kind, no, he just want to see Brother Fox and Brother Bear squirm. And squirm they do, oh yes, they do. The fox, he howl, and the bear, he moan."

John Tinker sticks his head down into the passageway, saying, "We've got the mouth of the harbor, Jacky, and we're fair for the channel."

"Thanks, Tink," I answer. I put El Gringo back into the coop and stand, fist to small of back as I straighten. "All right, Sister Girl and Brother Boy, let's get to our stations."

# Chapter 41

⚓ *Carnival! Joy! Dancing in the street! Bands every-where! Food stalls with mounds of steaming rice and meats! There is a conga line! And there's another! Let's get in that one—one-two-three, kick, one-two-three, kick! Yes! Here, Davy, hold on to my waist—one-two-three, kick! That's it! You got it! Oh, yes, Carnival!*

The sponges are sold, and the *mordida* set aside. While the *Nancy B.* was not stopped by the *San Cristobul* on our way in, I do expect a visit from Cisneros soon, anyway.

Dr. Sebastian is off to see his intelligence contacts but expects to join us for dinner at Ric's tonight, and Higgins is off with his university scholars—don't expect to see *him* for a while. Thomas and McGee are bringing aboard fresh water and wood, and Jemimah, with the help of Joannie and Daniel, is restocking the pantry. Me? I'm off to Ric's with Davy and Tink.

On the way, we stop at the La Pelea de Gallos Arena so I can set up a fight for El Gringo tomorrow—and yes, it is to be with the undefeated El Matador. The ringmaster smiles slyly as he takes my entry fee.

"*Gracias, Señorita.* The purse is two hundred pesos. *Buena suerte,*" he says, but I don't think he really means the good luck part. Well, we'll see . . . and two hundred pesos, hey? That'll stand my crew a lot of treats.

When we get to Ric's, it is blazing with life. The days of Lent are nearly upon the Catholic populace, and they are making the most of the time they have left before everything gay shuts down for forty days. I have on my blue dress, and for once, it doesn't stand out amidst all the colorful garments. It is low-cut, yes, but it ain't the lowest bodice around, that's for sure. Though I love my adopted town of Boston, I like the free and easy nature of this place, too.

"And what will you give up for Lent, Jackass?" asks Davy as we make our way through the merrymakers on Plaza de San Francisco.

"Oh, probably good sense, caution, forbearance," I retort. "I'd like to give up chastity, but I guess that ain't gonna happen."

On our way into Ric's, I warn Davy and Tink, "Lads, Cisneros will probably show up here. No matter what he says and does to me, you must hold back." I squeeze both of their arms. "And you know why."

"What I *don't* know, Jacky," says Davy, "is why you're going to sing in this place tonight when you've already got a fortune in gold stashed in your hold?"

"Because, dear Davy," I say, poking my finger into the air, "for one, until that gold is safely delivered to Boston, where Ezra Pickering can safely dispose of it to our best ad vantage, we are no richer than we were before. Right now it is just simple dead-weight ballast to keep our ship upright in the waves, and that's all it is."

Davy just grunts at that.

"And two," I say, adding a finger to the first, "we are here to keep our ears open concerning the doings of the Spanish Navy. If the *San Cristobal* comes out and sinks us, we will get no joy from all that gold, as we will be drowned and dead. And three"—another finger joins the other two—"I like doing it. So there. Ah, here's Ric now."

Señor Ricardo Mendoza comes toward me, arms extended, great smile upon his face. "*Nuestra cantante americana bonita,* say you will sing for us tonight!"

"Of course, Señor Ric," I say, and take his hands and place a kiss upon his cheek. "And now a table if you would."

We are given a fine table in the middle of everything, just the way I like it, and good food and drink are brought and we lay to. Davy and Tink are dressed in their new nautical finery and are catching some admiring female glances. I notice that Tink has caught the notice of the girl serving our table—a black-haired beauty whose glossy ringlets dangle about her ivory oval of a face. Tink notices, too. Her lips are full and red, and there is a blush in her cheeks. Her eyes are modest and shy.

*Right,* I say to my ever-doubtful self, watching the play twixt the two. *Real shy. Huh! I'll bet she scoped out Tink last time we were in and made sure she was assigned to this table. But, what the hell, she's a neat little piece, and Tink needs some female attention, so let's see what happens.*

We eat, we drink, we sing, and, yes, we dance, too. Davy and I are up doing a spirited hornpipe to a tune expertly strummed and drummed by the house band when Lieutenant Cisneros and a small group of Spanish junior officers come in and take a table close to ours. He does not take his eyes off mine.

Davy and I finish up with a flourish, take a bow, accept the applause, and head back to our table. Tink has gone off with the girl—I see that they are hand in hand and deep in conversation in an alcove across the room—and as we settle back in at our table, I am not surprised to see Cisneros on his feet and heading for me.

"Steady, Davy," I say, putting my hand on his arm. "Why don't you go have a drink at the bar during this? It'd be best, trust me."

He doesn't look convinced, but he gets up, casts a cold look in Cisneros's direction, and leaves.

The Spanish Lieutenant comes up and stands next to me, looking down.

"Lieutenant," I say. "You are here for *la mordida,* and here it is. Now go away." I fling the little bag of coins against his chest, and it falls back onto the table. "Go give it to your Captain. Perhaps he will pat your head."

As I suspected, he does not go away, but instead sits down and snarls, "*Cierre su boca, puta.* Shut up and listen. We know you were diving off Cayo Hueso. We also know that there was a British warship anchored next to you for the past few weeks. What is going on?"

"I am but a sponge diver. You have your 'little bite' from the profits of my labors. Take it and go away."

"What business did the *buque de guerra inglés* have with you there?"

"Why did you not go out and ask them? Are you afraid?

You have twice as many guns as the *Dolphin*. The English and the Spanish are enemies, I think."

His face darkens. "Believe me, if I were captain of the *San Cristobal,* that British boat would lie right now at the bottom of the sea, and I would spit on the graves of all who went down with it."

"You are such a sweet man, Cisneros," I say. "However, you might find it not so easy to sink a British frigate. They do, after all, have British sailors, and *very* expert British gunners. During an engagement, a lucky shot might even find your own fine *hidalgo* hide and lay it out flat."

"You haven't answered my question, *puta*. Why was that ship lying next to you?"

I give my head a toss. "The Captain of that ship and I have a . . . friendship."

He looks incredulous. He points his finger at my forehead.

"The captain of a British frigate makes his ship wait at anchor while he takes a whore-of-a-sponge-diver? I do not think so."

"Men take their pleasure where they find it. Surely you know that, being something of a man yourself. Not much of a man, but something. And I can do other things than merely diving for sponges. *Many* other things. And I am told I am very good at those things."

His face turns a pleasing shade of purple, and I fear for the glass that he clutches in his hand.

"So. If you did those things for him, you will now do those things for me. There are rooms here, and I will take you there."

"No, you will not."

"And why not?"

" 'Cause I said so is why. And because you hurt those poor sailor boys just for talking to me and made me watch."

"Poor boys, pah! They needed a lesson and I gave it to them." His gaze grows hotter. "And I gave a lesson for you, too, *muchacha.*"

"I can only hope that you, also, receive such a lesson someday. Although I do not take pleasure in such things, I will rejoice in watching."

It is too much for him. He reaches out and grabs me by the neck.

"You will do what I say, you—"

Then he looks up into the hard eyes of Davy, Tink, and Señor Ric, all of whom have been watching the proceedings. It is Señor Ric who says, "You know the rules, Señor. Patrons must not mishandle the señoritas. You must now leave my place."

Cisneros, furious, flings me back in my chair, releasing my neck.

"Do not think that this is over, girl," he says as he collects his men and stalks off. "No, it is not."

Davy and I head back to the *Nancy* to check on the reprovisioning and to rest up for the night's revels.

Tink, however, stays at Ric's.

# Chapter 42

⚓ I pick up El Gringo Furioso and take off his vest and stroke and smooth down his feathers. I put my hand around his neck and look into his beady little eyes and ask, "Are you ready, Gringo? You don't have to go if you don't want to."

He struggles in my grip and his eyes seem to say, "Yes. I want to go. Put me down. There's no one to fight here. Here's a peck for you and I hope it hurts. Now let's get on with it."

All right, Gringo, we will do that. But soon . . . Not right now.

Daniel and Joannie are bustling around, neatening up things, and I think they're doing it 'cause they think Jemimah might be finishing up her latest Rabbit Tale. I got to admire how she manages to stretch these things out and get the most work out of the kids because of it.

"Pleeeease, Jemimah, we got everything put away—all the wood, all the food, all the—"

"All right, chil'ren, you can sit and listen," she says, casting a warning eye on the pair. "But you be good now, y'hear?" She clears her throat. "Now, you'll recall, when we left the Big Woods, Fox and Bear was down in the hole, lookin' at certain destruction, and Brother Rabbit had sent for his church-lady wife to come up and say some words over the two doomed Brothers.

"By and by, Sister Rabbit, her Bible under her arm, come hoppin' up the road, her rabbit child by her side.

"'Husband,' she says, when she sees Brother Rabbit. 'Just *what* is goin' on here?'

"'Jes' look over the side dere, Sister Wife,' says Brother Rabbit, pointin' down. 'What you see?'

"She look down the hole at the fox and the bear, who look back up at her. 'Look like two unrepentant sinners to me,' says Sister Rabbit, wrinklin' up her bunny nose and re-memberin' when these two particular sinners had her by the ears and were danglin' her over their pot of boilin' oil.

"'Dat's right,' says Brother Rabbit. 'And they's about to go off to dere reward, so's I suspects they be repentin' real fast, and we'uns was thinkin' dat it'd be good iffen you could say some Scripture over dem 'fore the mens come up and shoots 'em.'

"'Hmmm ...,' says Sister Rabbit, and she open her Bible. 'Daniel in the lions' den would be good. Or how 'bout Shadrach, Meshach, and Abednego in the fiery furnace?'

"'They be good, but do the one about walkin' through de valley o' de shadow o' death,' says Brother Rabbit, ''cause that be where dese ol' boys be strollin' real soon.'

"So, while the fox he growl and the bear he wail, Sister Rabbit reads out that Psalm.

"'Dere. I hope dat makes y'all feel better,' say the rabbit, grinnin' all over his face. He cock up one of his ears. 'Is dat the mens I hear comin'? Best get ready, Brothers. Best git right wit' God.'

"'Oh, please, Brother Rabbit, please get us outta here 'fore the mens come,' bawls the bear, tears rollin' out of his eyes, his front paws clasped together in supplication. 'I ain't yet ready to meet the Lord!'

"'Brother Bear,' growls the fox, glarin' hard at the rabbit, 'shut yo' mouth and save yo' breath. Dat damn rabbit couldn't get us out of here, anyhow.'

"'Oh, yes, I could get you out, Brothers,' say the rabbit. 'But I ain't gonna. I gots me a whole fam'ly o' little bunnies now, which you ain't never gonna get a chance to chomp on 'cause o' the fix you in. I gotta look out for dem. Got responsibilities. Myself, I'll prolly miss outrunnin' you two and alla time making you look like the fools you surely be.'

"'What if we promises to never lay tooth nor claw on no rabbit ever again?' asks the fox. 'Will you get us out den?'

"Rabbit think hard on this. 'Hmmm . . . What you think, Sister Wife?'

"'If they swears on this here Bible, Brother Husband. *And* if they promises to come to church on Sunday mornin's and meetin' on Wednesday evenin's from now on. Reverend W. Crane was just sayin' yesterday that he was mighty concerned about these boys' spiritual growth.' Sister Rabbit sure enjoyin' the fun, too.

"'Oh, pleeeease!' wails Brother Bear.

"'All right,' agrees the rabbit. 'Pass 'em down the Good Book, Sister, but be careful.'

"Brother Fox gets on Brother Bear's shoulders and reaches up, and Sister Rabbit leans way over the edge with

Brother Rabbit holdin' on tight to her little white cottontail so's she don't fall down in the pit, and so the Bible is passed.

"'All right, boys! Now testify!' crows the rabbit.

"And the fox and the bear put their paws on the Book and makes the promises.

"'Now, you brothers know if y'all break yore promises,' says Sister Rabbit, 'you'll roast in Hell fo'ever and ever? Good. Now throw me back my Bible, and my good man will get you out o' dere, won't you, honey?'

"'Right,' says Brother Rabbit, turnin' to Rabbit Child, who's been hangin' about watchin' all this. 'Run on down to the pond and ask Sister Beaver to come on up here and maybe bring a few o' her brethren along wit' her.'

"'What he doin'?' ask Brother Bear. 'How dat gonna help?'

"'Shut up, Bear,' says Brother Fox.

"I'm gonna shut up, too, right here," says Jemimah. "Time to get ready for dinner. These men be gettin' hungry."

*Me, too.*

# Chapter 43

*Lieutenant James Emerson Fletcher*
*Onboard HMS* Dolphin
*En route to rendezvous off Key West*
*And not a moment too soon*

*Jacky Faber*
*At once my greatest joy and my greatest trial*
*Onboard her schooner the* Nancy B. Alsop *off Key West*
*Or, at least, I think she is—one never knows*

*Jacky,*

    *I do not know what I have done in this life to deserve the things that happen to me in regard to you. What should have been the simplest of love stories—I take your hand and you take mine—turns out to be the most tangled of knots.*

    We arrived in Kingston in good order—the ship in full dress, gun salutes and all that. There was great joy upon the ship, for good Captain Hudson has granted daytime shore leave for all trustable sailors aboard, the liberty to be accomplished in three rotating watch sections. As you well know, it is rare for a commander to let his men off his ship in these times of war, fearing that they will desert, so they love the captain all the more for it. Some pay was issued and the joyful anticipation was palpable.

Upon mooring, we piped the Governor aboard, and I am reminded that the pirate Henry Morgan was once made governor of this island by our own government. After all the bowing and scraping was done, this present Governor, General Sir Eyre Coote, invited Captain Hudson and Lieutenant Bennett to dine at his residence. We junior officers were invited to the Officers' Club on the base, an invitation we gratefully accepted. Several of the lads and I made preparations and, seeing the ship well-secured, set off in a state of high spirits.

We went by coach and we passed by the very tavern you and I dined in all those years ago. I must pronounce myself moved to see the place. And when I saw the wall, the wall upon which you stood that day, your dress blowing about you, I closed my eyes and saw you standing there yet, so young and wild and free, and so very, very beautiful.

At the club—an elegant palace built in the Spanish style, all high ceilings and swooping arches—we were graciously received and introductions were made. I cast my eyes over the crowd and saw that, while there were a number of blue naval uniforms, there were many more of army scarlet. I was being introduced to several of them when I received a jolt.

"Gentlemen, may I present Captain Lord Richard Allen, Sixteenth Dragoons?"

I stiffened because I recognized the name—and the

face—instantly, for I well remember when I came upon you and him together in the Mississippi River. That scene has been forever burned into my mind.

There were bows and murmurs of introduction all around.

"Mr. Fletcher. So good to see you again," said Allen, extending his hand and waving me to his table. "A glass of wine with you, Sir?" The wretched man was unable to keep a sheepish grin from his face. I gritted my teeth and sat down.

Wine was poured and dinner served, and a great spread it was—a fine treat after shipboard fare. I enjoyed it thoroughly, in spite of the awkward situation.

"May I hope that our mutual friend is safe and well?" Allen came right out and inquired.

"She is."

"It gladdens me to hear that. And do you know just where might she be?"

"She is on a scientific expedition."

He regarded me and my distinct lack of enthusiasm in answering his questions concerning you.

"If you require satisfaction, Fletcher," he said, "I am willing to give it."

I, of course, did wish to kill him for having laid his hands upon your person. But if I were to manage to slay all those who have similarly done so, I would have racked up quite a lengthy Butcher's Bill. So what I said was, "My Captain, whom I respect, has forbidden his junior officers to duel. Besides, I do not perceive that you forced your attentions on Miss Faber. She is her own person, and she has an open and affectionate nature as you might well have observed."

"Oh, yes," he said, a little too heartily for my taste. "And you must excuse me for being very fond of her. And furthermore we must be friends, you and I." He extended his hand to me.

I took his hand and said, "Very well, my Lord."

"Good, and you must drop that 'my Lord' stuff. I am not much of a Lord and we are similar in rank. I answer to both Richard and Dick," he said, grinning broadly.

I was finding it difficult to dislike this man.

The dinner dishes were cleared and more wine was poured.

"So, just where in the world is this 'scientific expedition' . . . Good Lord, is that Flashby over there? I never expected to see that particular blighter again. Last I heard of him was a splash as he went over the side of the *Belle of the Golden West*. Flashby! Come over here."

I looked over to see that Flashby had, indeed, entered the room and was startled to hear his name spoken. Upon recognizing Lord Allen, his face darkened, but he walked over to stand next to our table, his hands clasped behind him. Neither the Captain nor I stood up.

"Up to more nasty business, Flashby, eh, what?"

"I am here on His Majesty's business," replied Flashby, coldly.

"If you're involved, it's sure to be nasty, Flashbutt." It was plain that Allen was not at all worried about offending Flashby. It was equally plain that Flashby was furious . . . and extremely uncomfortable.

"I did not come here to be insulted, Mr. Allen," he said, his teeth clenched.

Captain Allen got to his feet and faced Flashby. "Then meet me at dawn. Name your second. Mr. Fletcher here will second me. And that's 'Lord Allen' to you, Flashby." There is silence from our table and from all near us, this being an outright challenge.

"I am forbidden from dueling in my current command," said Flashby, his nose in the air. "Perhaps some other time, my *Lord*. May I be excused from Your *Lordship's* presence? Good day, then."

Flashby turned on his heel and left the place, to a hum of conversation. A Royal Navy officer had refused a challenge— a serious loss of face . . . *and* a discredit to the Service, which does not go down well with those naval officers present, myself included. While I thoroughly enjoyed Flashby's humiliation, I did not like seeing the Service disgraced.

Allen sat back down. "Do you think he speaks the truth on that?"

"Yes, my Lor . . . yes, Captain Allen. He is Second Mate on HMS *Dolphin* and I am Third Mate on the same ship. Had Captain Hudson not imposed his rule, I should have called Flashby out long ago. I will do so when the restrictions are lifted."

"Hmmm . . . Well, don't expect that cowardly rascal to be around when that happens. He's a slippery bastard," said Allen. "So you've heard what he did to her?"

"If you mean that he repeatedly struck her and confined her in durance most vile? That he burned her leg and promised even more torture? Yes, if that's what you mean. If there was more, perhaps I do not want to hear of it."

"No. That was about the extent of it."

"She tells me you were instrumental in stopping the abuse, and for that I thank you."

"Ummm . . . Well, rest assured that she dealt out far more than she received," he said, chuckling at the remembrance. "But tell me the name of your ship again."

"HMS *Dolphin*. Why do you ask?"

A smile spread across his features.

"And where is our girl and her 'scientific expedition'?"

"Off Key West. We will rendezvous in four days."

"Um. So she must be gathering very valuable specimens," he said, and then laughed. "Oh, this grows so very, *very* interesting!"

"But why . . . ?"

"Because I, along with a squad of my men, have been assigned to your ship to guard something of great value." He lifted his glass to me. "We shall sail together, James Fletcher, and we will see just what our little friend is really up to."

*Good Lord.*

# Chapter 44

I'm tending to El Gringo over at the coop, hand-feeding him shelled walnuts—figure he could use the oil the nuts got in them to glossy up his feathers some, and maybe put a little more weight on him, which can't hurt—and Jemimah's over at the breadboard, mixing up flour and water and forming up loaves for kneading, and the kids are pleading for the rest of the story.

"So you remember that Fox and Bear are still down in that trap?"

Both heads bob up and down.

"All right, then you'll recall that Brother Rabbit done sent off his boy to fetch Sister Beaver and her crew, and by 'n' by Miz Beaver come waddlin' up the path, with Brother Beaver and other of the Beaver Clan by her side.

"'What chew want, Brother Rabbit?' she say. 'We gots work t' do. Dams don't build demselves, y'know.'

"'Want some chewin' done, Sister,' says the rabbit, gettin' up and goin' over and puttin' his paw on a sweet gum tree that he had picked out. 'Now iffen you and Brother

Beaver was to chew on dis side o' dis tree, it'll fall over dere and dat big ol' branch'll poke down into dat hole and doze Brothers'll be able to climb out.'

"Sister Beaver look down into de pit and say, 'Don't see de wisdom o' settin' doze two rascals free, but all right.'

"So she and her man commence to chawin' away, and by 'n' by the tree come down and the branch fall where it was supposed to and the fox and the bear was able to climb out, blinkin' in the sunlight.

"Brother Rabbit, not quite trustin' the conversion of Brother Fox and Brother Bear, take his child and head off down the hill and back to the rabbit shack.

"But Sister Rabbit, no, she stand her ground, as the newly freed fox and the bear tower over her, to test the strength of their promises, and maybe her own faith, too.

"'Today's Wednesday, Brothers. See you at Meetin'.' Then she tuck her Bible under her arm and hop off down the hill after her man and her boy. End of story."

There is silence for a bit and then Joannie asks, "What happened to those brothers after that? Did they keep their promises?"

"Well, child, Brother Bear, he go back to live with his mama, who give him a good spankin' for hangin' around with bad company like that Brother Fox and he promise never to do it again and he live out his life all happy, gettin' fat on eatin' berries and roots and apples and suchlike—but no bunnies, 'cause Brother Bear don't want to go to Hell for the breakin' of a promise to the Lord, nossir.

"And Brother Fox, he starts goin' to church and meetin's and soon he takes the Spirit into his heart and he put on the black hat and long frock coat and white collar of the preacher. Preacher Fox preaches all through the Big Woods and then goes to preachin' up and down the Big River and he got right famous and he never again ate another rabbit. End of story, back to work, both of you."

"Jemimah, do you mean that there ain't any more stories?" asks Daniel, a bit crestfallen.

"No, boy, I don't mean that at all. Y'see, when one wily fox step aside, another one will step up and take his place, and when one bear decide to lie back and smell the flowers, well, another mean old bear will come roarin' in, up to all sorts of rascality."

Jemimah chuckles deep in her throat. "And you can be sure there'll be one very smart rabbit on hand to confuse them both. Heh! No, Sister Girl and Brother Boy, the stories never end. Now back to work, both of you."

The kids scurry out and Jemimah brings her gaze to bear upon me.

"I hear things down below. Late at night. Things rustlin' about. Sets my mind to thinkin' . . . and what I think is, Brother Rabbit may be the smart one in the Big Woods, but you, girl, you somehow be the trickster in this here story. I know it to be true."

I don't say anything to that, just continue to stroke Gringo's feathers as Jemimah continues to knead the bread.

She's humming a tune as she does it and I say, "Jemimah. That song you're hummin'. It sounds right familiar. Will you sing it for me?"

She slaps a dough ball on the board and commences to

knead it. And she lifts her head and starts to sing and beat the bread at the same time:

> *Oh, the High Sheriff, he told his Deputy,*
> *Go out and bring me Lazarus. (Huh!)*
> *Oh, the High Sheriff, he told his Deputy,*
> *Go out and bring me Lazarus. (Huh!)*
> *Bring him dead or alive, Lord, Lord,*
> *Bring him dead or alive.*

I was right, I had heard the song before. On the way down the Mississippi River, work gangs on the banks would sing this as they brought their big hammers down on the rocks they were splitting. They would time the hammer blows to fit the song, and so make the work pass easier. Just like sailors sing shanties when they're raising heavy sails, and just as Jemimah does as she kneads her bread, grunting *huh!* and slamming the dough down where the hammers would come down.

> *Oh, they found poor Lazarus,*
> *up between two mountains. (Huh!)*
> *Oh, they found poor Lazarus,*
> *up between two mountains. (Huh!)*
> *And they brought him down, Lord, Lord,*
> *They brought him down.*

I'm noticing that the bread dough is taking a good deal of punishment, as Jemimah seems to be putting a good deal of anger into her *huh!* She sings on, her big voice filling the galley.

*And they shot poor Lazarus,*
*shot him with a great big number. (Huh!)*
*And they shot poor Lazarus,*
*shot him with a great big number. (Huh!)*
*Number forty-five, Lord, Lord,*
*Number forty-five.*

She pauses a bit to put another dough ball on the board, and then takes up the song again.

*And they taken poor Lazarus,*
*laid him on the commissary counter. (Huh!)*
*And they taken poor Lazarus,*
*laid him on the commissary counter. (Huh!)*
*And they walked away, Lord, Lord,*
*They just walked away.*

*Lazarus's mother,*
*she come a'runnin'. (Huh!)*
*Oh, Lazarus's mother,*
*she come a'runnin'. (Huh!)*
*Cryin', 'My only son, Lord, Lord,'*
*Cryin', 'My only son.'*

Jemimah stops singing, and she stops kneading, too, and just stands there for a while, her head up, her eyes closed.

"That was beautifully sung, Jemimah," I say, meaning it.

She nods and goes back to her task.

A thought occurs to me and though I know that I'm probably treading where I should not go, I ask, "Jemimah, you've told us some things about your children, but you haven't said anything about your husband. Where is he?"

She snorts. "He's either in Heaven or in Hell, but he's dead all the same."

*Oh.*

"How did it happen, if you don't mind me asking?" I say, as gentle as I can. "You can tell me to mind my own business and I will shut up and do that."

"No, child, it's all right. I will tell you." She takes a deep breath. "His name was Moses and everybody called him Mose. He was a big man and did the blacksmithin' work on the plantation, poundin' out hot iron and steel. Worked with the horses, too. Everybody liked him, colored and white, alike. When he was a young man, he run away twice, tryin' to get to freedom, but he was caught and brought back each time and whipped. After me and the children come along, he stopped tryin' to run away. He learned to get along, just like the rest of us."

She is quiet again for a while, then heaves a great sigh and goes on.

"He was good to me and he was a good father to the kids, too. Raised 'em up as good as he could—bein' a slave and all, you ain't got all that much say in things. Yes, he loved his children and that's what brought him down at the end. When things went bad and the plantation was bein' broke up, some men from Charleston come up to take our two oldest kids away. When Mose saw my Josh and my Rosie bein' bound up and put in the wagon to be taken off and sold, sumthin' happened in his mind and he rushed at the men and tried to set our chil'ren loose so's they could run off to the woods and maybe get away, but he didn't have much luck in that. They hit at him with clubs and told him to lie down and don't cause no trouble, but he wouldn't do it, no, he swung on the men with his big fists and when two of 'em was on the ground and he saw that they was bringin' guns, he re'lized what he had done and he run off into the woods, all crazy in his head.

"They sent out armed men on horses with dogs, and they run him down and they killed him. Shot him when he run and cut him down when he turned and tried to make a stand.

"They brought him back in a buckboard with his toes draggin' in the dust, and just like poor Lazarus, they laid him out all bloody on a plank, right there in front of me and what children were left. Did it as an example to us Nigras what would happen if we ever act up. We buried him that afternoon, and the next day they come and took the rest of my kids down to the Charleston Slave Market. In a few days, they come and took me there, too."

She paused for a moment, her eyes still closed.

"Mose thought he was strong as Brother Bear, fast as Brother Fox, and clever as Brother Rabbit, but he warn't none of those, no," she says, shaking her head. "But he was my good old man, and I miss him."

With that, Jemimah Moses takes off her dusty apron and hangs it up. And as for Jacky Faber, she who used to think she had seen some trouble in her life, well, I just sit there and don't say a mumblin' word.

# Chapter 45

I left Gringo's vest on him for the journey to La Pelea de Gallos Arena, and this time I put it on over his wings so he wouldn't flap about and waste his strength. Carnival is still in full swing and the bird's beady little eyes seem to take in the excitement that swirls all about. The place is packed, with crowds of people pushing and shoving to get in the still-open doors. Davy, Tink, and Daniel, who had come with us, go off to join the throng. Joannie, I keep by me.

Before we go in the contestant entrance, I put the little leather hood over Gringo's head to keep him from getting too excited at the sight of the other birds. Still, I can feel his heart thumping in the palm of my hand.

I'm given my fight number. It's three, my lucky numeral, and we settle down to await our turn. The other handlers look at El Gringo curiously—what with his tight vest and all. The others have their birds in cages and they flutter nervously within.

Soon Red Sash leaves the holding area, and shortly we hear a trumpet blast and then:

"*Señores y señoritas!* Welcome to La Pelea de Gallos Arena on the last day of the season! Tomorrow we shall all don our ashes and there will be no contests for forty days! But today, eat, drink, be happy, and place your bets! The first fight will be between El Pollo Feo of Rancho Verde, and Chucho from La Playa Hermosa! Handlers, to your positions!"

The doors swing open and the first two contestants are marched out. Through the open doors I can see that Tink and Davy have managed to worm their way to spots right on the rail.

"Joannie. When we go out, I want you to join Davy and Tink and Daniel. They're right there." The doors close. "And here"—I dig in my pocket and pull out a gold coin—"put this on El Gringo to win. You should get good odds. And I'll give you Gringo's vest when we get to the center."

She nods, and a roar goes up from the arena. The first two gladiators are definitely at it now.

I spy El Matador's handler sitting nearby with a cage next to him. He is a small man with a large mustache, and wears the loose white linen suit so favored in this country. I've heard him addressed as Señor Maza. I am sure he remembers me from the last match—female trainers are not all that common—and I know he is eyeing me with a certain smug confidence.

We'll see about *that*.

I unlace Gringo's leather hood and pull it off. I had made it to look like the hoods that falconers put on their harriers, and the effect is not lost on the other handlers in the place. I have their undivided attention.

Gringo shakes his head and looks about, fierce as any hawk. Then he crows out his challenge, loud and clear.

"Hush, Gringo," I say, stroking his head, his uncut bright red comb a taunt to all the bald heads sticking out of cages. "Save it for the ring." I reach up under him and massage his legs and thighs to loosen him up, something I have been doing of late and which he seems to enjoy, or at least tolerate.

I have found that, in any game, be it cards or sword-fighting or chess or whatever, part of the victory will be won by messing with your opponent's head in the lead-up to the actual battle. Make him lose his confidence, like.

In that spirit I remove the lead slugs from Gringo's vest, one by one, and drop them in my pocket. This also is not missed by the others, especially by El Matador's handler. Could it be that I have started a new kind of training for the gamecocks of Cuba? If so, I pity the poor things.

There is another roar from outside and then silence, which means the first fight is over. Sure enough, the doors swing open and two men walk in, one triumphant, holding his struggling gladiator with both hands, the other disconsolate, carrying a very limp and very dead bird in his. The men put their birds, both the quick and the dead, back in their cages, and the defeated pair make their exit through the back door, while the victors sit and await the awards ceremony that will happen when all the fights are done. The Spanish, like most of us, do love their ceremonies.

I pull another coin from my pocket and walk over to Señor Maza.

"*Buenos días, Señor.* It seems our fighters are to meet

again in combat," I say in Spanish. He nods. "Would you like to place a side bet on the outcome?" I hold up the piece of eight. "Even odds, even though your bird is heavily favored. Yes?"

He considers and again he nods, but he does not seem quite so confident now.

There is another trumpet call and two more men and their birds tromp out to meet their fates. I settle back down and undo the lacings on Gringo's vest, but I do not take it off just yet. Instead I reach in my pocket and pull out a few seeds and offer them to El Gringo. He pecks at them avidly. We didn't feed him this morning, wanting him to stay lean and mean and hungry. But I figure a bit of a treat now won't hurt, and it'll keep his mind off the other birds.

Again there is a roar as the second bout ends, so we stand up and get ready. The doors open, and two men come back in, bearing their now quiet burdens—both cocks are still alive, but just barely. Blood trickles down through the fingers of one of the men, and from his expression, his bird was clearly the loser.

The trumpet calls and we rise, and, next to Señor Maza and El Matador, we march into the ring.

When we turn and face each other, Red Sash gestures to me and calls out, "In this next bout, we present the challenger El Gringo Furioso from Rancho . . ."—here he squints at his notes—"Dove-coot . . ."

I raise Gringo up for the crowd to see and there are shouts of derision as well as comments on his peculiar garment.

"Look! He's already trussed up for the oven! Ha! Five pieces of silver on El Matador the Invincible!"

"Is El Gringo cold? Is he afraid? Does he even have any wings?"

"I think he is very handsome and dressed in the height of fashion," calls out one of the señoritas who lean out over the balcony. "Two pieces on him!"

*Thank you, Sister.*

I take off Gringo's vest and hand it to Joannie. "Go, girl." And she bounds across the ring and vaults over the rail and is collected by Tink and Davy. Gringo, freed of his vest, spreads his wings and crows out his challenge. The crowd cheers.

". . . and on this side is El Matador, the champion! From Hacienda Maza!

There is a roar from the crowd as Señor Maza lifts up his fighter.

*El Matador! Viva el Matador!*

"Engage!" shouts Red Sash, and we shove our game-cocks against each other to get them good and mad. They both shriek and try to slash at each other, their neck feathers straight out.

"Ready!"

Señor Maza and I both crouch down and place our fighters on the sand.

"Fight!"

We release and stand back while the cocks leap at each other, spurs up and slashing, beaks thrusting at each other's necks and eyes.

"*Olé!*" shouts the crowd.

"Get him, Gringo!" shouts Joannie from behind me.

Gringo takes an early slash on the wing from El Matador, but the wound is not deep and he presses his attack. No longer the weaker one, he is relentless in pushing back the other bird, back against the rail. El Matador takes a cut to the neck, and the blood flows. But the wound is not mortal, so he fights on against Gringo's furious onslaught—he is not called *el campeón* for nothing—he's got depth and he's got bottom. He angles for a weakness and he strikes back as he finds it. He lashes out with his beak and finds Gringo's untrimmed comb, grabs it, and holds on tight.

*Oh no! Was I wrong in keeping his comb uncut?*

Maybe I was. El Matador has him in a death grip and he does not let go as blood seeps out of Gringo's torn comb and trickles over his face.

*Come on, Gringo! You can get out of that! Fight!*

Fight he does. Just like a cat when losing a fight will turn on her back and rake her opponent's belly with her open claws, Gringo brings up his spurs, and with his strong legs, drives them deep into El Matador's breast and holds them there.

El Matador quivers, but still he holds on. Gringo pushes his spurs deeper . . . deeper . . . Then slowly El Matador opens his beak, tries and fails to make a last defiant crow, and falls back, done.

"Fight over!" shouts Red Sash, and the crowd roars. The champion is down!

I scoop up the victorious Gringo and hold him up to the cheering crowd, then hand him off over the rail to Daniel. "Get him back in his hood and vest! We've got to calm him down!" I can feel his chest heaving and his heart pumping wildly under my hand. I hear Joannie whoop as she runs off to collect our winnings.

The trumpet calls and I go back through the doors as the next two contestants come out, carrying their fighters. Señor Maza and what's left of El Matador go back through with me.

I watch him as he tenderly puts his fallen gladiator back into his cage for the last time. I think I hear him say, "Sleep, my son, you have died with honor," and I see something I didn't notice before—the sleeves and pant legs of his linen suit are frayed. It comes to me that Hacienda Maza is probably no more than a few cages behind an earthen-floored hut in the poorer section of this town, and that El Matador was feeding his master and his family.

*Oh, why must I be so mean and thoughtless sometimes?*

I approach him, intending to give my condolences, and he looks up and announces, his face a mask of shame, "Señorita . . . the wager . . . I cannot . . ."

I know he cannot cover the bet, so I say, "Put the money in the poor box at the Cathedral, a little at a time, over the year. And, here, add my bit for *los pobres*." And I give him my piece of eight.

He nods gravely and takes it as I sit down next to him to await the end of these proceedings.

There are four more contests and then there is the final awarding of the prizes. I collect my two hundred pesos and rejoin my mates.

"Well," I say, "not a bad day all around. The drinks at Ric's will be on El Gringo Furioso. Shall we go?"

Go we shall, but something is wrong . . .

"Where's Joannie?" I ask.

We look around, and she is not here. I look at Davy.

"Last I saw of her, she was off to collect your winnings," says he.

Worried looks all around.

*Joannie is missing and nowhere to be found.*

*Uh-oh . . .*

# Chapter 46

"We'll go to Ric's. Whoever has taken her would look for us there. Daniel, you take Gringo back to the ship and tell them what has happened. Have Jim make the *Nancy* ready to go on a moment's notice. If you receive any word there, run to Ric's and tell us. If Higgins is not aboard, send for him. Tink and Davy, come with me."

Daniel flies off and the three of us march grimly across the plaza to Ric's.

"What do you think, Jacky?" asks Tink.

"I think it's surely someone who knows us—either Cisneros or El Feo or someone of that ilk. I can't believe that some random scoundrel would just snatch a kid who looks like a wharf rat and think she might be worth something to somebody." Joannie was dressed in her sailor garb—loose white shirt, canvas trousers, hair braided in a pigtail, feet bare. "Hope not, anyway."

Both of them nod. "The poor kid," mutters Davy through his clenched teeth. "If anyone hurts her, I'll—"

"Steady, Davy," I say, putting my hand on his arm. "Let's see how this plays out."

"It could be," suggests Tink, "that she was nabbed for the winnings she carried. They were considerable, you know, since the odds were so high against you."

*Right, and if that's the case, we'll soon find her body in some alley with her head bashed in—please, God, NO!*

"We'll see, Tink. We can only hope she's all right," I say. "Here we are."

The Café Americano sign looms overhead as we enter.

"Davy," I say, "stay here by the door. Lounge about— look casual and maybe a bit under the weather. I'll take a visible table off to the side there and send you a drink. If someone contacts me, we'll want to question him further. You understand? Good. Tink, you take the back door— same drill. All right? Let's go."

The lads split off and I go to receive Señor Ric's greeting. He is about to ask if I will play another set when I cut him short with, "Trouble, Señor Ric. The little girl who sang with me has been kidnapped and I suspect I will be contacted here. Has anyone given you a message?"

"No, Señorita, I am sorry." Señor Ric seems genuinely distressed. Well he might—he has daughters, too.

"Thank you for your concern, Señor. Just give me a table off to the side, thank you."

I am seated at a table off center but still very visible. I doff my mantilla, accept a glass of wine from Señor Ric, and order some drinks for Davy and Tink. I notice that it is the same dark-eyed girl I had noticed before who is the one who takes the glass to Tink. Under other circumstances, I would have rejoiced. Now I just wait.

· · ·

It is early afternoon and the place is filling up. Still no word from Daniel, or from anyone else. I begin to despair. *Oh, Joannie, you were safe back in London! Why didn't I leave you there?*

Then I notice a man enter—a *campesino* by his dress—who looks around and then fixes his eye upon me. He comes over.

"Señorita Faber?" he asks, looking furtively about.

I nod and he drops a folded note onto the table, then turns and heads for the front door. I gesture to Davy and Tink and they follow the man out. I open the note and read:

*Jacquelina—*

*I know you will be glad to hear that El Feo sleeps with the fishes, and I am once more Captain of* El Diablo Rojo. *I also have it on good authority that you have been very naughty and have been taking much gold from the* Santa Magdalena *and not handing all of it over to your English friends. I would very much like to share in some of that gold that you set aside, for old times' sake.*

*Yes, it is true that I also have your little girl. Fear not, she will not be harmed. Not yet, anyway.*

*We shall meet you off Key West to discuss things.*

*Till then,* querida mia . . .
*Su amigo,*
*Flaco*

I stand and put some coins on the table and Señor Ric comes over. He puts out his hand and I take it.

"Thank you, Señor, for all your kindness," I say, "but I think this is goodbye for a while."

"So sad, Señorita," he says. "We did so enjoy your presence."

"I know I shall be back someday and we will sing more songs. Till then, *vaya con Dios, Señor Ricardo*."

I present my cheek for his kiss and he delivers it, and I'm out the door and looking for the lads. I do not have to search far. I hear squeals of pain coming from a side alley and I follow the sounds.

"*Señores. No me molesten, por favor! Soy solamente un mensajero simple.*"

Davy and Tink have slung the man up against the wall and Davy has his shiv at the man's throat.

"What's he sayin'?" asks Tink.

"That he is only a messenger. We'll see about that," I say, and then, in Spanish, I demand of the man, "Where did you get this note?"

"From *Diablo Rojo*! Please, let me—"

"And where was that ship?"

"At Bahia Honda. That is where I work. In the shipyard."

"Do you know Flaco Jimenez, the Captain of that ship?"

"*Sí.*"

"Did he give you this note?"

"No. Another man."

"Who?"

"I don't know, Señorita, I—"

I look over at Tink. "Maybe a little more persuasion is necessary."

Tink grins and pulls out his own knife and holds it up

before the man's terrified eyes and then drops it down and slides it between the man's belly and his pants and then pulls it away, cutting the drawstring of the man's pants. They fall to his knees.

Tink then lays the flat of the blade against the man's thigh and begins moving the razor-sharp edge toward his manly parts. The man shrieks in terror.

"Now, Señor," I say. "Before you become a *castrado*, perhaps you will tell me who gave you the note. Hmmm?"

"It was . . . it was *un hombre inglés*! A big man. He gave me some money. And that's all I know! *Madrecita! Por favor!* I beg of you!"

"He says an Englishman gave him the note," I tell the lads. "What the hell?"

They shrug, as mystified as I.

"All right," I say. "Let him go. We've got to get back to the ship."

They release him and he slumps to the ground, grateful, I am sure, to be still whole.

We run back to the *Nancy* and leap aboard. Upon seeing that everyone is back, I order the lines thrown off and the sails raised.

"We've got to get out to Key West. Flaco's got Joannie," I announce to all and thrust the note to Higgins. "Jim! Off on the Port tack! John Thomas, McGee, get up all the canvas you can! Move it!"

We edge away from the dock as Higgins stands reading the message. After a moment he says, "I don't think Flaco wrote this."

"Why not?" I ask, taking my post on the quarterdeck next to Jim Tanner at the helm.

"For one thing, I believe that Captain Jimenez, for all his charms, is illiterate. For another, this is very much not like him."

"To take a hostage, you mean? Come on, Higgins, we did it all the time. That's what pirates do. We took some ourselves. Don't you remember?"

"Yes, but this is somehow different . . . a young girl snatched on the land and held for . . . not ransom, but to force you to do something," says Higgins. "And here's another thing—the note mentions Key West. As a Hispanic, Flaco would say, 'Cayo Hueso,' 'Bone Key,' and not Key West. And how would he know about the *Santa Magdalena*? I see someone else's hand in this, Miss."

"The messenger did mention an Englishman. I don't know who it could be."

"Hmmmm . . ."

"Anyway, we shall see, Higgins. But first we've got to get out to Key West, and fast."

"Agreed, Miss."

"Are all the guns primed and loaded?"

"Yes, they are."

"Good. We might need them when we get there."

It turns out we need them much sooner.

We have a good, brisk, following wind and are fairly tearing out of the harbor when we approach the *San Cristobal* on our starboard side. There is a sharp report from a signal cannon and a boat is put in the water. It is manned and comes toward us. I put long glass to eye.

"Christ! It's that damned Cisneros! He means to board us for a search!"

The boat draws closer. There are six marines in the boat and Cisneros stands at the bow.

"Stop your ship!" he shouts when he is within range. "We have information! We will search you!"

*Not this time, you won't!*

"Keep going, lads! All speed!"

I leap back to the aft swivel gun, which I know is loaded with a three-pound ball, and after I whip off the canvas cover, I aim it at the bow of the approaching boat.

"I hope you can swim, Cisneros!" I shout as I pull the matchlock. His face registers some shock as—*crrrraaack!*—the gun fires and the front of the boat explodes in a cloud of splinters. Actually, I hope he *can't* swim.

There is a cheer from my lads and cries of distress from the *San Cristobal*'s boat, which immediately sinks down to its gunwales. I'm glad to see that the poor marines are able to cling to it and not perish, but I rejoice to see Cisneros drenched and shaking his fist at me.

"I'm sure that was very satisfying, Miss," says Higgins, looking up at the guns of Morro Castle, "but you know we must now run the gauntlet."

"We must see to Joannie, Higgins. I see no other way to do it."

Higgins looks at me in an appraising way, nods, then goes to his duty station.

Cannons are fired and signals are run up the mast of the *San Cristobal* and puffs of smoke appear at the gun ports of the castle. Then we hear the low rumble.

*Booooooommmmm . . .*

We hear the whistle of the shots before they plunge into the water not twenty feet off our starboard side.

A huge geyser of water drenches our deck and all on it.

"Left full rudder!" I shout. "Jim! They've got our range! Steer a weaving course!"

Two more twenty-pound balls drive into the water in the spot just vacated by the *Nancy*. Then we hear something from another direction.

*Barroooooommmmm . . .*

We turn to see that the battery at San Salvador de la Punta is firing on us now.

"They've got us in a crossfire, Missy! They've got to get lucky soon!"

As if to give credence to his words, the next shot from Morro Castle comes down on our starboard rail, shattering it, and the next one falls not five feet from our bow.

"They've got our range! Get ready!"

"Left full!" I scream. "Steer due west!"

The *Nancy* turns and heads straight for the battery at San Salvador.

"What are you doing?" shouts Davy.

"Trying to get under their guns!" I shout back. "They can only point down so far. We're going to get out of the channel and try to get over the chain that stretches over the side approaches to the harbor! We've got a shallow draft! We should be able to get over it!"

*Boooooommmmm . . .*

These shots from Morro fall short. We are now out of their range.

*Barrrrooooom . . .*

More shots, again from San Salvador de la Punta, and they sail overhead, touching none of our masts, doing us no harm. We are under their guns now and must only get over that chain.

"Daniel! Get up on the bow! Watch for rocks! Report the bottom!"

The lad races to the bowsprit and stares downward.

"No rocks . . . Wait! There's one! Go right!"

We do it and don't hit.

"Bottom coming up . . . looks sandy . . . Good God! There's the chain! We're gonna hit!"

Nothing to do but charge on. Silence . . . Then there is a grinding noise and the *Nancy* staggers.

She staggers but does not stop, though she leans way over. The horrible grinding continues, and I look back at the harbor to see that many armed boats have been launched to take us. *Come on*, Nancy!

There is a last groan and we slip over the chain and are free. I was worried that the rudder would catch, but it didn't, thank God.

There is nothing ahead of us but the blessed open sea.

# Chapter 47

*Lieutenant James Emerson Fletcher*
*Second Mate, HMS* Dolphin
*Rounding western tip of Cuba*

*Jacky,*

*God willing, we should rendezvous with you tomorrow and get this business done.*

Except for the fact that I was not graced with your fine and spirited presence, my time in Jamaica was most enjoyable. We were treated most courteously by the staff on the base and Lord Allen saw to it that I was introduced to all of his usual haunts. Some of them were quite . . . well, colorful, as you can well imagine, given Captain Allen's nature, with which I know you are well acquainted. No, my dear, I did not avail myself of all the temptations offered therein. Ahem. Enough said about that.

We brought Allen and his men onboard two days ago and left on the tide. At dinner that night, we all enjoyed his animated tales of your actions on the trip down the Mississippi. I had not previously heard of your time as an Indian maiden, nor the now famous wager for the kiss, nor the fight with the renegade savages, nor . . . Well, nor a lot of things. I suspect I shall have to wait for Amy Trevelyne's next literary effort, to be fully informed.

I find it interesting that the Green-Eyed Monster of Jealousy lacks teeth when one knows the other person involved, and especially when he turns out to be a perfectly charming, likable, and merry rogue, with no harm or malice in him. I did not even bristle when, well into the after-dinner Madeira, he took to referring to you as Princess Pretty-Bottom. Yes, I have grown quite a thick skin.

You will note from the above heading that I have received a promotion. It is true—I am now Second Mate of HMS *Dolphin*. Imagine that, third in command of the ship we boarded as ship's boys. Oh, I know that you have done far greater things, but still, I allow myself a bit of pride.

Actually, I shouldn't be all that proud. My promotion was occasioned only by the fact that Lieutenant Flashby did not return to the ship in Kingston. He disappeared our first day there and has not been seen since. Dr. Sebastian said that Flashby left a note saying he was off on urgent intelligence business, but I think he departed as soon as he heard that Allen would now be aboard, and he did not want to put up with the humiliation of Richard's constant insults. Whatever, it was highly irregular all around, and I am glad he is gone. Glad, too, is our former Gunnery Officer and my good friend Lieutenant David Ropp, who is now Third Mate. I wish him the joy of his new position.

Well, there goes Seven Bells and now it's time for me to

take the Fore Noon Watch. I will put down my pen and put on my jacket and go topside in the hopes that we shall sight the *Nancy B.* very shortly.

*I pray that you are safe and well.*

*Jaimy*

# PART V

# Chapter 48

There is no one, neither King's nor pirate's ship, at the rendezvous when we arrive, so we drop anchor and wait . . . and wait . . . and wait . . .

I chew my knuckle and anxiously scan the horizon. "Keep a sharp eye out in all directions, Lookout!" I call up to Daniel overhead in the crow's-nest, long glass held to his eye. It was not necessary to say that, for he could not be more attentive. After all, it is his girl who has been taken, but all aboard are tense.

Higgins stands at my side. "Can I get you anything, Miss? Something to calm you?"

"No, and thank you, Higgins. I'll be all right. I just wish he'd get here."

"So you still think it is Captain Jimenez with whom you'll be dealing?"

"Yes. That messenger who came to Ric's addressed me as Señorita Faber. Not Bouvier, which is the name I have been using down here. Flaco is the only one around who remembers me as Faber."

"Hmmm. Perhaps you're right," says Higgins. "But I do wonder about that mysterious Englishman."

"So do I, but—"

"Missy! Ship due west! Coming on fast!"

"Well, we'll find out now, for sure." I grab my own glass and head up into the rigging. "Battle Stations, everyone! Weigh anchor!" We will need maneuvering room and can't be tied to the bottom.

I climb up next to Daniel and train my glass at the approaching ship, which is now hull up over the horizon.

"What can you make out, Danny?"

"Nothing yet . . . Wait . . . I can see his flag . . . It's red! It's that damned pirate!"

"Steady, Danny. We'll get her back. Just keep your eye on him and let us know if you can make out anything. All right?"

He gulps and nods, while I head back down to my quarterdeck to find the sails up and drawing.

"Steer due north, Jim," I say to Mr. Tanner, at the helm. "Let's make him come to us."

"Aye, Skipper, due north it is."

"It's *El Diablo Rojo,* Higgins. I think—"

"On deck there!" shouts Danny. "I can make out Jimenez! He's standing at the mast!"

"That's a good sign," I say. "I can deal with Flaco."

"But . . . but the big ugly one . . . El Feo . . . has . . . has Joannie on the bow . . . with a pistol to her head."

I whip my glass back up. My heart sinks. What he says is true. Joannie, her hands tied behind her, stands next to El Feo, and he has the barrel of a pistol tucked under her chin.

*How could Flaco allow this?*

Then I see why. Flaco is not standing at the mast—he is *tied* to it. His face and shirt are bloody, and he is no more in command of that ship than am I. His attempt to retake his ship must have failed, and failed miserably.

*Poor Flaco.*

We are now in hailing distance.

"Slack your sails and bring your ship under our lee, else I will put a bullet in her head!" shouts El Feo. "Fire on us, and the same thing will happen!" I can see him clearly now. He is dressed in traditional pirate gear—boots and baggy trousers, loose shirt crisscrossed with wide leather belts to hold knives and pistols—but with a difference. The red turbanlike thing on his head is stuck full of feathers and plumes. I guess it is to take away from his extreme ugliness, or maybe he means to make his reputation with it. I don't know, and I don't care about the vanity of some murderous brigand.

"Why should we not?" I cry out. "You will kill us, anyway! I'd rather we all died together, for that is our way!"

"Very brave," shouts El Feo. "But it does not have to be that way. You see, we know that you have gold. And if you tell us where it is, we will let you go on your way."

I don't believe that for a second, but I try to play for time. The ships are now alongside. "I have no gold. It all went with the English ship."

El Feo grins, and it is not a pretty sight. "English, eh? Well, we have here an Englishman who thinks differently." As he gestures behind him, a man steps up, a man in a loose white shirt, black pants and boots, smoking a long cheroot.

"Hello, Faber. So good to see you again."

*Who? What?*

*Flashby? Oh no!*

I collect myself and say, "How did you get here, Flashby? You were supposed to be in Kingston, with the decent men." This I say in English.

"The decent men? You mean those fools who cannot see right through you as I can? Well, it was a simple matter of taking a swift boat to Santiago de Cuba, then overland on horseback to meet with my Hispanic friends, and here I am."

"What makes you think you can trust this scum?"

"My dear, I have been working with this scum for years—sending poor, unsuspecting merchant ships their way when it suited me, in return for their help when I needed it. You will recall that I was operating in this area well before you got here."

When I say nothing to this, he goes on.

"Actually, I have found it much easier to work with the ugly one here. Captain Jimenez had much too many scruples for a true pirate."

I look over at Flaco. Though his head hangs, he is conscious of what is going on. And if looks could kill, El Feo would be a dead man, ten times over. Flashby, too.

"Speak Spanish, damn you both!" orders El Feo.

"As you wish, Señor," replies Flashby, in perfect Spanish. He turns to me. "The ships will be brought together and made fast. Your men will surrender their weapons, then they'll go below to your forward hatch, where they'll be made fast. Then we shall talk further about the gold."

"What gold?" I say, chin up, sticking to my story. "All the gold went on the *Dolphin*. You were there, you saw, you know what went on."

"I know you for a piece of filthy gutter trash, but I do not underestimate your cleverness and low cunning. The idea that you would be picking up all that treasure from the bottom of the sea and not squirreling away something for yourself is beyond belief. It doesn't fit your profile, as we say in the intelligence business." Flashy continues, smiling broadly, "Isn't it grand how the shoe is now on the other foot, as it were, Miss Faber?"

The ships come together and grappling hooks hold them tightly beam to beam. El Feo's men leap over to herd my sailors at musket point toward the hatch. "You, too, Mr. Higgins," says Flashby, waving his own pistol about, grinning and plainly enjoying this.

Jemimah appears at my side. She has seen the desperation in my eyes and she grabs my arm and hisses in my ear, "What would Brother Rabbit do if he was in this mess, girl?" She bores her gaze into my eyes and then she hurries down below. I guess the pirates don't much care what an old black woman does, 'cause they don't stop her. I do not blame her for going to hide, for this is not her fight.

El Feo jumps onto my deck, dragging Joannie with him. There is a large bruise around her left eye.

"You said you would not hurt her, *bastardo*," I hiss.

"She bit me," says El Feo. "It is something she will not do again." He jabs the pistol into the side of her neck. "Lower your sails. Now!"

Joannie's face betrays no emotion. Her eyes are hooded, and she has taken on a look I know well. It is the mask of the street kid who has been nabbed by the coppers—don't ever give them the satisfaction of seeing you cry, no matter how you feel inside.

I nod to Thomas and McGee. They loosen the bunt-lines and my sails fall to the deck. Flashby comes up next to me and blows a puff of rancid smoke in my face. "This is going to be such fun." He chuckles. He puts his hand on my tail and squeezes. "Such fun." I cannot repress a shudder of disgust.

*Oh Lord, this does not look good.*

"Now, as for the treasure, you will now—*Yeeow! Mierda!*" squeals El Feo, suddenly under attack from above.

"Let her go, goddammit! Run, Joannie! Run!"

Like a small hawk sweeping out of the sky onto its unsuspecting prey, Daniel Prescott has leaped from the crow's-nest to land squarely on top of El Feo, and he's flailing away at him with a stout marlinspike.

"Take that, you ugly bastard! Let her go!"

El Feo roars and raises his pistol and . . .

*No! Don't shoot him! Oh Lord, no!*

. . . and brings it down hard on the side of Danny's head. The boy crumples to the deck, blood coursing down his cheek, and he says no more.

Joannie, momentarily freed, runs not for freedom, but to Danny's side. Her hands are still tied behind her and so she can do nothing but lean over and put her lips on his brow. I know she thinks us all doomed, so that kiss will be her last free gesture. Flashby leans down and grabs her by the neck and jerks her to her feet. So much for grace in the face of horror.

"I will take your men out, one by one, put them on their knees and cut their throats right in front of you," snarls El Feo, his foul breath hot on my face. "How would you like that, eh?"

*Lord, even if I tell him, he's still gonna kill us all!*

"And suppose we start with *this* one!" He points to Joannie. "Put her on her knees."

*No!*

El Feo's thugs use their spears and swords to push back my men. Then they take Joannie and force her to her knees before him. He grabs her hair, pulls back her head, and puts his knife to her defenseless neck.

"Are you ready to watch, *puta*?" Feo grins, about to draw the blade across.

*All is lost . . . No, wait . . . Think, girl! What was it that Jemimah said . . . ? Come on, girl—do what the rabbit would do! And I go deep in my mind and . . . Yes . . . Maybe it ain't over yet.*

"Stop! Let her go. I'll tell you," I say, hanging my head in seeming defeat.

"That is much better," says the brute, flinging Joannie aside. "So show me. No tricks now, or the blood from her throat will spill over your feet."

I take a deep breath and then say, "It is not here. You know that. Both *El Diablo Rojo* and the *San Cristobal* have searched my poor little ship and found nothing. No, they did not. Because the treasure is buried . . . buried on Cayo Hueso . . . right over there."

El Feo's gaze follows my point.

"Where over there?"

"You see that red cloth?"

"*Sí.*"

"There is a flat area behind the trees and then there is a lagoon. The gold is buried on the other side of it. I shall have to draw you a map. I . . . I have paper in my cabin."

"Good." He grabs me by the arm and flings me toward my cabin, and we all go in—El Feo, Flashby, Joannie, and I.

"So make the map, *muchacha*, and let's get on with this." He pushes Joannie onto my bed and forces me into my chair behind my desk. I open it and pull out a piece of paper. My pen and ink sit up top, ready for use. I take up the pen.

There is a knock on the door, and one of El Feo's men sticks his head in.

"All of them are down below," he reports. "We have a guard on the hatch. They cannot get out."

"Good. Now put down the lifeboats and be ready," growls El Feo. "We are busy here."

I dip my pen in the inkwell and begin to draw. Both El Feo and Flashby stand over me and watch.

"Behind the red cloth you will find an opening in the mangroves. Pull in there. Then you will see an open area and the remains of an old Indian camp. Beyond that will be a large shallow lagoon. Right here."

I draw in the various shapes, the scratching of my pen loud in the silence.

"You must walk all the way around this lagoon to the other side, for the gold is buried right here." I make a big **X** on the page. "We marked the spot with many long pieces of driftwood laid one across the other. You cannot miss it, and you will need many strong men to remove the logs. They are quite heavy."

El Feo nods and barks out, "*Hombres!* To me!"

His men pop their heads back in the doorway.

"Leave two men to guard here, and four men on *El Diablo*. Everyone else in the lifeboats. Get shovels."

"*Sí, Capitán.*" They leave.

El Feo stands over me.

"There are captives in the hold of *El Diablo* as well," he says, laughing. "Ten of Flaco's loyal men. We shall have fun hanging them, one by one, when all this is done. Including Flaco. He shall be last. And then maybe you . . . and her." He hooks his thumb at Joannie.

"You are an ugly man, Feo. Inside and out. You shall surely rot in Hell." I could not help saying it.

"Ha!" He laughs. "You think I care that you find me ugly? No, I do not. In fact, I like being ugly." He puts his hand in my hair and pulls my head back. "I like— no, I *love*—the look on the señoritas' faces when I take them. I love the disgust, I love the revulsion, I love to hear them cry."

Feo's men are soon back.

"All is ready, *Comandante.*"

"Good. Let's go . . . no . . . wait." He looks at my bed, then he looks at me. A grin splits his ugly face. "No . . . I shall stay here. I have . . . business with this one. You, *inglés,* you will go with my men to collect the treasure. I shall stay here and collect treasure of another kind."

Flashby goes to the door. "Very well, *Capitán,* I shall do that. But, if you would, save a little bit for me. Either one of them will do." He looks from me to Joannie. "Don't look so downhearted, girls. After all, it is just the fortunes of war. Cheerio, all. I do hope you'll enjoy this, Jacky, I really do."

The door closes and I hear sounds of boats shoving off outside. Then silence, except for El Feo's heavy breathing.

El Feo begins to unbutton his shirt. "Get on the bed, girl."

I look to the door.

"You think to run, eh? Well, there is no place to run to. Besides, if you fight, I will do her first. Do you want that? Ah, I thought not." Joannie, wide-eyed, struggles against her bonds on the bed but to no avail. Meekly, I rise and go to the bed. El Feo whips off his filthy shirt and flings it away, being careful to replace his feathered headdress. His massive chest is covered with whorls of thick, black hair, and I can smell his stench from where I sit.

There is a knock on the door.

"What?" he asks, irritated.

Two of El Feo's men enter. "Ask her, Captain, where is the rum. We are thirsty."

He looks to me.

"I do not allow spirits aboard my ship," I say, primly, and let my eyes go furtively to my medicine cabinet. The gullible fools do not miss that look.

They laugh and triumphantly go to the chest and pull out my bottles of tincture of opium and leave. *Drink deep, scum.*

El Feo doesn't say anything. Instead he turns around and catches me across the face with the back of his hand. I fall back onto the bed.

*I must bide for time, I must . . .*

"Cry, *puta*. I will like it very much when you cry."

I know what is coming, so I sit up and put on the Lawson Peabody Look—eyes hooded, chin up, lips together, teeth apart. It helps some, but those lips do tremble and those eyes do well up with tears.

"That's more like it," he growls and places his hand on my shirt and with one powerful downward pull, rips it off. I pull out my now-exposed shiv and launch it toward his throat, but he is too quick and strong. He grasps my wrist and forces the blade from my hand.

*Oh God, my last hope.*

"Now, this is just the thing, Señorita," he says, picking up my blade and cutting through the waist cords of my trousers and drawers and then yanking them down and off.

"Get back, you ugly son of a bitch!" shouts Joannie, and kicks at him with her feet. He merely laughs and flings her to the floor, and then he comes back at me.

"*Muy bonita.* Very pretty, *sí,* yes, it is," he hisses, and then undoes his pants.

*Oh Lord, please . . . no . . .*

El Feo rises above me and takes my knees in his hands, ready to pull them apart.

"Now cry some more, *pobrecita.* Oh, you will not?" *Bueno.* Suppose I do the little one first and make you watch? Eh, *muchacha,* will that make you cry? Eh?"

It will, and tears pour out of my eyes, and in a blind rage against this horror, I struggle and squirm, but I know it will avail me—or Joannie—nothing. A corner of my despairing mind hears the rattling of something . . . What? . . . A cage door? Then . . .

"*Cluck?*"

*What?*

Then . . . "*Cluck?*" again . . . and then . . .

"*COCK-A-DOODLE-DO!*"

And then El Gringo Furioso, in full fighting fig, launches himself at El Feo's feathered headdress, slashing away with spurs and beak.

Already blood is showing around Feo's cheeks and eyes, for Gringo is strong and he is fast.

*"Madre de Dios!"* Feo screams, clawing at the bird, but Gringo is relentless. It occurs to my half-crazed mind that Daniel, in his haste to get back to the ship after Joannie had been taken, had thrust Gringo back into the cage I kept in my cabin but had forgotten to remove his spurs. Now Joannie has managed to open the cage latch with her feet, releasing the bird to do what it does best.

*"Eeeeyow!"* screeches El Feo, but this time it is not solely because of Gringo. I sit up to see that Joannie has attached herself to Feo's calf with her teeth and is clamped on good and hard. He kicks, but she stays on.

Then the door flies open, and through my upraised knees, I expect to see Feo's men come to his aid, but I do not see that.

What I see is a large African woman holding the world's biggest frying pan over her shoulder. She booms out, "What you got on your mind to do to that little girl, you?" Then she swings the huge black skillet and brings it to the back of Feo's ugly head.

*BOOOOOOOONNNNGGGG!*

El Feo sits straight up, his eyes crossed.

"I don't think you got nothin' on your mind now, no," asserts Jemimah as she swings again.

*BOOOOOOOONNNNGGGG!*

The pirate's eyes roll back in his head, and he topples over and off the bed.

"Jemimah! Thank God!" exults Joannie.

*Such good friends!*

But no time for thanks now, and no time for clothes, either. I leap off the bed, grab my shiv from the floor, and, starkers, I head out the door.

El Feo's men are festooned about the deck, groaning and holding their heads. It is plain that after being made groggy by the opium, they have been easily dispatched by Jemimah and her skillet.

I run to the forward hatch, throw the latch, and shout down, "Come, lads! You're free! Quick now! No time to lose!"

I hear their scrambling feet on the ladder as I jump over to *El Diablo*. Flaco lifts his head and smiles as he sees me, knife in hand, coming to free him.

"*Un ángel de cielo,*" he says, "clothed in the finest of garments."

"Never mind that, you," I say as I hack through his bonds. "Go now and set your men free."

"What of the others? The traitors?"

I look toward the beach from which we hear screams, and, I swear, the crunching of bones. I'd like to think that a certain one-eyed monster, the one that tried to eat Joannie and lost an eye in the process, is the one that got Flashby. The beast certainly had a right to bear a grudge against us Brits, and I hope Brother Gator took great satisfaction in the taste of that particular Englishman.

"I do not think they will be back. But still, we must be quick!"

I leap back onto the *Nancy* and see my men pouring out of the fore hatch.

"Secure the ship! Tie up these rascals. Help Flaco with those over there! Jim, take us farther out to sea. Davy, Tink, haul that piece of dirt out of my cabin. Higgins, to me!"

And I dive back into my cabin, chest heaving, as El Feo is being hauled out. Higgins follows me in.

"Miss. I fear you were . . . ?"

"No. But it was a close thing."

"I am very glad you did not suffer that," says Higgins. "What shall you wear?"

I look at the remnants of my usual sailing gear lying on the deck and say, "I guess my uniform will serve. The *Dolphin* will be here soon and I must be presentable."

"Yes, Miss."

As Higgins goes to my chest to get my clothes, I pick up El Gringo, who has been strutting about the deck, seemingly very pleased with himself. I plant a kiss upon his cockscomb and say, "My hero," and put him back in his cage. "Much good food and many plump and comely hens are coming to you, Brother Rooster."

After I am dressed, I go back out on deck to find that I am just in time for an execution. El Feo has been brought back to his senses, enough to know that he is about to be hanged.

He stands on the deck of *El Diablo Rojo* with a noose around his neck, hands tied behind him, glaring about with hatred—and fear—burning in his eyes. There are four strong men at the other end of the line, ready to haul him up.

Flaco is once again in full command of his ship, and I am glad of it. Those sailors who had been drugged and clubbed have once again sworn allegiance to him and have been added back to his crew. They had stood in fear of El Feo before, when he had taken Flaco's ship, but they fear him no longer.

"Captain Faber," says Flaco. "It is your ship that took this brute down. Say the word."

I think of being merciful, but then I consider what he

was going to do to Joannie, and what he did to Danny, and what he was going to do to all of us . . .

. . . and I nod.

El Feo is pulled ten feet off the deck. He twists and kicks for a long time, for his neck is thick. Then it is over.

His body is left hanging for twenty minutes or so and then is lowered and pitched over the side.

The only words spoken were mine.

"It is a shame to pollute the bottom of this beautiful sea with your carcass. I am sure you are already in Hell, El Feo, and I wish you the joy of the place."

It occurs to me later that yet another skeleton will now rest with the *Santa Magdalena*. How many more will there be?

# Chapter 49

"So, Flaco. You will head back to Bahia Honda?" We are taking breakfast in my cabin. It is a cool and extremely lovely day, with sunlight streaming in the open windows and a gentle breeze blowing the curtains about. My torn sailor gear is being resewn, so, upon rising this morning, I donned my uniform shirt and trousers again. Actually, I suspect we shall see the *Dolphin* today, so I want to be dressed and ready. And, yes, I slept alone last night, though not for want of trying on Flaco's part. No, he had to be satisfied with a hug and kiss after dinner, which was a veritable feast that saw a lot of serious celebration on the part of both our crews.

"Yes, dear heart, if I must leave you, it will be to Bahia Honda I will go," he says with a sigh. "I must fill out my crew as I am short-handed right now . . . due to the cunning of a certain beautiful *bandida*."

"With the help of several dozen large and hungry reptiles," I say with a laugh. "Here, try the orange marmalade. It is very good." I spoon a good bit of it onto my toast and pop it into my mouth. *Mmmmmm . . . it is good to be alive and tasting orange marmalade.*

"Such a thing of beauty . . . and so refined," laughs Flaco, looking at the bit of golden jelly that had worked its way out of the corner of my mouth, but which I had managed to catch with my napkin before it hit my spotless white trousers.

"Umm . . . well . . . your pardon, Señor."

The door opens and Joannie enters with a fresh pot of hot coffee and refills our cups. I reach over and ruffle her hair. "Thank you, my wild and fierce little Cockney," I say fondly.

She blushes prettily and leaves, I'm sure, to go back to her Daniel. He has recovered completely from the late El Feo's blow, and Joannie has pronounced the lad her hero and informed him that he shall never lack for kisses. Not from her, anyway.

"Why do you not give me half of the gold, then we shall raise our flags together and raid this ocean like we did before?" asks Flaco. "No, we shall raid like *never* before! We can buy more ships! Big ones! I know I can rouse the mighty Chucho with the promise of a ship of his own. We can mount a fleet and take every port in the Caribbean. You can be *la gobernadora* of Santo Domingo and I will rule over Jamaica. We will throw out both the Spanish Dons and the English Bulldogs! Yes, and the French, too! We shall be the King and Queen of the West Indies, you and I."

"Although the notion is intriguing, Flaco, I'm afraid I have no gold to give," I say, putting my hand on his arm. "And I fear that the Golden Age of the bold buccaneer is over. The British and the French and the Spanish are just too strong, and now the Americans, too. There's just too many of them. Face it, *mi querido*, it might be time to think of a nice rancho somewhere. Take a pretty and loving wife, and raise beautiful children."

"If you were to be that wife, Jacquelina, I might even consider that awful fate."

I laugh. "Dear Flaco, I do love you, in my way, but you know I am promised to another. As a matter of fact, I expect to see him very soon."

He claps his hand to his chest. "Ah, that another man shall pluck this rare and beautiful flower. It is too much for my poor heart!"

"Oh, I think you'll get over that plucking, you rascal. Here, soothe your tortured soul with another fine sausage."

Above, on the quarterdeck, a mouth is put to the speaking tube, and I hear, "Jacky. Ship on the horizon. We think it's the *Dolphin*."

I rise and go to the tube. "Be right up, Davy."

"It is the British frigate, this 'Dol-feen'?" asks Flaco. I nod.

"And it has aboard your intended *esposo*?"

Again I nod.

"Then I shall go and sink it, and then you will be free to roam the oceans of the world with your Flaco," he says, standing and putting his hand on the hilt of his sword and puffing out his chest.

"Go and sink it you will not," I say, laughing at the thought of the little brig *El Diablo* taking on the mighty forty-four-gun British frigate, fully manned and ready. "But go you must, as they will be here very shortly, and they may have some questions as to why the famed Hispanic pirate Captain Flaco Jimenez is hanging about one of their research vessels."

"I will go, *mi corazón,* but I know that we will sail together again someday."

"I know we shall, God willing. Now give me a farewell kiss and be off. I prefer you take it here, rather than out on deck, as my reputation is already in tatters."

My crew, bless 'em, have not said one single word about that little romp I took yesterday, bearing my shiv and clad only in my tattoo, but I know the story will get out.

Flaco chuckles and smiles. "That image of you, in all your natural glory, flying toward me to cut my bonds and restore my honor will forever live in my memory. Know that, Jacquelina."

I give him a poke in the ribs. "Put that out of your mind and give me that kiss, then away with you, *amigo.*"

We embrace for a good long time, but then my better sense takes over and I push him away. "Come, let us go."

We step out into the light, and I look over to see that it is, indeed, the lovely *Dolphin* that is bearing down upon us. We can hear whistles and bells coming from her, and we know that she is Beating to Quarters and Clearing for Action.

"It is, indeed, time to go," says Flaco, noting that the distance twixt us and the frigate is closing quickly. He turns to me and, putting his strong arm around my waist, bends me over.

"To hell with your reputation, Jacquelina. I will have another kiss before I go."

He takes that kiss, then releases me and shouts, his white teeth gleaming in his rascally smile, "And I hope your man was watching!" Then he bounds over to his ship. *Knowing my luck in that regard, he probably was.*

"*Hermanos!*" cries Flaco. "Ungrapple the ships! Set sail! Let us go!"

I put my fingertips to my just-freed lips and regain my composure to look out at the *Dolphin*. Strange, I think, that she should go to Quarters for such a puny ship as *El Diablo*, which is showing every sign of running away. Odd, too, that she should be turning and heading up wind. *What is going on?*

"Missy! Another ship! A big one! Coming on fast!" comes Danny's call from the crow's-nest. I grab my glass from its cradle on the quarterdeck and leap up the ratlines to stand next to Daniel. Joannie is up there, too, and she asks, "What is it, Jacky?"

I have the glass to my eye, and I do not like what I see.

"It is the *San Cristobal*. She has come out."

I grab the buntline and slide down, shouting, "Battle Stations. Haul anchor! Raise sail! Move!"

Back on deck we hear the first low *booooom* come rolling across the water. Then another. *Booooommm.* Flashes of fire spit out from the starboard side of the Spanish ship.

Nothing yet from the *Dolphin*. I see that she is trying desperately to claw to windward of the *San Cristobal*, to gain the weather gauge, the position where a ship can rain down its greatest firepower, its broadside, on the enemy, while presenting that enemy no opportunity to do the same.

But it ain't working. The *San Cristobal*'s eighty-eight guns against the *Dolphin*'s forty-four just won't wash. The *Dolphin* will be brave and will fight to the last, and honor will be served. But it will not matter. It's going to be a slaughter.

There is another blast from the *San Cristobal,* and I see the foremast of the *Dolphin* coming down. Soon she will be helpless.

*Oh God! Jaimy . . . Captain Hudson . . . Lieutenant Bennett . . . all my friends . . . I must do something.*

*El Diablo Rojo* is still close alongside and I call out, "Flaco! If you love me, you must help us!"

Flaco, looking out over the sea at what is happening, says, "I love you, Jacky, but what can I do? A British frigate, and the *San Cristobal*? I am but a poor pirate, and a small one at that."

"You must take your ship along the lee side of the *San Cristobal* and pepper her with shot—enough to distract her captain while I close in and try to shoot off her rudder! Do this for me, Flaco!"

He still looks dubious.

Then I say it. "Flaco. There *is* a stash of gold. Help me here, and you shall have half of it! I promise!"

Now I see the gleam of his teeth. "I knew it! And that is much more like it, jewel of my heart! Lead on!"

"Battle Stations!" I shout. "Jim, steer for the *San Cristobal*! Higgins, my jacket! Daniel! Hoist the Jolly Roger! All speed! Let's go!"

And so, our pirate colors flying above us, the *Nancy B. Alsop* and *El Diablo Rojo* charge into the battle.

# Chapter 50

*Lt. James Emerson Fletcher*
*2nd Mate, HMS* Dolphin

*An Account of the Engagement Between*
*HMS* Dolphin *and* San Cristobal
*Recorded while still fresh in mind*
*in anticipation of review*
*by Navy Board*

We met the Spanish eighty-eight-gun man-of-war *San Cristobal* off the south coast of Key West, Florida, and immediately engaged him in battle. Due to Captain Hudson's expert seamanship, we were able to gain the weather gauge, but it did us little good, for the enemy's overwhelming firepower sent a wall of iron into us, shattering several gunports and bringing down our foremast.

I went forward to direct the cutting away of the fallen sail, which had collapsed over our port side and was dragging down our speed, making maneuvering very difficult.

Wielding axes, we finally managed to free the mess, in spite of the fact that we were being pounded relentlessly by the enemy's guns. That accomplished, I was heading back to the quarterdeck when we received a tremendous blast, and I was thrown from my feet. Rising, I surveyed the devastation all about me—men were crying out in pain, while many others lay quite still. The deck was slick with blood. I noticed that I, too, had taken a flying splinter in the calf of my right leg, but I regarded it as minor, considering the real suffering that lay all about me.

As I worked my way aft, I observed that most of our guns were still firing but had not caused a great amount of damage due to our lack of position. Now that we had steerage again, I hoped they would be more effective, but still I felt, with sinking heart, that we were doomed to destruction or capture.

I noted also that Captain Allen's squad had joined our marines in the maintop and mizzen top and with their muskets were peppering away at the enemy. Lord Allen himself stood among them reloading his long Kentucky rifle. I saw him raise, aim, and fire it, and then one of the snipers on *San Cristobal* fell from the high rigging. The man had scarcely landed on the deck before Captain Allen had reloaded and fired again. Although I have nothing but praise for the performance of the officers and men of the *Dolphin,* I must single out that cavalry officer for special mention, as his coolness under fire was remarkable.

Upon regaining the quarterdeck, I was distressed to see that our excellent First Officer, Mr. Bennett, was down. Two men with a stretcher appeared, and he was taken, unconscious, down to the orlop, where Dr. Sebastian had set up his surgery. I was sure the good Doctor would be kept quite busy.

"He's unloaded his port guns on us, Fletcher, and hurt us severely," said Captain Hudson, grimly, "and now he's turning to finish the job." He then faced forward and shouted, "Bear up, bonny boys! Steady, boys, steady!" There was a faint cheer at that, a very faint cheer, you may be sure, but a cheer from our fine men, nonetheless.

"Mr. Fletcher, see what you can do about— What the hell is *that?*"

The Captain was looking over my shoulder and I turned to look.

There, coming full tilt toward the mighty *San Cristobal,* was a small brig and an even smaller schooner.

*Good Lord.*

# Chapter 51

*El Diablo Rojo* heeled over smartly on the starboard tack and let loose his broadside into the port side of the *San Cristobal.* There were only six twenty-four-pounders, but the blast got the Spaniard's attention. Luckily for Flaco, the huge ship had just loosed its full port broadside at the poor *Dolphin,* and the gunners were a little slow in reloading.

I don't let myself think about what might be happening on the *Dolphin.* No, instead I fix my mind on the rudder of the *San Cristobal* looming up ahead. I've got Jim Tanner on helm, John Thomas and McGee tending the sails, Tink and Davy on the side guns, Higgins on the after swivel, and me on the bow chaser. Danny and Joannie are powder monkeys and have been told to keep their heads down when not engaged in their tasks. I have strapped on my sword and pistols and all others are armed as well.

Flaco whips his ship around and lets loose another blast at the big ship towering over us. It is good that the *San Cristobal* is so high, because when we are close in, as we both certainly are now, she cannot bring her guns to bear upon us when we come in low to sting her.

"Ready all!" I shout as we get near. We're about twenty-five yards away when I decide to risk a shot. I sight across the barrel, swivel it three degrees to the left, judge the up-and-down action of the waves, and then jerk the lanyard.

*Crrrack!*

I had been aiming for the upper pintle of the rudder, but I was high and missed, splintering only a few of the after boards.

*Damn!*

"Jim! Hard Right! Tink! Davy! Fire the port guns as they bear! Joannie, Danny, reload the chaser!"

The *Nancy*'s head swings over and . . . *Crrrack!* . . . *Crrack!*

The lads fire, then the smoke clears. I see that the enemy's rudder is damaged yet hangs in its gudgeons and still works.

"Reload! Davy and Tink, to the other side." The kids reload the spent guns, and the lads man the starboard guns.

The *Nancy*'s bow continues to come around. We are now directly under the fantail of the *San Cristobal,* and we have not escaped their notice. Angry faces peer over the side at us. I see that one of them is that vile Cisneros, glaring down at me with all the hate that is in him. I whip out one of my pistols and get off a shot at his face, but he ducks so I miss.

Then Spanish marines appear with their muskets at the rail of the big ship as we lie helpless below them.

*Uh-oh.*

# Chapter 52

*Lt. James Emerson Fletcher*
*2nd Mate, HMS* Dolphin

*An Account of the Engagement Between*
*HMS* Dolphin *and* San Cristobal
*Continued . . .*

Yes, gentlemen, it was Miss Jacky Faber, so often at His Majesty's displeasure, who was now sailing to the aid of one of His Majesty's ships, risking life and limb to do so. Although you gentlemen may know of my liaison with this young woman, and some may fault me for it, I must say that I was never more filled with pride than I was at that moment. Dear, brave girl. Yes, I thought her actions rash, but then I have often thought so in the past.

Sailing in company with her was a small brig, flying colors not generally associated with any known country, that was unloading broadsides into the flanks of the *San Cristobal* with both impunity and great rapidity, distracting the Spanish ship sufficiently to give us a much appreciated breathing space.

Captain Hudson squinted through his long glass. "What colors are they flying, Fletcher?"

"Uh . . . I believe they are pirate flags, Sir."

"Um . . . It looks like she means to knock off the enemy's rudder. Brave girl. Let us see if we can help her. We shall draw closer."

Brave? No, she has never been vaingloriously or foolhardily brave. Generally I have observed her to be primarily intent on her own personal survival—and that of her friends.

I put the glass back to my eye, expecting the worst and finding it. The Spaniard, noting the threat from her stern, had plainly ordered marine sharpshooters to the fantail.

"Allen!" I roared up into the mizzenmast rigging. "Concentrate your fire on the enemy's quarterdeck! They mean to shoot Jacky!"

Immediately the musket balls from Captain Allen and his men rain down on the fantail of the *San Cristobal*, and the personnel there scatter. There is, however, an officer there who rallies the men, and muskets are again pointed over the rail at the little schooner lying below.

There is a thump as Allen's boots hit the deck next to me. He bites a bullet out of a white cartridge and reloads his rifle. His other men come down from the rigging to join him.

"I think we would all be better off if the *Cristobal* didn't have its captain," he says and levels his gun and fires. Over on the other ship, the Captain of the *San Cristobal* clutches his breast and falls to his deck. "Not very sporting of me," he says, "but it is our Jacky we are concerned about here, eh, what?"

He reloads as the three vessels come together. I could see the seamen David Jones and John Tinker down below on the deck of the little schooner preparing to fire their guns at the enemy's rudder, and Jacky Faber calling out orders to others of her crew. The *Nancy B.*'s mainmast rigging is now lying against the side of the *Dolphin*.

"Will you be taking care of things up here, Fletcher?" calls Allen. He slings his rifle over his shoulder and climbs over into the schooner's ratlines and begins to descend. "I believe we'll be of more use below. Come along, men."

A moment later I hear him call out from below . . .

*"Fear not, Princess, the Cavalry has arrived!"*

# Chapter 53

I cannot believe my ears. Nor my eyes. I stand astounded.

"Richard! What the hell are you doing here?"

"I might well ask the same of you, my sweet little river nymph, finding you out here on the big broad sea," answers Captain Allen. "But time for hugs and kisses later, Lady Pretty-Bottom, as we have hot work to do here."

We are crammed up against the other ships now, fighting to get our starboard guns in position to fire on what has turned out to be a very sturdy rudder. Before, musket men had appeared at the rail and had rained shot down upon us, but aside from a graze to the side of Davy's face, no one was hit. Then the musket men above disappeared, probably because of the red-coated squad that had just climbed down to our deck.

"Sergeant Bailey. Align the men across the deck here such that we will fire in two ranks. If anyone shows their face above that rail, have the first rank fire, but have the second rank hold back, in case they think to shoot at us as we reload."

"Aye, Sor," says Sergeant Bailey, the old Welsh soldier who has heard all this many times before. "McDuff, Quimby, Jackson, kneel in First Rank. McMann, Merrick, Luce, stand in Second Rank. You heard the Captain."

Could it be? Archie and Willie and the rest of Allen's Dragoons from our trip down the Big Muddy? It is.

"I thought you might like seeing the lads again, Jacky, so I brought 'em along especially, like," says Richard, scanning the ships towering over us. Both vessels shudder as they continue to put broadside after broadside into each other. In addition, the *San Cristobal* also suffers the lesser but still deadly blows from *El Diablo Rojo*. " 'Course I didn't know we'd be getting into this dustup, but hey, fortunes of war, eh, Princess?"

A bullet hits the deck between Richard and me, digging a furrow into the wood. He looks up, spots the man who fired it, a figure far up in the mainmast, and raises his rifle and fires. The figure jerks, slumps, and falls.

"If you ever see Lightfoot again, Wah-Chinga, give him my thanks for pointing out the virtues of this weapon." He reloads, and then shoves one of his thin cheroots between his teeth.

"Jacky! Coming in range!"

"Fire when she bears, Davy!"

*Cccrrrack!*

Davy's aim is true, but the four-pound shot hits the upper pintle of the anchor and bounces off harmlessly. Harmless to the *San Cristobal,* that is, for the shot ricochets back across our own deck, almost hitting Joannie, struggling across with another heavy bag of powder.

*Damn!* That rudder was built strong! Probably the

builder thought about this possible eventuality, and curse him for his foresight! "Tink! Coming up on you! Try him!"

*Crrrack!*

Same result—point-blank range, but just some splinters. The rudder holds fast and now we are right up against it—no room to get away and fire again. *Damn! Me and my great plans! We are lost! Unless . . .*

. . . unless the *San Cristobal* does something really stupid.

A man appears at the rail above, and the first rank of Dragoons fires and chases him back, but not before he manages to fling something down upon us. It bounces once, twice, and comes to rest between Richard and me.

*It is a bomb, with a mere six-inch fuse fizzing ever shorter!*

Richard leans down and picks up the thing and regards it. "How kind of the Dons to provide me with a light." Then he holds the burning end of the fuse to his cigar and draws in deeply. "Ah, now that's much better."

"THROW IT OVERBOARD, RICHARD!" I scream.

"And waste this fine piece of ordnance?" he says, calmly, looking at the bomb sputtering in his hand. "Why, I figure we've got at least eight seconds left. However, I do believe that you all should take cover. Men, you, too."

"CLEAR THE FO'C'S'LE! GET BEHIND THE CABIN. IT'S GONNA BLOW!" I wail. "NOW!"

Everyone, soldier, sailor, ship's boy and girl, lunges for the scant protection behind the *Nancy*'s cabin, as Captain Lord Richard Allen walks up to the bow and says, "This is what you wanted to get rid of, Pretty-Tail? Very well. Let's just put this right here."

He reaches over and tucks the bomb in the notch behind the upper pintle of the *San Cristobal*'s rudder.

"That should do it," he says as he saunters back to join us. Meanwhile I have landed on top of Joannie, and she struggles to get her head up to watch.

"Keep your head down, fool, or you'll lose your eyes!" I shout as I push her back down and wrap my arms around her.

"Thousand six . . . thousand five . . . thousand four . . . thousand three . . ."

There is a brilliant flash of lightning and then a tremendous ear-shattering *CRAAAAAACK!* of thunder.

Allen had miscalculated by several seconds and all six feet two inches and one hundred and eighty pounds of him, more or less, comes flying over the top of my cabin to land squarely on top of me.

"Richard! Are you . . . ?"

No, he is not hurt, and his mouth has landed conveniently close to my ear.

"I believe this is where we left off, Princess?" he breathes into my ear and runs his hand in under my open jacket.

"I . . . can't . . . breathe . . ." wheezes Joannie from under us both.

I crane my head up and see that . . . *Yes!* . . . The rudder of the *San Cristobal* hangs loosely in its gudgeons for a moment, then falls with a great splash and floats away.

"Let me up, Richard! I must tell them!"

He rolls over, gets to his feet, and calls out, "All right, men. Form up. Same drill. Keep a sharp eye out. They might try that trick again."

I get up and Joannie manages to get a lungful of air into her thin chest.

"Joannie! Go down and get my Faber Shipping flag! Quick now!" She jumps up, sucking in air, and goes to do it.

Then I run across the deck to survey the damage. Yes, my foresails are in tatters, but that rudder is down! I leap up into my rigging and shout up to the *Dolphin*'s quarterdeck, "Captain Hudson! Pull away!"

Heads appear over the side to look over at me hanging there in the ratlines and I yell, "Get in front of his bow! His rudder is off!" I point down at the wreckage floating below. "He is helpless!"

I know I should not presume to instruct Post Captain Hudson on naval tactics, but my mind is in a whirl. *Thank God! There's Jaimy! Still standing! He does not look happy, but he is still yet alive and on his feet! Thank you, Lord!* Orders are shouted and the *Dolphin* pulls away from the crippled *San Cristobal*. Any seasoned man-of-war's crew would know that a nimble craft like the *Dolphin* will now easily stay in front of a lumbering, rudderless tub like the *San Cristobal,* pounding her to pieces with relentless broadsides while all the Spanish ship could fire is her forward bow chaser, that puny gun being quickly silenced by the *Dolphin*'s next broadside. The big ship shudders as another blast slams into her unprotected bows. Ten minutes later, she strikes.

The Spanish flag is hauled down.

"She has struck!" I scream, flying back down to my deck. "Davy! Tink! Get a grapple and a line so I can get up on her deck! Joannie! Daniel! Get the rope ladder! To me! Let's go!"

Tink swings a grappling hook at the end of a line that

lies coiled about the crook of his arm and lets fly. The hook disappears over the rail of the Spaniard and the line is drawn back and . . . *Hah!* . . . It catches on something and holds. I grab the line, and putting my feet to the side of the *San Cristobal,* begin to climb. I feel Joannie and Danny hauling up behind me.

"Careful, Princess," says Allen below. "They have surrendered, but they still can be dangerous. I wish you had let me—"

"Danny! When we reach the rail, rig the boarding ladder so the soldiers can follow us up! Here we go! Now!"

I have my head over the rail and I see that it is Captain Morello, who, though wounded, is the one who has hauled down his ship's colors. He lies on the deck, his flag wrapped about him, his breathing labored, blood leaking from his side. On the other side of the quarterdeck is a helpless helmsman, his wheel spinning uselessly in his hands. And there, too, is Lieutenant Juan Carlos Cisneros y Siquieros, his sword out, raging against what has just happened to him, his ship, and his Spanish honor.

Not being totally stupid, no matter what anyone says about me, I wait till Davy has rigged the boarding ladder and I feel Richard and his lads swarming onto the deck beside me before I venture onto the quarterdeck of the *San Cristobal.*

I dash over to the fallen Captain Morello and reach out my hand for his sword. He looks up in his pain, and seeing a person in the full uniform of the Royal Navy, hands the sword to me. I take it and stride back across the deck to Cisneros.

"I am Lieutenant Jacky Faber, His Britannic Majesty's

Royal Navy. You will surrender and give me your sword, *Teniente* Cisneros. *Now.*"

He gazes incredulously at my outreached hand and my uniform, then he hisses, "Surrender to a cheap whore! Never!"

He raises his sword.

"You struck, damn you!" I shout, stepping back.

"It was that coward who pulled down our sacred colors, not me! And if it is the last thing I do in this world, I am going to kill you!"

I can tell he is beyond all reason. As he begins his swing, I whip out my remaining pistol and fire, putting a bullet in him, high on the right side of his chest.

He staggers, drops his sword, and falls to the deck.

Richard comes up next to me.

"Remind me never to get on the wrong side of you, Princess," he says, and then shouts to his men, "Get these Spanish lads down below and lock them down tight! Shoot any that resist!"

None resist. At least they know the rules, even if their officer did not.

"Put up our flag, Danny. Quickly, now!"

A boat scrapes alongside, and armed British sailors swarm aboard. Then it is Jaimy who also stands by my side.

"What are you doing, Jacky? You can't just . . . ," says Jaimy, alarmed and perplexed as he looks up at my Faber Shipping flag now snapping at the masthead.

"Just watch, dear one, and you will see," I say. "I am settling an old score twixt the King and me." I pick up Captain Morello's sword from the deck and wait for Captain Hudson to come on deck.

It does not take long.

He bounds onto the quarterdeck and looks at me, and then up at my flag. He does not look pleased.

"Good afternoon, Captain. Welcome aboard," I say, saluting. "As you can see, I have taken this fine prize . . ."

He is positively glowering now. "*You* have taken this prize?"

". . . and I would take it most kindly if you would present this ship to King George in return for my late ship the *Emerald,* which caused some discord between His Majesty and me, a matter that I now hope is fully resolved."

I hand him the Spanish Captain's sword.

He is taken aback for a moment, and then he roars with laughter. "That I will do, Lieutenant Faber, that I will most certainly do!"

# Chapter 54

When the battle was lost . . . and won, things grew very quiet on the four ships gathered there on that bloody morning, except for the moaning of the wounded.

After the *San Cristobal* had struck her colors, Flaco brought *El Diablo Rojo* alongside and shouted up at me, "I think we are done here for now, Jacquelina, my sweet little cactus flower, and I will say, *adiós, mi amor.* I will see you *very* soon."

I stand between James Fletcher and Lord Allen as I wave Flaco off, thankful that neither of them knows a word of Spanish.

"You have some very interesting friends, Prin . . . Miss Faber," says Captain Allen, affecting a slight cough.

Jaimy turns toward me with a questioning look on his face, when I am saved from this situation by something far worse.

"Miss Faber?" comes a call from a young ship's boy below me on the deck of the *Dolphin,* which is now tight alongside us.

"Yes?"

"Dr. Sebastian sends his respects and asks if you might assist him below," says the boy. "Things are quite awful in the orlop."

*Ah. The Butcher's Bill is being totaled and it must be paid.*

"Joannie. Get my medical kit. All of it," I say, taking off my jacket and handing it to her. "Then come with me."

She climbs over the side and returns quickly, the bag in her arms. I look down at Jaimy's bloody pant leg. "You, too, Mr. Fletcher, shall report to Sick Bay. Ah. Thank you, Joannie. Let us go over to the *Dolphin*. Excuse us, gentlemen."

The surgery is filled with the dead and dying, the weak and the crying, as we wade into it. I see the Spanish casualties are being brought down as well as our own, and the place is soon jammed from wall to wall with wounded men.

"Ah, Miss Faber. So good of you to help," says Dr. Sebastian, up to his elbows in gore. "Take that table there. We will triage and give you the less severely wounded. Call me over for anything you can't handle. And you'd best put on one of those smocks."

I do it, and Joannie opens my medicine bag and begins laying out the instruments on a side table. On my instruction, she pours some pure alcohol into a shallow pan, and into it she puts needle and thread and several tools. Bandage rolls are at the ready, as well as a cup for laudanum— those unfortunate pirates had drunk up all of mine, but Dr. Sebastian has an ample supply. There is an especially awful shriek from the other table and then the sound of a saw cutting through bone. Joannie is ashen but relatively calm.

"All right," I say. "Let's get on with this."

．．．

*Lie back, sailor, that's it . . . Easy now . . . Well, that's not too bad. Have a sip of this. It will make you feel ever so much better. You'll feel the straps going on now, but don't worry. It's just to make sure you don't move while we take care of you . . . Bite down on this leather plug . . . All right, here we go . . . I'll hold and you sew, Joannie . . . A little bit more . . . Brave boy! Done!*

*Next.*

*Here we go . . . Up there, now . . . You'll have to turn over a bit . . . That's got it. Ready now . . . Good . . . Now the spirits of wine . . . All right, close it up. Tell the Bo'sun no work for you till we say so. There we go . . .*

*Next . . . and next . . . Good God, is there no end to this? No . . . no, I'm all right . . .*

*Next . . .*

*Joannie . . . I can take care of this one by myself. See that boy lying on the floor? Right. I fear his time is not long. Go over and kneel by his side and hold his hand . . . If he cries out for his mother, lift his head and put it to your breast. Go now . . .*

*Next . . .*

*Eduardo!* Mi amigo! *Rest yourself and let's see . . . Not too bad. How are the others . . . Jesus, Manuelo, and young Mateo? Ah good, I am so glad to hear that. I know they hate their confinement, as I have been similarly held. But that will be over soon, and you all will be proud Spanish seamen again . . . Hold still now . . . Some salve on your burns . . . There . . .*

*Next . . .*

*Ah, Joannie . . . you are back. I felt it would not take very long . . . that poor boy. But thank you, child, for doing what you did . . . Take comfort in knowing that you have eased the passing of another soul . . . Don't cry now . . .*

*Next . . .*

*Well . . . is it not Lieutenant Cisneros, unconscious . . . I'm afraid it is . . . Lay him back and take off his shirt. Hmmm . . . the bullet went in but did not come out the back. We shall have to probe . . . Wait, he is coming around—too bad for him . . . Here, Don Juan Carlos, drink this . . . What, I am the Angel of Death? No,* Comandante, *I may have been a thorn in your side but I am not that. I will do what I can to save you. Is he strapped in? Good. Bite down on this . . . Forceps, please, Joannie. Hold on, Sir . . . I put that bullet in you and I will get it out. Ready, now . . . Ungh! Got it. All right . . . douse the hole with alcohol and close him up. No, Don Cisneros, I did not do that for spite . . . It will help you heal. Now get him into the stretcher.* Vaya con Dios, Teniente, *for it is He, not me, who will now decide your fate.*

*Next . . .*

*Ah, Jaimy, it's about time you came down. I know, Duty and all . . . Well, welcome to the Society of the Flying Splinter, Jaimy. You are the third member of the Brotherhood to join that exclusive club, you know—both Benjy and I can testify to the pain of that particular wound. But steady on and we'll fix you up. Do you need the restraints? No? All right, take a sip of this . . . That's it . . . Now bite down on the leather. Joannie, take the scissors and cut open the pant leg . . . Hmmmm . . . Right, there's the little blighter. Pliers, please. Thanks . . . Ready, dear? . . . A quick jerk . . . There, it's out and the wound looks clean. Now for a splash of alcohol . . . I know, I know it hurts, dear, but I think it's good to keep off infection . . . What . . . What are you trying to say, Jaimy? Here, let me take that plug out of your mouth . . . What, you release me from my vow of marriage? You silly boy, is it because of Captain Allen? Oh, do be quiet, Jaimy, I swear. Sometimes you can be just too damned noble for your own good. Now open up again and bite down while we sew you up. Use a nice tight overstitch, Joannie. Make it neat, for I intend to be looking at that leg for a good long time. That's it . . . bandage now . . . not too tight . . . Good . . . Up with you now, dear one. I will see you later.*

*Next . . . and next . . . and next . . .*

Joannie and I stumble out of the orlop several hours later, stupefied and bloody. I put my hand on her shoulder and say, "A hot bath for us, Sister. I think we deserve it."

She says nothing, and I look down at her hard face and say, "You are wondering why I had you do that? Why I took you down into that hell?"

No answer, but I think I see her head give a quick nod.

"It's because I never want you to think of battle as anything fine or glorious or anything but pure butchery," I say, hugging her to me. "What you saw down there, Joannie, is the real face of war. Remember it when your own sons play at their games and wave around toy swords and vow to perform deeds of great valor. And remember that over there, too."

On both of the big ships, the dead are being prepared for burial. Those who have perished are sewn up in their hammocks by their mates and are lined up next to the rail, where they wait for the words to be said over them as they are slid off into the sea. Some of the Spanish sailors have been let out to accomplish the same sad duty with their own fallen comrades.

"And now I think some clean, hot water is just the thing for us." I cuff her head lightly. "And this time, I'll even let you get in first . . . but you'd better not . . ."

At this she laughs a little, and we go down into my cabin.

The next few days are an absolute flurry of furious activity. Repairs on the late *San Cristobal* go on day and night, and I see very little of Jaimy. I, on the other hand, am again going down in the bell and bringing up the last of the treasure from the *Santa Magdalena*. And, since I am back in my diving rig, a lot is seen of me, to the delight of many, it seems.

*Men, I swear.*

Captain Allen, since it is his job to guard the gold that is being brought up and transferred to the *Dolphin*, is always in attendance, it seems, and plainly quite pleased with both his duty and my choice of costume. Jaimy is totally consumed with work on the rechristened *Saint Christopher*, which is probably to the good considering his state of mind as concerns my lack of propriety. Poor lad, he should be used to it by now. And, actually, I think he is. 'Course, being the envy of every man aboard doesn't hurt, either. These men have been at sea a long time, and being the only girl of age aboard . . . well, I've generally found it to work to my advantage and now to the confirmation of Jaimy's reputation as a lad handy with the ladies.

"Born to be in the water, like the mermaids, nymphs, and naiades of old," Lord Allen pronounces grandly, as I come dripping back onto the deck of the *Nancy* alongside the latest net bag of ingots. "Come ye gods and behold the lovely Miss Jacky Faber in her proper element. Like unto the Rhine maidens and the Lorelei, singing songs and luring poor sailors to their doom . . ."

*Pretty poetic for a soldier, I must say.*

". . . and with a comely handmaiden by her side, as well."

By this he means Joannie, whom I have allowed to dive with me down to the *Santa Magdalena* herself, the girl having proved her mettle time after time on this journey. The first time down, I show her the stash in the cave and hold my finger to my lips. She grins and nods, and we bring up more from the wreck . . . and add even more to the stash.

Back down again . . .

And, no, Jaimy is not permitted to share my bed again, to my great sorrow. The mission is now considered too important to indulge the whims of young love, as the work on the *Christopher* and the *Dolphin* goes on around the clock. The only breaks we get are the dinners in Captain Hudson's cabin after the work of the day is done, and riotous dinners they are, in spite of the general exhaustion. I sit with Jaimy at my side and sometimes with Richard on my other side. Yes, the tale of my naked romp across the decks of the *Nancy* and the *Diablo* has come out—I blame Daniel . . . or could it have been Joannie? Who knows, and who cares, for it is too good a story to remain secret long. And if it causes the midshipmen to blush mightily in my presence, well, I wish them the joy of their imaginings.

*Boys, I swear . . .*

Toasts are proposed and drunk, stories are told, songs are sung, and there is much joyous speculation as to how much their prize money will be and what they plan to do with it. More songs, more wine, more . . .

. . . and then it is all done and over. It is time for them to go and for me to stay.

"I wish you the joy of your first command, Mr. Fletcher," I say, lifting my glass to him.

The repairs on the *Saint Christopher* are completed, and it will be leaving within the hour—and Jaimy will be on it. We have been allowed a short time together before departure, and Higgins has set us a nice table in my cabin.

Jaimy clinks his glass to mine, smiling. "That illustrious command will last only for the five or six days it will take me to get her to Kingston, and then a more senior officer will be made captain of the *Saint Christopher*. Junior Lieutenants do not command First-Rate, you know."

I take a sip of my wine and give him a warm look over the rim of the glass. "But, still . . ."

"Oh, that does not matter. In fact, I shall be glad to get rid of it," he says, leaning back and looking about my cozy little cabin. "Actually, Jacky, I was in command of this very schooner once during your absence last year, you'll remember. I consider that my first command, and I think I enjoyed that much more than I will in taking that massive tub down to Jamaica. I know that I have spent some of my happiest moments of my life right here in this cabin, with you."

*Me, too, Jaimy . . .*

"True, the *San Cristobal* does lack grace, but it should still bring much in the way of prize money," I say, determined to be practical and brave and not start outright bawling. "A three-decker, eighty-eight-gun First-Rate Ship-of-the-Line-of-Battle and a head count of six hundred prisoners? The officers and men of the *Dolphin* should be quite ecstatic."

"Yes, that will be prime, and the men are very happy, and I imagine the taverns of London will be overjoyed. But for you, Jacky? Will there be something for you?" He reaches over and puts his hand on mine. My eyes, the traitors, are starting to tear up.

"Probably not, but if it will settle the score between me and the Crown, I shall be content," I say, putting my other hand on his. "I am tired of running, and I do not need much in the way of money, Jaimy. I do have some . . . uh . . . modest investments in Boston, and I will go there to see what they have profited me. I will wait for word from you that my name has been cleared, and then I will come join you, no matter what."

Bells ring outside my door, and I know it is time. I rise and so does he.

"Put such mundane matters out of your mind, and give your lady a last kiss, Jaimy."

*Mmmm . . .*

"And make sure you put that salve on your leg, and say hello to Mairead and Grandfather, and to your family." *And no, I'm not going to cry, but oh, yes, I am . . .* "Oh Jaimy, kiss me again and hold me. Just hold me for a bit, just a bit, just a little bit longer . . ."

*Oh, Jaimy, why do we always have to be saying goodbye?*

# PART VI

# Chapter 55

The *Saint Christopher*'s sails fill first, and she falls off on the port tack on her way to Kingston.

I stand on the quarterdeck of the *Dolphin* to watch her go, my eyes glistening.

"There, there, Miss," says Captain Hudson, taking my hand and patting it in a fatherly way. "You'll see the unworthy young pup soon enough, I suspect. Goodbye, now."

"Goodbye, Sir," I say, craning my neck up to plant a kiss upon his cheek. "You could not be a finer man, and I am proud to have sailed with you."

He bows and says, "Mutual, my dear." He then turns and bellows, "Set sail, Mr. Ropp! For Jamaica, and not a moment to lose!"

Mr. Ropp—completely and absolutely delighted to be First Officer of a Royal Frigate at the tender age of what . . . ? twenty, tops? if only for a short while—manages what for him is a stentorian bellow. "All men to the buntlines! Raise the Main, the Fore, and the Mizzen! Top men aloft to make sail! Rig the Fore-and-Afts!" I am glad to see that they were able to fish the fallen foremast from the sea and rerig it so that our dear old foretop is once again over our heads. I would have been sorry for that holy old relic to be forever lost.

Professor Tilden is on deck, too, and I thank him for his kind efforts at educating me and for the use of his fine bell. I assure him that it will be taken safely back to Boston—though I don't tell him I have absolutely no intention of ever giving up that valuable thing. I am glad to hear that he and Dr. Sebastian have fully reconnected and are engaged in new scientific experiments.

He *tut-tut*s and suffers a peck on his cheek from me and then goes below, leaving me with those who remain on the deck amidst all the scurrying about in preparation for getting under way.

"Dr. Sebastian," I say, taking his hand. "I just know the new portfolio of specimens will be well received by the Royal Academy. And I did so enjoy working with you on the drawings."

"My dearest Jacky," he replies, and I know he is not comfortable with this. "You are the rarest of specimens, yourself, and . . . and my fondest wish is that we will sometime work together at some future date."

"I am sure we shall, Doctor." Planting yet another kiss on yet another cheek, I add, "After all, think of the specimens we have not yet collected. And there's always the South Seas, where we have not yet ventured."

He smiles and nods. Then he turns and goes down to his laboratory and back to his work.

Now a red-coated figure appears in front of me, and I put the palms of my hands on his chest.

"Richard."

"Goodbye, Jacky. We are off on the foam, and thanks to you, we are headed back to Merrie Olde England—at least for a bit—and the lads are heartily glad of that."

"Please say farewell to your men for me, and let them know I hold all of them in my heart . . . As I do you, Richard."

He puts his hands on my shoulders and says, "Do you think Mr. Fletcher is watching us right now, through his long glass?"

"Nay, Jaimy is too upright and noble for that. As I have told him, too noble for his own good, sometimes. So give me that kiss, my Lord Allen."

He does and then says, "I may not be noble, Princess, but when I am in your presence, I am certainly upright."

I gasp and give him a poke with my knuckles and look up at him through my teary lashes. "Away now, you dog."

He laughs. "Dog or Lord, it is all the same, isn't it, Pretty-Tail? And if things don't turn out just right for you in the way of Lieutenant Fletcher, well, that offer of a Ladyship is still open."

He still holds my shoulders, which are beginning to shake. "Off with you, rogue," I manage to say. "You have always tempted me too much. Long life and happiness, Richard, and I mean that. Be careful of yourself. Goodbye."

A quick peck on his lips and, knuckles to streaming eyes, I flee back to my *Nancy* and then up into her crow's-nest to watch them leave.

There are cheers and cries of "Puss! Puss! Puss-in-Boots!" as the dear *Dolphin*'s sails are raised, then fill in the gentle breeze.

I wave as they pull away, and I stay there to watch until they are gone.

The topgallants of HMS *Saint Christopher,* and then the HMS *Dolphin,* have scarcely disappeared over the horizon to the west when a new set of sails appears, to the east, with a red flag flying above.

It is *El Diablo Rojo,* as I knew it would be.

"Bring the bell back up," I order, climbing down to my quarterdeck. "Joannie, get into your swimsuit. Higgins, will you attend me in my cabin? We have one more job to do."

# Chapter 56

"Good Lord," exclaims Higgins in wonderment. "*Sixty* gold ingots? Ten pounds each?"

"Yes, as well as half of what we bring up today. I told Flaco that I would give him half the gold I had stashed," I say, hands folded on the table in front of me, like any innocent schoolgirl—like any innocent schoolgirl clad only in a swimming suit and ready to dive again for sunken treasure in the company of Hispanic pirates. "I just didn't tell him that I had *two* stashes."

"Hmmm..." Higgins is obviously thinking hard about the ramifications of all this. The expression on his face is not at all encouraging. Time for the full-bore charm.

"Dear Higgins, I know you as the most honorable of men, which is why I did not tell you of this before; and for that you must forgive me. Please listen," I implore, putting my hand on his and giving him the big eyes. "As a member of British Intelligence, would you not have been honor bound to inform them of my little ... exploit? Or at least try to dissuade me from doing it?"

"Who else knows of this?" he asks, curtly.

"Just those who had to know—Davy and Tink, for they were the ones who moved the gold from a hiding place on the bell and down to the bilges. Joannie knows about the stash below the salt. That's all."

Silence.

"Please tell me you understand, Higgins, and know that I could not bear to lose your love and friendship for anything in this world. Please."

Silence, still.

"And remember," I say, pressing on, "back on the Mississippi, when I had taken the bounty money from Flashby and Moseley, and you pointed out that, while it was blood money, it still belonged to the Crown, and told me I should give it back and I did. Do you remember that? I know you do. But this is different, Higgins, don't you see? This is Spanish gold that does not belong to the King, and that never belonged to the King. Hell, I must have hauled up at least a million pounds' sterling worth of gold for the King's coffers. Have I not paid my debt? Have I not?"

He nods, slightly, his eyes hooded, and I push on.

"And think of the others—Jemimah will now have the resources to free at least some of her children, Annie and Davy will be well fixed, as will Jim and Clementine. And we can think about buying a bigger ship to start our Transatlantic Irish-American scheme. And, although I know you would never allow consideration of financial gain to compromise your principles, you, Higgins, with your shares, will be *very* well off. A nice house in Cambridge, near the college, perhaps? Maybe a little something for your dad back in Colchester? Something to keep him in his old age? Hmmm . . . Oh, please, Higgins!"

He nods. "The stores of Faber Shipping were getting rather thin," he admits, a smile spreading across his face. "And I do have in mind a very nice little cottage located on the banks of the Charles. Beautiful grounds, and indeed quite handy to Harvard."

There is a knock and Joannie pokes her head in. "Jacky. Flaco's coming alongside."

"Good. Have the hands float the raft and hoist up the bell."

"Aye, aye."

I turn back to Higgins.

"And Joannie, too. Although she does not know it, I plan to enroll her at the Lawson Peabody School for Young Girls when we get back to Boston . . . and don't you *dare* tell her, else she'll jump ship."

Higgins rises, laughing. "Putting that child in that school may well be the hardest task you have yet assigned yourself on this voyage, Miss, but I wish you well in that." He pauses a bit, and then goes on.

"True, I owe allegiance to my country, and I honor my word. But my first allegiance will always be to you, Miss, and I hope you know that. Shall we go topside and join our fellow pirates?"

It does not take long for Joannie and me to pull up the treasure from my little cave on the side of the cliff that hangs over what's left of the *Santa Magdalena*. Just before we fill the last net bag, I once again put my finger to my lips and look at Joannie there hanging in the blue-green water beside me. Then I shove three gold ingots back into the cave to stay, should we ever need to come back and claim them. She looks at me and grins, bubbles coming out the sides of her mouth, with both thumbs up.

*You can take the girls out of Cheapside, but you can't take Cheapside out of the girls.*

As we're about to climb under the edge of the bell for the last time on this voyage, I feel Joannie poke me in the side. I look at her and she points down. There, down in the depths, where lies the treasure ship that has given up so much of its bounty, I see a sight that will stay with me forever—the canvas-covered body of one of the seamen killed in the battle, caught in the drift of an undersea ocean current, slowly settling onto the deck of the wreck.

I do not know if the sailor was British or Spanish—all I know is . . . more bones to lie silent with the *Santa Magdalena*.

Now we all gather about the glittering pile of treasure that lies on my deck—me and my crew, Flaco and the sailors who stayed loyal to him during his recent troubles.

The towel Higgins hands me, to dry off, is wrapped turbanlike around my hair. I then plop down cross-legged next to the stack of booty, reflecting on what a proper bunch of brigands we must appear to be.

Flaco, resplendent in red silk, cocked hat with gold trim, and striped pantaloons tucked into folded-down black boots, sits across from me, grins, and says, "You will notice, my sometimes truthful heart-of-my-heart, that I have sent Moto to take down your red marker, so you will not be able to come to this spot again, should you have left something down below. Eh?"

No fool, that Flaco . . . 'cept that I have taken at least

twenty-five bearings on every conceivable rock, tree, point, or outcropping . . . Hey, I could find my way back here in a leaky rowboat in the dark. But no matter—time to divide the spoils.

I smile and nod and turn to the business at hand.

The ingots, being all of the same weight, are easy to divide. The rest—the silver, the crosses, the necklaces, the gold chalices, the jewels in those two little casks—we parcel out one piece at a time.

*Davy, take this cross for Annie, I know she will like it . . . Yes, and one for Betsey, too. All right, Flaco, you can take those . . . and Jemimah, this ruby necklace, I think it will look good on you . . . Ah, an emerald for my poor self, and one for Joannie, too. Tink, if you come to see that dark-eyed girl again, well, this will help. And Perrito, a present for your ma-macita, sí? And Coyote . . .*

And so it goes. The cask of jewels is spread out, all twinkling in the sun, and I put my shiv down through the middle of the pile, dividing it in half. Any disputes are settled with a roll of the dice—and I didn't even use my loaded ones.

When we are done, there is only one small gold cross that lies between us. Flaco rattles the dice and tosses . . . five and three—eight. I pick up the cubes and roll . . . five and four—nine. I win.

I take up the cross, stand, and go to the rail.

"I believe we should give something back to her," I say, and drop it over the side.

It glitters as it falls and turns through the water and then is gone. I like to think that it comes to rest on that poor sailor who lies down below.

"That settles things between us, I believe, Captain Jimenez," I say.

"Except for a final embrace, my slightly damp little mermaid," says the grinning buccaneer, his arms spread wide.

I put my arms about his waist and nuzzle my nose into his neck, making the bells on his braids tinkle merrily.

"Come now, Flaco, off with you. Maybe someday we shall sail together again."

"I know we shall, *mi corazón*."

"*Adiós, Flaco, mi amigo.*"

"*Vaya con Dios, Jacquelina, mi amor.*"

*El Diablo Rojo* has gone over the southern horizon as the *Nancy B. Alsop* weighs anchor and heads east then north toward Boston.

I stand up in the crow's-nest and look out over the sea. Jaimy's over in that direction and is safe, for now, or as safe as one can be in this world, and for that I am glad. The bell is secured below, and my crew is happy with their new-gotten gains, even though most of them do not yet realize the extent of their good fortune. All, however, are looking forward to going back to their home port, and to friends, to lovers, and to family.

Me, too.

The wind whips my hair about my face, drying it from my last dive. I take a deep, deep breath and look down upon my world—my sturdy little ship, my good friends, and the calm sea—and I realize one thing, one very great and glorious thing . . .

*I am free . . .*

# Epilogue

It's dark in the bilges of the *Nancy B.*, down by the heavy ballast that keeps the ship upright in a blow, where five of us are gathered—Davy, Tink, Higgins, along with a very mystified Ezra Pickering, and me. Tink holds up a lantern and all that can be seen in the gloom are the wolfish grins on the faces of my crew.

"Shine the light down here, Tink," I say, crouching down and pulling out my shiv. "Watch this, Ezra."

I reach down and draw the blade over the top of a gray bar and a gleam of rich yellow appears.

"What?" asks Ezra. "Is it . . . ?"

"Yes, Ezra, it is gold. Pure gold."

"How much?

"About six hundred pounds."

"Six hundred pounds sterling?"

"No, Mr. Pickering," says Higgins. "Six hundred pounds of actual gold."

"Six hundred pounds! Good Lord! I doubt the Commonwealth has that much gold in its treasury! I am staggered!"

Ezra habitually wears a slight smile on his face, but I suspect that that little smile has been wiped off for the moment.

"Who knows of this?" he whispers.

"Just us four . . . five now," say I.

"Hmmm . . . And the rest of your crew?"

"No. Although we intend to give all their fair share, we felt it best that we talk to you first. We have given out pay—some gold, many jewels—and all are happy. In fact, we have set aside a nice gold watch chain with emerald fob for you—a diamond stickpin as well—and we hope you will like them. Yes, all are quite happy . . ."

*Well*, almost *all are happy*, I reflect, as Ezra silently collects his thoughts. Upon arrival in Boston, I had a joyous reunion with Amy Trevelyne, tempered by the fact that brother Randall had not yet returned from the wars in Germany and there was no word of him. Amy, however, remains cheerful, or as cheerful as she ever gets, and already had pen and paper in hand and has been taking notes on my various travels. Jim is snugged up with Clementine, and Davy with Annie, while McGee and Thomas are off to the Pig and beyond. Jemimah has bought new clothes and we have hired investigators to search for her children down south and to see about buying them out of slavery. And El Gringo has been given an honored retirement at Dovecote. He's been put out to stud, as it were, and provided with a proper harem. So the other roosters had better watch out because even though I've taken off his silver spurs and hung them up, I've not thrown them away—for his son might want the use of them someday.

Yes, everybody's quite happy . . . everybody 'cept poor Joannie . . .

"But, Jacky, I don't wanna go to school!" she wails as we get out of the coach in front of the Lawson Peabody School for Young Girls. "I wanna go back to sea with you!"

"Hush now, Joannie," I say. "We are not yet heading back to sea, and there are things you must learn if you are to get on in this world: Comportment, Horsemanship, Etiquette, and Management of a Household. Art, Science, and Music, too. You will learn them right here, just as I did. Up the stairs now, down this hall, and into this office. That's it . . . head up now."

Both attired in the Lawson Peabody School uniform— black dress, black stockings, and white silk shawl gathered about the shoulders—we enter.

"Put your toes on that white line . . . you see it? Good. Now wait—you shall have to get very good at waiting in this world. Ah. Here she is."

A rustle of black silk and a presence enters the room.

"Ah, Miss Faber. Good to see you again. And this is . . . ?"

"Miss Joan Nichols, Mistress, late of London. I would appreciate it if you would take her on."

"I see. I expect that you will vouch for her character?"

"Yes, Mistress."

"Very well. Good day to you, Miss Faber. I will now take Miss Nichols and introduce her to the rest of the girls. Please do come back later and recount to us your most recent . . . travels. I am sure we will enjoy hearing of them."

I give Joannie a kiss on her damp cheek and leave the office.

As I go, I hear Mistress Pimm say, "Miss Nichols, we

here at the Lawson Peabody affect a certain demeanor . . . Stand up straight now and lift your chin as if you are delicately balancing a book on your head. All right. Now, lips together and teeth apart. Now drop your eyelids down halfway, projecting a look of languid confidence . . . That's good, not perfect, but acceptable. My girls call it the Lawson Peabody Look. It is possible that someday you will, too."

I go out the door and back down to the harbor, leaving Joannie to her fate.


A cough from Ezra brings me back to the present in the bilge of the *Nancy B. Alsop*.

"Ahem . . . and yes, Ezra, it's all legal . . . sort of."

I give him a quick summary of just how I got this hoard, and Mother England's possible interest in it. He nods, thinking . . .

He then says, "My word . . . This will have to be handled very secretly, and very, very carefully." More nodding, more thinking. "Subsidiaries . . . trusts . . . holding companies . . . phantom corporations . . ."

"Well, dear Ezra, that is your department. Me, I'm going out shopping."

"Shopping?" he asks, somewhat dazed by all this, as I'm thinking, *Ha, Ezra! I got you this time!*

"Yes, Ezra," I say as I prepare to go back up into the glorious sunshine of a perfect Boston day. "For a ship. A big one."

*Oh, it is so very, very good to be rich!*